Therese Dotray-Tulloch

Therese Dotray-Tulloch

For Opossum Falls

Also by Therese Dotray-Tulloch

Life on Pleasant

For Opossum Falls

Therese Dotray-Tulloch

Therese L. Dotray-Tulloch

For
Opossum
Falls

ISBN: 9780615633428   Soft cover

Therese Dotray-Tulloch
theresetulloch@gmail.com

To **Lucy and John Dotray**

The foundation of our home was built upon their love, and they continually filled it with joy, laughter, and life lessons. I will forever be grateful for the gift of life they've given me, the wonderful home I was raised in, and their constant support and love.

Therese Dotray-Tulloch

To say the least, a town life makes one more
tolerant and liberal in one's judgment of others.
Henry Wadsworth Longfellow

Home, the spot of earth supremely blest,
A dearer, sweeter spot than all the rest.
Robert Montgomery

Life is an adventure in forgiveness.
Norman Cousins

Therese Dotray-Tulloch

Prologue

She grabbed the little girl and ran.

She supposed she should take some small amount of satisfaction from knowing that when the time came, she simply grabbed her and ran. She didn't think too overly long about it; she didn't feel scared; she didn't panic. For the first time in a long time, she didn't even think about The Event before putting her current predicament in the forefront of her mind and comparing it and all of her feelings with what she had better do now. She bent down, looked straight into the chocolate-brown eyes gazing back at her so trustingly, and hissed, "Let's go!"

Holding on tightly to the chubby little hand, still sticky from unraveling fruit roll-ups, she grabbed her purse through the passenger window and ran straight into the marketplace. She couldn't do anything to cover her noticeably blond curls, but the little girl's shiny black mane fit right in with the hordes of humanity conducting business in the typically busy marketplace. By the time the police officer looked up from entering her driver's license information into his computer, she was long gone. As the officer rushed into the crowd, glancing left and right while standing on tiptoe to see farther into the impenetrable crowd, he chided himself for allowing her pretty face to cause him to let down his guard. The shoppers closed in around him and he knew he wouldn't be able to find her again in that place. Glancing down at the little plastic driver's license he still held in his hand, he memorized her name. "Alright, Helena Elizabeth Anderson, let's see what you've got going on to cause you to run from an officer of the law like this," he said to himself.

What he would soon find out would make him feel sick to his stomach; he would often think about it at odd times of the day and night. The police officer would wonder how such a lovely, fair-haired woman could live with herself while hiding such a horrendous secret.

For Opossum Falls

Therese Dotray-Tulloch

Chapter 1

By the time Laney was finally able to slip off her mauve Pick and Pay smock, grab her purse from under the counter, and shout her farewells to old man Schluter, Pick and Pay's pragmatic owner, she was already twenty minutes later than she'd told Cathy she would be.

"Enjoy yourself at your first Sugar Beet Queen Pageant, Helena," Mr. Schluter called as she headed out the door. No matter how many times she'd corrected him, he always preferred to call her by her full name, rather than the nickname 'Laney', which she much preferred. Deciding she no longer had time to go home and change like she'd originally planned, she looked down at her casual, white blouse, hastily tucked it into her comfy black jeans, then looked askance at her functional white sneakers which made standing for eight hours at the checkout counter at work bearable. There was nothing she could do about her shoes at this late hour, she decided, not if she wanted to make it to the pageant on time.

Walking with purpose the three blocks down Main Street to the high school, Laney thought about how good it felt to stretch her long legs and move. The street was crowded with townspeople and visitors alike, all turned out to enjoy the first night of the three-day harvest festival, so she stayed close to the curb to make haste. Laney smiled and waved at many whom she recognized as regular Pick and Pay customers. All of the shops on Main Street were staying open to take advantage of the much higher than usual foot traffic around town, whether it made sense to their particular business or not.

The Chit Chat Café was so crowded there was a line extending out the door. The accountant's office had hired someone to parade around in a foam dollar-bill costume that stood nine feet tall. The eyes in the costume were cut right where George Washington's eyes were located on the dollar bill, except they were turned sideways giving the normally complacent-looking former president a rather shifty look.

The Chamber of Commerce was a hub of activity as volunteers turned up to receive this year's complimentary volunteer work shirt. This was a source of pride for many of the locals; tee shirts from Sugar Beet Festivals past were often seen around town as people worked in their gardens, at the Anytime Fitness Center, and chaperoning on field trips. This year's tee shirt was beet red, as they often were, but did not depict a picture of a large beet on the front as had been done so often in the past. It was hard to make a beet look attractive, therefore, most of the townspeople, though grateful for the economic success of the local beet factory, were tired of wearing one. This year's design was of a beet sliced up into thin rectangular strips called cossettes which is how beets were cut up at the factory a mile and a half out of town. Outsiders would think it was a picture of shoestring potatoes turned pink, but the locals knew better.

Outside of Just Screw It, the hardware store owner stood holding a big sign with the Wal-Mart logo circled in red with a slash through it. "Hey, Mr. F, I'll take one of those," Laney said as she reached for one of Mr. Fassbinder's homemade buttons with the same crossed out Wal-Mart logo on it. "Actually, I'll take two. I'm sure Cath will want to wear one, too."

"Help yourself, Laney. Take as many as you need, I can always make more," Mr. Fassbinder said as he handed her a bright red flier that he had also printed up. "Be sure to read this fact sheet about how Wal-Mart is killing off Main Street America. Support America, not Wal-Mart!" he said loudly trying to attract attention to himself.

Laney looked back to see Jeanine Westerly glaring hostilely at them. Jeanine ran the Chamber of Commerce. She had spent much of the past year trying to lure Wal-Mart to open a Superstore on the outskirts of town. She had done her research well, had compiled boxes full of meticulous notes as to why Wal-Mart was needed here, and had pulled out all the stops when the white limousine carrying three Wal-Mart executives rode into town to meet with Jens Jenson, the mayor. Bringing Wal-Mart to town was to be her greatest coup and now here was that meddling old hardware-store owner making a fuss about boycotting Wal-Mart and supporting the local mom and pop shops; yeah right. Small town stores were a dime a dozen. Jeanine wanted the excitement of being able to shop at a huge, big box store which should be her right as an American citizen. Realizing that she was still clutching on tightly to the extra, extra-large tee shirt Robby Benson was trying to take from her, she took her eyes off of the activity in front of Just Screw It's storefront and smiled largely.

"Be sure to take a shirt for Beth, too," Jeanine said as she grabbed another XXL shirt from the box and handed it to Robby. "We'll see you both at your usual shift in the beer gardens after the parade on Sunday, right?"

Laney kept walking as she attached Walter's 'For Opossum Falls' button to her blouse and didn't stay around to listen to Robby's explanation to Jeanine as to why he wouldn't be able to work his usual shift on Sunday. She knew that Robby had agreed to help Mr. Fassbinder at the new booth they had set up at the end of the parade route so they could pass out more information about the negative impact Wal-Mart store openings have on the thirty-mile radius surrounding one of the newly opened retail complexes. Robby and Beth Benson owned the local meat market, Let's Meat. Beth's grandfather had opened the original meat market back at the turn of the twentieth century, and they had been using the same recipe for skin-on wieners ever since. The Bensons would be passing out complimentary beef sticks with slashed out Wal-Mart buttons poking out of them. They knew their neighbors well enough to know that their consciences wouldn't let them just eat the beef sticks and throw the buttons away. They would feel obliged to wear the buttons at least for the remainder of the festival in compensation for the tasty treat from Let's Meat. The more visible the buttons with Wal-Mart's logo crossed out with an angry red slash through it, the better.

Rounding the corner, Laney stopped abruptly at the sight of a long line of women snaking from the school doors halfway down the street. The atmosphere was jolly as clusters of women stood about visiting and laughing, waiting with no apparent sense of impatience for the doors to open to allow them into the auditorium for this year's Sugar Beet Queen Pageant. About two-thirds of the way up from the end of the line, she spotted Cath listening with her head inclined forward to better hear what the short woman standing in front of her was saying. Cath was wearing black leggings with a zebra-patterned long, silk blouse fastened with a shiny, ebony belt and sexy, stiletto-heeled sandals. As usual, her short black hair was styled impeccably making her look younger than her thirty-four years. She broke away from the other woman when she saw Laney approach and greeted her with a kiss on the cheek and a hearty laugh.

"This, whatever you're wearing, is only okay because this is your first ever Sugar Beet Queen Pageant and you obviously didn't get the memo that said 'Everyone dresses to the nines' for this sophisticated happening in town." Cath gestured towards Laney's feet. "Oh God, are those nursing shoes you're wearing? Thankfully, they're opening the doors to let us all in now so I don't have to stand next to you much longer while you're wearing those old-lady monstrosities on your feet," and she hooked her arm through Laney's and squeezed affectionately to take the sting out of her words. "Don't worry; the auditorium will be dark so no one will be able see your tootsies for much longer!"

Cath knew that Laney could wear a flour sack and still manage to look adorable. Despite her long legs, she was barely five and a half feet tall, petite and fine-boned. Her large, blue eyes were set deeply above her delicate, slightly upturned nose, and her wide mouth with full lips lent her a sensuous air. Her naturally blond hair with golden highlights held soft curls which fell gently to her shoulders. Cath had no idea what had caused it, but there was a sadness that surrounded Laney, a burden weighing upon her shoulders of some unspeakable grief or wrong. There was anguish showing in the glimpse of her soul seen through her sapphire-colored eyes, and Cath hoped that one day Laney would consider her a good enough friend to share her sorrow.

Cath, too, had known heartache in her life, but she'd already told Laney all about her numerous miscarriages and her inability to carry her babies to term. Late one Friday night, the first warm spring evening of the year, after emptying a bottle of merlot and while they were halfway through the next one, Cath had told Laney all about her first pregnancy and the months of bed rest she'd endured after her uterus was sewn shut to try to slow the premature labor. They had cried together when she'd described the horror of realizing she hadn't felt the baby move inside of her for awhile, the agonizing experience of seeing the lifeless body on the ultrasound screen confirming her suspicions, the unspeakable nightmare of living with her deceased baby still inside her, as she waited a whole week for the cruel twist of nature to at last send her body into delivery mode, after months of threatening early labor, and finally, the anguish of giving birth to death.

Only as one who lives with her own sorrow can, Laney accepted the burden of Cath's sad story with complete and utter understanding. She didn't try to fix it or make it right; she didn't belittle the tragedy by placating her with meaningless platitudes; she didn't compare the death of this forever-unborn child with one already held and born as if that somehow made it the lesser of two evils. She had taken the mason jar Cath was drinking wine from out of her hand and set it down, reached for her and hugged her with both arms wrapped tightly around her, and cried with her, heartfelt sobs choking them both until at last, tears and snot smearing both of their faces, she'd gotten them Kleenex to wipe themselves off and then refilled their glasses.

They had met at the Pick and Pay shortly after Laney had moved into town and started cashiering there. Laney had complimented Cath's hair and asked her where she got it cut as she was overdue for her own haircut. Cath had thrown back her head and laughed her trademark hoot as she proceeded to rummage around in her oversized, teal purse, at last extricating a slightly torn business card with *Cathy's Clip and Curl* written on it above a picture of an open pair of scissors. "I work out of my home but Eric, that's my husband, fixed up the basement real nice so I have a permanent hair station down there with a private entrance, so business and home lives do not have to overlap. Don't know how desperate you are, but my last appointment is at five this afternoon, so you could come any time after that."

Laney had showed up at seven that night, fifteen minutes later than she'd planned, as she'd gotten lost on the gravel road. She wasn't used to rural driving yet. First of all, when giving directions, the locals never used street names or addresses. Instead, they always gave the names of people who lived or used to live at or near by a certain destination. Second, distances were never mentioned, so Laney always found herself turning much sooner than she was supposed to because she simply was not accustomed to everything in the country being so much farther apart than in the city.

Deciphering at last Eric and Catherine Hanson's name on the mailbox, Laney turned down the driveway and was surprised to drive at least half a mile over a creek, up and down slight hills with sugar beets growing on either side of the road before finally rounding the corner in front of a lovely, old clapboard farmhouse complete with a white-trimmed wraparound porch. As she turned off the engine, the cheerful sound of the crickets' melodic chirping filled the expansive bucolic silence. Abundant flower gardens lined the sidewalk while hanging baskets of cascading scarlet and white petunias hung from the porch. With the sweet smell of phlox wafting in through the open car window completing the magical scene, Laney sat for a moment breathing it all in and feeling as close to contentment as she'd felt in a very long time.

The feeling that she was being observed woke her from her reverie causing Laney to turn her head slightly to see who it was. Noticing nothing at first in the rapidly descending dusk, Laney did a double take as she spotted the statue of a dog leaning slightly to the left in the middle of the lawn. Not a very attractive lawn ornament, she thought to herself, although she supposed it was better than those ridiculous cutouts made to look as though the woman of the house was bending over in her yard flashing her behind at you.

Gathering her purse, Laney stepped out of the car and began moving up the charmingly meandering sidewalk to the door with the sign *Cathy's Clip and Curl* above it. Stepping off the sidewalk, Laney thought she would straighten the tilting dog statue. Approaching the figurine more closely, she was impressed with how realistic the matted hair looked as well as the mismatched ears, one perched upright while the other folded down giving the puppy a rather jaunty look. What in the world kind of dog are you supposed to be anyway, she thought as she studied the medium-sized brown dog with large white spots randomly tossed across its back. Just as she was about to reach out and level it, the dog 'statue' tilted its head slightly to get a better view of her. Laney gasped in surprise just as Cathy shouted out the window, "Don't worry about Bon Jovi, he wouldn't hurt a fly!"

Bon Jovi continued to gaze unflinchingly up at her in his calm, nonjudgmental manner until at last Laney reached out to pet him. His disproportionately long tail began thwacking the ground at this point and Laney couldn't help but laugh. When he collapsed onto his back, she bent over to give him a good stomach rub all the while admonishing him for tricking her into thinking he was a sculpture. Discovering that an appreciation for Jon Bon Jovi and his music was another thing the two had in common, Cath told Laney all about naming the poor dog after Eric had seen him a couple of years ago hanging out at the sugar beet pile a few days in a row seemingly having been abandoned.

The two women found endless things to talk about while Laney got her hair cut that first time; Laney had ended up staying till the cuckoo clock struck twelve and they both marveled at how time had flown by. "You still haven't told me how or why you chose Opossum Falls to settle in, but I can tell you, you're like a breath of fresh air around here, and I, for one, am so glad you did," Cath said as she walked Laney to her car. "You know, I feel like I've known you all my life already even though we've just met today. Why, Laney Anderson, I feel like we are kindred spirits. I have a feeling we are going to be friends for a long, long time."

Laney looked up then and gasped as she clapped her hands over her mouth whispering, "Oh my god, what is it?"

Cath followed her gaze, looked up and sighed, "Oh, sweet, the Northern Lights are out tonight. Aren't they lovely? I'd better call Marge." She noticed the rapture on Laney's face. "Do you mean to tell me you've never seen the Northern Lights before? Have you lived in the cities your whole life? Well, you're in for a real treat." The sky to the north was pulsating with brilliant flashes of green, a continuous rippling of bright color lighting up the horizon.

Laney interrupted her by shrieking and grabbing her hands to twirl her around in a circle on her front lawn. Bon Jovi joined in by circling around them in the opposite direction, growling sporadically his low, throaty bark. "I have always wanted to see the Northern Lights! ALWAYS!!" Laney shouted without taking her eyes off of the sky. "Do you know they're named after Aurora, the Roman goddess of the dawn, and Boreas, the Greek work for wind: Aurora Borealis? They're said to look like a windy dawn! And, look! Look! They're gorgeous! It's like a fluorescent emerald curtain moving across the sky! You are right, Cath, this is a wonderful, good sign!"

Before Cath knew it, Laney was crumpled up on the lawn crying, the dog by her side thumping his tail in sympathy. Cath had supposed they were tears of happiness, at the time, but now that she knew Laney better, she had changed her mind and was pretty sure they were actually tears of sadness. She had told Laney about their Northern Lights' telephone chain saying she would add Laney's name to the list and excused herself to go inside to call Marjorie Peterson to alert her of the arrival of Northern Lights. No matter what time of night the gorgeous, rippling phenomenon was spotted, the chain would start phones ringing around Opossum Falls to those on the list who never wanted to miss the opportunity to witness the astonishing sight.

~~~~~~~~~~~~~~~~~~~~~~~~~~~~~~~

"Thank goodness you got here so early, Cath," Laney said as they squeezed through the doors of the auditorium with the rest of the crowd and hastily entered a row and fell into two available seats in the middle before someone else grabbed them. "There will never be enough seats for everyone outside lined up to see the pageant."

"That's right. I have been forced to stand through the entire pageant before just like those who didn't arrive early enough will have to do tonight. Believe me, it's much more enjoyable and doesn't feel half so long when you're not on your feet."

Laney was surprised when the pageant began and Dick McGhee, the local attorney turned emcee, asked for any past Sugar Beet Royalty to stand. She thought Cath was joking when she started rustling to her feet next to her, but the next thing Cath was waving to others in the crowd who were standing, also, about ten percent of the audience it seemed. "Why, Cathy Hanson, you never told me you were nobility before! All this time, I should have been kissing your ring in greeting instead of pecking your cheek!"

"Don't you be cheeky," Cath whispered back, pinching Laney's cheek. "The only reason I don't still wear my crown is because I was only Miss Congeniality, not queen or first or second princess. The judges didn't vote for me at all; my fellow contestants did. That doesn't really count."

"Don't be absurd. Being voted by your peers means even more, if you ask me, especially when you consider the candidates are all at the most difficult age of 17! Seriously, well done, Cath. I guess you haven't changed all these many years later; I would still vote for you as Miss Congeniality!"

"Shhhhh, quiet!" Cath whispered back with a sparkle in her eye. "I don't want to miss any of Dick's jokes. They are always in unbelievably poor taste. I mean, seriously, doesn't he even think to run the jokes past someone first before saying them in front of an entire crowd? So off color they're practically gray."

Hours later, the crowd filed slowly and calmly out of the auditorium in a much more leisurely fashion than when they had entered it. A sweet, blond girl named Sally Olson, who had played Beauty and the Beast on her harp, had been crowned queen despite the fact that Mr. Olson, dressed as the beast, had tripped onstage during the crucial segment when he was supposed to be escorting his daughter around the stage to show her off in the best possible light in front of the judges. Sally had very regally lifted up the hem of her sparkling yellow evening gown and stepped over the crumpled form of her father sprawled onstage, never taking her eyes off of the judges as she dazzled them with her magnificent smile. As Cath and Laney strolled out of the high school, they overheard Marge Peterson walking behind them ask her companion to explain the joke Dick had told about the couple who went to see the doctor to help them with their erectile dysfunction problem.

In her dream, Laney woke up to Scott's lips brushing her forehead as he kissed her and set her morning cup of freshly ground, dark-roast coffee on the bedside table. "Rise and shine, sweetheart, I hear Gabby making morning sounds already."

"Mmm, the coffee smells great, thanks, honey." She spoke sleepily as she pushed herself up into a sitting position and felt comforted just holding the warm cup in her hands. Scott was already dressed. Laney thought once again how handsome he looked in his white, button-down shirt and diagonally striped navy and red silk tie. Scott liked to get up early and enjoy a cup of coffee while reading the front page of the paper before bringing Laney her coffee to enjoy in the comfort of their queen-sized bed. Not being a morning person, Laney loved the luxury of sipping on her first cup of coffee before she even had to step out of bed.

Laney and Scott had met at Gustavus Adolphus College in St. Peter, MN. She had first noticed Scott at orientation when the incoming freshmen were forced to play several ice-breaking games to encourage them to make new friends quickly to counteract the inevitable loneliness they would feel living away from home for the first time. Fair-haired and broad-shouldered, Laney was admiring Scott's polite manner as well as his strong physique while listening to the instructions of the coordinator. Half of the students were told to remove a shoe and place it in a pile in the middle of the group. Then the other half of the group was instructed to select a shoe and find the rightful owner of that shoe, and in that way to strike up a conversation. Laney spotted the tan walking boot she felt sure she had seen on Scott's foot and pulled it out of the mound, walking toward him with a ready grin on her face. Another blond was already approaching Scott with the shoe that actually did belong to him, and Laney exclaimed, "Oops," as she looked around the group to see whose shoe she actually was holding. A large, sweaty girl wearing jeans and a plaid shirt was awkwardly stepping from one foot to another on the outside of the circle and, sure enough, Laney realized she was holding the girl's missing boot. Not until the following semester when she walked into Western Civilization History class did she have the opportunity to finally talk to Scott. She saw him sitting in the front row of class with a vacant seat next to him, so she hustled to it and slid into the desk. Turning to face her, Scott greeted her and asked, "What do you know about this prof?"

"I've heard she's really tough," Laney answered. "Maybe we could study together?"

Three years later, they got engaged. They waited until after graduation to get married in Christ Chapel on Gustavus Adolphus' campus. After that, Laney taught at an elementary school in St. Paul while Scott went on to study law at William Mitchell. He passed the Minnesota bar exam three years later and was immediately hired at Faegre and Benson.

Shortly after they moved into their new home in Eagan, Laney found she was pregnant. Celebrating their fourth wedding anniversary, Laney waited until they were at dinner at Forepaughs to share the exciting news with Scott. When they raised their wineglasses to toast their four happy years of marriage, Scott noticed that Laney didn't even touch her wine. "What's the matter? Is the wine too sweet for you? We can order another bottle of something else. How about a Cabernet?"

Laney covered Scott's hand with her own and said, her eyes shining with tears of joy, "I'm not drinking, because I can't. Well, not for nine more months anyway." As the realization of what she was saying dawned on him, Scott reached across the table to kiss her. Laney smiled blissfully as she murmured through the kisses, "We're going to have a baby, Scott! You're going to be a father!"

Up until the final weeks, Laney loved being pregnant. Initially, when she wasn't showing yet, she was tickled to be walking around with such a wonderful secret inside of her. She had never felt more fulfilled. She sensed she was truly experiencing what it meant to be a woman. She marveled at how tender her breasts felt, how nauseous she became just whiffing the scent of coffee, how ravenous she was at all hours of the day and night. She had never been in better shape before, either. No matter how cold it was outside, she would run four miles a day, then speed walk as the end of her pregnancy neared. She knew without a doubt that she was having a little girl, not because the ultrasound said so, but because she sensed her little girl within her the second the little blue stick of the pregnancy kit told her she was pregnant. Scott picked out a boy's name, Michael, but Laney knew they wouldn't use it, not this pregnancy anyway. Gabrielle Rose was to be her daughter's name and Laney knew she would never, ever love anyone more than she loved this miraculous little creature growing steadily inside of her.

Laney ate so healthily throughout her pregnancy that in the entire nine months she didn't touch any processed food at all. She used yeast to make her own yogurt each morning, squeezed fresh fruit to make her own juice, bought fresh fish from Byerly's seafood counter to sauté for dinner, and even grew herbs in the sunny, south-facing bay window above the kitchen sink to spice up her food. Not only did she avoid all alcohol and caffeine, she didn't drink pop, either, but just added a splash of cranberry juice to sparkling water when she felt she needed a treat.

She took yoga classes specifically for pregnant women and learned to concentrate on the breath she drew into her solar plexus, focusing on nourishing her increasingly mobile daughter within her. Reading that it would help develop her daughter's mind, she listened to Mozart every single day, concentrating on his violin sonatas and symphonies. A fine musician herself, Laney also played Mozart's concertos on the piano for an hour every day that she was pregnant. When she paused in between pieces, the baby would begin to kick and move within her. "Look, she wants me to keep playing!" she would exclaim incredulously to Scott, and he would come over and place his hand on her stomach, wanting to be a part of the experience, too.

In the end, when even bending over to tie her shoes became difficult, Laney marveled at nature's clever solution to ease her worries of delivery and giving birth: by making the last days of pregnancy so incredibly uncomfortable, she was finally ready to get this baby out no matter what. Having vowed to ingest no drugs whatsoever while giving birth so as not to risk injuring her daughter, Laney struggled through eight hours of labor with Scott and her wonderful midwife by her side before Scott reached for her hand and placed it between her legs while he spoke with unbridled emotion, "Feel our baby's head, Laney. It's coming!" Pushing with all her might, Laney half-laughed, half-cried Gabrielle's name as she at last welcomed her baby girl into the world.

Both Scott and Laney fell head over heels in love with Gabby, as they soon came to call her. They marveled at how absolutely dull their lives B.G., Before Gabby, now seemed. No wonder the human race kept on propagating itself; having a baby was the most wonderful experience in the world. With Scott's wholehearted agreement, Laney extended her six-week maternity leave indefinitely. She could never, ever leave Gabby with someone else to witness her first smile, hear her first words, and help with her first steps. Even during Gabby's naptime, when Laney knew she should be straightening up the house or doing laundry, she would often stand by the crib and stare down at the little miracle she had grown inside herself. She would see Gabby kick out or twitch in slumber and she would place her hand on her empty stomach and almost grieve at Gabby's absence from within her, knowing that she would have been feeling that movement had she still been carrying Gabby. When the baby was fussy, which she hardly ever was, she would lay her down in the bassinet next to the piano and softly play Mozart's C Major piano concerto #21. Gabby would stop crying and lie still allowing herself to completely tune in to the music. Laney knew she was taking comfort from hearing the same music she had heard while she was safely cocooned in watery confinement within her mother's womb.

Therese Dotray-Tulloch

Gabby was only six pounds, three ounces, at birth. She was born with the loveliest head of silky blond curls, so fair as to almost be white, each curl brushed with shimmering gold highlights so fine-looking, complete strangers would reach out to fondle Gabby's fair tresses. Laney didn't even mind the intrusion into her baby's space, because Gabby absolutely thrived on human interaction. She seemed to think she was put on this earth to be admired and cooed over. If by chance the person within Gabby's sight was not greeting her or commenting on what an adorable little creature she was, she would wriggle about and make baby noises as if to say, "Hello! I'm here! Please notice me!" And always, Gabby would be noticed, and the person would go away happier than when they had first come in contact with her.

Laney was always being told what an incredibly beautiful baby Gabrielle was. Her lovely, wide-set eyes were a striking cerulean blue framed in long lashes. They sparkled as she interacted with others and seemed full of mischief and fun. Her nose was upturned just the tiniest bit giving her an adorably perky look. Her lips were full and her smile was almost constant. Before she'd learned to talk, she would make a squeaky noise when she smiled and her infectious happiness spread wherever she and Laney went.

~~~~~~

That morning, after Scott had brought Laney her coffee, she heard Gabby chatting to herself over the Fischer-Price monitor and she couldn't resist going to get her to bring her back into bed with her. Scott came, too, and together they slowly pushed open Gabby's bedroom door and spied on her for a moment without her realizing it. She was laying on her back gazing up at the animal mobile hanging over her crib. She was kicking her chubby little legs and sucking on her thumb while singing a song in gibberish, appearing to be talking to the animals in the mobile swinging above her. Scott squeezed Laney's hand and she could feel his eyes upon her, but she couldn't bear to take her eyes off of her beautiful baby girl. Just then, Gabby turned her head and saw them. She squealed with delight and flipped herself onto her stomach, kicking her little legs to push herself over to the side of the crib. Grabbing onto the bars on the side of the crib, Gabby pulled herself up to standing and laughed with delight to see both of her parents peeking into her bedroom. They laughed joyously back as Laney rushed in to pick the little girl up out of the crib and hold her high in the air above her, crying, "Good morning, Sunshine!" while Gabby giggled and shrieked with pleasure.

Scott kissed them both good-bye and headed downstairs to grab his briefcase and leave for work. Laney stood at the changing table and removed Gabby's diaper, keeping up a constant dialogue with her as she put the dirty diaper in the hamper the diaper-service would take away and clean. While Gabby stretched her legs up towards Laney's face, Laney reached out and pretended to bite Gabby's toes, part of their diaper-changing ritual as she said, "De-licious! Let me have another bite of those tasty toes!" while Gabby responded with gales of laughter. Nibbling on her baby's fat little digits on her feet, she smacked her lips to make Gabby giggle even harder.

Picking up her precious little daughter, Laney was surprised to feel Gabby put her chubby little arms around her neck and say, "Mama." She closed her eyes and breathed in the wonderful smell of baby powder and freshness, relishing the feel of Gabby's tight grip around her neck. Laney felt the weight of her baby on her chest as she slowly awoke from her dream. The pressure was so great, she thought her heart would break in two. Holding nothing in her arms but her pillow, she closed her eyes and wondered how to find the strength to get up out of her lonely bed.

Therese Dotray-Tulloch

Chapter 2

Marge Peterson knew all about the struggles of forcing oneself to get up out of bed to face the day when all one wanted to do was to lay there and feel sorry for oneself. A widow for just over a year now, Marge was a native of Opossum Falls and could trace her family lineage all the way back to the founding father of the county, Joseph Renville.

Of French and Dakota descent, Renville was a friend and leader to both whites and Indians alike. After serving as a captain in the War of 1812, he continued to work as a government interpreter, scout, and church leader as he set up a trading post in the area back in 1833. Marge liked to think she got her ability to get along with just about anyone from her ancestor Joseph.

In 1856, the first land claim in Renville County was registered to Louis LaCroix, another French Canadian. He was soon followed by the

Irish, Scots, Germans, Swedes, Fins, Norwegians, and Bohemians. They settled where timber and good water were located, built homes and cleared the land to begin raising crops in the rich, black soil. Situated near the Minnesota River Valley, Opossum Falls in Renville County is right in the middle of a fertile agricultural area known for its high productivity.

Marge grew up just down the street from where she lives now on Dogwood Avenue. Her French Canadian mother married Albert Bakker of German descent, editor of the Opossum Falls Digest, so Marge grew up being dragged to newsworthy events as far back as she could remember. She had sat in on city council meetings, school board sessions, and countless basketball games in the packed school gymnasium. She went to see firsthand the devastation caused by frequent tornadoes and knew that Opossum Falls suffered from a much higher number of tornado touchdowns than the national average. She helped her father present the town's New Year's baby with all of the gifts the area merchants donated and helped deliver the hams to the winners of the Easter raffle. It had been a wonderful way to grow up, and it gave Marge a genuine appreciation for and interest in her hometown of Opossum Falls which she never outgrew.

She left home to study Library Science at Augustana College in Sioux Falls, and then came home to marry her high school sweetheart, Charles Peterson. They lived together in the Dinkytown area of Minneapolis while he finished his optometry studies but couldn't wait to get out of the cities and settle back down in Opossum Falls as soon as he was finished. Charles bought a building on Main Street which Marge helped him convert into *Eye Care for You*, the clinic where he fitted contact lenses and glasses for Opossum Falls' residents. Marge worked at the clinic with Charles as receptionist, accountant, housekeeper, and inventory manager. She kept an eye on the upcoming trends in the size and shape of eyeglasses and also continued to stock little, round wire-rimmed glasses, even when they were out of style, because she knew their fellow townsman Henry Johnson liked to wear them.

Theirs was a successful partnership in all possible ways. Charles and Marge truly enjoyed each other's company and thought nothing of spending all day side by side at work and then coming home and enjoying the evening together, too. Besides running the eye clinic, they also raised three wonderful children. The kids learned to work at the clinic, also, while they were growing up and Marge liked to think it taught them to have a good work ethic throughout life.

Marge was one of those women who never complained about her children during her child-rearing years. She had truly enjoyed every stage her kids went through. Naturally, she found some years easier than others, but she thought of it all as a unique opportunity to experience the process of life. Each three years apart, the kids were near enough in age to have grown up to be close, but far enough apart so that they never felt as though they were in competition with one another.

Still, though she had tried hard to always live in the moment, it seemed as though the years just flew by. Even though everyone had warned her, had said "Enjoy these years, they go so fast!" and she had really been aware of that, looking back she felt as though the kids were born, blink, they were starting school, blink, they were going to prom, blink, they were getting married, blink, they were gone.

Zach was the oldest, and he embodied all those characteristics typical of the first born. Organized and responsible, Zach put his leadership skills to good use in his job as Vice President of Development at Cargill in Minnetonka, a suburb of Minneapolis. Amanda, the middle child, never had to worry about being overlooked on account of being the middle child in the family as she was the only daughter and therefore held a special place in Marge's heart that would never be usurped. Tough but loving, Amanda always managed to keep up with her brothers yet still stay soft and feminine, too. Amanda taught in nearby St. Cloud, but she and her husband, a professor at St. Cloud State University, were temporarily living in South Africa while he finished his fellowship at the Energy Research Centre at Cape Town University. Tyler, the baby of the family, personified many of the youngest child's traits. Strong-willed and fiercely independent, he was currently living in Ecuador working on agricultural conservation as a Peace Corps volunteer. On their most recent Skype chat, Tyler had told Marge that he was considering extending his two-year contract by signing on for a third year. He had wanted to make sure she had no problem with that before he actually committed to it.

Marge's children were very thoughtful that way, still asking for her advice and opinion even though they were all independent adults now. Marge forgot that sometimes, and if she were upstairs putting towels away in the linen closet, she would walk past Zach's old room, and her heart would leap in her chest as she realized that he would never live in his bedroom again. Walking down the stairs, she would walk to the far right side of the staircase as if Tyler's ninja turtles would still be lined up there ready for him to jump into action to inhabit the complicated make-believe world he'd created for his plastic action figures. Marge had only recently finally thrown out the fluorescent orange, turquoise and purple nail polish that Amanda had worn for a while, realizing that Amanda had long outgrown that funky stage.

Marge had loved raising her family and always said she had no right to be sad when the kids moved out; wasn't that the goal, after all, to raise children capable of becoming independent and living on their own? She would've felt she was a failure if her adult-age children were still at home living under her roof. Until the discovery of colon cancer during Charles' routine colonoscopy, Marge and Charles were truly enjoying learning how to be just a couple again. Charles' diagnosis quickly changed all of that.

By the time the physicians at the Mayo clinic in Rochester diagnosed Charles' colon cancer, they told him the cancer was so advanced that there was nothing they could do. They gave him two weeks to live. He died a week later. Everyone told Marge it was a blessing the disease acted so quickly so Charles didn't have to suffer long. Marge knew she should agree; for Charles' sake she should be glad that the cancer didn't drag on for him but instead consumed him so rapidly. But sometimes, when Marge sat on the deck enjoying her morning coffee, she wished she had had more time to take care of Charles. She wished she had known it was going to be their last Christmas together, their last trip to Mexico, and their last time making love. Everything had happened so fast, they had barely had time to decide whether or not Charles wanted to be cremated.

~~~~~~~~~~~~~~~~~~~~~~~~~~~~~~~~

On this late September morning after Marge had opened the mail, she found herself sitting in her car in her driveway unable to back up any farther. Even if she just touched the gas pedal with her right foot, the most awful screeching noise ensued and stopped the Toyota from reversing. Marge leaned forward and let her head rest on top of her hands which were still clutching tightly onto the steering wheel. She squeezed her eyelids closed and felt hot tears seep underneath her eyelashes. Suddenly, there was a tapping on her window and she heard a voice enquiring, "Excuse me, Miss. May I help you?"

Sitting up abruptly, she hastily wiped her eyes with the back of her right hand while with her left, she rolled down the window. "Hello?" she managed to get out.

"If you like, I can get that branch out from underneath your car. It sounds like its good and stuck. I don't think you'll be able to get it out by driving over it. You might even puncture something under there and you don't wanna do that."

"Why yes, thank you, that would be much appreciated," Marge said through the open window. The black-haired man continued to look at her expectantly with kindness and sympathy showing through his deep brown eyes.

Finally he questioned again, "Miss, would you like to get out of the car?"

Marge felt flustered as she reached for the door handle and hastily opened the door, saying, "Of course, thank you."

The man held out a hand to assist her out of the car and when she reached for it, it felt warm and strong in hers. When she stood up, she faltered a moment and found herself falling backwards until the car stopped her from toppling any further.

"Are you alright?" the man asked with genuine concern on his face. "Here, let's get you seated." He guided her over to the porch and helped her sit in the rocking chair facing the front yard. "Would you like me to get you a glass of water?"

"No, thank you, really, I'll be fine in a moment," Marge murmured, feeling anything but fine. She closed her eyes and tried to find some inner strength but instead felt as if she really were about to cry again. "Maybe a glass of water would be nice. Just go on in, the door's open."

When he left to go inside, Marge tried to pull herself together. She took some deep, cleansing breaths to calm herself. Then she decided it probably wasn't the smartest thing in the world telling a complete stranger to go inside her house to get a glass of water. She knew her kids would scold her when she told them about it, if she told them about it. She tried to remember how she'd left the kitchen, if it was messy or not, then remembered she had just bolted out the door after the mail had arrived and she'd read the shocking letter. Tears flooded her eyes again as she thought about the letter, just as the man opened the door carrying a glass of water as well as some paper towels. "I thought you might need these, too," he said.

He bowed politely as he handed her the glass. He was neither short nor tall with broad shoulders, thick, black hair, and beautiful bronze-colored skin. He was in his mid-fifties and carried his age extremely well.

Marge thanked him, took a few sips of water, and then wiped her eyes with the paper towel. The man was already bending over beside the car trying to dislodge the branch. Marge was embarrassed to see what a huge branch it was. She had been so distraught when she'd gotten into her car that when the garage door opened and she saw the branch through her rearview mirror, she thought if she hit the gas hard, she'd be able to just drive over it. Seeing the size of it now, she realized how foolish she'd been.

The man stood and wiped his hands on his jeans before coming back to the porch. "I think it's best if I use my chainsaw to break up the branch a little before I try to pull it out. I have one in the back of my truck." Marge just nodded her approval, happy to continue sitting in her rocker.

A few minutes later, after the chainsaw roared to life, he made three separate cuts, then bent down and easily slid the branch out from underneath the car. He stayed down awhile obviously checking to see if she'd done any permanent damage to the undercarriage of her car. Seeming satisfied that she hadn't, he then proceeded to pick up the branches and carry them with the chainsaw. That was when Marge first noticed the truck that was parked at the end of her driveway. It was a dark green Ford pickup with a ladder attached to the side. A lawn mower and other gardening tools filled the back where the man placed the chain saw and branches.

Approaching her again, Marge saw that the logo on the man's shirt matched the one on the door of his truck, *JC's Landscaping*. "Did you know one of your brake lights is out?" the man said, "That has nothing to do with today, but I just thought I'd tell you, in case you didn't know it."

Marge's smile was a little shaky. "No, I didn't. Well that was good timing, I suppose, you driving by just as I was dragging a fallen branch around under my car."

His eyes were sympathetic as he smiled and reached out his hand. "I'm Juan Carlos," he said, pronouncing 'Juan' with a soft 'h' sound.

Marge held out her own hand, saying, "Marge Peterson. Pleased to meet you. And please forgive me-"

"Don't worry," he interrupted her, "you don't need to explain."

"No, but I'd like to," Marge continued. Juan Carlos stood in front of her looking uncomfortable. "You'll think I'm just a scatterbrained, foolish woman. You see, I just learned some rather shocking news. I mean, well, my husband is dead." Juan Carlos' eyes widened in shock. "No, no, that's not the shocking news," Marge rushed on before she sounded even more irrational. "He passed away just over a year ago. He died of cancer. We found out he had colon cancer and he died a week later. But, well, I just learned from the insurance company and their billing department that he actually knew he had cancer long before I did. He knew, but he chose not to do anything about it, no chemo, no radiation, no treatment at all. He knew, but he never told me."

Juan Carlos didn't say anything; he just continued looking at her with those kind eyes.

"Our own doctor, Dr. Smith, was the one consulting with him, according to the insurance claim. I just opened the letter and was going to confront Dr. Smith when the branch stopped me," Marge finished and sighed heavily. "On second thought, I think I'll call and make an appointment first. Or perhaps I'll invite the doctor over for coffee so he can help me understand." Suddenly realizing how much she was sharing with a complete stranger, Marge blushed, and started to apologize again.

Juan Carlos bowed slightly, saying, "I am very happy to have been of service to you," and turned around to walk slowly toward his truck. Suddenly, he turned back again and returned to face Marge, saying, "I'm sorry for your troubles."

And then he was gone.

Chapter 3

Walter Fassbinder watched the pickup truck drive away from Marge Peterson's house and wondered what landscaping work she was having done. Having been Marge's next-door neighbor for more than thirty years, he knew pretty much everything that happened over there. Knowing what an avid gardener Marge was, he was surprised that she needed help from a landscaping company. Then he realized she had probably just been getting some help with downed branches after the heavy windstorm that had passed through the previous night. Kicking himself for not going over there to check up on her, Walter hesitated at his front door, wondering if perhaps he should stop over there now to see if she'd like to join him for lunch. Afraid he would start to annoy her if he pestered her too often, he decided to carry on with his own plans.

Walter took his mail out of his mailbox and tucked it under his arm to read while he waited for his lunch at the Chit Chat Café. He strolled the few blocks to Main Street enjoying the warm September sun. The tips of the maple trees were just starting to turn color, and Walter noticed a hint of the smell of fall in the air. He saw there were a couple of pickups parked in front of Just Screw It, and he had to restrain himself from walking over there to be sure his customers were getting the help they needed from Karen. Karen had been working for him for over twenty years, and she practically knew his floor layout and inventory better than he did. Still, he had been a fixture behind the counter of his hardware store since the day he bought it. Concerned for his health, his kids had convinced him that he should retire, or at least semi-retire. He'd agreed to try it out and had been only working half days since the beginning of the month. He had to admit, he liked having the time to organize his "Boycott Wal-Mart' campaign. He also liked being able to eat lunch every day at the Chit Chat.

The bells above the restaurant door jingled as Walter opened it, causing everyone to turn to see who had walked in. First to greet him was Bianca, three plates balanced on her left arm with a coffee pot in her right, "Hey, Mr. Fassbinder, be right with you," she called out to him. The gentlemen bellied up to the counter, Dick McGhee and Henry Johnson, paused from eating to nod in his direction, as did the mayor, Jens Jenson, who was eating at a table with his brother, Jerry. Jens and Jerry owned 'J & J's Ductwork', the heating and air conditioning business in town. In a booth by the window sat Cathy Hanson. The other booth was empty, so Walter headed that way just as the door tinkled again and Laney walked in. She greeted Walter and headed over to Cath's table, apologizing for being late due to a rush at the Pick and Pay just as her lunch break was due to start.

Bianca brought Walter a cup of coffee and confirmed that there were still plenty of plates of the special available, pork and dumplings, which Walter predictably ordered. Walter enjoyed the daily special every day of the week except for Wednesday. They served chicken or beef chow mien in an effort to expose the town to a little cultural diversity. 'Worldly Wednesday' it said on the menu, but Walter wanted none of it. Betty Larson could make a terrific hamburger hot dish and her fried chicken was to die for, but her attempts at Chinese cooking fell flat.

Walter opened his mail while he waited for his lunch and eavesdropped on the conversation of the two women sitting in the booth behind him. Their impromptu lunch was a result of Cath having to come into town to pick up some parts at the implement store for Eric. Laney asked what exactly an implement store was, and

Cath was laughing and trying to explain when the door flew open and two little boys burst in. They were jabbering loudly in Spanish apparently right in the middle of an argument.

"Hey, you two, enough! You can't barge in here and interrupt everyone's lunch this way. What's going on?" Bianca scolded them.

"But, Tia, we just got yelled at by an old lady in a big, black car. She said we couldn't play outside on the sidewalk and why weren't we in school, anyway? We told her we came home for lunch and she told us to go inside and have lunch, then, because the street was no place for us to be."

"Yeah, and I said it was none of her business where we played but Manuel grabbed my arm and wouldn't let me finish but dragged me in here, instead."

The two boys were dressed the same in their jeans, hooded sweatshirts, and tennis shoes. At ten and eight years old, they looked up at their aunt expectantly. They were a part of Bianca's extended family, which seemed to consist of endless numbers of nieces, nephews, cousins and the odd grandparent, who all seemed to come and go randomly over the years. Bianca and her husband Anthony had two children of their own, Jesus Maria and Anita Beatrice.

Bianca sighed and seemed at a loss as to how to answer the boys. Looking up at the clock above the counter, she was saved by the time, and said, "Never mind, it's time for you to head back to school, anyway. Did you finish the sandwiches I left out for you?" As they nodded their heads in unison, she continued, "Good, then hurry on back to school."

The boys shouted acknowledgment to Bianca's instructions and ran back out the door.

"Sorry about that," Bianca called through the serving window into the kitchen. Betty Larson handed her two pieces of banana cream pie for the men at the counter and said, "Don't worry, I'd be upset, too, if old Mrs. Grabow stopped to yell at me."

There were a lot of chuckles in response to the Chit Chat owner's comment, but soon Cath's voice rose above the laughter. "Please do not mention that woman's name to me today! That is all I've been hearing about for the past week, Mrs. Grabow this and blanketty-blank Mrs. Grabow that. It's all I can do to stop Eric going over there and strangling her!" The Grabow's and Hanson's were neighbors, and their fields stood side by side. Apparently, Mrs. Grabow was threatening to sue the Hanson's over some herbicide drift which had wafted over from the Hanson's sugar beet field onto Mrs. Grabow's newest venture: a field full of grapes.

Catching Dick McGhee's eye, Cathy said, "I know, I know, Dick, I'm not supposed to talk about it in public. But, shoot me for saying so, when old lady Grabow is outside tidying up her walk, clutching her broom with her big black sun hat on, tell me I'm not the only one who sees a remarkable resemblance between her and the cackling wicked witch of the West!"

Walter turned around and leaned his arm on the back of his booth. "I would have to say, I am inclined to see a resemblance there myself. Not just in looks, but in behavior as well." Walter held up an envelope from his stack of mail and pulled out the folded-up letter from inside. Enjoying the attention from everyone in the café, he spoke loudly and deliberately. "I just received this in my mailbox this morning. Seems Mrs. Grabow is considering unleashing her attorneys on me, as well, if I don't desist and immediately halt any more of this;" here, he cleared his throat and began speaking in a high, squeaky voice a la Mrs. Grabow, "ridiculous and totally out of step with the rest of the nation, negative publicity about Sam Wal-Mart and the opening of a superstore in our humble town. Opossum Falls would be lucky to have Wal-Mart open up a store here. I'm sure I would feel this way whether the potential Wal-Mart were to be built on my property or not!" Putting the letter back in the envelope, Walter finished up, "Oh, and by the way, rumor has it that the property for the proposed superstore is supposedly selling for three and a half million dollars!"

"Dios mio," Bianca said as she crossed herself after setting Walter's pork and dumplings down in front of him. "What would old lady Grabow ever want with so much money anyway? She doesn't have any children, and her husband is dead and gone three years already."

"Keep hiring attorneys to scare the crap out of the rest of her fellow townsmen, perhaps?" Cath stood up and air-kissed in Laney's direction. "Time to head home with my 'implements' for Eric. He's going to wonder why it's taken me so long. Shh, mum's the word! Bye, all." The door jingled as Cath exited.

A minute later, Laney stood up to leave, too, just as Tom Larson came out of the kitchen to join Walter in his booth. "Didn't you like the soup, Laney? You've left half of it in your bowl," Tom said disapprovingly.

"It was delicious, Mr. Larson. The bowl is just much too big for me," Laney explained as she headed back to work.

"How's the search for prospective buyers going, Tom?" Walter asked out of the side of his mouth as his cheek bulged with dumpling.

"As bleak as when we started a year ago, Walter. I don't know how much longer Betty and I can do this," Tom sighed as he stirred sugar into his coffee. "My back won't be able to hold up much longer, and Betty's hips are getting so bad, she has to pull up a chair right next to the stove. I'm thinking we can stay open through the winter, but if we don't have a buyer by next summer, we might just have to close the doors, new owner or not."

"And leave Opossum Falls without a restaurant on Main Street? Wouldn't that be a shame?" Walter crooned.

"Indeed it would, but gosh darn it all, Betty and I deserve a little relaxation in our old age, too, don't ya know. We've been baking and cooking back in that kitchen for longer than you've run the hardware store, Walt. We'd like to turn the business over to someone else willing to run it, but if there's no buyer, there's no buyer, and that's that."

"And anyhow," Henry Johnson said as he headed for the door, "Wal-Mart is bound to have some kind of fast food available once they open up their doors!"

Walter didn't even hesitate but threw his biscuit right at the back of Henry's head hitting him so soundly, it knocked off his hat.

Therese Dotray-Tulloch

Chapter 4

Emma Grabow slammed the door of her Lincoln Town car and marched into her kitchen mumbling to herself. She was so angry she didn't even notice the hummingbird sipping nectar at the feeder outside her kitchen window, normally one of her greatest joys. Emma loved watching the antics of her resident hummingbirds. Especially now, when she knew her days of watching birds was limited, as soon the cold would force them farther south until the harsh Minnesota winter passed and the birds were able to return to the north again. Fuming with frustration, Emma grabbed her broom and stepped outside to sweep her front sidewalk, a task which always seemed to calm her. Grasping tightly onto the wooden handle, she vigorously swept back and forth ridding the walk of the first leaves to fall off the large oak tree shading her front yard.

Upset at seeing the Mexican boys out of school and hanging around
Main Street, she had felt it her civic duty to stop and reprimand them.
At least they actually did go to school, or so they said. She stopped
sweeping suddenly and realized she should have swung by the school
to be sure those boys actually were registered. Then, driving past her
vineyard before turning down her driveway, the damage to the vines
closest to the Hanson's property was so pronounced, she almost cried.
The arrogance of these farmers; just because Eric Hanson farmed
thousands of acres of sugar beets and she had only three acres of
grapes did not mean his fields were somehow more important than
hers. She had posted signs which said 'No Drift', had sent letters to all
of her nearby neighbors detailing the vulnerable nature of grapes and
why they had to be particularly careful when using herbicides, had
even offered to teach a Community Education class about planting
grapes, the newest Minnesota crop which was practically guaranteed to
make a profit, all to no avail. Not a single person had signed up for
her Community Ed class. Eric Hanson or someone had hired the
helicopter to spray herbicide on his sugar beets, and the fact that there
happened to be a southeast wind that day pushing the contaminant
right onto her precious grapes meant nothing to him. Well, she'd
show him. She'd contacted her lawyer, and he'd assured her that
precedent had been set and that she should have no trouble
whatsoever winning remuneration. All she needed was proof and
official verification that the reason her grapes weren't growing and the
leaves were shriveling was because they had been sprayed with
Roundup.

Marching back indoors, she didn't even notice Cathy Hanson drive by.
She went straight to the phone and picked it up, asking for the
number for the United States Department of Agriculture. She was
going to get proof of the wrong done to her and she knew just how to
get it, too.

~~~~~~~~~~~~~~~~~~~~~~~~~~~~~~~~~

Laney finished her shift at the Pick and Pay but still stayed there as
long as she possibly could. She finished putting out the newly-arrived
magazines and flipped through them for a while pretending to be
interested in the recipes for successfully baking a twenty pound turkey.
She offered to clean up the jar of pickles that Otto Schroeder
accidently dropped. After bringing in the carts that had been left
higgledy-piggledy out in the parking lot, Mr. Schluter had turned her

around and pushed her gently back out through the door, saying "Go home, Helena. It's a beautiful evening and you know we don't have very many more of those ahead of us before we start calculating wind chill. Go out and enjoy it!"

Laney had attempted to smile as she said, 'Alright, alright, I'm going," but the smile quickly left her face as the reality of going home to her empty apartment hit her and she knew she couldn't face it. Not tonight. She walked down Main Street and saw many of the shops were already closed for the day. She kept walking as the sun dropped quickly out of the sky. By now, the days were growing shorter. The sun seemed to move so much more quickly as it fell out of the sky than it did all day long as it traversed the sky, but she supposed that was just because at sunset you could measure the sun's movement against the horizon.

She had managed to get through another day. She tried to bolster her spirits by commending herself for being strong, but then, she wasn't feeling very strong. Not wanting to be alone this evening, she continued walking around Opossum Falls. She walked from one end of town to the other. She saw the streetlights come on, she heard car doors slamming as people got home from work, she watched the lights slowly come on in the houses she walked past, the warm lights looking so inviting from the outside.

It cooled down considerably once the sun had set, and Laney was beginning to wish she'd carried a sweater with her. With a heavy heart, she wondered if she'd have to give up soon and face her empty apartment, when she found herself approaching the library. The lights shone cheerfully from inside the old brick building and Laney couldn't resist going inside. Not only would people be there to prevent her from experiencing the solitude she so wanted to avoid on this night, but there would also be the comfort of being surrounded by books, sometimes the most wonderful friends a person could ask for. Everything about the place beckoned to her with promise as she walked up the stairs and went inside.

The librarian was on the phone when Laney walked in, so she just smiled at her and headed toward the fiction section of the library.

Slowly walking past the shelves of books, Laney loved to recognize the titles she'd already read, pull them from the shelf, and read the back or the front inside cover to remind herself exactly what the book had been about. Holding a Kent Haruf book in her hand, she smiled as she remembered reading about the two old bachelor farmers, when a frustrated expletive from the librarian caused her to look up.

"Oh, sorry, I'd forgotten anyone was in here," the librarian apologized. "Did you need help finding anything in particular?" When Laney assured her she was just browsing, the librarian continued, "I'm in a bit of a pickle because I have half a dozen people waiting in that room down the hall, and their tutor just canceled. I would help them myself, but I have to stay at the front desk."

"What is it they need tutoring in?" Laney asked.

"English, actually. They're adults, most of whom speak a little English, but they need help with basic reading, writing, and such. Marge Nelson comes in once a week to work with them, on a volunteer basis, but she just called to say she couldn't make it tonight, for personal reasons. She's never canceled on me like this before. I feel really bad; I know some of these people make quite an effort to get here and it seems like such a waste to have to just send them home."

Laney set the book back on the shelf and said, "Well, I speak English."

The librarian laughed and said, "Oh, please don't think I was hinting, though I realize now that it really must have sounded that way. I'm Cindy, by the way."

"I'm Laney. No, I know you weren't hinting. It's just that actually, I would be happy to help. I have nothing going on, this evening, to speak of...."

"If you really mean it, that would be fantastic! Come on, I'll introduce you to the group right now. They usually just work for an hour or so and are ready to head out between seven and seven-thirty."

Laney was glad she didn't have any time to get nervous or to change her mind. She followed Cindy down the hall and soon found herself standing in front of four women and three men, all of Hispanic origin, sitting around a large table. They listened politely as Cindy explained what had happened and who Laney was. Cindy shut the door quietly as she left the room. Laney took a deep breath and smiled hesitantly at the group. One of the men raised a hand and asked, in a strong accent, "Mrs. Marge no coming this night?"

The others murmured, "Yes, where Mrs. Marge?" and Laney realized that they hadn't understood a word of what the librarian had said. She laughed and spoke much more slowly, explaining that she would be helping them tonight.

"So, what were you planning to work on tonight with Mrs. Marge?" Laney asked. Taking the workbook that the woman named Maria held out to her, she read aloud, "Banking in English."

"Yes, what mean 'check bounce'? How my check bounce, please, Mrs.?"

Laney laughed as she pulled up a chair and began explaining the simple nuances of English to the eager group. "You definitely do not want your check to bounce," she began.

An hour later, Laney found herself saying good-bye and promising to come back again to work with Marge Nelson sometime. She was straightening up the chairs when a couple of new women walked in, one of them saying, "Oh, hello, you're new to book club!"

Cindy, the librarian, followed them into the room saying, "This is Laney. She was just helping out with our English class. But Laney, you're more than welcome to stay and join our book club, too. We meet the first Thursday of every month and absolutely anyone is welcome. Well, we say that, but we never expect any men to come. We haven't been disappointed yet, either," she finished with a laugh.

While they'd been chatting, a few more women had walked in. Laney felt grateful for her good fortune in stumbling upon the library this evening. After hearing that the book they were about to discuss was *Jonathon Strange and Dr. Norell*, Laney couldn't resist taking them up on the offer to join them for the discussion. Coincidently, she had even read the book.

There ended up to be about a dozen women who turned up. Laney
had seen some of them at the Pick and Pay and around town, but
she'd never spent time with any of them before. They were all very
welcoming and seemed genuinely excited to have a new member
attending their book club. They explained that they had been meeting
as a book club at the library for over fifteen years. It was a lovely
gathering of women aged mid-thirties through mid-seventies. Laney
felt so glad to be there. They spent about half of the time talking
about the book, and the rest of the time just chatting about their lives
and the goings on around town. When it was over, Marianne offered
to give Laney a ride home, which she accepted.

Waving good-bye as the car pulled away from the curb, Laney took a
deep breath before digging her keys out of her purse and slowly
walking up the stairs to her apartment. She was glad not to have
another long evening stretched out ahead of her. Tonight, maybe
she'd even be able to fall asleep without too much trouble.

In her dream, she was watching Gabby play on the edge of the lake. She was wearing a little one-piece bathing suit, white with tiny yellow ducks scattered across it with a pink ruffle above the rose-colored stripes covering her lower half. She was wearing a diaper underneath her bathing suit giving her the look of having an enormous bottom. She wore a pastel-colored plaid bonnet tied beneath her chin. She had a green plastic bucket with a matching spade and she was busy digging with the tiny shovel, using both hands to carve out a hole in the sand. Dipping the bucket into the lake which she could reach from her sitting position, Gabby then dumped the bucketful of water into her hole. Reaching to fill up the bucket again, she turned back to the hole and found the water had all seeped out already. Nonplussed, Gabby filled the bucket with water, poured it into her hole, and repeated the process dozens of times without tiring. Only the sudden appearance of a couple of ducks swimming into view caused her to pause. Gabby watched the ducks for a while, mesmerized by their paddling feet visible in the clear lake water. Slapping her spade in the water, she shouted, "bah!" causing the ducks to spread their wings and with a few fearsome flaps, ascend into the air. Watching them fly off to the other side of the lake, she stared until the ducks circled around and landed a safer distance from the little girl playing in the water. This caused Gabby to squeal with delight and she turned back to look at Laney to be sure she'd seen them, too.

"Yes, you scared the ducks, didn't you, silly girl?" Laney said. "Can you say 'duck'?" But Gabby had already gone back to her task of filling her bottomless hole with water. Laney watched her daughter contentedly, marveling at her patience in repeating the same task over and over again yielding absolutely no results. In the distance she heard a familiar tinkling and she watched Gabby with interest knowing she, too, would recognize the sound when she heard it. Calmly filling the bucket with water, Gabby was intent on her task when she froze midmovement. Throwing the bucket aside, she screamed and twisted onto all fours, crawling just as fast as she could on the pebbly sand up to where Laney sat, laughing.

"Ay, ay!" Gabby said as she pointed towards the approaching ice cream truck.

"What is it?" Laney asked, feigning ignorance.

Putting her sandy hands on either side of Laney's face, Gabby looked tellingly into her eyes and repeated her nonsensical words which clearly said 'ice cream' to her mind. She pointed again excitedly in the direction of the hypnotizing music. "Alright, come on, then, let's stop him," Laney said as she reached in her bag for her billfold.

Picking up Gabby, she held her easily on one hip as she brushed the sand off herself, tugged her bathing suit cover down, and walked up to the young kid running the ice cream truck. "We'll take a Sundae cone please. Do you have one without nuts?"

"Yeah, that would be the vanilla fudge chocolate," he said as he opened the lid and dug into his cooler. "And how about you, Mom, don't you want an ice cream treat, too?" He was cute, with his baseball cap turned backwards, his summer suntan, and his friendly, hazel eyes.

"What are you, on commission or something?" Laney laughed as she took the cone for Gabby but held it carefully out of her reach.

"Actually, I am," he admitted unashamedly. "I had to buy my entire inventory from the get go. So, you see, if you don't buy a treat from me, I'll be stuck eating ice cream till kingdom comes and won't be able to afford the books I need for school next semester. So, what do you say?" He tilted his head inquisitively.

"You're good!" Laney laughed again. "Alright, how about one of the mint chocolate cones, do you have any of those?" After settling up, he thanked her and pedaled off while Laney hollered after him, "Stay in school, alright?"

She went back to the water's edge and sat down with Gabby right between her legs. She opened both of their cones and let Gabby hold hers all by herself, making sure she never let it get near the sand. The Schwann's ice cream was delicious, as usual, and Laney thought what a lovely additional benefit it was to having kids, that you got to eat all sorts of treats you might not expose yourself to otherwise. Gabby had just as much ice cream on her face, neck, chest, and running down both arms as she had inside of herself, Laney was sure, but when she tried to take it away from her for a second to splash water on her to clean her off, Gabby screamed and reached for the remainder of the soggy cone. "Alright, alright," Laney admonished as she quickly handed the cone back to her. "Finish up and I'll clean you off afterwards."

That's what they call a sugar-high, Laney thought to herself as she leaned back on both elbows while Gabby gobbled up the last of her cone. Sitting in the shallow water, they managed to clean themselves off while having fun splashing at one another. Gabby tried to master Laney's trick of punching into the water with her fist, followed by her other hand slapping at the water that rose up as a result of the punch creating a loud, pleasing 'crack', but she was too slow. Over and over again, she tried, finally getting so frustrated she started to cry in aggravation. Knowing just what to do, Laney carried her back up the beach and lay down with her on the blanket, humming softly to her as she did so. Gabby's cries quickly turned to whimpers. Within moments, she was asleep, one minute sucking vigorously onto her thumb, the next so soundly asleep, her thumb slipped soundlessly out of her mouth onto Laney's chest. Gazing down at her, Laney's heart overflowed with love.

Laney felt the weight of her baby on her chest as she slowly awoke from her dream. The pressure was so great, she thought her heart would break in two. Holding nothing in her arms but her pillow, she closed her eyes again and wondered how to find the strength to get up out of bed.

Therese Dotray-Tulloch

Chapter 5

Marge got out of bed and went straight to the kitchen, determined not to waste another day in self-pity and recrimination. She went to the fridge and took out the butter to soften, then went into the pantry and gathered flour, sugar, baking soda, chocolate chips, and oatmeal, all the ingredients she would need to make her signature oatmeal-chocolate chip cookies. She preheated the oven and got out her favorite ceramic mixing bowl but then just stood at the counter, her mind circling back over the awful truth that her husband had lied to her. What kind of a wife was she, after all, if her life's partner knew that he was dying and not only kept the information from her, but also denied himself treatment and any chance of curing himself of his fatal disease? This made a mockery not only of Charles' death but also of the life they had shared together for so many years. The ugly reality of that was like a punch to her gut, and Marge found herself staggering backward, stopping only when she'd backed into the warm stove. The ringing of the doorbell shook her out of her reverie, and glancing into the little mirror in the hallway, she brushed her bangs out of her eyes and scolded, "Pull yourself together," as she opened the front door.

She was surprised and not just a little pleased to see Juan Carlos standing at the door, a pair of work gloves in his hand. "Good morning, Juan Carlos," she said at the exact same time that he was saying, "Mrs. Peterson."

"Oh, I'm sorry," she said, flustered, "I don't know your surname."

"It's Ramirez, but please, call me Juan Carlos," he said with a grin, rolling the r at the beginning of his name naturally, pronouncing the second r almost like a d.

"Ramirez," she repeated, completely anglicizing the name. They both laughed. "No, I can never get those 'R's right in Spanish. Well then, you must call me Marge. Please, won't you come in?" She opened the front door wide but Juan Carlos was already shaking his head.

"No, Marge," he said, pronouncing it almost like march, "I've just come to see if you'll let me finish what I started yesterday."

Seeing her face reddening with embarrassment at the remembrance of the awkwardness of yesterday's meeting, Juan Carlos quickly hurried on.

"When I was here before, I couldn't help but notice that the branch on the driveway wasn't the only one damaged by the windstorm. If you look, you can see there are a couple of other branches that don't look very stable. They could get blown down in the next strong wind and break a window or worse. I have all of the equipment, I'd be happy to take care of them for you."

"No, I mean, yes," Marge stammered. "No, I hadn't noticed the branches, but yes, I would appreciate the help, most definitely." Marge looked up at the large elm tree as she spoke and did indeed see some other branches dangling.

"Then I'll get started right away," Juan Carlos said as he backed away.

"This may take a few hours, so I hope you won't mind the noise."

Marge shut the door feeling lighter in spirit. Heading back into the kitchen, she proceeded to make the cookies feeling more purposeful now that she had someone with whom to share her finished product.

After a couple of hours, Marge went back onto the porch and set out coffee and cookies. Calling to Juan Carlos when there was a pause in his chain sawing, she asked if he had time to take a break.

"I certainly do, if it includes some of those delicious cookies I've been smelling," he said as he was climbing down the ladder. "If you hadn't invited me soon, I'm afraid I would have had to go looking for you, perhaps with some made up injury just to give you a chance to offer me some cookies."

Marge laughed and suggested he go wash up in the little bathroom just off of the kitchen. She sat down and poured out two cups of coffee from the thermos, rocking gently in the rocker while she waited. A few minutes later, Juan Carlos came back out the door, a half-eaten cookie in his hand. "Please forgive me, I simply could not wait even one minute more. Mmm-mmm, I think the taste is just as excellent as the aroma which has been driving me crazy all morning! Normally, I am not so rude as this, but I think I have been under the spell of your cookie smell!"

Marge laughed delightedly, motioning to the other rocking chair for Juan Carlos to sit in, saying, "There is plenty more where that one came from, so please, eat!" She handed him the plate full of cookies and he took one, and then two more. "Do you need cream or sugar in your coffee?"

"I am sorry to admit I like equal portions of coffee, milk, and sugar! Where I come from, everyone takes coffee this way. Black coffee, no, no, I have never been able to drink it that way."

"I'm so glad," Marge said as she pushed the sugar bowl toward him and poured a generous amount of cream into his cup and then into hers, too. "I have to admit, even at my age, I totally fall under peer pressure and take my coffee however the person I am with takes it.

Lately, it seems, everyone has given up smoking and taken to drinking coffee black. I have learned to drink it that way, but I love to have an excuse to doctor it up with cream when I see someone else rebellious enough to do so!"

"Oh, Mrs. Peterson..."

"Marge, please," she corrected him.

"Marge, let me show you, this is how we take the cream in our coffee," and he proceeded to empty the little creamer first into his cup and then into hers changing the black coffee to a light brown.

"Wonderful!" She took a nice, slow sip of her coffee, and nodding her head said, "Oh dear, Juan Carlos, I think you're going to be a bad influence on me." When he threw back his head and laughed, Marge's heart skipped a beat and she realized with surprise that she felt happy, happier than she'd felt in a long time.

Marge went in to get more cream and Juan Carlos finished off the plate of cookies while the coffee break stretched into forty-five minutes. They chatted about a variety of things. Marge was surprised to learn that Juan Carlos had lived in Opossum Falls for a very long time. In fact, he'd been coming there to work in the sugar beet fields since he was a little boy. They chatted about family and how a lot of his family lived in Piedras Negras, just over the border from Eagle Pass, Texas. Seems he had been married once but he wasn't anymore, that he had one son who died but left behind a little granddaughter. When Marge confided that she didn't have any grandchildren yet but was looking forward to the day, Juan Carlos agreed that they made having children worthwhile.

Pushing himself to his feet, he said, "Well, thank you for the break, but now I must get back to work."

"Juan Carlos," Marge asked, "Would you be interested in joining me for lunch? I have some leftover chicken. I'm not at all used to cooking for only one yet, and I was planning to make some chicken and wild rice soup." Juan Carlos hesitated for just a second.

"Oh, I understand if you don't want to," Marge waved her napkin, feeling embarrassed.

"I would be honored to join you for lunch, Marge," Juan Carlos said with a bow. "I noticed that the trees lining the back fence by the alley could use trimming, as well, so I have enough to keep me busy for a few days, at least. They are getting close to the electrical lines and you don't want to be at fault for a power loss. I will just let my previous appointment for this afternoon know that I won't be coming." He took his cell phone out from his pocket and walked back toward his truck to make his call.

~~~~~~~~~~~~~~~~~~~~~~~~~~~~~~~

Walter noticed that the JC Landscaping truck was sitting at Marge's for the third day in a row. Karen had come down with the flu so he'd had to fill in at Just Screw It for her shift as well as his own. He hadn't had a chance to check up on Marge but just kept seeing that truck there as he came and went. Karen was back at work this morning so Walter decided he'd go over and invite Marge to join him for lunch at the Chit Chat. Patting on an extra-generous amount of after shave, he studied himself in the mirror. "Not bad, not bad at all you ol' tiger," he said to himself as he brushed his eyebrows down a little bit. He thought he was one of those lucky men who seemed to get more handsome with age. His white hair made him feel much more distinguished than his brown hair ever had. "Now, let's go visit the cougar," he said to himself in the mirror, raising his eyebrows up and down suggestively.

Walking up to Marge's front door, he snapped a red flower out of her garden and held it out to her when she opened the door. "For you, my good neighbor."

"Good grief, Walter, I prefer to enjoy my Salvias where I planted them in my garden, if you don't mind," she said with a laugh, plucking the flower out of his hand. "Come on back, I've got food on the stove in the kitchen I have to keep an eye on."

Walter followed Marge back to the kitchen, admiring the sway of her hips as she hurried down the hallway. She looked good in her mustard-yellow Capri pants with a black, fitted blouse falling to just below her hips. Marge always managed to look elegant even when she was just home cooking, and Walter had always admired that about her.

Even at her age, she was still a fine looking woman. He loved how she kept her blond hair cut fashionably just above her shoulders, the nails on both her hands and feet polished prettily in soft pink. He sighed, wondering if he'd given her enough time to mourn Charles' death and if he could put the moves on her at last.

"What are you up to, Walter? Do you need me to sign any more petitions to help stop Wal-Mart from ruining Opossum Falls?" Marge had a twinkle in her eye which Walter took to be a good sign. She seemed really happy today. Perhaps she had missed him and was glad he'd stopped over. She lifted the lid off the frying pan and began to stir the contents.

"Wow, something smells good," Walter complimented, thinking maybe he could save a few bucks and skip the fried chicken at the Chit Chat today. "What are you making?"

"It's a new recipe. I'm making chicken fajitas with rice and refried beans on the side," Marge was saying as Walter came to stand behind her to sample her cooking. His heart started racing as he found himself standing so close to her. Suddenly, he decided to take the chance and he nuzzled the back of her neck, placing his lips gently against her skin. Marge was so surprised, she froze. Just then, Juan Carlos's voice was heard through the back door, "Your attempt to cook Mexican smells wonderful, Marge." He stopped abruptly as his eyes took in the scene at the stove.

Marge dropped her spoon and turned around, but Walter didn't move so she found herself pressed flat against him with the stove behind preventing her from moving. "Juan Carlos," she began, but he was already out the door. "I must be going," he said without turning around, "Good-bye."

Marge was so flustered she didn't quite know what to do. She stared at Walter incredulously and wondered why her heart was racing so in her chest, why she was feeling so sad and disappointed that Juan Carlos had just left and wouldn't be joining her for lunch as he had for the past few days.

Her speechlessness carried on for so long, it made him uncomfortable. Walter cleared his throat at last, and said, "Sorry about that, Marge. Your kitchen just smelled so good, and you, too, that I just got a little carried away, I guess." Marge heard the rumbling of Juan Carlos' truck as he pulled away from the curb while Walter was murmuring, "I don't really eat much Mexican food, but I'm willing to start."

Walter looked so chagrined that Marge gave him a small smile and said, "Well, would you like to stay for lunch, then?"

"Si, señora," he replied to which Marge laughed.

Lunch turned out to be a wonderful affair. Besides the chicken fajitas, Marge had made pineapple upside down cake for dessert. They sat in her kitchen chatting and laughing while the time just flew by. Walter helped her clean up even though she tried to stop him, thinking these little touches were sure to put him in her good graces. It wasn't till after he'd gone home and was gluing sticks onto his protest signs to make them easier to carry that it occurred to him that the JC Landscaping worker had called Marge by her first name and had been walking through the backdoor as if he owned the place. Walter didn't feel very good about that, and he decided he'd have to have a word with Marge about it just as soon as he got the chance. She was a widow living alone now and she had to be careful about those sorts of things. Then again, Walter smiled to himself, maybe she wouldn't be living alone for long.

Therese Dotray-Tulloch

Chapter 6

Bianca Gonzalez shut the door to the Chit Chat as the last customer left and she turned the sign around so the word 'Closed' faced the street. Filling the plastic ice cream pail with hot water, she splashed some vinegar in it and began to wipe down each table. She hummed to herself as she worked efficiently and thoroughly, washing off the chairs as well as the tables. Bianca took great pride in the little café and always made sure everything was absolutely spic and span.

Standing at just over five feet tall, Bianca was short but very sturdy and solid so she never gave the impression of not being tall. She had beautiful, thick, black hair which she kept in a long, tight pony tail which cascaded down her back from the crown of her head. Her skin was olive colored and so smooth there wasn't a blemish to be found. Large, brown eyes with thick black eyelashes were the most prominent feature on her round face, until she smiled, which was often, with her contagious wide smile full of nearly perfect white teeth. Her limbs were compact and strong, but she had exceptionally tiny little hands with stubby fingers, so small that she still shopped for winter gloves in the children's department.

A hard worker, Bianca arrived at the Chit Chat earlier than the Larson's these days because she liked to have everything perfect before she opened the doors. She had been born in a border town in Texas, just across the Rio Grande from Mexico, but like many in her situation, had had ties to Minnesota all of her life. Born into a migrant worker's family, she had traveled back and forth on the road from Texas to Minnesota more times than she could count. Her father worked in a canning factory in Southern Minnesota and oftentimes her mother did, too. Starting in June with the pea pack, they would stay through the end of the corn pack in October. When they were little, the kids would all come, too, and spend their days playing in the backyard in the trailer park where the company provided housing for the seasonal workers.

Loading up the ancient station wagon to drive back home to Eagle Pass, the kids loved to count states as they crossed from Minnesota into Iowa through the harvested corn and soybean fields, the freshly-tilled earth a rich, shiny black. They entertained themselves by playing the License Plate and the Alphabet games as well as I Spy and Twenty Questions. They would drive briefly into Missouri before entering Kansas, then through the flat, dusty plains of Oklahoma dotted with the monstrous-looking oil diggers. They would perk up when they crossed the Texas state line but still were barely half-way home. Driving through Fort Worth, Austin, and San Antonio, they sang songs, and the closer they got to home, the sillier their songs became. Finally leaving Interstate 35, they turned South onto US 57 for the last hundred miles to Eagle Pass.

The twin sister to Piedras Niegras on the other side of the river, Eagle Pass was the first U.S. settlement on the Rio Grande, originally called Camp Eagle Pass. Occupied by the Texas militia, they were meant to stop the illegal trade between Mexico and the U.S. during the Mexican-American War. After the war, trade between the two countries flourished and Fort Duncan was built upstream of Eagle Pass to supervise that trade.

A sleepy town during the hot summer months when a huge chunk of its population heads north to find work, winter finds it a lively, hopping place when the migrant residents return home and find jobs in construction or as mechanics to tide them over till it's time to head North again. During elementary school, Bianca, her siblings, and all those in their situation would always arrive about a month after school had already started. The teachers in Eagle Pass would have to work doubly hard to enable all the migrant-worker kids to catch up. It was too hard to miss the crucial first weeks of class in high school, so Bianca's father started going to Minnesota by himself in the later years, living without his family for at least four months out of the year.

The migrant workers had a hard life. They worked extremely hard, long hours every day either in the sugar beet fields, cutting asparagus, husking corn, or packing peas. They stayed in dormitories or trailer parks, often ten to fifteen workers crowded into tiny rooms with no air conditioning and sometimes with no cooking facilities. The local parks in the small towns where they worked became the kitchens for the migrants over the summer months and the smells of cooking corn tostados over little charcoal grills wafted throughout the warm summer nights.

Bianca had vowed she would escape the migrant worker's life, so she studied hard at school with dreams of working in the hospitality industry at the Hyatt Regency Hotel in downtown Houston. She had gone on a school trip once and had taken the glass-walled elevator up thirty-three floors to the famous Spindletop restaurant in the Hyatt to enjoy the 360-degree view of the city. Bianca had decided that was where she wanted to work. She started practicing cooking, specializing in Southwestern fare; her family came to love her cooking so much, that they all blamed their round plumpness on Bianca.

Even their dog, Picapiedra, loved Bianca's cooking. His full name was Pedro Picapiedra, Fred Flintstone in Spanish, because his paws were so chunky they looked just like Fred's block feet and because Bianca's Papa had loved to watch the Flintstones when he was growing up. Part basset hound, part golden retriever, Picapiedra looked exactly like a basset hound wearing hairy, salmon-colored pajamas. One spring evening, a huge tornado ripped through Eagle Pass and Picapiedra was sucked out the garage window where the family was hiding from the storm. Afterward, they couldn't find him anywhere. Bianca's Papa put up posters all around town and drove his old station wagon up and down the streets calling, "Pedro, Pedro Picapiedra!" all over town. Shouts of "Bilma," Spanish for Wilma, would follow him down the street, bringing a little humor to the devastated town that was nearly incapacitated by the deadly tornado.

A month after the tornado had passed through and just before Bianca's Papa was due to travel North again for pea pack, Bianca's brother called from outside, "Papa, come quick!"

Hurrying through the front door, the family was met by a most astounding sight: Picapiedra dragging himself down the street, trying to get home. His two front legs were broken and he had numerous cuts and scrapes from the escapade, but his tail was wagging vigorously and he appeared absolutely ecstatic to be home again. Where the tornado had dropped him out of the sky, they would never know. Nor would they ever be able to figure out how Picapiedra managed to drag his heavy body home crawling with his front legs broken in multiple places, but crawl home he did, to the great relief of Bianca's Papa. Bianca's brothers teased her that it was because of her good cooking and all of the leftovers that Picapiedra had grown to love. Secretly, Bianca thought that they were right. Bianca's Papa wanted to change the dog's name to Milagros, which meant 'miracle', but the family talked him out of it, saying it would be cruel to change his name when he had crawled so far and long to get back to the only place where he could be called by his real name, so Bianca's Papa conceded.

He would not give in, however, in his determination to take the dog with him to Minnesota that year. Refusing to be talked out of it, he placed Picapiedra in the front seat for the eighteen-hour drive, lifting him out so he could perform the necessary duties when needed, feeding him fast food along the way. The housing provided at the canning factory normally didn't allow pets, but after hearing Picapiedra's incredible story, they allowed the dog to stay. He became the mascot for all of the workers, looked after by whichever gentle caregiver wasn't working during that particular shift.

The year that Picapiedra traveled to Minnesota was also the year that Bianca got pregnant and all of her dreams of having a sophisticated job in a fancy hotel were put on the back burner. Anthony Gonzalez was the father; a neighbor and classmate in Eagle Pass, they'd been sweethearts since middle school. After they got married and Jesus Maria was born, Anita Beatrice arrived just eleven months later. For one month, the two children were the same age, and Bianca would tease them and call them her terrible twins. With two kids to feed, Bianca and Anthony turned to the only work they knew, joining the other seasonal workers in Minnesota. After a few years of traveling back and forth between Texas and Minnesota, Anthony got a permanent job at the sugar beet factory in Opossum Falls. Bianca was thrilled to put down roots and call the appealing little town home.

Opossum Falls was used to having Mexicans come work in the sugar beet fields every summer. They stayed in rather ramshackle dormitories and apartments above the shops on Main Street. The school organized a summer program to give the kids some structure while their parents worked in the fields all day. The town put up with the unusual activity of kids playing in the streets late into the evening on the long summer days. When all of the beets had been harvested, the seasonal workers drove back down south and Opossum Falls returned to its comfortable status as a small, Midwestern rural community of European stock.

When workers like Anthony Gonzalez were hired by the beet factory fulltime, some of the local residents didn't know what to make of it. Veronica Schroeder suggested that they live in Willmar where other Mexicans lived and just commute to Opossum Falls for work. She argued that their children would surely be much happier surrounded by other kids just like them. Marge Peterson was so infuriated by that comment, she suggested that Veronica move to South Africa where the idea of apartheid originated and she could be surrounded by other people who thought like she did. Back and forth the arguments raged.

In the meantime, Bianca and her family moved into a spacious, three-bedroom apartment above the hardware store, enrolled the kids in school, joined the church, girl scouts, and boy scouts, and gradually became accepted in the community. Anthony was a dependable, hard worker, Bianca was friendly and out-going, and the kids were normal children with slightly darker skin than the rest of their classmates in

Opossum Falls. With the passing of time, people who were inclined to discern such things noticed it less and less in the Gonzalez' family. When her kids got a little older, Bianca went to the Chit Chat to ask if they would consider hiring her. She told them of her love of cooking and how she specialized in southwestern fare.

Tom and Betty Larson had owned and worked at the Chit Chat Café for over thirty years, most years running the place completely on their own. Oh sure, their kids had always helped out, first by sweeping the floors and doing the dishes, eventually by taking orders and finally even helping with the cooking. Betty passed down all of her recipes to her kids and trusted them to follow them religiously to duplicate exactly the comfort food the Chit Chat was patronized for. Now, of course, their kids were long gone working at high tech jobs in Chicago and Silicon Valley, rarely using the recipes that Betty had so painstakingly written down for them. Tom had been about to say no to Bianca, to repeat his longstanding speech about the Chit Chat not being a job for them but more like their own kitchen which they opened up to their friends day after day to share meals together, when Betty shushed him.

"For Pete's sake, Tom, this isn't a hobby for me, it's a job. I'm on the far side of my sixties by now with seventy peeking right around the corner, and you know what, I'm getting kind of tired." She'd looked at Bianca then and she'd liked what she'd seen although she had to squash the whole 'southwestern' cooking idea right away. "Minnesota bland is what our customers want," she'd told Bianca, "we don't have spicy or zesty, we serve mild and bland. We'll start you out doing dishes and see what happens from there."

Five years later, Bianca was waitressing fulltime and had become a much-loved figure at the Chit Chat. Betty didn't think anyone knew it, but more and more Bianca was doing the cooking for the restaurant, too, making the soups in advance and cooking up the daily specials. Without making a big deal of it, she was slowly introducing a few more spices into the familiar dishes, and even Betty didn't know why but she would find herself saying, "The Hamburger Hot dish is really tasty today; must be the Benson's hamburger meat cooking up lean and juicy." Bianca kept tossing in a bit more cumin here, Mexican oregano and cilantro there to the continued delight of the Chit Chat patrons.

~~~~~~~~~~~~~~~~~~~~~~~~~~~~~~~~~~~

Bianca was just finishing up sweeping the floor when there was a sharp rap on the locked Chit Chat door, and glancing up at the clock, Bianca hurried over to let her daughter in. "Hola, hija, you're late today. You'll have to eat quickly."

"Dance line practice went about twenty minutes longer than usual," Anita Beatrice said as she tossed her heavy backpack filled with books onto the chair and collapsed into the one right next to it. "I'm beat!"

"You stay put and I'll bring your supper right away. You need to eat fast so you're not late for your shift at Pick and Pay." Bianca put the food that had been warming on the stove in front of her daughter.

"Oh, my gosh, this soup is amazing! What is it?" Anita said as she gobbled it down.

"Taco soup," Bianca said proudly, "The whole huge kettle went so quickly, I had to put that bowl aside for you before noon to be sure you'd get some."

"Taco soup!" Anita Beatrice chuckled, "You are going to turn this town into Mexican food lovers yet, Mom, just you wait and see!"

Bianca poured herself a half of a cup of coffee and filled the rest with milk as she sat down across from her daughter while she chatted about her day at school. As she listened, she marveled at the fact that this beautiful young woman was her daughter and at how quickly life was going by. Wasn't it just yesterday that she had been comforting her little girl when she'd fallen off of her bicycle? Anita Beatrice's thick, long hair had a lovely natural wave, and her intelligent, brown eyes sparkled with interest at everything life set before her. She was planning to go to college the year after next in St. Cloud and Bianca was so proud of her. She studied her pretty face while Anita Beatrice chatted and tried to freeze the moment in her memory knowing how much she would miss these regular day to day moments when her daughter moved away.

"So, next week everyone votes for Homecoming candidates and a lot of my friends think I'll be one, for sure! I don't, but I'm sure Matthew will! The quarterback is always a candidate, but even if he weren't quarterback, Matthew is so popular and good-looking he would definitely be a candidate anyhow. So, when can we go shopping for a homecoming dress?"

Anita Beatrice sat for a few more minutes while she finished her dinner and then left to go to work as a cashier at Pick and Pay. Bianca quickly finished cleaning up the Chit Chat so she could get home to start preparing dinner for the rest of her family. She was thinking of serving chili relleno as she locked up the backdoor.

Chapter 7

Jens Jenson took the bag from Laney and purposely grabbed onto her hand instead of the bag, squeezing tightly while trying to convey some meaning as he stared into her eyes. Annoyed, she pulled her hand away without trying to be obvious about it and turned to face her next customer. The mayor was always trying to get Laney alone, but she was totally disinterested and baffled that he couldn't see that. Did he think his position as mayor gave him extra privileges? The fact that he was a married man made Laney so angry she wanted to scratch the skin off of his hand the next time he tried to get her attention at the grocery store. What a creep. He was really enjoying the attention he was getting from the Wal-Mart team as they worked out the details of opening up the superstore in town. Knowing how anxious Jenson was to have Wal-Mart in Opossum Falls, Laney imagined he was giving them huge tax incentives.

Emma Grabow was next in line looking as impatient as always. Laney greeted her politely and rang up her items thinking how sad it looked when single people shopped: tiny cans of vegetables, the smallest containers of milk and ice cream, just a couple of bananas and grapefruit. She smiled as she handed over Mrs. Grabow's groceries and was pleased to get a gentle one in return which took years off of the woman's face. It was a lovely form of human kindness giving a smile and one was almost always rewarded instantly with one in return.

Anita Beatrice was working at the cash register two aisles down chatting and laughing with each and every customer and helping to make Pick and Pay a happy place to be. In between, Shannon Fischer was working at a cash register, too, but she hardly interacted with the customers at all. Laney had noticed that she was looking rather pale so she called across the aisle to her and said, "Break time! Go sit out back and catch some fresh air, Shannon."

Shannon knew it wasn't time for her to take a break yet, but she felt like she was about to throw up any minute so she smiled gratefully at Laney, locked up her cash register and fled out the back door. Laney, looking worried, watched her go until a bag of chilies rolled down her conveyer belt. She looked up to see Marge Peterson unloading her grocery cart onto the conveyer belt.

"Mrs. Peterson, I hope you're feeling better!"

Explaining that she hadn't really been sick but just needed a 'personal day', Marge got a chuckle out of using the trendy, new term. She thanked Laney for taking over her English class at the library the other day and invited her to come back to class anytime. So much of what the non-native English speakers needed was just someone to converse with to get that useful one on one practice, so Marge tried to express to Laney how sincere she was in inviting her back. "We could be co-teachers, you and I."

Laney was flattered that Marge was being so nice about it and felt sure she would help out again the following week. She was still struggling to keep her head above water by staying busy. Surrounding herself with such kind people was exactly what Laney needed. She was about to say so when Mrs. Peterson turned excitedly to the man unloading his groceries behind her, "Juan Carlos, hello! I was hoping I would run into you again."

"Mrs. Peterson," he said stiffly without looking up. Laney didn't recognize the extremely handsome man removing groceries from his cart but she greeted him warmly and waited for Mrs. Peterson to step through to the aisle so he could come closer to the cash register but she wasn't budging.

"Juan Carlos, I believe you left something at my house when you ran out so quickly yesterday," Marge said in a teasing tone.

Juan Carlos looked up then with a puzzled look in his beautiful brown eyes, "No, I don't believe that I did."

"Yes, you did," she replied with a big smile on her face and Laney realized with surprise that Marge was flirting with him. Juan Carlos was trying unsuccessfully not to smile back at her. Laney could almost feel the magnetic pull between the two of them as they looked into each other's eyes across the grocery cart. With a crooked grin, Juan Carlos finally gave in and asked, "What, then? What did I leave behind?" He pronounced the 'w' with the distinct 'hw' sound.

"Your lunch," Marge replied triumphantly, "Surely you remember I was attempting to make fajitas for my first time ever?" Juan Carlos laughed while she continued, "But maybe that's why you ran out so quickly, because it was my first time?"

A flicker of embarrassment crossed Juan Carlos' face, "No, that is not why I ran out."

"Well, you won't believe what I just bought," Marge continued brightly while ignoring his discomfort, "Hot red chilies!" She lifted them out of the grocery bag for him to see. "I found a recipe for enchiladas that I'm dying to try. I'll expect you tomorrow for lunch and will not accept 'no' for an answer!"

Juan Carlos looked like he was going to melt on the spot and that saying 'no' was the farthest thing from his mind. Smiling warmly back at Marge, he told her to expect him first thing in the morning and that he would work in the yard until lunch time. His eyes followed Marge closely as she walked away. Continuing to ring up his groceries, Laney made idle chit chat. "Looks like you've got a little one in the house.

Animal crackers, Captain Crunch, popsicles; someone is going to be happy to see you when you get home."

Juan Carlos smiled at her and looking into his eyes Laney thought, no wonder Marge Peterson has fallen for him. "Yes, my granddaughter, Isabella Rose. She's turning five years old next month." And just like that, Laney felt it happening again. She felt herself descending rapidly down a long black tunnel and she was back at the time of The Event. She closed her eyes and tried to block it all out; she couldn't bear to experience it again. She felt strong arms around her and a voice in her ear saying, "Let me help you. Please, Miss, sit down here."

Laney opened her eyes as Juan Carlos was slowly lowering her into a chair that seemed to have materialized out of nowhere. Laney saw concerned faces all around her and she was so embarrassed, she wished the ground would open up and swallow her right then and there. She kept repeating that she was alright, really, but Mr. Schluter insisted that she take a break and go sit at the picnic table out back.

Although the sun was out, it was still chilly, so Laney pulled on her jacket as she went to join Shannon at the picnic table. A black walnut tree shaded the picnic table and from time to time dropped its heavy nuts onto the table with a loud crack. Shannon was playing with one of the nuts as she sat shivering at the table, tossing it back and forth between her red-chapped hands.

"Be careful with black walnuts," Laney advised, "They'll stain your hands so you'll never get the black off."

Shannon caught the nut and looked down at the palms of her hands which were indeed covered in dark smudges. She sighed heavily. "That's just great. I mean, what else can possibly go wrong?"

"Having a bad day?" Laney asked, grateful not to have Shannon asking about her and why she had suddenly joined her on break.

"Mmm, you could say that."

"Care to talk about it? I mean, I know we don't know each other well, we're just co-workers, but sometimes that's exactly the sort of person to confide in. No preconceived notions, expectations, opinions, you know," Laney said. Shannon stared off toward the bushes deep in thought. "But, believe me, I understand if you don't want to talk about it."

After a long pause, Shannon turned her head to look at Laney. Her eyes were filled with tears, but her voice was completely calm as she said softly, "I'm pregnant."

Laney reached her hand across the table and held onto Shannon's, "Oh, honey, that's nothing to cry about. Being pregnant is like being given a precious gift. You just need to figure out what you're going to do with it, that's all."

Like a dam bursting open, Shannon started talking and there was no stopping her. Laney quickly realized that she must have been the perfect person for Shannon to talk to. Shannon's father was the pastor at the Lutheran Church in town. A strict and rather bull-headed man, he was married to a meek-mannered, rather dull woman who usually went along with whatever he said. They were into their forties before Shannon was born, and she was raised in the spotlight of the church and made to feel as though whatever she did was a reflection on the church. With little freedom and hardly any joy, Shannon grew up in Opossum Falls where everyone knew her as the Minister's daughter. It wasn't until the past summer when she was accepted into the People to People Ambassador Program and managed to talk her parents into letting her go that she was finally able to spread her wings and fly.

For three weeks, Shannon traveled with a group of kids her age to Europe to act as a young ambassador of the United States. Unfortunately, having been raised under such strict conditions that she'd never had to make any choices on her own, her first taste of freedom nearly killed her as she said 'yes' to just about everything. Traveling around Italy, France, and England, Shannon couldn't soak up enough of the history and culture of these fascinating places she'd only read about in books. She also wanted to absorb as much of the night life as possible, so whenever any of the kids wanted to sneak away from the chaperones at night, Shannon went, too. She tried alcohol for the first time, as well as drugs and sex. She had the time of her life and for the first time didn't have to worry about her actions reflecting badly on her father, the minister, or his church. Until those actions caught up with her, that is.

Shannon had come home from Europe full of stories of being serenaded in the gondolas in Venice, walking among the tombstones of Normandy, riding the Eye in London, but she never told anyone about her escapades at night. She was actually relieved to live within the strict rules her parents outlined for her, and she felt sure that when she went away to college the next year, she would be more in control and would never let total freedom get out of hand like that again. And then, she missed her period.

The first month she didn't menstruate, she tried to tell herself that traveling by air and crossing time zones had thrown her off schedule and that she had nothing to worry about. By the second month, the volleyball season had started. This year, the new volleyball coach wanted the girls to be in top physical condition, so he was having them run four miles a day, something the volleyball players had never had to do before. Shannon blamed her lack of menstruation on her sudden and excessive physical activity. This month, Shannon knew she couldn't avoid it any longer, and she drove into Olivia where she was less likely to be known and bought a home pregnancy kit. While using the bathroom in the Subway restaurant, she found out for sure what she had already suspected: she would be having a baby in March.

Dropping her head into her hands, Shannon whispered to Laney, "I don't even know who the father is." Laney put her arm around the distraught girl's shoulders and waited for her to continue. "I mean, he could be one of three. They were all in the People to People group with me." She started to cry then, and Laney just patted her back until she'd finished. When she lifted up her face at last, Laney handed over a Kleenex from her pocket and told her she had black walnut smeared all over her face, too, now and that she'd better wipe it off. Shannon sniffled loudly asking, "Do you think I'm an absolute whore?"

"Of course not. I think you made some bad choices and acted out of character because you were giddy with the first taste of freedom you've ever had. But now you need to look forward and decide what you're going to do."

"I can't tell my parents. I absolutely can't."

"Yes, you can. You have to."

"But it will kill them. They'll die of shame. They'll kill me! I can't do it to them, I just can't!"

"Shannon, look at me. Your parents love you. They will be hurt and disappointed, that's true, but this will not kill them. What would be even worse for them is if they thought you couldn't come to them with your problems. Go, talk to them. And Shannon, don't forget to keep holding your head up high. You're pregnant. It is not a life threatening disease and you have not committed a crime. So, stop beating yourself up, okay?"

They walked back into Pick and Pay to head to the front of the store to finish their shifts. From time to time, they would manage to catch each other's eye over their cash registers and the heads of their customers and they would smile. Problems, no matter how big, feel infinitely smaller when shared with a friend.

Therese Dotray-Tulloch

The bouquet of balloons was obstructing the view through the rearview mirror, in Laney's dream, but causing great entertainment for Gabby sitting in her car seat next to the colorful latex decorations. She kept slapping at the balloons and dragging her fingers tightly across them so the most unpleasant screeching sound was generated making Gabby laugh and laugh. Laney was about to scold her, but then, realizing this was, after all, Gabby's special day, she stopped herself and put up with the noise until they pulled up in front of the zoo.

"We're here, sweetheart, let's go!" Laney carefully removed Gabby from her car seat while Scott began unloading everything else from the car: balloons, food, presents. He was also the official videographer so he began filming the party right away, documenting everyone's arrival and Gabby's pleasure as she welcomed every guest as though she were royalty and they her devoted subjects. Laney slipped on her own party hat to get Gabby's attention.

"Hey birthday girl!" she called to her. Gabby immediately started grunting and reaching for the pointy, paper hat Laney was wearing. "Look! I have one here that's just for you! She pulled the little elastic string underneath Gabby's chin and adjusted the hat in between her two silky pigtails. Gabby smiled delightedly and looked up with her eyes as if she would be able to see the hat on top of her head. "You look beautiful!" Laney cooed.

Just then, Gabby felt the tightness of the elastic band under her chin making her uncomfortable, and before Laney could stop her, she'd grabbed it with her little fist and stretched it as far as it would go, saying "Oweee, oweeee!" Unable to pull it any farther, she let go and the resulting SNAP caused Gabby to howl in pain and shock. Huge crocodile tears rolled out of her eyes and her chin trembled with indignation as she repeated, "Owee, Mommy, oweeee!" over and over again, looking at Laney with hurt, distrustful eyes.

"Oh, honey, I'm so sorry," Laney said as she smothered Gabby's chin with kisses. Gabby continued to whimper, her lips thrust in a disappointed pout. "Who wants to wear this silly ol' hat, anyway?" Laney asked as she pulled off her own hat, too, and stuck it on top of Gabby's on the picnic table in front of her. Immediately forgetting her sting, Gabby reached excitedly for the two hats and put one inside the other over and over again marveling at the magical way they fit so snugly together. "Why do we spend so much money on ridiculous toys when the simplest things entertain our brilliant daughter so effectively?" Laney asked Scott, looking directly through the camera lens. He shrugged his shoulders in response and Laney carried

Therese Dotray-Tulloch
on directing the party.

After eating the picnic lunch Laney had brought, playing games, and opening the presents, everyone sang 'Happy Birthday' to Gabby while Scott and Laney carried the cake with one birthday candle shaped like the number one on it over to Gabby. Gabby smiled happily from her booster seat attached to the picnic table and reveled in all the attention she was receiving from friends and family. When the song was finished, Laney encouraged her to make a wish and blow out the candle. Gabby blew and blew but somehow no air was accompanying all the noise she was making and the candle flame continued to flicker. "Like this, Gabby, see? Whoooooo." Everyone tried to show her how to successfully blow out a birthday candle. Finding no success, they invited some of the older kids to help, and Gabby clapped her hands with glee when the flame was blown out. The Bundt cake was frosted swimming-pool blue and there were little paper umbrellas as well as teddy bear graham crackers with little swim suits frosted onto them lounging all over the 'pool'. Gabby grabbed the stick of gum serving as the diving board and hastily stuffed it into her mouth while she kept her eyes on Laney's face. She was never allowed to have chewing gum. Everyone burst out laughing, Gabby loudest of all, as she chomped happily away on the normally forbidden treat.

After putting away the picnic and presents, they walked from the picnic grounds at Como over to the zoo section of the park. Gabby loved the zebras and the giraffes and she kept pointing at the lions and calling "Kitty" in her own fashion. Finally, the party ended with everyone riding the merry-go-round. Gabby was exhausted by this time and she practically fell asleep on the beautifully painted horse with the open mouth exposing huge, white teeth. So Laney slipped her off the horse and carried her to the carriage on the carousel. Sitting with Gabby in her arms, the cheerful waltz music playing as they went round and round, Laney couldn't imagine a better birthday for her precious one-year-old daughter. It had been a perfect first year. Laney felt the weight of her baby on her chest as she slowly awoke from her dream. The pressure was so great, she truly thought her heart would break in two. Holding nothing in her arms but her pillow, she lay in bed and wondered how to find the strength to get up.

Chapter 8

Walter swept up the last of the broken glass at the front of Just Screw It Hardware Store and sighed heavily while peering out the gaping hole where his window used to be. He was expecting the guys from Window World any time now. Walter grabbed the whisk broom and dust pan and began brushing broken glass off the shelves, too. He hated to think how much it was going to cost to replace his big storefront window. Shaking his head, he admonished himself to not even think about the cost because he had no choice, he had to have a storefront window on Main Street. What else was he going to do, put boards up? Still, this was by far his most expensive set-back yet.

Ever since he'd started his *Stop Wal-Mart* campaign, he'd been receiving warnings to quit it. They began as harassing phone calls at all hours of the day and night, at first just to the store but soon after on his home phone and cell phone, too. Walter wasn't intimidated by the phone calls at all. In fact, he rather enjoyed the attention he got talking about them at the Chit Chat, and they even brought more customers into Just Screw It who wanted to hear firsthand about what was said over the phone. Next, there were splattered eggs all over the front of his store windows. That hadn't been fun to clean up, but with hot water and metal scrapers, he and Karen had managed to get it all off before the day was through. The graffiti painted on the windows was much harder to remove. The words "MAIN STREET IS DEAD" were painted in blood red. When garbage was strewn all across the sidewalk, Walter started to worry that customers would now be deterred from entering the store, so they had cleaned everything up as quickly as they could. He started locking his garbage bin. This morning he'd gotten a call from Dusty of the Opossum Falls Police Department to meet him at the store as there appeared to have been a break in. Walter knew they wouldn't find anything missing. Instead, he found a large brick with his logo *Just Screw It Hardware Store* inside of a red circle with a slash going through it wrapped around it with a rubber band which had been tossed through the window.

It flabbergasted Walter that a company as huge as Wal-Mart would resort to such tactics. He had gone to Dick McGhee to see what could be done about it, but the lawyer had assured him that there was absolutely no way a company as big as Wal-Mart would allow itself to get caught up in something like this. He'd asked Walter if he could think of anyone else who might hold a grudge against him and be attempting to hurt his business, but Walter had said no, that was absurd, he had never had any enemies. Dick had told him to just keep his head down and to try to stay out of trouble. Walter had kicked into gear and started protesting Wal-Mart's presence in Opossum Falls even harder by taking out ads in the Opossum Falls Daily Digest, setting up a booth at the Sugar Beet Days' Festival, attending city council meetings, and passing out information at football and volleyball games and anywhere large groups of Opossum Falls residents gathered. Then, the other businesses that were supporting Walter's campaign to stop Wal-Mart from opening in Opossum Falls started getting attacked, too.

First it was Eye Care for You. Marge Peterson had supported Walter right from the start as soon as they'd heard of Wal-Mart's plans, so it was no surprise that her business was the first to be targeted after Just Screw It. She had hired a young optometrist from Granite Falls to work at Eye Care for You after Charles' passing. A rather mousy young thing, she'd called Marge in tears when she'd arrived at work one morning to find the eye clinic had been broken into and garbage spread all over the waiting room. Thankfully, none of the expensive eye equipment had been touched. Marge just marched on down to the clinic with rubber gloves and had gotten rid of the mess, sending the first patients of the day over to the Last Chapter Bookstore and Coffeehouse for a cappuccino and scone on the house while they waited for the waiting room to be cleaned up.

Next, all of the windows at Pick and Pay had been spray painted with graffiti with phrases like: 'Wal-Mart's fruit will be fresher' and 'You pay more at Pick and Pay and Pay and Pay and Pay'. Then, Donna's Donut Shop had eggs and tomatoes thrown at the windows. Finally, the Chit Chat Café had a small fire started at the back just off of the kitchen. Luckily, Bianca's son, Jesus Maria happened to be walking by, so he managed to put it out before the police, having been called by passersby seeing the smoke, arrived at the scene. And now, Walter's huge store front window, the original window from when the old brick building was built back in 1898, had a brick thrown through it.

After Window World arrived and began installing the new window, Walter left Karen behind the counter at Just Screw It and, briefcase in hand, he walked down the street to the Chit Chat for lunch. Passing by the Chamber of Commerce, he saw Jeanine Westerly sitting at her desk gesturing wildly with one hand while talking on the phone. As soon as she saw Walter, she swiveled her chair so that her back faced him. He continued past the accountant's office and walked into the Chit Chat where sympathetic greetings from his friends welcomed him.

He ordered the hamburger hot dish special and sat down by Marty Bleak of Bleaks' Funeral Home. Martin Bleak had been born into the business and growing up he was taunted by his peers with cries of 'Marty the Mortician'. Supposing that his parents had chosen his name for the nice alliteration, Marty had embraced his profession, helping out in the funeral home on Main Street over the years as he was growing up, and then taking over completely when his Dad passed on at the age of sixty-eight after suffering from a stroke. Mortimer Bleak had collapsed while he was putting the final make-up touches on after embalming ol' Judge Johnson. Had he been discovered sooner, he likely would have recovered at least partially from his stroke, but he lay next to the Judge for over eight hours before the Judge's family finally arrived for the viewing. Thinking that the mortician was her grandpa, the Judge's granddaughter had cried out: "Look, grandpa got out of the box!" to the horror of her family. When they started to call for an ambulance, Marty stepped up and said, "Rigor mortis has already set in so I think we know he's dead already. Why bother with the ambulance? Let's just move Dad into the hallway until we finish with the Judge and then we'll get Dad his own casket." He'd been running the business successfully ever since.

Having been raised in the funeral business, Marty had a very accepting view of death. Dealing with dead bodies on a daily basis removed much of the distastefulness, so to Marty it was all in a day's work. In fact, Marty had a terrific sense of humor and he was anything but morbid. He liked to brag that he had the quietest customers around. When asked, "How are things?" he would likely answer, "It's pretty dead around here." He often chatted pleasantly with the deceased bodies as he worked on them and sang along with his favorite oldies, the Bee Gees, who were always blaring loudly in the background. He seemed to get particular satisfaction singing along to "Ah, ah, ah, ah staying alive, staying alive!"

With cremation growing in popularity, Marty had gone to the bank to take out a loan to add cremation facilities to the Bleak Funeral Home by extending the building to the east out back. Rather than losing money while more and more families chose cremation for their loved ones, Marty talked local mourners into having a viewing of the body first whether the body was to be cremated or not. With the growing expansion in size of many of his clients, Marty stocked up on what he called 'Doublewide' caskets. He thought that many of us spend so much of our lives worrying about being overweight; we should not have to worry about it in death.

When he joined Marty at the Chit Chat and in light of his own troubles, Walter asked him how his business was doing. "People are dying to get in," Marty said as he wiped his chin. "Mmm, this empanada is delicious! Betty's never had this on the menu before."

They discussed Walter's next strategy in his 'Stop Wal-Mart' campaign. Walter had made copies of a map with Opossum Falls in the center and a circle around it. Evenly spaced throughout the circle were towns listed where Wal-Mart stores already existed: Willmar, Litchfield, Hutchinson, Redwood Falls, Marshall, and finally, only twenty miles away, Montevideo. On the back of the map, underneath the name of each of those towns, Walter had listed the names of the businesses that had gone out of business since Wal-Mart had opened in those towns. Then, he also listed the names of businesses that had closed in the neighboring towns around those towns where Wal-Mart had opened.

Opening up his briefcase, Walter removed the thick pile of research he had done on Sam Walton and the Wal-Mart Corporation. He had the biography of Sam's life stating that he had been born on March 29, 1918, married to the same woman, Helen, till he died of bone cancer in 1992. He was forty-four years old when he opened his first Wal-Mart store. Walter had numbers showing how Wal-Mart sales had tripled every five years since 1986, how the Wal-Mart workforce is nearly three times larger than the U.S. Army, how Wal-Mart is currently larger than any company ever has been in the history of the world. He had statistics to prove that while a new Wal-Mart might bring cheaper prices to Opossum Falls, the subsidies that Wal-Mart would extract turned it into a very bad deal for them as taxpayers, because Wal-Mart was no longer even the tiniest spur to economic growth.

Walter had a copy of a full page ad that Wal-Mart had placed in the Flagstaff, Arizona newspaper after facing opposition from the Flagstaff city council. It featured a 1933 photo of Nazi supporters piling books into a bonfire in Berlin. The copy read: *Should we let government tell us what we can read? Of course not. We can read what we choose because of the limits the constitution places on government's ability to restrict our freedoms. So why should we allow local government to limit where we can shop? Or how much of a store's floor space can be used to sell groceries?*

"Can you believe this?" Walter asked Marty after letting him see the ad. "I don't know what is more offensive; their using Nazis in their ad campaign or trying to get us to believe that freedom to shop is as important as freedom of speech." He showed Marty his copy of Al Norman's book, *Slam Dunking Wal-Mart! How You Can Stop Superstore Sprawl in your Hometown.* "This book has been super useful, as was *How*

Wal-Mart is Destroying America (and the world) by Bill Quinn. Most of my ideas on how to keep Wal-Mart out of Opossum Falls have come from them."

While Marty flipped through the books, Walter told him about some of the court cases Wal-Mart has been involved in over the years. There was a current one in the news about a 15-year-old girl arrested for shoplifting at the Wal-Mart in Davenport, Iowa. Apparently, she hadn't shoplifted at all but had checked out through the self-serve aisle. She was practically beat up by the store security and then by the Davenport police. Her brother, who had been shopping in the grocery section of the store and was checking out separately there and had given his sister his credit card, tried to help his sister by calling 911, but then he was arrested too, for disturbing the peace. The girl's lawyer asked to see the security tapes, but both Wal-Mart and the Davenport police refused to hand them over presumably because they did not want to cause a Rodney King type riot. So far, there had been no comment from Wal-Mart, not even regarding the three thousand dollar medical bill the poor girl incurred after the event.

Marty read from a newspaper clipping he picked up, "*Rob Walton, Sam's eldest son said, 'after Dad was gone, we made a real strong commitment to keeping his name and his philosophy in the tops of minds around the company.'* Awww, ain't that sweet?" They finished lunch and discussed the details of the protest. Marty agreed to be there the following Saturday when Walter would be at the proposed Wal-Mart site confirming he would have his camera with him.

"And I'll have my Depends on," Walter joked, but he was only partially kidding.

Chapter 9

Emma Grabow finished washing the dirt off her hands and went to the stove to put the tea kettle on. She placed her hand over her lower back and massaged the ache a little bit. She'd been out working in the garden for hours and these days her back was sure to let her know all about it. The cannas had all been pulled up and were spread out on a shelf in the cellar so they wouldn't get moldy over the winter. She knew some who complained that cannas were too much work, planting them every spring, removing them every fall, but Emma felt it was worth it. A lot of things in life were like that. It took work to make beautiful things grow, and maybe sometimes it was because of the work you knew you'd put into it that you really appreciated the splendor of the thing. Besides, Cannas weren't native to Minnesota. They came from Central America. Emma got a kick out of cooperating with Mother Nature, asking her to grow her lush tropical plant with its luxuriant foliage in the harsh Minnesota climate if she promised to take it out and keep it safe over the winter. Who could pass up a bit of the Caribbean in the middle of a Midwestern backyard?

Emma had also covered her Applejack rosebushes with leaves and had put bundles of hay around them. The roses had been developed by Dr. Griffith Buck at Iowa State University to survive in Minnesota's climate in a low-maintenance landscape. The Applejack was a lovely pink rose. Emma had planted one at the end of each row of grapes in her vineyard. They looked gorgeous blossoming there as the Applejack roses lasted all summer, but their beauty was not why Emma planted them.   Roses are even more susceptible to powdery mildew, leaf spots, rust and the dreaded black rot than grapevines are. Every vineyard owner knows that by planting roses in the vineyard, they have the equivalent of the canary in the mineshaft, as it were, and the moment damage is detected on the rosebush, action can be taken to save the vineyard.

The whistling of the teakettle was Emma's signal to put a couple of teabags into her porcelain teapot and pour in the water to let them steep. She breathed in the aromatic smell of Earl Grey. She'd tried some of those loose teas sold at the Last Chapter but she grew tired of all of the finagling of straining the leaves or using fancy metal loose tea holders, then all of the messy clean-up, not to mention that hours later she would invariably see that she had a tealeaf stuck to her front tooth. She would stick to her simple, standard teabags, thank you very much. Some of the flavors of those new teas were so strange, too, and tasted just like freshly clipped grass cuttings or, worse, overly sweet perfume. The fact that her standard favorite Earl Grey tea was one fourth of the price convinced her that she could just go back to what she'd always enjoyed. Just because something was trendy and new didn't necessarily make it better. While she waited for her tea to steep, Emma thought about how the Chinese had been drinking tea for thousands of years. She knew about the popular Chinese legend of the Emperor of China, inventor of agriculture and Chinese medicine, who had been sitting around drinking a bowl of boiled water when a couple of leaves blew in from a nearby bush. The emperor had taken a sip of the brew and been pleasantly surprised. It had probably taken thousands of years to perfect the ideal little prefabricated teabag, and now the trend was to go back to the more 'natural' loose tea. Emma shook her head disapprovingly. One of the joys of growing old was having roots deep enough to prevent you from being blown around by every new trend that cropped up.

Carrying her teapot and teacup on the plastic, floral tray, she went out to the sunroom and sat in her favorite chair looking out onto her birdfeeders. Jingle Bells, the cat, immediately jumped into her lap, and Emma lovingly rubbed his head. She was glad to have the large, ginger-colored cat warm her up a bit. She had gotten a little chilled working outside, so she resisted the temptation to sit out on the porch. She knew she would regret it come January when she had no option as to where to enjoy her afternoon tea, so perhaps she'd have her second cup outside after she'd warmed up a bit more. They were in the fields today lifting the sugar beets; Emma loved watching the harvest. Otto had always loved the excitement of bringing up the beets so this time of year always brought back lots of good memories for Emma.

She smiled as she watched the Gonzalez boys head down her driveway on their bikes to ride back into town. They were good workers, those two, and she was glad she'd acted on her instincts and approached Bianca about hiring them to help after school and on the week-ends with the animals and yard work. The more she had thought about them hanging around Main Street all of the time, the more she worried that they would eventually get into danger. Not because they were born troublemakers, as some of her fellow townspeople thought they knew for sure, the same people who desperately wished the town could go back to the way it was when it was first settled by their Norwegian and German forefathers. Rather because it was only a matter of time, if kids were left unsupervised for too long with no structure, that they end up like in the *Lord of the Flies*. She realized the thing to do was to give them something with which to occupy themselves in a productive manner. Work had always been her salvation, so she decided to offer it to those boys, too.

Bianca had originally said yes, but then had called Emma and said there was no way to get the boys out to the farm, so as much as she regretted it, she would have to say no. Anthony couldn't leave the Sugar Beet Factory to drive the boys out and the Chit Chat was always busy right when school let out so Bianca couldn't get away then, either. After pondering over the problem, Emma had gone to Walter at Just Screw It and asked him to purchase two bicycles appropriate for boys their age. Walter was surprised that she was giving him her business, she knew, but for heaven's sake, it wasn't personal, their feud over Wal-Mart. Oh alright, maybe it was, but still, she wanted the bicycles and she might as well save herself the trip and get them right in Opossum Falls. Besides, it might gain her some points with the local business owners, not that she cared much about that.

The look on the faces of Manuel and Alonso when Emma told them the bikes were theirs was heartwarming. They'd both just stood there, their mouths agape, till one of them had shouted, "Dios mio, these bikes are ours!" and they had run over and hugged Emma, their tan little arms sweetly circling her waist. Blinking back tears of surprise, Emma had gruffly told them she would expect them by eight the following morning wearing clothes they could expect to get dirty in.

Emma lived one mile south of town on a gravel road. Besides the milk truck, there was never much traffic on the road unless it was harvest time. She gave the boys explicit directions to always bike as close to the ditch as possible on the wrong side of the road facing traffic, especially when biking on the two slight hills where they could be hidden to oncoming traffic. Reminding them that every car that passed them was a potential spy reporting back to her where the boys had been seen on the road, she felt confident the boys were behaving and riding straight to the farm and home again. Walter had been instructed to obtain sturdy bikes with nice fat tires to make biking on gravel both easier and slower; that helped keep the boys safe, too.

They were good workers, too; Emma had to give them that. They were so close in age that everything was a competition between them and Emma got a kick out of seeing them work harder and faster to try to top the other brother. Alonso, the eldest, seemed to really take to the animals. He enjoyed feeding the chickens, pigs, and sheep and wasn't at all afraid of reaching his hand in the roost to bring in the eggs. Millie, the Border Collie, stuck to him like glue, and they became fast friends.

Sipping her tea, Emma surmised that she could easily have grandsons exactly this age herself. Perhaps she did. Emma's heart clenched in her chest as she drew in her breath and felt the familiar pang of regret. Nearly four decades later, the sadness she felt about her loss continued to haunt her and she smiled ruefully to herself thinking that if the old adage, time heals all were true, then it had better hurry up because soon she would be running out of it.

Born and raised in Opossum Falls, Emma's Grandfather had been instrumental in getting the old Milwaukee Railroad to come through Opossum Falls thereby ensuring its continued existence. The fight had been between Opossum Falls and nearby Vicksburg, a sweet little village perched on the banks of the Minnesota River which had been settled by veterans of the Civil War and named after the battle of Vicksburg. Emma's grandfather had won the conflict and soon Vicksburg disappeared. Its few buildings consisting of the general store, post office, and blacksmith shop were picked up and moved to the nearby town of Sacred Heart. All that remained of Vicksburg now was the old cemetery which was reported to be haunted. Visitors to the graveyard claimed to hear a woman's voice crying for help and in the spring the flowers that grew there were said to bleed. Every Halloween, the local teenagers headed out to scare themselves at the site and came back to tell stories of a head stone that glowed in the dark among other horror stories.

Emma's father had been the president of the Farmers and Mechanics Bank in town and was a prominent figure in Opossum Falls while she was growing up. At one time or another, he was also the president or chairman of the parish council, Rotary Club, city council, school board, and County Commander of the American Legion. When Emma was a junior in high school, she'd gotten pregnant on Prom Night. Like many of her generation, she had had no idea that she could actually get pregnant the first time she had sex. Her parents were mortified and absolutely forbade her to even consider keeping the baby. When she began to show, they sent Emma to a home in Minneapolis where other unfortunate girls in her situation were kept practically like prisoners. They spent their days embroidering or knitting gifts for their babies which they wouldn't be allowed to keep anyway. When the lights were turned off at night, the girls would whisper about their chances of escaping to be able to raise the babies growing inside of them. Some had tried to run away but were always found and brought back. There were no single mothers in the country during this era.

When the time came to give birth, the doctor would be summoned and the delivery made. Tiny cries of newborns would cause their nipples to tingle in anticipation of nursing, but that is all they would ever hear as the newborns were immediately whisked away to the homes of the infinitely more deserving adopting parents. The new mother disappeared as well before any of the remaining mothers-to-be had any chance to talk with her or to ask her questions about what giving birth was really like and if she had gotten to see her baby at all or hold it in her arms for even a moment before it was taken away.

After a long labor of intensive back pain, Emma gave birth to a boy with a full head of thick, blond hair. She cried out to the nurses begging them to please let her hold her little boy for just a moment, but they turned their backs on her believing firmly in their convictions that it would be easier for the girls in the long run if they didn't have the memory of their baby's face to haunt them. Besides, they also felt the girls had brought their troubles upon themselves by being so promiscuous in the first place. Emma continued to cry and to bleed which eventually caused her to pass out. When she came to, there was no sign that she had ever produced a baby in the room at all; the little suitcase she had brought with her to Minneapolis was packed and ready to go by the door. The doctor came to see her before she left to tell her that there had been complications and he was afraid the chances of her having any more children were slim to none.

Emma found herself back in high school with four months left before graduation. Steadfast Lutherans, Emma's parents thought it best never to mention the disgraceful circumstances that had led to her absence during the latter part of her pregnancy. Her classmates had been told that she had a sick aunt in Minneapolis she had had to go live with and take care of until she died. The father of Emma's baby never even suspected a thing. The drama of high school and all of the excitement that went with it interested Emma not at all after she was forced to give up her son. The once popular, outgoing girl turned into the recluse the townspeople now assumed she had always been.

No longer interested in going to college, much to her parents' chagrin, Emma began raising animals in the backyard of her parents' home. They were respectable townspeople who seldom had to get their hands dirty, and all of a sudden their daughter was acquiring farm animals. She turned the garage into a makeshift barn and had a chicken, rabbit, duck, cat, pig and a sheep. She only wanted animals that were already pregnant and she was fascinated in watching them give birth. She watched Annette, the pig, for hours on end as her little piglets squealed and fought their way onto her tits. She loved to see how the baby chicks followed their mama around and how the cat would lick and clean her kittens for ages while they slept and then, as they grew bigger, even as they tried to escape.

All the while she watched and worked with her animals, Emma never stopped thinking about her little boy. For the first year, she celebrated his monthly birthday and tried to picture exactly what he looked like then and what he would be doing: lifting up his head, smiling, turning over, and crawling. She had no one she could talk to about her grief as her parents refused to discuss it and wouldn't let her tell anyone as it would cause such embarrassment to the family's reputation. While her friends were all heading to the Gibbon ballroom to dance and party, Emma stayed home and took care of her baby animals.

When she was at the feed mill one day buying grain for the chickens, she ran into her father's friend, Otto Grabow. A widower who farmed sugar beets a mile south of town, he told Emma that his deceased wife had raised chickens and all sorts of farm animals and perhaps she'd like to come and see if she could use any of her old equipment. He'd gotten rid of all of the animals at the time of his wife's death. Visiting him at the farm, Emma realized that Otto was flirting with her. She fell in love with the farm instantly and gradually grew to love Otto, too. Her parents were devastated that she could throw herself at a man twenty-five years her senior but, of course, that was the frosting on the cake for Emma. The only downside to his being so much older was that he passed away and left her alone when she was only fifty years old.

She still celebrated her son's birthday every year and tried to imagine what he would be doing now and how he would look. On Emma's fortieth birthday, she'd driven to Minneapolis and found the home for unwed mothers where she'd given birth to her one and only child. It had been turned into a New Horizon Daycare Center and no one there could tell her anything about where the babies may have gone or through which adoption agency. Emma resigned herself to the fact that she would never know her son but still, she never stopped thinking about him. Did he know he was adopted? Did he wonder why his birth mother had given him up for adoption?

Sipping her tea, she watched the slow dance of the tractor and the loading truck move round and round the vast field, always keeping in step and staying close enough for the immense amounts of sugar beets to be lifted from the tractor and dropped into the loading truck. Emma thought about her son as she so often did. She rocked in her chair and hoped, as she always did, that her son didn't think she had given him away because she didn't want him and she wished from the bottom of her heart that he was happy.

Chapter 10

Eric Hanson could see the bedroom light on over at Emma Grabow's place and he wondered what she was doing up at four-thirty in the morning. He was sitting high up in his tractor which afforded a sweeping view of the neighborhood surrounding his one hundred sixty acre farm. Bon Jovi was sitting next to him on the wide leather tractor seat, and Eric rubbed his head and chatted with him to help keep himself awake. He had been at work since one a.m. getting the beets out of the ground, and he would work around the clock as usual during the sugar beet harvest. He was certainly used to it by now as he had been born and raised growing sugar beets right on this very farm. Eric's grandfather had been one of the first in the area to plant sugar beets in the late 1920s. He'd mostly planted soybeans, but he set aside fifty acres for sugar beets. He had heard that the Sugar Mill down in Chaska was paying well for sugar beets, so he thought he'd give the new crop a try.

In the 1960's, two significant events occurred that inspired Eric's father to devote the whole farm to sugar beets. First, there was a technological breakthrough when the Monogerm seed was perfected which dramatically improved the way in which sugar beet plants were cultivated and, second, President Eisenhower's administration permanently barred the importation of Cuban sugar into the United States creating an immediate demand for a significant supply of sugar beets. Eric had grown up cultivating sugar beets and driving the tractor during the harvest season. He knew that every acre of land could potentially produce thirty tons of beets. Eric not only worked his own one hundred and sixty acres but he rented three hundred and twenty more in the nearby area.

This year's harvest was just beginning and Eric was all geared up for what could well be his most productive harvest season ever. He sold his beets to the Minnesota Sugar Beet Cooperative Sugar Company which had opened up a processing plant outside of Opossum Falls in 1971. The Chaska processing plant had recently closed due to cost prohibitive alterations that the plant would have had to make to keep up with the newly established Pollution Control Agency's regulations. Minnesota Sugar Beet Cooperative Sugar's processing plant in Opossum Falls was one of six factories throughout the Midwest comprising twenty-eight hundred farmers harvesting four hundred thousand acres of sugar beets which, during an average year, brought in ten million tons of sugar beets.

Because there were hundreds of thousands of beets being harvested within a small window of time, each Minnesota Sugar Beet Cooperative Sugar farmer was assigned a harvesting shift in order to ensure an orderly process at the piling stations and factory. Eric's shift started at one a.m. and would continue until one p.m. unless he received a weather shut down order. Beets were harvested within a weather temperature gap between twenty-eight to sixty-five degrees. This was because the temperature of the beet itself was crucial and checking the beet temperature with a probe was critical. If the beets were harvested too warm or too cold they could slowly start to decay while they were piled up at the piling stations before being processed at the factory. As every beet pile was worth around ten million dollars each, the risk of decay was to be avoided at all costs. It was especially frustrating when it might be a beautiful day with the sun shining and the threat of rain in the forecast. Then the factory would announce a shutdown because the beet temperature was too warm, so instead of harvesting in ideal conditions, the harvest would take place in the rain. Harvesting in the mud was no fun, but Eric certainly had done it many times before.

The past few days had been dry which made field conditions excellent for harvesting. Unfortunately, they had also been hot which had warmed up the internal temperature of the beets. Eric would stay tuned to the local radio station to listen to the daily sugar beet report. If there were to be another industry-wide shut down, he would get a text message on his cell phone so that all of the farmers would know to stop at exactly the same moment. Eric really hoped he wouldn't because he knew the longer the harvest was put off, the more chances they had that rain or even snow would interfere and make getting the beets out of the ground much more difficult.

The leafy tops of the sugar beets were mowed off so that the beets could easily be popped out of the ground. Eric drove the tractor which pulled the digger, concentrating so that he was always lined up just right to pluck the beets out of the ground. Right next to him, Juan Carlos was driving the open box truck. The beet lifter and truck had to work as a single unit. It was as if Eric and Juan Carlos were involved in an intricate ballet so that the waterfall of beets coming off the conveyer landed in the truck and not on the ground. The truck couldn't stray too far from the tractor. A small screen in Eric's John Deere assured him they were lined up properly, and they used walkie-talkies to communicate their every move.

Outside of the rig, it was still pitch dark. Eric drove, carefully following the rows while the digger lifted up the beets onto the grab roll. The purpose of the grab roll was to separate the mud from the beets, and then to convey the beets to the back of the harvester. From there they fell into the Ferris wheel, made the big trip up to the top of the wheel, and finally dropped down to the elevator chain where they were conveyed out to the truck. Juan Carlos' voice came over the walkie-talkie. "I'm full up; time to head over to the piling station." His truck was now full of about fifteen tons of beets. Eric waited while Juan Carlos pulled away and another open-box truck slid in next to the digger to take his place.

"Hey, Mr. Hanson, I'm back." Eric recognized Jesus Maria's voice over the walkie-talkie. Both vehicles began moving as they executed their well-orchestrated dance.

"How are things at the piling station?"

"Not bad at all. I had to wait about fifteen minutes, max. Then I weighed in, dumped, and weighed out in less than twenty minutes."

Because sugar beets were harvested twenty-four hours a day, it was necessary to have a place to keep the beets when the factory couldn't possibly keep up. These were called 'piling stations' and they were open around the clock during the season. As the harvest went on, there would be millions of beets stacked up to four stories high with seventy thousand tons of beets in one pile. Over the winter, the piles would slowly diminish as the sugar factory removed the beets. In the meantime, the sub-zero temperature would be good for the beets. A frozen beet was less likely to rot. There would be fans at the piling station to keep the air flowing through the piles so that the beets wouldn't warm each other up and prevent the freeze from setting in.

Eric was pleased to see the hot pink line just over the horizon to the east. He yawned and rubbed his eyes, one at a time, so as never to lose sight of the straight row of beets he was following. He appreciated that just when he was about to get so tired he could barely keep his eyes open, the sun would rise and he would be stimulated by the beautiful world awakening all around him. Being a farmer, Eric loved this time of the day. He could never understand how his wife, Cath, could sleep right through it day after day. She claimed to appreciate the sunsets much more, explaining that, after all, they were basically the same thing only in reverse. Looking back at their house, Eric could see the lights on and knew that this was a rare day because Cath was up already, getting ready to help out at the Chit Chat during the busy harvest season. Bon Jovi was awake now, too, perking up with the brightening sky and waving his tail from time to time.

Eric couldn't help but smile when he thought of his wife, Cathy. He had fallen in love with her back in high school, when she was running for Sugar Beet Queen and her talent had been reciting a poem she'd written about sugar beets. He made her repeat the poem at the end of every harvest season, reminding her that was precisely the moment she had stolen his heart. Wrapping a sheet around her otherwise naked body, she would hold a sugar beet in front of her with both hands while she proudly recited her poem.

> Among the vegetables most elite
> I bow before you when we meet
> Oh, how you make my anxious heart beat
> Not even foul weather dare to you defeat
> The thought of you makes my mouth secrete
> You have Saturn, god of agriculture beat
> I love to walk upon you with bare feet
> How quickly you grow with rain, sun, and heat
> Why, I would rather eat you any day than meat
> Whatever food adds you then becomes a treat
> Whether cane or beet our taste buds do you cheat
> Being your queen would be so neat
> Best of all is that you are so sweet
> I most solemnly do repeat
> Best of all is that you are so sweet

Cath had not been crowned queen, but Eric liked to tease her that she had been the queen of his heart ever since. She had gone to live in St. Cloud for a couple of years after high school attending beauty school. Eric would drive up to visit her every other week-end and they would hang out at the White Horse eating sausage and potato pie while planning their future. Eric was already taking over his family beet farm while his parents were moving into a condo in Opossum Falls, spending a couple of months of every winter down in Texas. Cath was looking forward to living in the country. She wanted to work out of her home and raise gaggles of children. It had all turned out exactly as they had hoped, except for the children part.

Eric could not believe the hurt that he experienced seeing the woman he loved in pain. The death of their unborn child and every miscarriage following that tragedy killed a little of his wife's happiness and pierced Eric to the core. Enough now, he had told Cath after the last miserable miscarriage, enough of this merciless torture. We are going to have a baby, but not like this. Just recently, they had gone to see Dick McGhee to enquire about the process of adoption.

Outside of the tractor windows, the world was slowly taking shape as it got closer to sunrise. Bon Jovi barked and Eric saw a shadow running across the freshly-mowed beets. It was one of the many ginger-colored cats that lived in the barn. They were semi-wild cats kept to keep the mouse population down. Earlier that spring, when Eric was first priming the tractor after it had sat all winter in the Quonset hut, he came across a litter of kittens under the hood. Eric kept a small oil pan heater on the tractor, and the smart mama had known a warm spot when she saw one, but she was not happy at all when he removed her and the kittens from their cozy nest. The next day, as he checked his oil under the hood again before taking out the tractor, he saw they were back again. The mama cat had laboriously dragged each of the kittens back underneath the tractor hood!

Like fire on the horizon, the sun peeked up from the edge of the earth to the east. Eric watched it in brief increments as he concentrated on driving his tractor straight to be able to lift the beets out of the ground with minimal damage. In seconds, the hot orange ball was fully visible perched on the rim of the world. Eric reached for his sunglasses and sighed knowing it would be a long day as he watched the sun inch its way across the big sky while he continued to pluck his beets from the progressively warming earth.

~~~~~~~~~~~~~~~~~~~~~~~~~~~~~~~~

Bianca turned up earlier than usual at the Chit Chat and began cooking up sausage and bacon as well as brewing coffee. She put out the sidewalk sign that said, 'Beet Season, Have a Safe Harvest' on one side, and 'Buckle Up, Drive Safely' on the other. The harvest season brought in lots of extra business to the Chit Chat either in take-out meals when the harvest was on or with overflowing booths and tables if the sugar company ordered a shut down. She was glad that Laney and Cath were coming in to help prepare boxed lunches and wait tables.

While Bianca started boiling the potatoes and dicing onions for hash browns, she thought about what had happened to Anita Beatrice, and she got so angry, she started chopping the onions more and more forcefully. The Senior Class at Opossum Falls High School had voted for the junior nominees for the Homecoming Royalty. Anita Beatrice had been one of the five junior girls nominated. Anita Beatrice was shocked and flattered beyond belief; there had never been a Hispanic nominated at the high school. Of the five boys nominated, one of them was Matthew Stevenson, the Opossum Falls football quarterback and therefore one of the most popular boys in town. Matthew had been coming over lately and spending time with Anita Beatrice. Bianca could tell there was a bit of romance in the air.

Homecoming week was full of activities at Opossum Falls High School. The kids got to dress up in different themes for school each day; there was a traditional bonfire outside of town after the girls' volleyball game, there was a powder-puff game, a tag football game played by the girls, and finally, there was the parade down Main Street shortly before the football game was to start. It was no surprise when Matthew was voted by the entire high school to be homecoming king. In all honesty, it wasn't a surprise, either, that Anita Beatrice didn't win homecoming queen. What was a surprise was the cruelty of the posters hung around the school encouraging the student body not to cast a single vote for the 'Mexican chica'. Written in both English and Spanish in bold, black magic marker, they were hung up throughout the school and stapled to telephone poles in the parking lot and around the block and read, Go Away, Marcharse, No Mexican Queens in Opossum Falls. Anita Beatrice had tried to keep it from her mom but one of the teacher's had called to forewarn Bianca of the trouble her daughter was having. Anita Beatrice had tried to shrug it off, saying she knew it was just a small group of idiots and that most of her classmates didn't feel that way. Still, when the votes were cast and Vanessa Schmidt won, rumors went around that Anita Beatrice didn't even win ten votes. To make matters worse, Vanessa was Matthew's old girlfriend; he had broken up with her and she had not been happy about it one bit. She was thrilled to have the opportunity to clutch on to Matthew's arm as much as possible throughout the homecoming week's festivities.

Laney and Cath burst into the Chit Chat together talking and laughing loudly as if it weren't the wee hours of the morning. After shouting out greetings to Bianca, they put on their aprons while they told her she wouldn't believe what they had just seen. They had seen Jeanine Westerly out in the alley behind Donna's Donuts. She was carrying a bag of some sort which may have been a trash bag. When she saw their headlights, she hid behind a tree in the backyard. They drove super slowly down the alley as she edged her way around the tree trying to keep out of sight. "I was so tempted to put down my window to shout, Yoo-hoo, Jeanine, but Laney wouldn't let me," Cath laughed.

"What were you doing driving down the back alley?"

"Who cares what we were doing! What was Jeanine Westerly doing, that's what I want to know! Actually, we had a perfectly good reason for driving through the alley. This poor city girl," she put her arm around Laney's shoulders, "has never seen an opossum; can you imagine that, Bianca? I have counted at least eight sightings since Laney confessed her secret to me, but this was the first time Laney was actually with me when I thought I saw one slink down the alley. It ran up a tree when we got close to it and of course, it would be willing to stay up there all day rather than face us."

"Actually, I'm pretty sure it was just a cat," Laney whispered loudly to Bianca as she began to make toast.

"I heard that and it is so not true," Cath shot back, "While it's true that opossums have some interesting cat similarities, like, for example, when an opossum is done eating it will clean itself just like a cat will, however, it is actually more like a skunk in the way it secretes a really foul-smelling, stinky odor when it's frightened. So don't you go trying to pick up any weird-looking cats, Laney." Cath continued while she began chopping up tomatoes, "Another fun fact every citizen of Opossum Falls should know is that, when cornered, an opossum will often pretend to be dead hoping that it will then be left alone. That's where we got the phrase 'playing 'possum'."

Throughout the busy morning at the Chit Chat, Cath would continue to amuse Laney by spouting out more opossum facts. She had just made her laugh by stating that the opossum's naked ears, nose and tail were so susceptible to freezing that they would often fall right off and that Laney should keep her eyes open for them. A man who was sitting alone at the counter, wiping the remaining egg off his plate with a piece of toast, smiled up at Laney and asked her what was so funny. Laney told him while staring at the bit of yellow yolk he had stuck in the corner of his mouth. "You can impress your friend with this," he told her, the bit of yolk moving up and down while he spoke, "opossums can eat rattlesnakes and other poisonous snakes because they are resistant to venom!" He spoke in a conspiratorial whisper which made Laney laugh.

He looked very out of place in the Chit Chat during the harvest season as he was surrounded by farmers and truck drivers. His brown hair was cut neatly and every hair was in place, noticeable because it definitely wasn't 'hat hair' which practically every other man in the place sported, their baseball caps sitting next to their plates or hanging on the back of their chairs. He was wearing pressed, khaki trousers and a pale blue, button-down shirt. He wasn't wearing a tie but it looked as though he might have been. Only his boots looked as though they may have been worn in a beet field. They were a deep brown and looked comfortable, as if he'd already put a lot of miles on them. Laney looked into his deep-set grey eyes and thought they looked familiar. Once upon a time, she thought, she would have liked his boyish, open face. Those days were over, she reminded herself as she walked away and began wiping down the counter. Cath looked over at him. Setting down two plates at the booth closest to the door, she walked up to the stranger and asked, "Are you from immigration?"

He reluctantly pulled his gaze away from Laney. "What, me? No, no I'm not," he answered her seriously.

"Good, because we don't think too highly of you immigration boys, especially at this time of year when we have a harvest to get in and sugar beets to be processed," Cath had her hands on her hips and spoke crossly.

"Can't say as I blame you for that," the man said. Cath continued to stare down at him, not sure if he was making fun of her or not. She wanted to ask him what his business was in town but she supposed she didn't have the right. Instead, she tapped the corner of her mouth and cleared her throat to help him catch her meaning.

"Excuse me?" he looked up at her uncomprehendingly. She tapped again at the corner of her mouth but when he still didn't get it, she grabbed a napkin and wiped at the egg stain on his mouth for him. His face turned red as he thanked her and asked for his bill so he could settle up. He also asked if he was correct in assuming that if he just stayed on this road, he would get to Emma Grabow's vineyard. Cath told him to just keep heading south. As he was about to leave the Chit Chat, he suddenly remembered to ask for the receipt. Cath looked at him askance thinking he was an immigration agent needing the lunch receipt so he could get reimbursed. "Look," he said, understanding her skepticism, "I do work for the government, but not in immigration. I'm Pete Oetzmann, USDA," and he held out his card to her for proof.

"Cath Hanson, and that's my friend, Laney Anderson, whom you can't seem to take your eyes off of." Her eyes twinkled as she made him blush again. She studied his card and said, "Actually, Emma Grabow is my neighbor. We live on the farm just south of hers. Your card here says your title is Crop Protection Services, Mr. Pete Oetzmann. What do you want to see Emma for?"

"I'm afraid I'm not at liberty to say. But I'm sure Mrs. Grabow would be happy to discuss it with you if you asked her," Pete said as he stood up to leave.

She gave a sharp laugh, "You don't know our Emma, then."

Cath watched him go. While she was glad that he really wasn't an agent for Immigration and Customs Enforcement, something didn't feel right about her next door neighbor seeing someone from Crop Protection Services, either.

The Mexican sky was a cerulean blue, in Laney's dream, with brilliant white nimbus clouds floating majestically across the seemingly endless ceiling of sky. The mountains in the background were so clear that the different ranges appeared to be stacked up like playing cards. Above the screams and shouts, Laney knew she could hear the constant rumble of the Pacific Ocean if she listened closely enough, but she was enjoying the squeals coming from Gabby instead.

They had arrived in Puerto Vallarta three days earlier on a direct charter flight alive with the atmosphere of vacationing Minnesotans eager to escape the frigid cold of winter for a week of Mexican sun. Scott and Laney took turns holding Gabby throughout the flight. Gabby loved being read to; she drew pictures with her new set of washable markers, and played make-believe with her favorite doll, Anna. Making sure she swallowed juice from her sippy-cup during takeoff and landing ensured that Gabby's ears kept popping so she never fussed once during the three-hour flight. The three sisters sitting behind them loved playing with Gabby all through the flight as she spent a good portion of time entertained by standing on Laney's lap and looking backwards at the girls. "She's such a good baby," they exclaimed, "and what a flirt! Have a good week, Gabby, and we'll see you on the return flight next Saturday!"

It did seem as though flirting was exactly what Gabby was doing quite naturally. She was such a hit with all of the staff at their glorious Mayan Kingdom Hotel that it seemed everyone knew her name; she had the run of the hotel for the week. "Hola, hola," Gabby called out wherever they went. "Buenos Dias, Gabrielita, la mas Bonita," they'd respond. Once, in the elevator, a sour looking elderly couple resisted Gabby's charms and pointedly looked away from her as she tried to engage them in salutations. Speaking with a flat, Midwestern accent, the woman asked, "What kind of a vacation is this when you bring your baby and all of the work of taking care of her with you to Mexico?" Laney was too stunned to answer until the elevator doors opened and the couple shuffled out, "A family vacation," she hollered after them just as the elevator doors closed, holding Gabby even tighter in her arms.

The waves at the beach frustrated Gabby in their relentless manner of knocking her down as she tried to toddle into the water, so they took a break to go to the nearby water park for the day. Gabby screamed with delight as she sat on Scott's lap and flew through the tubes of the giant slides, picking up speed as they went along until they landed in the pool at the bottom of the slide with a splash! After countless descents down the slides, Gabby was thrilled to discover she had her own individual little pool to spend the rest of the day playing in, complete with an attached mini elephant slide serving as her entrance to the pool.

Holding her doll, Anna, on her lap, Gabby would slide down the elephant slide and splash into her own pool, careful to keep Anna's head up out of the water. Then she would stand up and throw the doll into the water causing more than a couple of horrified gasps from walkers-by before they realized that it was just a doll she was throwing and not a real baby. Gabby would grin up at them triumphantly and say, "Baby swim!" and they would laugh with her which is exactly the response for which she hoped.

Laney sat in the lawn chair next to the pool with her P.D. James book on the table next to her, but she didn't get more than a couple of pages read as she kept an eye on Gabby. She sipped through the straw in her coco loco, a tasty concoction served in a big green coconut with pieces of pineapples and grapes stuck to the outside of it with toothpicks to create a funny face. Gabby laughed when she saw it, and then pulled a pineapple chunk off and sucked on it, nodding her head vigorously and saying, "Mmm-mmm, good," her new favorite phrase. Quick as a flash, she started walking down the path, her chunky legs picking up speed as she awkwardly placed one foot in front of the other, holding her arms out to the sides for balance and swaying back and forth like a miniature Frankenstein monster. "Gabby," Laney called as she jumped up from her chair and chased after her which naturally only caused Gabby to move even faster as she giggled and hustled away from her.

"Mommy's gonna get you!" she said as she stomped loudly right behind her, and Gabby screeched and tried to move even faster with her newly acquired skill of fast-walking. Laney scooped her up then and swung her around in a circle till they both got tired, saying, "One of these times you're gonna run so fast, you'll fall, you silly girl." Gabby pointed at the funny clown garbage receptacle whose mouth was the opening to insert trash into, and Laney leaned in so Gabby could drop the pineapple rind into it. All the while, Gabby was vigorously shaking her head with her little blond curls wound up even tighter than usual from being wet from the pool, repeating, "Me no fall."

On their last evening in Mexico, they went to the beach and found seats at the table closest to the front to watch the Mexican Fiesta Extravaganza. While Laney and Scott feasted on authentic enchiladas and chile relleno, Gabby enjoyed sucking on an ear of corn and eating rice with her fingers. Once the show started, Gabby was utterly enchanted by the lovely costumes of the traditional dancers and squealed when the long skirts on the beautiful senoritas twirled faster and faster as they moved around. She clapped her hands when the vaquero performed tricks with his lasso and jumped in and out of the large circle while the rope never stopped moving.

She was mesmerized by the actors when they wore masks and acted out the hunt for survival of their ancestors. Only when the dancing horse appeared and the music got louder and louder as the musicians played faster and faster while the horse continued to kick up his hooves did Gabby get scared. She turned her face around against Laney's chest and refused to watch any more. During the finale, when the dancers were back on stage with the musicians playing, the horse, offstage, thought they were still playing for him. He kept on prancing, taking the attention away from the dancers onstage. The audience couldn't help laughing while the relentless horse danced on, but even then Gabby wouldn't turn her face around.

Realizing that she must have fallen asleep, Laney kissed the top of her silky head, and felt the weight of her baby on her chest as she slowly awoke from her dream. The pressure was so great, she was afraid that her heart would break in two. Holding nothing in her arms but her pillow, she lay in bed and looked up at the ceiling, wondering how to find the strength to get up and face yet another day.

Therese Dotray-Tulloch

Chapter 11

Pete stood on the sidewalk and watched a couple of trucks filled with sugar beets drive by. He tilted his head back to admire the clear, blue sky and thought, what a perfect day for harvesting. Pete felt good about his job and was proud to be a government agent, but days like today made him long to be out on a tractor plucking the fruits of the earth. Climbing into his pickup truck, he put the windows down and put the truck into gear. The fields were looking good; it was great that they weren't too muddy for the harvest. The temperature still felt pretty cool, too, so perhaps Minnesota Sugar Beet Cooperative wouldn't have to order a shutdown of the harvest on account of the internal beet temperatures heating up too much. Pete smiled to himself as he remembered the frustrations of being shut down when there were still beets sitting in the ground which needed to be harvested.

Not that Pete was a country boy by any means. He had grown up in a suburb of the Twin Cities, an only child to parents who were a bit older than most of his friends' parents. He'd attended Bloomington-Jefferson High School and graduated somewhere in the top hundred out of five hundred graduates. His Dad was originally from the Fergus Falls area and still had lots of relatives farming there. Every summer, Pete would go stay on his grandpa's farm to help with the farming. He had lots of cousins living on farms of their own near grandpa's, and they thought Pete was crazy. They were country kids who loved spending time in the cities. Some of them would have loved to have gotten out of helping with fieldwork to spend time hanging out in Bloomington with Pete. Instead, here was their city slicker relative willing to give up his summer in the city to help out on the farm.

Pete loved every bit of it. He loved the plowing and the planting in the springtime, the spraying and cultivating in the summertime and the harvest in the fall. His parents always let him miss a week of school during the harvest and sometimes even two if the harvest got backed up. Pete's grandpa had been a widower for a couple of decades by now, so they would live like a couple of bachelors; the first one up in the morning would make the coffee, whoever wasn't in the field would cook up some dinner to take out to the one on the tractor in the late afternoon. They would sit in front of the TV on those summer evenings watching the Twins play baseball, and during the commercials they'd talk about history and politics. Pete loved his grandpa so much and he knew that his love of country life was deeply entwined with his feelings for his grandpa.

When Pete graduated from high school and tried to think about what he wanted to do with his life, all he could think about was farming. His parents tried to discourage him, pointing out that farming was difficult enough for those lucky enough to inherit the land and the equipment needed to farm. To start with nothing as Pete would have to do was well-near impossible. Still, Pete couldn't envision himself doing anything but working with the land. To get as close as he could get to farming, he decided to study Agriculture at the University of Minnesota's St. Paul Campus. Four years later, he started working for the United States Department of Agriculture, gradually working his way up to becoming an agent for Crop Protection Services.

Driving south on Highway Six, Pete watched the sugar beet harvest and realized how much he missed working with the land. He was proud of the work he did although much of it involved sitting behind a desk and researching the best seeds or herbicides for a particular farmer in his jurisdiction. Most recently, he had helped develop an app called Soil Web which provided soil survey information to farmers in a mobile form which was particularly useful for those working out in the field, just like he wished he were. Pete worked out of the Fargo, North Dakota USDA Research Station. His department had gotten a letter from Emma Grabow last week indicating her belief that herbicides had drifted onto her vineyard causing irreversible damage. Pete was there for the initial visit just to be sure it was necessary for his whole crew to drive down to investigate the alleged damage.

Spotting *E. Grabow* on the mailbox, Pete turned right onto the driveway and then stopped the car. To his left, the vineyard stretched prettily up a slight slope, the ten-foot rows of grapes uniformly stretching out of sight. To the right was a pretty, little pond with a couple of Canadian geese lazily swimming around inside. Farther down the driveway and off to the right, Pete admired the homey farmhouse with the wrap-around porch. The grass was perfectly mowed, the mowed rows diagonally pleasing as they crisscrossed the ample lawn. Pete sighed and thought that he liked this Emma Grabow already, or at any rate, he appreciated her beautifully appointed farm. Walking over to the white fence surrounding the vineyard, he could see at a glance that there had definitely been herbicide drift which had stunted the growth of the grapes.

Pete got back into the truck and drove the rest of the way down the driveway. The farm looked even more impeccable up close. Pete continued driving past the farmhouse and followed the driveway as it circled around. He passed the enormous Quonset hut which obviously housed the farm equipment. Next to that was a low rectangular-shaped building which was most likely the chicken coop. It looked as though it had just been painted the same beautiful red as the stately barn standing next to it. The sidewalks leading out to the buildings were immaculately swept. Even the windows on the barn looked as though they had just recently been washed.

Pete was getting out of the truck when two boys appeared, one of them struggling to carry a scruffy-looking, ginger-colored cat. The boy was very wisely holding the cat straight out in front of him, so no matter how much the cat extended its claws and flailed its paws around, the boy wouldn't get scratched. "I'll get the door for you, Alonso," the smaller boy shouted, as he raced ahead to open the side door leading down to the basement.

"Hello, that's quite some cat you've got there."

"Yeah, it is," Alonso bent his arms a little as the weight of the cat was getting to him, but the cat's near miss as it swiped at his chest caused him to renew his efforts to hold the cat straight out in front again. "It's not mine though; it belongs to old Mrs. Grabow." He kept walking, turning his head to shout over his shoulder, "We found him back of the chicken coop trying to get in."

Pete waited while the boys threw the cat indoors and quickly shut the door again. "Good job keeping it out of the chicken coop. Cats and chickens are natural enemies, you know."

"Yeah," the younger boy shouted excitedly, "and we get to keep all the money from the eggs from Mrs. Grabows chickens! She even said so! She told us, right, Alonso? As long as we feed the chickens and collect the eggs ourselves, she don't care what we do with the eggs! So, at first I was scared to put my hand in to see if there were any eggs in there. It's dark and I didn't know what I would touch! But Alonso, he said he wouldn't share the money if I didn't help, so, that first time, I just closed my eyes and slowly reached my hand in till finally, I felt it. An egg! It was so warm on account of the chicken had just gotten off of it. That's what we gotta do first, get the chickens off of their roosts. Some of them, they do not want to get off, neither!"

Pete couldn't help but smile at the boy's enthusiasm. "So, what happens to the eggs next?"

"We sell 'em to the Chit Chat. Our aunt works there and she asked the owner and he said he would pay market price for them as long as we cleaned 'em up a bit before bringing them there because they don't want to scare any customers if a little piece of hay got into their breakfast."

Pete was trying hard not to laugh out loud at the little boy's keenness. "I just came from the Chit Chat."

"Did you have any eggs? If you did, you had one of our eggs 'cause that's the only kind of eggs the Chit Chat makes!"

"As a matter of fact, I did have eggs and I was thinking right while I was eating them that they, quite possibly, were the best eggs I had ever had in all my life!"

"Of course they were," the little boy nodded with gusto. "That's what I've just been telling you!"

The boys explained how they carried the eggs home in the big baskets they each had attached to their bikes. After cleaning them, they took them over to the Chit Chat. They hadn't spent any of the money they'd earned from the eggs yet, either, so they explained to Pete that they were practically rich already.

Just then, the back door opened and a woman wearing jeans and a sweatshirt stepped out. Walking towards them, she scolded, "Do you boys think I'm paying you just to stand around and jabber? Don't you have work to do?"

"Yes, Mrs. Grabow, sorry, Mrs. Grabow." The two boys hurried back to the chicken coop.

After calling after the boys that it was nice meeting them, Pete reached in his back pocket and introduced himself to Emma Grabow, handing her his card as he did so. He had phoned ahead, so she had been expecting him. They shook hands, each taking note of the strength and firmness of the other's grip. "They were just putting the cat in the house, by the way," Pete explained by way of defending the boys. "They didn't want it to get after the chickens."

"Jingle Bells has about as much desire to chase chickens as I have to go bungee jumping," Emma said dismissively. As Pete raised an eyebrow at her, she finished, "No, I'm not interested in dropping off of some cliff or bridge to be shot up as if by a slingshot and then to bounce around until someone comes to rescue me, thank you very much."

"What cat doesn't want to chase chickens, though?"

"My cat," Emma said as she ended the discussion.

They walked over to the vineyard and Emma showed Pete where the damage had occurred. He assessed the situation, and then assured her that he would be back with his crew to take samples of the damage to the grapes. Shaking hands once again, Pete got back in his truck and headed north.

She was trying to decide exactly who it was Pete had reminded her of as Emma watched him go. She should have asked if he was from around Opossum Falls and if he had relatives in the area. Looking down at his card, she didn't think the name Oetzmann rang a bell, but certainly there were plenty of Germans living in the area. She was sure she would have a chance to find out exactly where Pete Oetzmann came from while they tried to sort out the problem with her grapes. At any rate, he seemed to be a very nice young man and she felt sure she would enjoy working with him.

As Pete got back onto the highway, he thought he saw Jingle Bells, the cat, across the road running away from Emma Grabow's farm, then realized that he must have been mistaken because there was no way the cat could have gotten out of the house and onto the road ahead of him. As he drove, he followed behind a truck loaded with sugar beets until it turned off into the piling station. Pete looked at the mountain of sugar beets with interest but kept on driving north.

As he drove through Opossum Falls again, Pete saw the woman from the Chit Chat walking unhurriedly down Main Street; Laney, he remembered her friend calling her. Acting on the spur of the moment, he decided to take advantage of one of the loveliest benefits of being in a small town, and he pulled up to the curb and rolled down the passenger window. This would not have been so well-received in the Twin Cities or indeed, even in Fargo, but here in Opossum Falls, he knew that the gesture felt just right. Laney glanced at the car which had pulled up beside her, and she recognized the driver who had recently been at the Chit Chat. She smiled tentatively at him and walked up to the window, "Need some help?" she offered, thinking he might need directions again.

"Can you tell me where I can get some nice takeout food or maybe a deli?"

"Well, one of the gas station sells pizza, another one sells subs, there's the Chit Chat which you've already been to, the corner bar does burgers and other fried foods, and Pick and Pay has a deli. But its sugar beet harvest you know, so no matter where you go, you'll likely have a bit of a wait."

"Last question, what do you feel like for dinner tonight?"

Laney raised an inquisitive eyebrow. She had been told to leave the Chit Chat as Betty Larson was in the kitchen and Anita Beatrice had turned up after school to help out, too. Cath had needed to get home to get supper ready for Eric and his crew who were busy with the sugar beets. Laney was feeling tired, but even worse she was feeling the beginnings of the panic that had so ruled her life lately. She had dreaded going home and being alone. Feeling like an empty shell, she had been trying to decide what to do with herself. She knew that back in Minneapolis, she likely wouldn't have even considered the invitation to dinner from a perfect stranger. But then again, like many women, Laney was a keen believer in her intuition. It didn't take her long with a person for Laney to feel pretty sure whether or not he or she was good or bad, or someone Laney would want to spend time with. While The Event had shaken her very foundation, she still felt able to depend upon her perception of someone.

The sandy brown-haired gentleman with the kind face was no threat to her, Laney sensed that right away. His company might save her from another sad evening reflecting on the unimaginable turn of events that brought her to this point in her life. Smiling a bit wistfully, she knew she couldn't be good company, however, and she pretended to misunderstand his invitation and bade him farewell. Pete sat for a moment thinking how totally out of character this was for him but that for some reason he simply could not let this woman just walk away. Her eyes had been so full of sorrow just now that he had an inkling of some unbearable tragedy that surrounded her. He eased his foot onto the gas and drove slowly besides her, speaking through the downed passenger window, "Miss, I don't mean to bother you, but I am a stranger in town and I would appreciate a little company. Don't misunderstand, I only mean like a dinner companion. I have to stay in town tonight for work purposes and it's promising to be such a lovely fall evening, I hate to spend it indoors in a generic motel room."

Until just moments ago, Pete had been planning to return to Fargo, but he thought the 'stranger alone in town' scenario might generate a little sympathy. Laney kept walking as she gave it some thought. He sounded sincere enough. Maybe she should stop thinking about herself for a change and do this stranger from out of town a favor. He drove slowly beside her and said, "Well, what do you think? I even know a couple of good jokes I could share with you. What do you say?"

"Actually, I get a discount at Pick and Pay. They have a seafood salad that's to die for," Laney said as she leaned down to open the passenger door.

~~~~~~~~~~~~~~~~~~~~~~~~~~~~~~

At the piling station, Juan Carlos weighed in, dropped his load of beets, weighed out, and was back on the road in less than half an hour. After he exchanged trucks back at the farm, he headed home. Eric had invited him to stay for dinner, but he had turned him down. He knew Tia Juanita would have a hot supper ready for him, he planned to spend a little time with his granddaughter, and then he was planning to crash. He had worked over eighteen hours straight, and he was exhausted. He would have to set his alarm for just after midnight and start his shift with Eric Hanson all over again at one in the morning. Juan Carlos wasn't complaining, however. He loved helping out with the sugar beet harvest. The long hours gave a real boost to his income and helped keep food on the table during the lean winter months when his landscaping business was slow. He had barely stopped the truck underneath the sprawling oak tree when Isabella Rose came running out of the house shouting.

"Abuelito, mira! Look what Tia Juanita and I found!" She pulled Juan Carlos over to a box on the porch and in a hushed voice said, "Look, we're keeping him till he gets stronger." Inside was a medium-sized black bird with pale yellow eyes and a long tail. Its feathers shone with purple, green and blue iridescence on its head and a rich bronze sheen on its body.

Tia Juanita stepped onto the porch, wiping her hands on her apron. She was short and round with a beaming face and a cheerful countenance. She had come to him via the mysterious underground communication system that caused help to turn up when work was available, and she had been taking care of Isabella Rose for four years now. She was a typical Hispanic woman of a certain age who could have been forty or seventy or any age in between. She lived in a small room in back of the kitchen. Juan Carlos didn't know what he would do without her.

"This bird, he smashed into the window with a loud bang while Izzy was eating her lunch," Tia Juanita informed him. "We ran outside and found him lying on the ground, not moving. We thought he was dead!" She spoke with a strong Spanish accent but was diligently speaking English around Isabella Rose as Juan Carlos had requested.

"But he's not dead, abuelito, see? And I gave him water and some of my sandwich and now I'm catching flies to feed him 'cause Tia Juanita says he eats bugs." The bird stared suspiciously at them blinking his eyes and looking around in small, jerky movements. He held one wing slightly aloft as though it pained him, or perhaps he was drying it off.

Juan Carlos sat on the porch step and pulled Izzy close to his side. The trees around the house were filled with cackling grackles migrating south for the winter. Twice a year in spring and fall the birds would come through in their huge flocks filling the neighborhood with their twittering. All of a sudden, the birds would all stop chirping at once and the silence would be stunning in its absence of tweeting. Then the choir would start up again as one. As Juan Carlos was describing how the grackle was a great imitator of other bird sounds, the bird in the box suddenly spread both wings and lifted itself gracefully out of the box and flew into the overhead tree, joining the rest of its flock. Izzy shrieked in surprise at first, and then clapped both hands in approval at the bird's rapid recovery. Juan Carlos congratulated his granddaughter on her doctoring skills and for providing the bird with a safe place to recover from its encounter with the window.

"But now what am going to do with these?" she asked innocently as she opened her little fist to show the three dead flies she clutched inside. Juan Carlos chuckled as he scooped her up in his arms and pretended to shake her upside down to force her to drop the dead flies while she shrieked with laughter. Overhead, the chorus of grackles started up again and seemed to laugh right along with her.

Chapter 12

Minnesota Sugar Beet Cooperative factory was in high gear. At this time of year, they were working at full capacity and Jeffrey Schroeder was in his element. Manager of operations, Jeff was at his best when the plant was full, every single machine was operating, and hundreds of workers were getting the job done. Jeff took a beet from the first load of the season to come into the factory and he kept it on his desk throughout the busy harvest season. Whenever a machine would break down, which, of course, always happened when they were being worked around the clock, or there would be a squabble among the workers, which there always was, especially between the seasonal help and the permanent employees, Jeff liked to hold up the beet with one hand and a little packet of sugar such as you would use in a cup of coffee in the other.

"This is it, people; this is what we're here for. It's not rocket science; it's food science. The sugar comes in the door looking like this," and Jeff would hold up the beet, "and goes out the door like this," up would go the packet of sugar. "As quickly and as smoothly as possible. Let's do it!"

Jeff liked to point out that making sugar from sugar beets wasn't actually a manufacturing process. The manufacturing had already been done by the 'Man' upstairs with a bit of water, sun, and dirt.

The processing plant handled twelve hundred tons of sugar beets a day, one hundred and fifty thousand tons a year. Jeff had calculated that the average time for a beet to enter the factory and get turned into sugar was sixteen to twenty hours. He was trying to keep the time down to sixteen hours consistently.

The first stage of the process was washing the beets. Then the beets were sliced into French fry sized slices called cossettes which were soaked in hot water to get to the sugar inside. After the pulp was separated, the remaining liquid was treated with lime and carbon dioxide and then was filtered. This was pumped into enormous evaporation tanks and filtered again. From there, the sweet essence was placed into boiling tanks to be boiled. Finally, the remaining substance was freeze dried leaving only granulated sugar in the end, ready for packaging. The final step was to have the sugar pass over a magnet and then through a metal detector to be sure that any metal which may have rubbed off from the equipment would be removed from the final product.

The factory had equipment capable of packaging the newly processed sugar into teaspoonful packages all the way up to twenty-five pound bags. Some was distributed in five and ten pound bags. The majority of the sugar, however, was shipped by bulk in rail cars or semi-trailer trucks.

At this time of year, there were over five hundred people working round the clock at the processing plant comprised of permanent employees as well as the temporary help who were necessary during the harvest season. The co-op provided electricity and water in a huge area set aside for RV's and campers for the temporary help to live in while they worked. There was some dormitory-style temporary living available, too, but that was mostly used by the Latinos, the migrant workers from Mexico, Ecuador, and Guatemala.

There were groups of retirees from Florida, Texas, and Arizona who made an annual pilgrimage up North to work in the sugar beet harvest year after year. They would drive up in their RV's and appreciate the free trailer site, electricity and water. Some of them had been farmers in some capacity or another; most of them were originally from the Midwest. They planned their vacations around the sugar beet harvest, combining the trip with a chance to see their families and friends. Family members would come together to work in the plant, at the piling stations, or as drivers in the fields. They worked hard and enjoyed the supplement to their retirement income.

Many of the Latinos also had a long history with harvest in the Midwest. They had been coming to work in the fields and factories since back when all of the cultivating had to be done by hand. Many of them were part of the circuit that picked asparagus in Washington, cultivated sugar beets in Minnesota, then on to Wisconsin to work in the lettuce fields before returning for the sugar beet harvest. Some of these workers also had campers which they lived in while they worked, but many of them did not. They lived in the dorms, cooked their suppers on the charcoal grills out back or dined in the plant cafeteria which put on good food at reasonable prices.

Jeff wasn't supposed to admit it, but he suspected some of these workers weren't exactly legal citizens, and he knew the entire co-op administration knew it, too. They demanded to see papers, of course, and every employee, temporary or not, had to present their social security number. Whether or not they were actually legitimate social security numbers, he couldn't really say. The Hispanics were hard workers and the co-op needed their help. That's all Jeff knew, and he intended to keep it that way.

~~~~~~~~~~~~~~~~~~~~~~~~~~~~~~~~~~~~~~

Pete woke up the next morning at the Sheep Shedde in Olivia feeling very chipper. He whistled as he shaved in front of the bathroom mirror. The previous evening he had spent with Laney had been remarkable. Pete hadn't had much experience with women; he was the first one to admit it, so perhaps he didn't have much to compare it to. It's not that he wasn't attractive; he had had plenty of women over the years coming on to him and making themselves available to him. It was his lack of interest that was the challenge, of course, but for Pete it wasn't an act. He truly was not very interested. He had even had a couple of relationships last for around six months. Pete had always known those relationships weren't going to work out, however. He had never felt exactly in tune with those women; they hadn't engaged him at all, and certainly not in the way that he'd felt connected to Laney last night. His heart beat a little bit faster as he thought about the way she'd looked at him when they had said goodnight. Damn, if only he was a more confident man, he would have leaned in and kissed her. He had been sorely tempted.

After picking up supper from the Pick and Pay, a bottle of wine from the liquor store, and a blanket and glasses from Laney's apartment (he had been made to wait in the car, Laney realizing she had to show at least a smidgeon of common sense and not invite a complete stranger up to her apartment), Pete had backtracked to the creek he had crossed near Emma Grabow's place. The creek was an offshoot of the Minnesota River to the south of them; a rambling little stream where small rapids appeared in slight differences of elevation along the creek's path. Pete had noticed a County Park sign off of the highway where he and Laney had found the perfect spot to spread their blanket at the water's edge. One of the best things about Minnesota was that you never had to go far to find yourself on the water's edge. With its fifteen thousand plus lakes as well as the Minnesota River, the Red River, and the mighty Mississippi, among others, Minnesotans liked to brag that their state had the most shoreline of any other state in the continental United States. Its ninety thousand miles of shoreline was more than the states of California, Florida, and Hawaii combined.

Sitting on the water's edge, Pete had felt comfortable with Laney right from the start. They had chatted easily all through supper. Sharing the enormous slice of German chocolate cake complete with coconut frosting, they had fought over the remaining crumbs left on the plate. Enjoying the bottle of red wine from the nearby Glacial Ridge Winery, they had talked easily long after the sunset while the bats darted about overhead nabbing the last of the mosquitoes before the cold weather set in. They had talked about growing up in the Twin Cities, their college years, and their new home towns. They had talked about their families and how unusual it was that they were both 'only's', that is, the only kids in their family. Pete had shared that his mom had begun to display signs of Alzheimer's and how hard this was on his dad. Pete felt it wouldn't be long before they would have to find a home to place his mom where professionals would take care of her. She had gotten away from his dad a couple of times already and the twenty-four/seven care was wearing on his dad. Living in Fargo, Pete felt too far away to help much. If Pete had noticed that Laney was holding back and leaving out a big chunk of her life, he was polite enough not to pry on what he was hoping was their 'first' date. There would be time later to find out all of Laney's secrets, he hoped.

It was when the harvest moon was rising, casting its surreal light over the romantic rural scene that Pete felt melancholy settle over Laney and she went someplace in her mind where he was not invited. They sat in reflective silence for a while. In some unfathomable way, Pete felt like he was home. After a while, they packed up their things and drove back to Opossum Falls. It was on the way back that Laney remembered Pete's promise of a joke, saying that she would love to end the perfect evening with a laugh. Pete panicked for a moment because the truth was that he was not a natural joke teller and he could hardly ever remember the jokes he heard. Worse, he remembered parts of jokes but not the whole thing so he might get up to the punch line and then not be able to remember what it was. Playing it safe, he thought he would tell a short one that gave him little room to screw up. "What does a fish say when it hits a brick wall?"

"What?"

"Dam."

"Up until exactly ten seconds ago, this had been a surprisingly wonderful evening," Laney said with a chuckle as Pete pulled up in front of her apartment and put the car in park. When he turned to face her to ask if he could walk her to her door, she thanked him and said she was fine walking to the door alone. Looking into each other's eyes, a tremor went from Pete's heart to Laney's and back again. They both felt it, and a tiny gasp escaped Laney's lips as it took her by surprise. She'd smiled then, and said softly, "Good-night, Pete," and she was out the door.

Pete finished shaving and patted his cheeks with a towel. Now, he thought, facing himself in the mirror, how can I turn Emma Grabow's vineyard problems into a reason to spend more time in Opossum Falls?

Chapter 13

Brandon Hopkins hated Mexico. Not that he'd ever been there, but still, he couldn't stand the way so many Mexicans had sneaked their way into the country and were now taking jobs that real American citizens should have. He hated it when someone tried to point out that Mexicans were working at the jobs that no one else wanted. He didn't care. They had no right to be here. And when he was asked what he had done to deserve to live in this country, he'd sneered, "I was BORN here." The fact that he, personally, had done nothing because, obviously, being born here was just a stroke of luck, and nothing he had actually done to deserve the good fortune to be living in this country, never registered with him.

Born in lower, middle class Chicago, Brandon was raised in a family that thought the country belonged to whites and everyone else should just get out. His father had worked in a factory job where the majority of workers were black and he was a miserable, frustrated racist. He took out his frustrations at home, beating Brandon on a regular basis. This led to his being a bully all through high school. Brandon had taken a two-year law enforcement course before applying to the Immigration and Customs Enforcement Agency. He was accepted and went to Glynco, Georgia for twelve months of training where he worked extremely hard and gained a reputation for being ruthless.

U.S. Immigration and Customs Enforcement, known as ICE, used to be the investigative and intelligence resource of the U.S. Customs Service and the detention and deportation leg of Immigration and Naturalization. At one point, even the Federal Air Marshals were a part of ICE, but they were eventually moved back to TSA. ICE was formed as part of the Security Act of 2002 following the September 11th attack of the World Trade Center and is responsible for border control. ICE enforces the nation's immigration laws and ensures the removal of undocumented aliens and permanent residents who have committed serious crimes from the United States. ICE employs an estimated fifteen thousand employees in four hundred domestic and fifty international offices.

Brandon Hopkins considered himself the uniformed presence of immigration enforcement within the interior of the United States. For the past five years, he had been a part of Operation Community Shield in St. Paul which targeted violent street gangs and took full advantage of ICE's broad law enforcement powers including the unique and powerful authority to deport criminal aliens. This included both illegal aliens and legal permanent resident aliens who, for whatever reason, were no longer welcome in the U.S. Brandon's fellow ICE agents had complained over the years of his excessive use of unnecessary force. This trend toward violence finally came to a head when a gang member Brandon had arrested died in jail as a result of trauma to the head. Charges were never filed, but Operation Community Shield no longer wanted Brandon around.

The gang member's death was certainly not the first casualty to occur in an ICE detention center; in fact, there have been over a hundred deaths that ICE has counted since 2003. Some were a result of neglect, like the sad case of the tailor from Guinea whose fall resulted in a head fracture while he was being held in isolation while an ambulance wasn't called for over thirteen hours. Others were suicides like that of the Salvadoran who had no previous history of mental illness. Just prior to being arrested by ICE, he had had surgery after a motorcycle accident that resulted in metal pins being placed in his leg. He was on painkillers, but ICE refused to give them to him. Before committing suicide, he wrote a letter to his mother telling her of his inability to take the pain anymore. One detainee died in detention of kidney disease, another of pancreatic cancer which had been left untreated until the day before she died. ICE was known for its ruthless brutality and for shuffling its troublesome agents around from one area to another.

Brandon was transferred out of Operation Community Shield and sent to New Mexico for a while to work on border patrol. He had been back in the Midwest for only a few months before he got involved in an immigration raid at a meatpacking plant in Worthington, MN. Once again, ICE was named in a lawsuit over the alleged abusive and illegal tactics used by agents during the raid, and Brandon had been identified as one of the worst culprits of the abuse. He apparently had ordered female Hispanic workers to disrobe while he hurled racial epithets at them while at the same time allowing the white workers at the plant to simply go about their business during the incursion. The raid had been a part of a six-state rampage that led to the arrest of almost thirteen hundred Hispanic workers including over two hundred in Worthington alone.

Worthington is a town of about fifteen thousand residents near the Iowa border. After the raid, two hundred thirty workers were taken away in buses from the plant. Most were charged with being in the country illegally with about twenty of these facing criminal charges of identity theft. Without the opportunity to go back home to collect their things, even though many of the workers were parents with kids left in daycare, most of the 'illegal's' were immediately deported with only a few sent to jail in Atlanta to await immigration court hearings.

There was another lawsuit filed against ICE which Agent Hopkins was also involved in on behalf of some Hispanic residents in Willmar, a town close to Opossum Falls. These residents claimed that agents broke into their homes without warrants and that they were illegally detained by ICE; more than a dozen of these plaintiffs were children.

Carefully reassembling his SIG-Sauer after taking it apart to clean, Brandon once again admired the double action trigger which allowed him to fire repeatedly without pause. He holstered the pistol while he put on his ICE jacket. Brandon was on preliminary reconnaissance duty at the sugar beet factory outside of Opossum Falls. He had driven by earlier during a shift change and his initial assessment had been that there were an awful lot of brown faces in the crowd. What were the chances that all those working at the factory were legal U.S. citizens? He snickered to himself feeling confident that he would be sending some illegal aliens back to their own countries before he was through with the Minnesota Sugar Beet Cooperative. "Adios and good riddance," he said under his breath as he walked out to his car.

~~~~~~~~~~~~~~~~~~~~~~~~~~~~~~~~~

Walter knocked on Marge Peterson's door with high hopes that their walk to the library together might result in some intimate conversation, but those were soon dashed when she answered the door with Laney Anderson in tow. Explaining that Laney had agreed to co-teach her English as a Second Language class at the library from now on, Walter made a mental note that he need not continue coming up with pretexts to accompany Marge to the library on the evenings she had class anymore. Greeting the ladies with his usual enthusiasm, he carefully hid his disappointment and stuck out both of his elbows for the women to take his arms. After jostling about trying to walk three abreast on the sidewalk, Laney let go and graciously offered to walk behind Walter and Marge. Marge quickly dropped Walter like a hot potato, too, and stepped back to walk with Laney chatting eagerly about the personalities of the students in their English class. Feeling every bit the third wheel that he was, Walter walked awkwardly in front of them one minute walking much too fast and getting too far ahead of them, the next strolling so slowly that they accidently stumbled over his heels. Arriving at the library at last, Marge and Laney greeted Cindy at the front desk and headed back to where a roomful of eager students awaited them.

Attempting to salvage what had rapidly turned into a failure of an evening, Walter decided to sit in one of the rather dilapidated arm chairs donated to the library some years ago and to catch up on some of the newspapers from around the area. He subscribed to the Opossum Falls Digest of course, so he had already read that one at home. At the library, he liked to read Willmar's West Central Tribune, the Olivia Times Journal, and the Granite Falls Advocate Tribune. He greeted the mayor who was already sitting there flipping through Newsweek.

Walter and Jens' relationship had once been much friendlier. They had been in the Lions Club together and had sat together through numerous county commissioner meetings. They both always worked the last shift in the beer gardens Saturday night during the Sugar Beet Festival, easily the busiest shift and the one where trouble would most likely be caused. They were there to keep an eye on the locals so they didn't get into too much trouble on the craziest night of the year in Opossum Falls. Each of them had driven home his share of drunks during that potentially dangerous week-end to try to keep accident levels down. Since the proposal to open a Wal-Mart in Opossum Falls, however, the two friends now stood on opposite sides of the fence. They had engaged in several discussions to try to persuade the other to try to see their point of view, but these eventually became so heated that they had ceased and desisted and now pretty much just ignored each other. Jens was determined to claim the opening of the biggest store in Opossum Falls' history during his reign as mayor, and he was not going to let anyone or anything get in the way of that goal. Walter felt equally resolute about keeping small town America vibrant and strong by keeping Wal-Mart out so the small businesses continued to thrive. Each man was clandestinely scheming so his plan would succeed.

While they steadfastly ignored each other in the library, the noises from Marge and Laney's English class increased in volume. There was music blaring and sounds of thumping and clapping could be heard. Walter glanced inquisitively over at the librarian, but Cindy appeared oblivious to the unusual sounds coming from the English class. The mayor, too, acted as though nothing out of the ordinary was happening. Following their lead, Walter went back to reading the paper even as the floor vibrated and laughter boomed from behind the classroom door.

Therese Dotray-Tulloch

Laney pulled into the empty parking spot and in her dream, she shifted into park and exclaimed, "It's our lucky day, Gabby, a parking spot close to the entrance."

"Dark," Gabby answered, and Laney told her that it wasn't really dark out, the parking ramp just made it look that way. Opening up the back of her minivan, Laney pulled out the stroller and unfolded it, pleased as usual with how easily she could open up the fancy stroller and glad that her girlfriends had all pitched in for her baby shower to get her such a valuable gift. Gabby was playing with her fingers and singing her own version of "Itsy-bitsy Spider" when Laney went around to her door and unbuckled her car seat to lift her out, saying, "Oh, my big girl, you're getting so heavy!"

"Heavy," Gabby repeated. Laney was fascinated with the ease with which Gabby was acquiring language. She seemed to be listening so carefully these days to all that was said around her, and she would constantly repeat words, and just by saying them, it seemed they were lodging themselves into the word bank inside of her head and just like that, they were added to her vocabulary.

"Really heavy but in a good way, not fat, I mean, substantial. I don't want you to be anorexic, Gabby."

"Rexic, Gabby," Gabby repeated, as Laney strapped her into the stroller.

"Oh shit," Laney said, "Now I've done it, setting my poor girl up for years of therapy already." She headed towards the mall entrance.

"Shit," said Gabby, and Laney stopped pushing the stroller and bent down in front of Gabby and said, "No, don't say that, sweetheart, that's a bad word. Mommy shouldn't say it, either, but definitely you can't say it, okay?"

"Mommy, shit?"

Laney tried not to laugh as she was about to scold Gabby and explain some more, but the wind was howling through the ramp so instead she stood up and started walking again pushing the stroller in front of her thinking, never mind, hopefully Gabby would forget the word as long as she didn't use it in front of her again. Parenting was so much more complicated than she ever thought it would be.

A couple of older women were walking ahead of her, and one of them held open the door for Laney to push the stroller through, while the other one held open the next door. "Thanks so much," Laney said.

"We remember those days," one of the ladies said. "Enjoy them, they go by so fast!"

"Oh, I will," Laney responded, "I do," at the same time that Gabby was looking up from her stroller, repeating, "Fast!"

The ladies laughed and carried on through Nordstrom's while Laney pulled over to the side to take off her coat, and then bent down to remove Gabby's hat and coat and stuff them all in the back of the stroller. "Let's get our shopping done first, Gabby, and then we can play."

Finding exactly the shirt she wanted for Gabby, she made her purchase and then wandered halfway around the enormous Mall of America pushing Gabby until they arrived at a giant soldier made out of Legos.

"Stop!" Gabby hollered, and Laney laughed, saying, "What do you say?"

Gabby answered, "Stop, peas," which was how she said 'please', and she tried to climb out of her stroller.

"Hold still, silly goose," Laney said as she bent down to unbuckle the belt and lift her out of the stroller. Gabby's feet barely touched the ground, and she was off, hurrying over to one of the tables set up perfectly for someone her size with buckets full of large Legos beside them. Gabby grabbed a bucket and began assembling the Legos, carefully connecting the large, colorful pieces together. Nearby was a taller table where the older kids worked with the smaller Legos making more complicated creations. Laney sat down on a bench to watch while she agreed with the woman sitting there already that having the Mall of America to bring kids to in the middle of winter was a perfect place for them to be able to play without having to freeze outdoors.

When they left Legoland, they took the elevator up to the third floor food court. Gabby got some chicken nuggets while Laney had a salad. They sat at a table looking down onto Nickelodeon Universe, the world's largest indoor theme park. Gabby squealed every time the roller coaster went by. Laney bribed her with a promise to ride on the Ferris wheel if she finished her lunch. Taking the elevator back down to the first floor, they strolled around the nearly hundred acre shopping mall until they got to the Ferris wheel. Leaving the stroller down below, Laney carried Gabby as they rode the escalator up to the entrance to the Ferris wheel on the second floor. She liked this one, the largest indoor Ferris wheel in the world, because it consisted of sturdy big tubs with hard umbrellas on top as opposed to the typical rides that were nothing more than flimsy seats that rocked too easily as the giant wheel circled around. Climbing into the roomy tub, Laney held on tightly to Gabby as the ride began and they rode high up to the ceiling. Gabby clutched onto Laney and was too frightened at first to make a peep. After a few turns around, she relaxed her grip a little and pointed at a few things as they went around, but her little body was still tense with fear throughout the entire ride. After they disembarked, Gabby squirmed in Laney's arms until she put her down. Gabby stretched up her little arm until Laney took her hand and they stepped carefully together onto the escalator. Gabby never took her eyes off of the moving stairs. At the bottom, she kept both feet completely still so Laney had to lift her up at the last moment when the stair they were standing on disappeared.

"Where go?" Gabby asked, her voice squeaking, her little hands raised in bafflement. Laney tried to show her how the escalator just went round and round but Gabby wanted to actually see where the stair went. Trying to avoid a tantrum that would surely result if Gabby got too frustrated this close to nap time, Laney distracted her by showing her the Ferris wheel they had just been on, pointing out how high they had gone.

"See, what a brave little girl you were, riding so high on the Ferris wheel!" Gabby stuck her thumb in her mouth as she tipped her head backwards to see the top of the giant Ferris wheel. Reaching with her other hand, she pointed upwards, and pulling her thumb over to one cheek while still keeping it in her mouth, she said, "Sky."

"Yes," Laney agreed looking out the huge skylight over the Mall of America, "That is the sky up there." All the way through the mall as they walked back towards the direction of their car, Gabby pointed so Laney could name the object for her. Just outside of Nordstrom's, Gabby pointed at the bust of a man in the foyer. "Hero. He was a hero, Gabby." She stopped to read about Tom Burnett, the Minnesota native who acted so heroically on September 11th who, with the help of some of his fellow passengers, crashed Flight 93 in the Pennsylvania countryside rather than allow it to fly to Washington, D.C. to crash there and kill who knows how many innocent victims.

Back at home, after they had finished cleaning up after supper, Laney told Scott to go sit in the living room to wait for a special surprise. She pulled Gabby into her bedroom and pulled the bag out from under her bed with the shirt in it that they'd *bought earlier at the Mall. Slipping the shirt on over Gabby's footed pajamas, she sent her out into the living room while she grabbed her phone and started videotaping.*

Scott smiled when he saw her and said, "Look at you, Gabby, did you get a new outfit?" He tilted his head to the side while he tried to read the words on the tee shirt. "I'm... the... big sister?" he said, and the seconds ticked by until suddenly he repeated in excitement, "I'm the big sister! Wheeeeeeee!" and he scooped up Gabby who shrieked with pleasure as he twirled her around the room. "You're the big sister! Mommy's gonna have another baby!" Then he pushed the camera away from Laney's face and leaned in to kiss her gently on the lips, all the while Gabby chanted, "Big sister, big sister!"

"Really, Laney?" Scott asked, "How are you feeling? Have you been to the doctor yet?" He pulled her close for a hug. Laney laughed in reply telling him that she felt fine. Picking up Gabby, she sat with her in the rocking chair and proceeded to tell him all of the details of their expanding family.

Rocking Gabby in her arms, Laney felt the weight of her on her chest as she slowly awoke from her dream. The pressure was so great, she was afraid that her heart would break in two. Holding nothing in her arms but her pillow, she lay in bed and looked up at the ceiling, wondering how in the world she would find the strength to get up and face another day.

Chapter 14

Juan Carlos slowed down as he drove around one of the last of the huge trucks hauling sugar beets as it turned into the piling station. He touched his horn lightly and waved at the driver as he passed him, lifting two fingers off the steering wheel in the time-honored tradition of the country driver. He looked approvingly at the mountains of sugar beets and thought the farmers should be happy with the harvest this year, depending on how the sugar content in the beets measured up, of course. He had finished helping Eric Hanson with his harvest and was now concentrating on his landscaping business again. He always loved helping out during harvest season though.

Juan Carlos was often nostalgic during the sugar beet harvest. He remembered growing up and working as a *betabeleros*, Spanish for a sugar beet worker. Now, although he loved helping out during the harvest season, he was glad that he'd gotten out of field work and into landscaping. Patting his truck, he chided himself, "That's right, jefe, you are your own boss, now."

The Ramirez family had been *betabeleros* from the Crookston area in northern Minnesota, some of the first in the area. Sugar beets had long been grown in Europe, not for human consumption but to feed livestock. It wasn't until 1802, when the first sugar beet extraction factory started operating in Prussia, that sugar beets were grown for human use. The sugar beet was brought to the U.S. by German immigrants in the early nineteenth century. When the consumption of sugar began to rise in the early twentieth century, sugar beet production increased rapidly. In 1918, a farmer near Crookston successfully planted sugar beets. After the Second World War, the price of wheat plummeted, so even more farmers decided to plant sugar beets. The root crop flourished in the light soil with its good drainage. This Red River Valley surrounds the Red River which flows north into Canada and separates North Dakota from Minnesota. Some three hundred miles long and forty to fifty miles wide, the Red River Valley of the North (as opposed to the south where the Red River separates Texas from Oklahoma) now produces fifty percent of the sugar beets in the U.S. market.

Juan Carlos' father had been recruited from Texas by the American Crystal Sugar Company in the late nineteen forties. *Betabeleros* were paid more than any other seasonal agricultural worker, but cultivating sugar beets was difficult, back-breaking work. The first couple of years, his father cultivated the sugar beets on his knees with a short-handled hoe. By the 1950's, the hoe was obsolete, and the sugar beet harvest was mechanized. Working for one of the biggest sugar beet farmers in the area, the Ramirez's were needed year round to maintain the three hundred acre farm. They lived in a trailer house on the farmer's land. Juan Carlos' father worked for the same farmer for over twenty-two years.

Despite the federal law that stated that all workers should be at least fourteen years old, Juan Carlos, like all of his six siblings, started working at the age of ten. The work was grueling and everyone in the family put in long hours, especially during the cultivating and harvest seasons. At school, Juan Carlos also worked hard and was determined not to continue being a *betabeleros* for the rest of his life. He did love working with the rich, black soil of the Red River Valley though.

After graduating from Crookston High School, he went to Texas Tech University to study Landscape Architecture.

Coming from Minnesota, his four years living in Lubbock were a real challenge. The searing heat, the lack of lakes, and the constant wind made him long to be back up north. His Texan classmates made fun of him, the Mexican who thought he was a northerner, but he didn't care. He did enjoy spending time with his grandparents and cousins while he was in Texas, and there he met his future wife at a cousin's quincianera, a huge fiesta held for girls on their fifteenth birthday. He got married in Our Lady of Guadalupe Church in Lubbock just after graduation and immediately returned to Minnesota with his bride. Working back in the sugar beet harvest until he could find a job in the landscaping business, Juan Carlos was happy to be back, but his wife was miserable. In fact, she didn't like anything about Minnesota: the mosquitoes, the cold, nor the snow. Right after their second wedding anniversary, she told Juan Carlos that she loved him but not enough to stay and she packed up and headed back to Texas. It wasn't until after she'd left him that she told Juan Carlos that she was pregnant with his child.

Their son Miguel grew up spending half of his time in Texas and the other half with Juan Carlos in Minnesota. Miguel settled in Texas to marry his girlfriend as soon as they realized she was pregnant, and they had an adorable little girl, Isabella Rose. On one of their trips up North, they were involved in a pile-up on Interstate 35 in an ice storm while driving through Iowa. Slammed from behind, their car was pushed underneath a semi truck. Both Miguel and his wife were killed but miraculously, little Izzy, asleep in her car seat in the back seat, survived with barely a scratch on her. Miguel's mother was completely devastated by her son's death and was incapable of caring for her granddaughter, so Juan Carlos took the little girl in. With Tia Juanita's help, they were raising her as best they could.

After working for a landscape company in Fargo for a few years, Juan Carlos moved to Willmar when a job opened up for him. After about ten years, he'd decided it was time to venture off on his own and he had set up JC Landscaping. He bought a comfortable trailer home and settled in Olivia. He worked hard and built up a nice clientele in the surrounding area, but he was always looking for more work. Whenever storms passed through, he would drive by neighborhoods to see who needed help with branch removal or maintenance. He often employed high school boys to help with his business and to give them some experience as well. Bianca's son Jesus Maria had worked for him all summer long and was still helping out on Saturdays and after school. When the snow began to fall, JC Landscaping became a snow removal business and, depending on the winter, they were usually kept plenty busy all season long. Still, it was a struggle, and as Juan Carlos got older, he began to keep an eye out for something else he might do that wouldn't be quite as physical as his landscaping business.

On this Saturday in late October, Juan Carlos and Jesus Maria had been laying a brick path at a house on Eucalyptus Street. Juan Carlos left the boy there telling him he would return in the late afternoon to see how far he'd gotten while he drove over to Marge's house for lunch. He smiled happily to himself as he pulled into Marge's driveway. He could not possibly imagine where this relationship was headed but he was certainly enjoying the ride. Lifting the burnt-orange mum plant out of the back of his truck, he whistled in response to the cardinal perched on an overhanging branch as he walked down the sidewalk to Marge's front door. His eye scanned her front garden professionally and he thought his choice of mum color would fit in nicely with the plants she already had.

Marge was just taking the salmon loaf out of the oven when Juan Carlos rang the doorbell. Removing her apron, she glanced quickly into the hallway mirror before answering the door, smoothing down her hair as she did so. She'd decided that she would make one of her favorite dishes for Juan Carlos this time and stop with the Mexican cooking for a change. If he found her salmon loaf bland, he could always sprinkle cayenne pepper on it. Not that he needed to be any hotter. Marge surprised herself with thoughts like these which seemed to be occurring the more she saw of Juan Carlos. Everything about this relationship surprised her. It was good, she thought, at her age, to be surprised. She smiled eagerly as she pulled open the door.

Marge and Juan Carlos chatted easily over lunch. They had moved beyond family histories and were now talking about their favorite authors and who they were reading now. Juan Carlos was telling her about his Zane Grey novel when there was a frantic rapping on the back door, accompanied by someone shouting Juan Carlos' name. Marge jumped up to open the door. Jesus Maria was there dripping with sweat from having run all the way from Eucalyptus Street and panting heavily, "Juan Carlos, we need to go help. There's been an accident at the piling station. Some of the kids were horsing around and got trapped under the beets!"

"Let's go," Juan Carlos said as he was already putting his arm into the sleeve of his jacket.

~~~~~~~~~~~~~~~~~~~~~~~~~~~~~~~~

Marge baked a couple of spice cakes while she waited for Juan Carlos to come back. She would deliver one of them to the family of whoever was involved in the accident at the piling station. Comfort food helped in any situation. Every woman with an ounce of sense knew this already, and if the men didn't consciously know it, they always ate the food anyhow. She frosted the cakes, licking the last of the frosting off the knife.

The darkness descended quickly; Marge had just turned on the reading lamp on her side table as it had gotten too dark to read. She laid her book down in her lap and concentrated on the little girl, Sally's, plight in *Whistling in the Dark*, author Lesley Kagen's first novel. Marge loved to read an author's first book. Kagen was in her fifties already before she published her first novel. Marge felt first books were filled with stories the author had been saving up over a lifetime, and she felt privileged to be sharing them.

She stopped and listened closely as she thought she heard footsteps. A soft tapping followed. Marge stood up and went to the door. One of the many joys of living in a small town was that Marge never felt nervous about answering her door no matter what time of the day or night. She pulled open the door and her heart leapt at the sight of Juan Carlos standing there. He looked exhausted, holding his hat in his hands, and before he could say anything, Marge reached out and pulled him into the house. Without even thinking about it, she leaned in and very gently touched her lips to Juan Carlos'. Her open mouth clung to his for a long moment and she felt desire well up from deep inside her. Juan Carlos began to respond, but Marge recollected herself and, gently placing her hand against his chest, she pushed him away.

He drew in a deep breath while his eyes slowly crinkled into a lazy smile, "Wow," he said quietly.

"I, I'm sorry, I have no idea where that came from," Marge stammered, flustered.

"Well, let's see if we can find out," Juan Carlos said as he put his hand on Marge's lower back and drew her towards him. Looking into her eyes, he was just about to touch his lips to hers again when rapid footsteps followed by a brisk knocking on the door followed. Marge pulled quickly away and opened the door to Walter, who was talking even before she had the door all the way open.

"Marge, there's been an accident at the piling station." He looked over at Juan Carlos and feigned surprise, but of course, the JC Truck at the curb was precisely the reason Walter was there. "Hello, Juan Carlos, are you here about the accident, too?"

"Sure," he answered, glancing at Marge while a deep red flush crept over her face, "I just came from there, actually."

"Good, you can tell us all about it then firsthand," Walter said as he started to sit down, "Marge, have you got anything to drink? Stronger than tea, if you know what I mean. It is Saturday night, after all."

Marge got drinks and served cake while Juan Carlos told them all about the accident at the sugar beet piling station and the condition of the injured boy. At this time of year when the beet harvest was nearly finished, the sugar beet pile stood twenty feet high and about a hundred and fifty feet wide. The local kids knew better than to play in the dangerous, unstable piles, but it had always been hard for them to resist, and over the years kids had gotten hurt almost as a rite of passage.

That day, a group of high school kids were playing around in the back of the pile where they couldn't be seen from the road. They were daring each other to see who could climb the fastest to the top of the pile of beets. Travis Ibsen had gone first. As he was scrambling up the mountain of beets about three quarters of the way up, he stepped into a hole between the beets and sunk through. For a stunned moment, his head and one arm were seen poking out of the beets. A high-pitched, terrified screech escaped from the boy before gravity won and pulled him into the bowels of the hill of beets. The kids who were watching Travis from the loading dock sprang into action. The boy who had been using his cell phone to time Travis' climb quickly used it to call 911 for help saying that a kid had slipped into the pile of beets at the piling station and was buried underneath a hundred-fifty thousand tons of sugar beets.

Matthew Stevenson was a junior at Opossum Falls High School and was the quarterback of the football team. Football season was over and Matthew was enjoying a few weeks off from practice before the basketball season started. He was a starter on the team, or he would have been. As soon as Travis disappeared, Matthew leapt from the loading dock planning to scramble up the mountain of beets to aid Travis. The six foot drop from the loading dock onto the concrete below did not bode well for Matthew. The snap of his femur breaking could be heard all the way up the pile. The same boy called 911 again to update the emergency operator. The news had spread quickly throughout Opossum Falls and Jesus Maria, concerned for his classmates, had run to Juan Carlos to see how they could help.

By the time they arrived, Matthew had been taken away by ambulance, but the buried boy had only sunk deeper into the pile. There were plenty of air pockets in a pile of sugar beets, so suffocation wouldn't occur nearly as quickly as it would in a pile of corn or wheat. It was important for the boy to remain calm and breathe. With the entire Opossum Falls Fire Department there to help, enough beets were eventually removed so that the boy could be safely lifted out. Tragedy had been averted for Travis, but it looked as though Matthew Stevenson's wouldn't be playing basketball this year.

After a second helping of spice cake for each of them, Walter accompanied Juan Carlos down the sidewalk to his truck and kept up a steady stream of chatter with him through the window until finally Juan Carlos gave up and drove away. Walter looked back up at Marge's house, but she had shut off the front light already, a sure sign that she was no longer open for visitors. Walter walked slowly down the sidewalk to his house next door, admiring the many stars filling the night sky. Venus, named after the Roman goddess of love and beauty, was awfully bright tonight hovering near the horizon.

Walter let himself in the door and thought about love. He walked over to the fireplace and stood in front of the photograph of him and his wife, Berniece, on their fiftieth wedding anniversary. The breast cancer that would take her life must have already been spreading within her when this picture was taken unbeknownst to them. She had made jokes about what a relief it was to have her breasts removed because it was so annoying, now that they were as flat as pancakes, the way she would sweat underneath them. She admitted she had been using deodorant underneath her sagging breasts and was pleased that would no longer be necessary. Berniece was such a card and always had been. Her sense of humor was what had drawn Walter to her in the first place. Theirs had been a home filled with laughter and fun; Berniece had been a great mom raising their three children. She had fought hard, but the cancer had won, and as she lay dying, it was Berniece who was comforting Walter, making jokes up until the bitter end.

"I have had a great time, and am not even sad to go," Berniece had told him on her deathbed. "What a relief that I don't have to worry about watching us both grow old and ugly. Walter, you must promise me that you won't be sad for long. Go on one of those internet sites and find yourself a new woman, someone to make you laugh who still has breasts." Walter had promised her, and he had tried to honor her wishes and not be sad. The children had all moved away ages ago but they were still very good to him and they came home often enough. He enjoyed his life in Opossum Falls and especially his new project to stop Wal-Mart. Still, he missed Berniece greatly and knew she would have relished this challenge to beat back the big boys. Basically, Walter was tired of feeling lonely. With overwhelming sadness, he forced himself to be honest and acknowledge that Marge wasn't interested in him. Admitting to himself that he literally had nothing else to lose, he decided to waste no more time and to put the next phase of his Stop Wal-Mart plan into action tomorrow.

Chapter 15

Anita Beatrice arrived at the Renville County Hospital in Olivia to visit Matthew just as most of the boys' basketball team as well as Coach Martin were leaving. Coach did not look happy as he gnawed on his signature Cuban scowling as he exited the room, desperate to light the cigar as soon as he was out of the hospital. Anita's brother, Jesus Maria, chided her not to tire the poor guy out as he needed his rest. Anita leaned over the bed and kissed Matthew gently on the lips, tears flooding her eyes as the shock of seeing him in a hospital gown looking pale and with his leg held up in a sling from the ceiling affected her greatly. Matthew tried to shrug it off, but he was feeling pretty emotional himself, not least of all because he now knew he would be missing out on the entire basketball season, all because of stupid kids' stuff goofing around on the sugar beet pile and his heroic effort to jump off the loading dock. The painkillers were making him drowsy, so the two held hands while Anita sat in a chair pulled next to his bed and tried to comfort this boy she loved so much.

Matthew had stood by Anita Beatrice's side during the homecoming fiasco when some of the town rednecks had tried to shun her due to her race. While she hadn't won homecoming queen, the fact that she had been nominated as a candidate was a fine precedent. During the homecoming dance, Matthew, as King, had to dance the first dance with the homecoming queen, Vanessa Schmidt. When all of the homecoming candidates came out to dance halfway through the first dance, however, Matthew quickly sidled up next to Anita and traded partners leaving Vanessa furious with her mouth hanging open in shock and Anita delighted as Matthew twirled her away in his arms. Later, he took off his crown and placed it on Anita's head which won unexpected applause and whistles as the student body opted to show support for Anita and disproval for the racial prejudice which had reared its ugly head.

Anita chatted idly while she kept Matthew company. She told him about how busy the Chit Chat had been during the sugar beet harvest and how pleased her mom was at how some of her Mexican dishes had been so well-received. She talked about her job at Pick and Pay and then she filled him in on Shannon Fischer.

The rumors had started to fly around the school that Shannon was pregnant due to her being sick in the morning and the little bulge that had begun to show through her volleyball uniform on the normally pencil-thin high school senior. Shannon realized she had better confess to her parents before they heard it from someone else first. She couldn't even imagine how ashamed her father would be if one of his parishioners came to inform him that his own daughter had sinned so profoundly that she was pregnant. It wouldn't have been any immaculate conception either.

Dinner at the Fischer house was always a sit-down affair. Struggling to finish the slice of meatloaf on her plate, Shannon had poured more catsup on it and continued to push it around with the peas and carrots while feeling her mom's eyes upon her. Listening to her father discuss his disappointment in the youth minister at Norwegian Lutheran Church and how combining the Wednesday night religion classes with the Catholics was simply not working out, Shannon sighed and put down her fork, pushed back her plate and announced that she had something to tell them. Her father, unused to being interrupted, harrumphed a bit while her mother set her fork down, too, to pay attention. Not knowing how to soften the blow, Shannon had come right out with it. "I'm pregnant. I'll be having a baby sometime in March."

Her father had practically gone into convulsions, as she'd expected, ranting and raving about how this would look in the eyes of the church and how would he ever be able to hold his head up standing in front of the pulpit. Shannon took the abuse with her head bowed, not trying to defend herself, feeling smaller and smaller as her father's voice grew larger and larger. Her mother's firm, "That's enough now, Clarence," surprised her because of its authority as well as the use of her father's seldom used first name. Normally, her mom called him 'Pastor,' but perhaps in this instance she was thinking of him more as a husband and father than as the head of the church. When she had their attention, Shannon's mom said quite simply, "Shannon's human, just like the rest of us, so it's only natural that she's allowed to make her share of mistakes. The good lord understands this and so shall your parishioners."

The unexpected silver lining to her pregnancy, Shannon quickly realized, was the new understanding and closeness she began to share with her mom. She accompanied Shannon to the doctor, brought her shopping for maternity clothes, and even took her to counseling to help her figure out exactly what she was going to do with the baby. She was, in every possible sense, exactly the mom Shannon needed at this time in her life. Shannon still hadn't decided what would happen to the baby in March, but she knew she had her mom's support no matter what. Shannon's mom treated her with such dignity and respect that the rest of the town seemed to follow right along. Interestingly enough, even Pastor Fischer became more well-liked and respected as the news of Shannon's pregnancy got around. His illegitimate grandchild made him less fearsome and judgmental, fine qualities for a minister of God.

As she sat by his hospital bed, Anita realized that Matthew had fallen asleep. She let go of his hand to take *The Poisonwood Bible* she was reading for English class out of her book bag. She read until the nurse came in to tell her that visiting hours were over.

~~~~~~~~~~~~~~~~~~~~~~~~~~~~~~~

Pete had been on his second cup of coffee with Emma Grabow when the rest of his team turned up. He was surprised at how annoyed he felt to see them simply because they were interrupting the pleasant time he was having chatting over coffee in Emma's cozy kitchen. The coffee itself was delicious, a dark roast which must have been pretty recently ground. It was brewed strong, just the way he liked it. When Emma had offered to fry him up a couple of fresh farm eggs, his pleasure had been so obvious that she hadn't even waited for him to answer, she just chuckled as she reached overhead for one of the frying pans dangling from above the island in her kitchen. The theme of the kitchen was apples, so the wallpaper, curtains, towels, and even the dishes all displayed candy red apples with tiny, lime-green leaves. Pete got a kick out of the apples painted on the plastic rectangles over the light switches, thinking, 'this is a woman who pays attention to detail.'

Pete and Emma chatted easily. After she'd gotten his family history out of him, Emma had told him all about her husband, Otto. Pete was especially interested in his job as a sugar beet field man. While Emma cooked, she explained how Otto's job as a field man had been threefold. First, he had had to recruit farmers to grow sugar beets. Second, he had provided all of the technical assistance for the farmers as well as advice on which seed types to plant, on farm implements, pesticides, and herbicides. Third, he had been the intermediary between the growers and the Mexican migrant field laborers. During the nineties, Otto had been working with about ninety growers. Of course, he had had a small acreage himself, part of which Emma had converted to grapes after Otto's death.

Pete thanked Emma for breakfast and headed out to the vineyard to join his crew. His four associates were wearing lab coats with paper guards over their mouths. They pulled on disposable, plastic gloves and began collecting samples of the soil, leaves, petioles and grapes. They were looking for the residue of an herbicide which had drifted from the nearby beet fields, but Pete already knew from experience what it was going to be. He could tell by the curled up leaves that the culprit was Roundup. The giant Monsanto had developed a genetically modified sugar beet engineered to resist glyphosphate, the herbicide marketed as Roundup. The farmers in this area were undoubtedly using Roundup on their beets.

What most farmers didn't realize was that any sort of pesticide or herbicide drift was actually considered trespassing. There had recently been a case whereby an organic soybean farmer had successfully won a suit against a co-op that had sprayed Roundup on fields adjacent to his. The case went all the way to the State Appeals Court which endorsed the lower court ruling that herbicide drift is the equivalent of trespassing. The Co-op had to compensate the organic farmer for lost income, legal fees, and punitive damages. Pete would be informing Emma that she, too, would have the right to take the guilty farmer through the courts. Assuming the outcome was what Pete expected it to be, starting at the lower courts and all the way up to the Appeals Court, Emma would be compensated for the damage done to her crop of grapes.

After dividing the affected areas of the vineyard into a grid, the agents got to work and spent the morning gathering samples from select areas of the grid to get the widest variety of examples for testing. Jingle Bells, the cat, followed them around the vineyard obviously happy to have the company though too cool to show it. He would scratch at the dirt and make a nice bed for himself to lay in languidly until suddenly snapping at an unsuspecting fly. Except for his thick tail constantly lifting its tip up and down, he looked completely relaxed. When a rabbit was spotted farther down the row, Jingle Bells took off like a flash in pursuit.

When all of the necessary samples had been collected, the four agents loaded them into coolers and drove off back to Fargo. Pete went back up to the farm house to inform Emma that it would take a few days for the lab work to come through, but he would be in touch with her just as soon as he knew anything. As he waited at the front door for Emma to answer, he petted Jingle Bells' head as he lay all curled up on the rocking chair on the porch. "You deserve a rest after your active morning, don't you Jingle Bells," Pete said scratching under the grateful cat's chin. The cat looked back at him through slits of eyes as if he hadn't moved a muscle all morning.

"Active morning, my eye. He hasn't left that chair once, useless creature," Emma said as she answered the door with a hot pad holder in one hand. "You're just in time for lunch, Mr. Oetzmann. I've got some homemade pork sausage which I made when ol 'Wilbur passed on, and I'm serving it up with sauerkraut. A good German like you won't be able to pass that up, now will you?"

Pete paled as he made his excuses. He had just been reading about the Prime Minister of the Central African Republic, Jean Bedel Bokasa, who had, unbeknownst to the French diplomat Robert Galley, fed him human flesh at his extravagant coronation banquet. When Emma clarified that Wilbur was, in actual fact, just like in Charlotte's Web, a pig, Pete expressed his condolences on the loss of the pig and said he would be delighted to accept the invitation to lunch. They spent an enjoyable lunch hour sitting in the cheerful apple-filled kitchen, because the bees were too bad at this time of year to eat lunch out on the porch. Emma had been canning the last of her tomatoes all morning so the counter was covered in quart-sized jars filled with tomatoes, salsa, spaghetti sauce, and tomato juice.

Pete shared with Emma the difficult time he was having with his mom's Alzheimer's and how hard it was that she hardly ever recognized him anymore. It was also worrisome knowing how hereditary the disease was. Being an only child, Pete talked about all of the responsibility he felt with regards to his parents. After a while, he pushed back his chair and patted his stomach.

"Don't take this the wrong way," Pete said as he wiped the last of the Dijon mustard off of his chin, "But I have to say that I'm glad Wilbur moved on. That sausage was fantastic! The spices were just right."

"Glad you liked it. I'm sending you home with a jar of my spaghetti sauce, too, because that is loaded with the sausage."

Just then, the little pet door pushed open and Jingles walked regally into the kitchen completely ignoring Emma and Pete as he strolled past them into the mudroom where his litter box as well as his food was kept. Moments later, the slam of the basement door at the back of the house was heard. "What are those boys up to now?" Emma wondered as she went to the window to find out. "Alonso, what's going on?"

"Not to worry, Mrs. G., we was just putting Jingle Bells down the basement so he wouldn't bother the chickens while we was trying to collect the eggs."

Emma's eyebrows descended as she looked with a puzzled expression at Pete. The sound of scratching, as though the job at the litter box had been successful, came from the mud room. Pete got up and went to look, "Um, Jingle Bells is right here."

"I told you he doesn't chase chickens," Emma said smugly to Pete before she shouted out the window again, "Boys, can you come here a minute?"

The brothers raced each other to the back door, fighting to pull open the screen door while pushing the other out of the way shouting: "I won!" "No, I won!"

"Look what I've got, boys," Pete called to get their attention, and they saw him cradling Jingle Bells in his arms. They both turned and looked towards the basement door where they had just deposited the cat they thought was Jingle Bells, the surprised looks on their faces comical in their parody of one another.

"But, we just put Jingle Bells down the basement, like we always do," Manuel said.

"Oh dear," Emma said, "I don't particularly like that 'like we always do' part."

Holding the cat at such an angle that he finally stepped gracefully out of his arms, Pete said, "Come on, let's see who we've got down the basement then, shall we?"

As in the style of the traditional old farmhouses, the basement wasn't accessible from inside the house. They had to walk outside and enter the basement from a door on the side of the house. Emma reached in first to feel along the wall until she came to the light switch. Otto had added that feature shortly after he and Emma were married. She hated having to walk down the basement stairs in the clammy darkness and feel around above her head until she felt the chain descending from the ceiling to turn on the single light bulb, sometimes waving both arms over her head for long minutes trying to make contact with the elusive chain.

The group walked down the wooden stairs to the cellar which was used completely for storage. The water pump, heater, and softener were down there as was the furnace. The other two walls were covered from floor to ceiling with shelves filled with all sorts of Emma's canned goods. She canned everything from her own garden like cucumbers, beans, beets, peppers and tomatoes, of course. She also canned fruits such as peaches, pears, and plums. She made jellies and jams from rhubarb, strawberries, grapes, blueberries, raspberries and gooseberries. Looking at the shelves made Pete's mouth water, but Manuel's "Shit" followed by, "I mean, shoot, sorry, Mrs. G." drew his attention downward.

Piles of excrement were scattered all over the cement floor, and in the corner, where the huge bags of cat food that Emma had delivered to the basement by the feed mill were kept, was a bag that had been torn open by cat's claws working tirelessly at the paper bag until it ripped. No one said a word as they took in the ominous sight before them.

"So, if you just put the mystery cat down the basement now," Emma asked the obvious, "why is there so much cat poop all over the floor? And who tore open this bag?"

The boys looked at their feet, too miserable to answer, so Pete added helpfully, "Emma, I saw the boys put a cat we thought was Jingle Bells down the basement yesterday, remember?"

"But that still wouldn't account for quite so much of this, well, *crap*, would it?"

Alonso finally spoke, never taking his eyes off the ground. He mumbled so that Emma had to ask him to repeat himself and to speak up. "Mrs. G., we been putting Jingle Bells down the basement for over a week now."

"For over a week?"

Just then, Pete noticed a slight movement from one of the top shelves. Looking down on him through curious eyes was a cat looking practically identical to Jingle Bells. Sure enough, a little further down the shelf was another 'imitation Jingle Bells', and then another. "Well, what do you know," he said, chuckling.

All four of them stared up at the shelves in surprise till they heard a scrambling sound from below and the newest addition to the basement started crunching hungrily on the cat food in the enormous bag. They all started laughing then, the boys collapsing on the floor and Emma laughing so hard she had to wipe the tears with her apron. "This explains Jingle Bells' recent obsession with the basement window. Can you imagine what a glorious place for a stray cat to end up?" Emma said in between gasps of laughter. "All the food you can eat! And look, the dripping from the water softener even provides freshly filtered water for them!" which caused a fresh wave of laughter from all of them.

It was amazing how much each of the cats resembled Jingle Bells. They were thinner, of course, and not quite so tame, but they were all ginger-colored tabby cats. Later, after the boys had cleaned up the poop and Pete had put a fresh litter box down the basement, Emma started to change her tune as she began fuming at Eric Hanson again.

"It's all Hanson's fault. When I found Jingle Bells on Christmas Eve, he was a scrawny little kitten who had obviously been hit by a car, according to the vet, with ear mites, fleas, and an infection in his jaw. I went around the neighborhood to ask if the cat may have come from any of my neighbors' farms. I had my own cat at that stage, good ol' Phukett, and I didn't want her to have to put up with a feisty new kitten in the house. The neighbors all said no, they'd never had a cat like Jingle Bells. I remember Eric distinctly saying, "No, m'am, we've never had any ginger-colored cats around here! What a fraud. They must be his old barn cats that are now tempted by my chickens. Well, I'm going to drop them right back off at his place. You just watch me."

After Pete got her to calm down and convinced her that it would accomplish nothing as the cats would easily find their way back to Emma's, he suggested the boys make up some posters to put up around town announcing they had free cats to give away. This was the time of the year when the mice started to move indoors so they were to be sure to mention in the posters what good 'mousers' the big tomcats were.

Bidding farewell to Emma at last, and thanking her again for the delicious meals, Pete promised her that he would ask around at work to see if he could find any takers for the numerous Jingle Bell imitators.

Chapter 16

Walter lay in bed and reminded himself to appreciate the soft, comfortable mattress and his favorite down pillow. He spoke to his absent, deceased wife as he often did when he awoke in the morning after fifty-one years of habit. "Well, Berniece, looks like this is really it; my times to show this town what I'm really made of, to 'shit or get off the pot,' as it were, excuse my French. Can I admit that I'm scared stiff?" Walter patted the empty pillow next to him where his wife would have been laying, no doubt telling him to toughen up and get on with it already. "Yes, dear, you are quite right," Walter said to his partner in spirit, and he swung his legs over the side of the bed and slowly stood up.

He took his time packing his backpack, knowing that the nights were cold already and the days growing shorter by the minute. He put in long johns, a flannel shirt, and some extra socks. He went to the kitchen and filled his soft-sided cooler with the items he'd picked up at

Pick and Pay yesterday. He punched in Marty's cell phone number and only said, "Yup, I'm heading over now....uh-huh........thanks, Marty." He was halfway out the door when he turned around, walked straight over to the fireplace and grabbed his favorite photo of Berniece. Shoving it into his pocket, he walked briskly out the door and down the walk.

Marge was out in her yard pulling up the tomato cages and taking down the pea fence. She called out to Walter as he went by, "Good morning, Walter. Isn't it a beautiful day today? We have to appreciate the fine weather while we can. We know what's coming, don't we?" Noticing his bags, she asked, "Where are you off to? Do you want me to keep an eye on your place while you're gone?"

"You know, Marge, that would be great, thanks," Walter said as he hurried on his way. Marge sat back on her heels and watched him walk away thinking how unlike Walter it was to be going somewhere without telling her all about it. She wondered what he was up to. Walter felt badly about deceiving her, but he knew she'd find out soon enough where he had gone. He wanted to get things ready before garnering the publicity that was his ultimate goal.

Walter had just finished grabbing the items that he needed off of the shelves at Just Screw It when Marty arrived to help him carry them. They drove off in Marty's car to the proposed future site of Wal-Mart.

It was the northern-most edge of Otto Grabow's property. Since his death, Emma had leased out the land. She was now working with the city, of course, to offer the sweetest deal they could come up with so Wal-Mart would open a store there. In anticipation of this, they had erected a big sign proclaiming, "Future site of Wal-Mart.' Walter had kept covering up the sign with black plastic but someone, most likely Jeanine Westerly, removed it every time he put it back up. The proposed supercenter would take up nearly two-hundred thousand square feet of Emma's land.

 Right in the middle of the future site stood a majestic Red Oak tree. It was to this tree that Walter was headed. *Quercus rubra*, or Red Oak, grew all throughout Minnesota, some as tall as one hundred and twenty feet. The mighty oak on Emma's property was just beginning to turn colors of yellow, red, and tan. As was typical of oaks, this tree was a gorgeous shade tree and Otto had enjoyed many lunches sitting beneath the generous, outstretched branches. Knowing how slow-growing oak trees were, Otto had resisted the temptation to take it down even though it had been a hassle driving around it to cultivate and harvest the sugar beets year after year. Still, over time he had come to appreciate the tree more and more.

Unfortunately, Wal-Mart had no such compunction. The tree was smack dab in the middle of its projected site and so it was destined to come down.

There were so many reasons why Walter was against Wal-Mart moving into Opossum Falls, but the imminent removal of this lovely old oak tree was the final straw. Standing beneath the magnificent old tree, Marty and Walter tipped back their heads to gaze up its regal trunk.

"Do you know what 'tree fiddy' is?" Marty asked.

"No, never heard of it."

"Oh, about three fifty," Marty said, still looking upwards without even a hint of a smile.

Walter turned his head to look at him. "Man, you must have learned that at mortuary school. Even when you're being funny, you keep that funeral director's somber composure. I am impressed."

Marty grinned and slapped Walter's back, but quickly turned serious again as he asked his friend, "Are you sure you want to do this, Walter?"

"I've never been surer of anything in my life," he said with false bravado, "Well, except when I asked Berniece to marry me, of course. Here's my extra cell phone. Thanks for keeping it charged up for me." He stuck out his hand for him to shake which Marty clasped and then with his other arm, gave Walter an awkward, man to man hug.

Walter climbed up the wooden boards they had nailed to the tree as steps earlier. Higher and higher he rose until he was almost thirty feet high. He clambered onto the makeshift tree house he and Marty had constructed over the past few weeks in preparation for this day. It was an eight foot square platform. Walter spent a few moments hooking up the pulley system they had worked out, and then he tossed the cable down to Marty who attached the basket to it. They spent the next half hour raising and lowering the basket as Marty sent up an inflatable mattress, sleeping bag, tarp, Walter's bags, a battery-powered lamp, and a lawn chair.

"Okay, Marty, time to take down the stairs," Walter hollered down.

"Gee, Walter, are you sure that's necessary? What if there's an emergency of some sort and we need to get up to you quickly? I mean, I don't mean to scare you, but you are approaching your 'twilight' years and, believe me, in my line of work, I am constantly witness to the fact that taxes aren't the only unavoidable truth we'll all face eventually. Can't we just leave the stairs where they are?"

"We already talked about this and you agreed, Martin Bleak. I don't want every Tom, Dick, and Harry climbing up those stairs to try to talk me out of this. Next thing you know, all the church ladies will be bringing me hot dishes and Pastor Fischer will think it's his duty to clamber up here to console me. Marty, please, it's what I want. I've thought long and hard about this and chose my partner in crime carefully because I knew you'd be able to do this for me, for the cause. Hurry up now before someone sees you."

Marty climbed reluctantly up the wooden steps and removed the top step first, tossed it to the ground below him, descended a step, and removed the next one, lower and lower until he was standing on the ground again using his hammer to pull out the nails on the last couple of steps. He took his time picking up the pieces of wood, shouting his most recent joke to Walter.

"So, did you hear about Sven being so sick? Everyone was sure he was on his death bed, when the next thing you know, the smell of Lena's baking got him out of bed. He went straight to the kitchen, got out a plate and a big knife and was just about to slice into the beautifully frosted chocolate cake that was sitting on the counter when Lena snapped, "Put that knife down. You're not to cut into that cake."

"Why not?" Sven asked.

"It's for your funeral!"

As Walter chuckled, Marty saluted him and, as planned, drove off so Walter would be alone when the media arrived.

Marge was right; Walter thought as he looked around, it really was a perfect fall day. The sky was that brilliant blue which made the colors of the changing trees all the more spectacular. There were stately white clouds off in the distance seemingly frozen in place. The sun moved like dancers on his platform as the spots shone through between the colorful oak leaves, the slight breeze causing the shadows to sway. He was surprised at how quiet it was high up in the oak tree. Walter blew out his breath and felt surprisingly elated. After weeks of planning, he was finally really here. It was really happening. Instead of feeling scared like he thought he would, Walter felt good. Looking around him, he suddenly threw his head back and laughed. By golly, it wasn't just the young folks who were changing the world. Even at his age, Walter was making a difference and boy did that feel good.

The view from up there was quite something. There in the south was Emma Grabow's farm with the pretty grape leaves framed by the trellises in the vineyard changing color. Beyond that was the Hanson farm, the fields around them all lifted clean of sugar beets, the rich, black soil so dark it looked to have been burnt. More and more fields as far as his eye could see, some still harvesting, the tractors looking small and slow from up there. He was quite sure he could make out the Minnesota River off in the distance. To the north, Walter looked out over Opossum Falls. How sweet and inviting the little town looked. All the shops on Main Street looked so tidy and useful. Why, everyone should come up here, he thought, momentarily regretting his decision to have Marty take the stairs away, to see what a perfectly functional little town Opossum Falls was and how it had absolutely no need for Wal-Mart to come in and destroy it. He stretched up on his tiptoes to try to see his house, enjoying the brilliant red of his sugar maple shading his yard so effectively.

The sun inched slowly through the sky and bit by bit morning became afternoon. Walter was a little surprised that his presence up in the tree hadn't been discovered yet, and he stood up to take a leak off of the corner he was designating to use as a bathroom. Just as he was zipping up, he saw a white news van approaching with the letters WCCO painted largely on the side. Smoothing down his silky, white mane, he made a mental note to himself to have Marty bring him a small mirror. It wouldn't hurt to make sure he looked good if he was going to be on national television, after all. Remembering Andy Rooney, he also tried to flatten his eyebrows with both of his thumbs.

Walter had prepared a statement which he read from the bowels of the tree: "Symbolizing strength and courage, the oak has long been considered the mightiest of trees. The ancient Romans thought oak trees were lightning magnets and thus connected the oak tree to Jupiter and his wife Juno, the goddess of marriage. In this way, the oak is a symbol of fidelity and fulfillment. How then, can we allow ourselves to be unfaithful to this symbol of conjugal contentment? Socrates thought the oak tree was an oracle tree. The Druids used to eat the acorns of the tree to prepare themselves for prophesying. That the leaves of the oak tree contained the power to heal and renew strength they doubted not. Nor should we.

I, Walter Fassbinder, of sound mind and body, do hereby protest the cutting down of this mighty red oak tree in respect for the tree as well as in vehement protest to the proposed building of yet another Wal-Mart Supercenter." He actually paused here to noisily spit. "Said supercenters, which are becoming ever increasing in number, are blights upon our rural and suburban landscapes. In unprecedented numbers, Wal-Mart has continued to erect vast supercenters at breakneck speed. Since 2005, it has expanded the amount of store space in our great country by over thirty percent. It added more than one thousand, one hundred supercenters which were almost all built on land that had never been developed. The irrepressible chain now has nearly seven hundred million square feet of store space in the U.S. plus another two hundred eighty seven million around the globe. Its U.S. stores and parking lots cover roughly sixty thousand acres. I ask you now, do we need another Wal-Mart?

Statistics are clear what has happened to other businesses in a community once Wal-Mart moved in. There are ample studies which also show what happened to retail wages after Wal-Mart turned up drawing on more than fifteen years of data on actual store openings. Wal-Mart drove down wages with an annual loss of at least three billion dollars; yes, that's three BILLION dollars in earnings for retail workers.

Standing in this beautiful tree, I feel privileged. There is wildlife all around me and it is good. I look down on the small but vibrant town of Opossum Falls and I shudder to think what our Main Street will look like in a year or two if Wal-Mart is allowed to build on this spot in my town. Yes, I am against Wal-Mart, but, more importantly, I am FOR Opossum Falls. Now it's your turn. It comes down to this simple question….Are you for Wal-Mart, or are you for Opossum Falls?"

There was a moment of reverential silence when Walter finished speaking. The lovely newscaster with Spanish blood somewhere in her background actually had to wipe tears from her eyes before giving the nod to the cameraman to stop shooting at Walter high up in the tree and to focus on her. "There you have it, folks, Walter Fassbinder, high up in the Red Oak tree asking you to choose if you're for Wal-Mart or for Opossum Falls. To vote online, go to WCCO.com and click on 'Poll" to select your choice." Angela continued to smile into the camera till she heard, "Cut, that's a wrap," then she tipped her head back to tell Walter he'd done a terrific job. He was wearing a headset with a microphone which they had sent up in his basket. She asked if he had a safe place to keep the headset, by safe she meant dry, and he said yes he had a waterproof Rubbermaid bin. She suggested he just keep the headset then which he took to be a good sign meaning that they wanted to hear more from him in the future. They packed up the van and pulled away, leaving Walter alone up in the tree once more.

~~~~~~~~~~~~~~~~~~~~~~~~~~~~~~~~

When the WCCO crew came into Pick and Pay, they had already stopped at many of the other businesses to try to capture local sound bites to add to the segment of Walter's story which they were planning to air on the five o'clock news. They had also stopped to talk to a few of the townspeople out on the street. Walter's protest was now well-known around town and the anti-Wal-Mart sentiment firmly outweighed any positive feedback for Wal-Mart at this stage of the investigation. The crew was loading up on drinks and snacks to take back to the hotel in Olivia, and they thought filming cashiers and asking their opinion would make for good copy.

Pete had stopped by the Pick and Pay as he always did after he had first stopped at Laney's apartment and she wasn't at home. He was describing his interview with one of the old beet farmer's in Emma Grabow's neighborhood who had practically greeted him with a shotgun in his hand, so displeased was he to see a government agent in his backyard. Laney was laughing and about to suggest he invest in a bullet-proof vest when she saw the WCCO cameras. The smile vanished instantly from her face which grew white with fear. She turned directly on her heel and fled through the store to the backroom. Pete was stunned, but quickly looking around, realized that everyone else was focused on the hubbub surrounding the familiar face of the newscaster and had not noticed Laney's flight. Reaching across the checkout counter, Pete carefully removed the key to Laney's cash register so she wouldn't get into trouble for abandoning her post, and he followed Laney's trail to the back of the store.

Shannon Fischer had that special glow about her which pregnant women gain in the midst of their pregnancies. Her hair had thickened and turned surprisingly wavy with gorgeous highlights shining like corn silk before detassling. Her face had filled out and her rosy skin radiated. She couldn't button her lavender Pick and Pay smock any longer but it looked cute over one of her Dad's white shirts. The cameraman was enjoying flirting with her while he explained that she should look right into his camera when the red light was on. The reporter, Angela, asked her a few questions while she was checking out groceries.

"Walter, or 'Mr. F,' as we call him, is a terrific guy and we all think the world of him. His store, 'Just Screw It,' always gives great donations to any fundraising the school or churches are doing. He donated ten Emergency Kits for cars for the post prom party store, and every year when the volleyball team sells frozen food, he always stocks up. He even puts toilet paper on sale during homecoming week! You know, for teepeeing!" Suddenly remembering where she was, Shannon added, "And so does Mr. Schluter here at Pick and Pay. Do I think Walter's crazy for protesting from the gorgeous oak tree sitting right smack in the middle of Wal-Mart's proposed site, no, I don't, In fact, I think he's chill."

"What do you think of his 'Pro-Wal-Mart or Pro-Opossum Falls' stand?" Angela asked.

"I think it's dead on. We do have to make a choice. And I think the world can never have enough trees, but we certainly can have too much retail space." Veronica Schroeder had just said that very thing when Shannon had checked out her groceries as they exchanged gossip about the rumors surrounding Walter that were flying across town. She didn't think Veronica would mind her sharing it on WCCO. "I'm definitely Pro-Opossum Falls," Shannon finished, smiling directly into the hot cameraman's lens.

"And I'm Angela Weaver, live from Opossum Falls." She smiled at Shannon when the camera lights turned off. "You were great, kid, a real natural. You should seriously think about a career in broadcasting." Shannon said good-bye and couldn't stop smiling for the rest of her shift.

Pete caught up with Laney wrestling with her coat in the employee back room. He was flabbergasted by her reaction to seeing the camera and reporters. Her eyes were frantic as she looked with fear behind Pete to see if he'd been followed.

"Oh my god, they found me. I have to get out of here," tears were falling from her eyes as she moaned.

"Laney, no one is here for you. They're talking to Shannon. It must be about the protester outside of town."

"Are you sure?" Laney held her breath, unable to believe him. When he nodded his head, she collapsed at the table and covered her face with her hands. Pete stood there, his heart beating rapidly as he wondered what the hell was going on. He sat down across from her and reached out his hand. She reached slowly with one hand and held onto his. "Please," she kept her eyes downcast as she spoke in a whisper. "Please don't ask me to explain. I can't talk about it."

Pete couldn't think of anything to say so he just sat there holding her hand, wondering what he was getting himself into but knowing that he simply could not walk away. When she finally raised her head, her eyes spoke her unbearable sorrow while she said, "If you ask, I'll never be able to see you again."

Her threat was spoken so forlornly that Pete reassured her immediately, "Laney, you don't have to worry about me. Do you want me to say you're sick and I'll take you home?"

"No, just let me know when they're gone and I'll go back to work. I'd rather work now, I need to. It helps me so much, to, you know, stop me from thinking about things too much"

When Pete came back to tell her the whole WCCO crew was gone, Laney got up to return to her station, taking her key to the cash register back from Pete. "Thank you," she told him, "for everything." Pete, feeling stunned at what he'd just witnessed, watched her walk out the door.

The baby gave a determined kick inside her, in Laney's dream, and she laughed as she stroked her tightly-stretched stomach while scolding her unborn child, "Must you always grow active right when I finally sit down to rest?" The baby responded with a long, slow movement, so Laney reached for Gabby's hand and placed it on top of the bare skin of her belly saying, "Feel this, look how anxious your little brother or sister is to get out and play with you."

"Baby, kick!" Gabby said in her loud, toddler voice. Laney noticed how Gabby very seldom just spoke normally but everything she said was shouted with enthusiasm as if the world was just much too exciting to talk about it in a regular voice. Putting her face right next to Laney's tummy, Gabby hollered, "Baby come now! Now, Baby, come play!"

Laney laughed and told Gabby she was sure the baby heard that, who didn't, but to lean back and listen to Mommy read now. They had spent the morning making Valentine's Day cookies to surprise Daddy with when he got home from work. Gabby had wanted to help with every step of the process: stirring the softened butter and sugar together, cracking open the eggs, beating them in, cautiously measuring the vanilla, soda, and salt before adding it into the flour and carefully stirring it all together, rolling out the dough after it had chilled a bit and then cutting out the heart-shaped cookies. Laney had turned the cow-shaped timer for eight minutes and Gabby would bellow, "Cookies, out!" whenever it sounded.

Laney always marveled at how quickly time passed when she was taking care of Gabby and of how little she actually accomplished. She didn't care however, and luckily Scott didn't either. After lunch, Laney was exhausted already and was happy to put Gabby down for a nap, promising her that they would make pink frosting, frost the cookies, and sprinkle red sugar crystals on them after naptime. She told her to go choose a book for Laney to read to her before her nap.

Gabby already had a stack of favorite books which Laney and Scott would read to her. Laney's favorite was a beautiful hardcover book called, Baby's Favorite Bedtime Stories, with pastel drawings on the cover and all throughout the book. Filled with lovely poems, stories, and even song lyrics, Laney read that book over and over to Gabby till they both knew it by heart. This afternoon, Gabby had chosen a Little Golden Book *called* Mommy's Little Helper. *The pictures were so old-fashioned and sappy, but Laney loved how that meant nothing to Gabby at all. She wondered how soon Gabby would become concerned with what was in style and what wasn't, when peer pressure would make her concerned about* what she liked or not. For now, it made her happy that one of Gabby's favorite books was such a simple one. Having outgrown the rocking chair this late in the pregnancy where she and Gabby used to sit and read, they now sat on the couch while Laney read to her. Laney put her feet up on the footstool and Gabby nestled into her side, leaning forward while Laney put her arm around her. The moment Laney started to read, Gabby popped her thumb into her mouth and with her other hand, twisted a curl of hair round and round her finger while listening intently to the story she had heard at least a hundred times already. When she wasn't so sleepy, Gabby would loudly pop her thumb out of her mouth to repeat a line from the book, to question something, or simply to say, "Gabby do that!"

Laney felt a bubble welling up inside of her which she recognized as overwhelming happiness. What a tremendous thing it was to be a mother and to love your child so much. There was so much joy in this sturdy little person beside her which rubbed off on everyone and everything around her. From the moment she awoke in the morning, Gabby was full of wonder and chatter. Every day was filled with new discoveries. Laney's world had never before seemed so marvelous.

Laney rubbed her huge belly while she wrestled with the conflicting emotions she felt for the life she carried inside of her. How could she possibly ever love the next baby as much as she loved little Gabby? Their lives were so perfect right now and they simply couldn't be any happier. How would they deal with the disruption the new baby would bring with it? This pregnancy, while slightly more uncomfortable due to the fact that she was now running after a toddler, had gone just as smoothly as her first pregnancy. This baby felt much bigger though and she carried it much lower. Also, although she'd opted out of the ultrasound technician's willingness to tell her the sex of the baby, she felt nearly certain this baby was going to be a boy. With Gabby, she had felt right from the start that she was carrying a girl. She didn't know how, but she knew to trust her instinct which was so often right.

Now, her intuition was telling her not to worry, that she would have enough love to share with both of her children. She was finding it hard to believe, however, as Gabby began to drift off to sleep before she'd even finished reading the book. Laney was embarrassed to admit to herself that she actually resented her unborn baby for the love he would be taking away from Gabby. Gently stroking her back as she slept, Laney felt the weight of Gabby as she slowly awoke from her dream. The pressure was so great, she was afraid that her heart would break in two. Holding nothing in her arms but her pillow, Laney lay in bed and looked up at the ceiling, wondering how in the world to carry on and face another day.

Chapter 17

Holding his anger in check just long enough to say good-bye, Brandon waited until he heard the click on the other end before slamming down the phone, then picked it up and slammed it back down once more for good measure. How dare they, he fumed to himself, trying to project a new and improved image, my ass. Brandon thought back to the raid in Worthington when hundreds of ICE agents had stormed the factory, helicopters hovered overhead, and buses were lined up to haul the illegals directly away from the raid. He continued to stare at the phone, unable to believe that his supervisor had really just informed him that he was on his own for the raid he was planning at the Sugar Beet Factory.

Apparently, with a new administration in office, ICE wasn't allowed quite the free hand it had enjoyed up until now. The tree huggers and bleeding hearts were broadcasting all sorts of statistics about wrongful deaths, unconstitutional, yadda, yadda, yadda. And then there was the unfortunate incident in Long Beach, where the ICE Agent went ballistic when he was being reprimanded for being too rough while arresting suspected aliens, and he started shooting at his deputy commander. Another ICE agent stepped in and shot the shooter, his colleague, dead. Not such great publicity for Immigration and Customs Enforcement, for sure.

Finally, there was all the hoo-ha from down in Southern Minnesota regarding the local police who refused to honor ICE's request to hold those detainees that, with time, ICE felt sure they could drum up dirt on.

Brandon felt disgusted at this low key approach to fighting illegals. He remembered the Postville Raid down in Iowa and had wanted to conduct his raid exactly that way. At that time, Postville was the largest single raid of a workplace in U.S. history with nearly four hundred workers arrested with false identity papers. They were subsequently charged with identity theft using stolen social security numbers, and most of them served five months in prison before being deported. Best of all, thought Brandon, was that the scum who had allowed the aliens to work there in the first place was sentenced to twenty-seven years.

Brandon would like to see Jeff Schroeder behind bars. He knew the supervisor at the beet factory was aware that he was giving jobs to illegal aliens; how could he not know it? But attempting to raid the factory on his own, Brandon scratched his head as he contemplated exactly how he was supposed to get it done. If he had more time, he would continue to petition his supervisors that he was absolutely certain there were undocumented workers in Opossum Falls. But the sugar beet harvest was now over, and while the factory was still working at full capacity to get the beets processed, Brandon knew that things were slowing down and many of the illegal workers would soon be heading back to Guatemala or Mexico or wherever. If he wasn't going to get any help from ICE, then what the hell, Brandon thought, might as well head out and raid the factory now.

Brandon picked up the phone again and called the Opossum Falls' police station. When the dispatcher answered, he asked to speak to Dusty. Telling him that he was on his way to the factory, he told Dusty to bring whoever was on duty to meet him there for backup. Then, he adjusted his gun and walked out to his car, spitting on the sidewalk as he passed by.

Meanwhile, Dusty and a couple of the other local cops headed over to the Chit Chat. They flirted with Bianca as she served them. They had no intention of helping the ICE agent raid the sugar beet factory. If they could have, they would have instead warned the workers that ICE was coming. Dusty and his fellow officers were a part of this town. They knew the workers and they knew their families. Immigration was not their fight and they stayed as far away from it as they possibly could.

News that a suspected ICE agent was in the factory spread quickly throughout the massive workplace when Brandon arrived at the sugar beet factory, The workers had long had a plan in place to secretly broadcast the news as efficiently as possible and each shift practiced every so often just to keep it viable. The code name was Operation Yellow, and the message that flew in whispers from person to person was 'Yellow, for sure'. When it was only for trial purposes, they had spread the phrase 'Yellow, for practice' around the factory floor. In Spanish, the word 'ice' is 'hielo' pronounced more or less as 'yellow'. The word 'sure' was pronounced by many of the workers with a heavy ch sound so as the news spread, the ch, ch, ch sounds danced around the factory like dandelion seed in the wind.

There was not a single undocumented alien working at the sugar beet factory who wouldn't have changed his or her status in a heartbeat if they had been allowed to. Likewise, if these aliens had been able to find work in their own countries sufficient enough to be able to support their families, they would have chosen to stay at home. They worked illegally because they had no other choice; the key word being 'worked', not 'illegally'. As employers across the country could attest, these immigrants worked hard.

In a country such as Ecuador, the greatest source of money coming into the country was not from exports but rather from Ecuadorians sending their paychecks home from the United States and all across Europe, too. Entire villages in Guatemala and Mexico survive on the money sent home to family members from relatives working outside of those countries. It is quite a feat, when you think about it, that many of these workers barely seem to make enough money to survive and yet they still manage to consistently send at least a third of their paychecks, and oftentimes more, back home to their native villages.

The difficulty of working as an illegal alien takes its toll; at any given moment the life they're leading in the U.S. could be terminated. They know that they could be pulled over on the slightest pretext, a missing headlight, or for not wearing a seatbelt, and their illegal status would be found out and they would be placed in jail and deported. All illegal aliens are forced to drive without a driver's license, of course. Although many illegals have worked for years with false social security numbers, the money from their paychecks going into social security month after month, but they will never receive any of that money back in the form of a social security check as the number they're using isn't actually theirs.

There are countless heart-wrenching stories of parents being deported while their children remain behind. Anyone born in the United States is automatically a citizen, so the children can stay but the parents must go. After the raid in Worthington, a number of children were simply deserted at daycare while their mothers were deported. There is no fund to help reunite abandoned children back with their parents who have been deported.

Brandon followed the sign that said 'office' while he glanced around the factory, wondering what that strange 'ch' sound was. He walked briskly and with authority knowing that he had to act fast before any of the workers tried to escape out the back door. Damn, he wished that he had backup. In his favor was the fact that all previous raids had been conducted with dozens of agents so once the raid was announced, they would assume, wrongly, that Brandon wasn't alone and hopefully he would be able to round up all of the illegals without violence. But then again, Brandon was more than ready to show force if he had to.

Jeff was instructing Anthony Gonzalez, the forklift driver, to stop what he'd been doing to help unload the shipment of paper rolls for the single serve portion pack machine when Brandon rudely interrupted them. Handing over the paperwork which authorized him to request to see the documents of each worker at the sugar beet factory, Brandon said, "I insist on your immediate assistance," just as pulsating music began blaring over the intercom.

Jeff said, "What?" while Brandon repeated the sentence which Jeff could hear no better the second time. Jeff pointed to his ear and then overhead before holding out his hand in the universal sign for 'stop'. Brandon was about to protest when suddenly, one of the women stepped out of line and belted out, "While the storm clouds gather far across the sea," in a lovely strong voice, singing along with the music being played over the intercom. A few other women stepped out to sing the next phrase along with her, "Let us swear allegiance," more joined in, "to a land that's free," and then a dozen men were singing, "Let us all be grateful for a land so fair," with even more joining in, "As we raise our voices in a solemn prayer,"

"I'll be damned," Jeff chuckled, and then he shouted towards Brandon's stunned face, "It's a flash mob!"

Everyone in the factory joined in now, first whipping off their hairnets and hats with a flourish, singing, "God bless America, Land that I love, Stand beside her, and guide her through the night with a light from above. From the mountains, through the prairies, through the oceans, white with foam, God Bless America, my home, sweet, home, God Bless America, my home, sweet, home."

Brandon was flummoxed. He had been about to rant and rave and order the music stopped when they began singing the well-known chorus that was familiar to him. Wouldn't it be awfully unpatriotic for an agent of the federal government to interrupt and halt the singing of 'God Bless America'? He stood there frozen in indecision for a moment till he realized that Jeff was bellowing out the song beside him, so he removed his cap, held it over his heart, and joined in the impromptu song. As the music carried on, the men were repeating the verse while the women broke into a dance of some sort and they were holding hands and twirling in a circle. Brandon stood there awkwardly with Jeff, his hat still over his heart. When the music ended at last, during the applause, Jeff went straight into his office and announced over the intercom that Agent Brandon Hopkins of the Immigration and Customs Enforcement Agency was there to inspect their documents. He said it would be against the law for anyone to leave the building, and then he proceeded to describe the order in which they should suspend their work to present their papers to the agent.

Returning to face Brandon, Jeff asked him, "Do you have any idea how much an interruption like this costs the company, Agent Hopkins?"

"Well, maybe if you didn't hire illegals, you wouldn't have to worry about me needing to shut you down like this."

"Ah-ah-ah, careful now, Hopkins. Our constitution does still stipulate that we are innocent until proven guilty, correct? If I were you, I would be careful what you say."

"Are you threatening me?"

"No, I'm just warning you. Everything you do and say is being recorded and I would hate to see you lose your job on account of unprofessional behavior." As Jeff spoke, he pointed to Anthony Gonzalez who had suddenly become a videographer when Jeff had handed him the camera as he exited his office.

Brandon had to stifle a string of cuss words as he acknowledged the camera and carried on with the raid, telling himself that Jeff may have won the battle but he was going to win the war. He looked towards the door, wondering to himself, "Where the hell were Dusty and the rest of his keystone cops anyway?"

 Four hours later, the last of the employees walked away from Agent Hopkins, folding their papers back into their pockets, and Brandon sat back in his folding chair stupefied. Not one single employee of the Minnesota Sugar Beet Cooperative was working illegally, not one! If he hadn't seen it with his very own eyes, he never would have believed it. In fact, he still didn't believe it. Something was wrong. He wasn't sure how, but he knew that he had been diddled. Aware of the camera on his every move, Brandon thanked Jeff for his assistance, apologized for the inconvenience, and walked purposefully from the building. Outside, he struggled with what to do with his anger without killing someone. He kicked the tire of his car so hard, he may have broken his toe.

When their shift ended, the workers filed out of the factory as usual. It wasn't until they reached the parking lot that they gave each other sly winks and satisfied smiles. The women from Marge and Laney's English class at the library couldn't wait to report back how successful their flash mob had been. Not only had they performed the song and dance even better than during practice, all of their co-workers who were not fortunate enough to hold legal papers in their hands had managed to slip out unnoticed while Agent Hopkins stood with his hat over his heart singing along to *God Bless America*.

Therese Dotray-Tulloch

Chapter 18

Laney lay in bed unable to sleep. Staring up at the ceiling, she watched the Daddy Long Leg spider in the corner. She didn't like spiders, but she wasn't particularly afraid of Daddy Long Legs. Besides, she would rather be able to see where this one was and know it was there than wonder about its whereabouts. She used to be terrified of spiders, but it was funny how everything is put into perspective when something happens in your life that truly does terrorize you.

Laney sighed and decided she may as well get up. She was afraid to fall asleep because she knew that she would dream. She didn't mind the dreams; in fact, she loved them. For a while, after The Event, all she wanted to do was sleep so that she could live in the world of her dreams. She entered her dreams and she stayed there, sometimes for weeks at a time. Now, even though she could hardly believe she was thinking this, she was actually trying to get better. Inside her dreams was exactly where she wanted to be, but waking up and having to realize all over again that she had only been dreaming, and that she had to face the world as it was now, was too hard.

Laney knew she was still a long way from recovery, but wrapping her robe around herself, she acknowledged that it was as if she was emerging from a heavy fog and finally, finally she could start to make out shapes at the end of the tunnel. For so long, she had lost all will to live. She had been so sick for a while. She couldn't really remember most of that time. When it was obvious that she had become a danger to herself and those around her, she had been committed. For a long time, she had lived in a drug-induced sleep. When the doctors began forcing her out of her zombie-like state, she had resisted it with every ounce of her being. She had wanted to die. She didn't like to remember those days at all.

Then one day, her doctor had told her that they had done all they could for her and that it was time for her to move on. Weaned off of the drugs that had helped her through, she recognized that to survive she could not go back to the life she had been living at the time of The Event. Checking out of the hospital alone, she had fled to the Greyhound bus station in downtown Minneapolis and looked at the names of the destinations. She wasn't feeling hopeful or excited, so she did not want to choose a place that would give her false expectation, like Belle Plaine or Grand Rapids or Aurora. She didn't want the optimism from a place with the word 'new' in it like New Prague, New Ulm, or New London. When she saw the name Opossum Falls, she had practically snickered at its appropriateness for her. When cornered, opossums fall into a death-like state. That is exactly what Laney had done. She was living, though barely, in a death-like state. She went to the counter and purchased a one-way ticket. In the hours she had before the bus left to Opossum Falls, Laney walked to the Target downtown and bought a suitcase which she filled with a set of sheets, towels, toiletries and some clothes.

Riding the bus through the flat countryside, the sameness of the fields felt right to Laney. She had not wanted to live, but she didn't deserve to die, either, and escape the hell on earth which was her doing. She would be completely anonymous in Opossum Falls, she hoped, as long as no one recognized her from the publicity. She hoped enough time had passed that the nightmare of her fifteen minutes of pain-filled fame had been forgotten already in a town as far removed as Opossum Falls.

The only apartments available in town were basically for assisted living, but that was fine with Laney. Her building was filled with sweet old ladies who walked carefully down the hallway pushing their walkers. Despite Laney's intentions to keep completely to herself, it wasn't in her nature to be unfriendly, so it wasn't long before Laney was carrying groceries for her neighbors, bringing up their mail, even walking the Cairn terrier next door when it's owner got the flu.

Working at Pick and Pay and residing at Parkview Estates, Laney was ever so cautiously learning to live again. Part of her fought this and continued to remind herself that she did not want nor deserve to live. Another part of her was beginning to allow herself to feel. She would never let herself forget the enormous guilt she carried like an over-laden backpack on her shoulders. She knew she still had unfinished business to attend to with which she was not yet strong enough to deal. But now, for the first time since The Event, she began to feel as though one day she might be.

Laney's downstairs neighbor, Constance, had been on her way to her bridge club one afternoon, when she had dropped a bottle of wine, the drinking of which was apparently a ritual with her bridge group. The blue bottle shattered all over the sidewalk and Laney had rushed out to help clean it up, sending Constance on her way so she wouldn't be late for bridge. The deep red cabernet outlined the broken shards of glass. Laney paused in the midst of sweeping thinking how much more beautiful the bottle looked in pieces than it had when it was whole. It was a revelation for her to realize that something in pieces could be okay, too. She might never be whole again, but maybe that would be alright. Sweeping up the broken glass, Laney took it up to her apartment, washed it, and although she didn't yet know why, she kept it.

Not long afterward, Laney was on her way to work when she walked past a garage sale. On the lawn was a round, glass tabletop with a wrought-iron stand such as is often used on a patio or deck. Laney suddenly knew what she wanted to do. Approaching the owner, she asked if she could pay for the table and pick it up on her way home from work. In typical small-town fashion, the owner offered to deliver it to Laney's apartment for her. That suited Laney just fine and she thanked the woman and paid her, telling her where she lived and that her apartment was unlocked, as usual.

Beside the large, green Waste Management dumpster behind Pick and Pay, the employees got used to seeing Laney breaking glass bottles. Whenever an unusual or pretty-colored bottle arrived at the store, Laney would confiscate it, and when it was empty, she would smash the glass and take it home.

Wrestling as she often did with insomnia, Laney would sit at her little round table arranging the shards of glass into a mosaic. As she worked, she thought about Pete and how kind he had been when she'd had her melt down at work. Who knew what he was thinking about the secrets lurking about in her past. Probably, she had scared him off good and she would never see him again. The thought made her wistful and sad. Working on her mosaic, however, always made her feel better. Slowly, she was creating a masterpiece of color and beauty. Sometimes she added a pretty stone she had found or a piece of shell. Cath had given her a tortoiseshell hair clip that had shattered when she'd accidently dropped it and she'd put that in, too. Working on her montage was soothing to her. There was something comforting about putting broken pieces together. They didn't have to fit exactly together to work.

~~~~~~~~~~~~~~~~~~~~~~~~~~~~~~~~

Marge Peterson couldn't sleep that night, either. Ever since menopause, Marge had grown accustomed to finding herself wide awake at odd hours of the night. She knew there was no point at all in just laying there, so normally Marge would throw off her yellow and peach Irish chain quilt and get up to sit and read in her rocker until she felt drowsy again. Tonight Marge allowed herself the luxury of laying there for awhile and acknowledging just how happy she was. She sighed heavily and stretched out her arms, exclaiming with surprise when her left arm landed on top of her new housemate. She turned on her side and began petting him, saying, "I'm sorry, Pumpkin, I forgot you were here."

The large, orange tabby cat opened one eye to look at her for a moment, and then as if she weren't important enough to warrant further attention, he slowly let it close again. Marge laughed at how he acted as if he owned the place and had been living with her forever.

He began to purr loudly while she scratched under his chin. She liked having a cat again and was glad when Juan Carlos had surprised her with it. He had seen signs up around town offering free cats to good homes, good mousing cats, too, and he had thought of Marge and how she'd told him she had seen the tiny droppings of a mouse leaving evidence to his presence in her pantry. Juan Carlos had dropped off the cat right before dinnertime so Marge had been able to persuade him to stay and dine with her. Juan Carlos. Just thinking his name made her smile.

Marge wondered how it had come to pass that she was in love again. She did love Juan Carlos. She liked admitting it to herself, even though she had no intention of letting anyone else know about it, or at least, not yet. She had loved her husband, Charles, for such a long time. He was a decent man and theirs had been a good marriage. It certainly hadn't been perfect, by any means, but they had always tried to show one another the respect and kindness they deserved. His death had come about so quickly, for her at least. She had gotten over the fact that he had kept his illness a secret from her. She understood that he had done it to shield her and to enjoy what little time he had left on earth in as normal a fashion as possible. What would Charles think about her loving another? She knew that if she were in Charles' position, she would never begrudge him a companion and she would expect him to love again.

Lying in bed, watching the moonlight move slowly across the ceiling, highlights of her life with Charles passed before Marge's eyes like an old fashioned slide show. She thought about memories and how very comforting they were to her. She had read once that every time you remembered an event in your life, you had the potential to change it a bit. Then, the next time you remembered it, you were actually remembering the memory, not the event itself. That was why so many people remembered the exact same incident so differently. They had each eventually created their own individual memories. Marge reflected on many of the memories she shared with Charles.

The big tomcat was now lying in the crook of Marge's arm. Scratching behind his ears, she thought about honor. She wanted to honor the memory of her dead husband. Did being in love with another man lessen that honor? She didn't think so. In fact, she could even take the argument in the other direction and say that being in love and wanting to share her life with another man again showed how much respect she had for the state of marriage and the companionship it implied.

Marge thought that was really what she enjoyed most about her relationship with Juan Carlos: the companionship. After being a partner for so many years, she did not like being alone. Juan Carlos was fun to be with, he made her laugh, she enjoyed talking with him, he was a good worker, and she was very, very attracted to him. She smiled when she remembered the way he had kissed her when he left her. He made her feel so alive. She knew she wouldn't be able to resist him much longer. If she were honest with herself, she would admit that if he weren't such a gentleman, she would have already pulled him into her bed; it seemed he was the one resisting her. She stretched luxuriously next to Pumpkin practically purring herself.

Out the window, she glimpsed a soft pink glow on the eastern horizon and realized with surprise that the sun would be rising soon. She thought of Walter out in his tree and wondered how he was surviving. Dear Walter; who knew she was living next to such a political activist all these years? Berniece would be so proud of him. Throwing off the covers at last, much to the cat's annoyance, Marge decided she would get up and make a nice, hot breakfast to take over to Walter at the proposed Wal-Mart site. Standing at the window, Marge stood in her sun salutation yoga pose, repeating it three times. Opening her arms wide to welcome in the world around her, reaching up to open her rib cage and her heart, bending low because it stretched her low back and felt so good, Marge felt near tears just because she was so happy. The entire eastern sky was glowing scarlet now as a new day dawned.

~~~~~~~~~~~~~~~~~~~~~~~~~~~~~~~~

Walter lay on his back tucked into his sleeping bag and wondered if he had ever before felt so alive. He had been sound asleep when the lovely call of a cardinal pulled him bit by bit out of his dream after first becoming a part of it. He had been dreaming he and Berniece were with the kids in the Boundary Waters Canoe Area. This unspoiled wilderness area comprised two hundred miles of islands and lakes separating Minnesota and Canada. Motorized vehicles were not allowed in the BWCA so the pristine landscape was silent but for the calls of nature and the soft paddling of the canoeist in the brisk, clear lake water. Where the small streams connecting the lakes were too rock-filled or at too great of elevation differences, portages became byways for campers to transport their canoes.

Walter and Berniece had spent their honeymoon in the boundary waters. They had made a ten-day loop, putting in at Sag, and then logging ten miles worth of water underneath their canoe each day to complete the hundred mile trip. Chatting, singing songs, getting to know one another while they paddled through the lakes by day, they got to know each other differently in the little pup tent they put up each night. Their muscles grew strong as they paddled hour after hour. Their skin grew browner and browner. The first time Berniece flicked off her bikini top to paddle topless, Walter had almost dropped his oar. With Berniece up in the bow, Walter lustfully watched her tan, bare back for hours on end as she firmly stroked her paddle through the water.

The portages got easier as the trip went on, and as they became more physically powerful, it was easier to lift up the canoe, and the packs grew lighter as they gradually diminished their supplies. The first day of the trip, they'd paddled for eight hours to find the dot on the map signifying a campsite, that being a clearing for a tent with an iron grate over a fire pit. They had cooked dinner over the wood left by the previous campers, a courtesy imparted by every camper in the boundary waters ensuring that no matter how dark a night might be when you arrived, a cord of firewood would be available to build a fire.

Their only experience as lovers having been following their wedding the previous night at the Normandy Village Inn in downtown Minneapolis, they were anxious to enjoy the pleasures of one another's bodies again as soon as possible. Feeling completely isolated on the only campsite on the entire lake underneath the vast canopy of stars with the waxing moon glowing gently in the east, they decided to leave the tent inside its canvas bag laying their sleeping bags under the birch trees beneath the stars. Lifting Bernice's moist tee shirt up over her head, Walter had reached behind to unhook her bra and had gasped at the beauty of her breasts newly released from their harness. Desperate to enjoy the novel sensation of running hands over precious new skin, they hastily removed their clothes and had fallen into one another's arms onto their sleeping bags. Their lovemaking was fervently passionate and the resulting waves of orgasmic pleasure were soon washing over them. So caught up were they in each other's body, that until their heavy breathing finally slowed, did they become aware that indeed, they were not alone. Hundred of mosquitoes had been present during their lovemaking and had left their marks all over the newlyweds' tender nakedness. The buzzing was so loud it was as if they were camped beneath a jumbo jet taking off. Looking at each other with clarity at last, they realized that they were not seeing splotches of moonlight on one another's bodies through the trees overhead, but patches of mosquitoes enjoying their evening meal. Simultaneously feeling the pain of multiple mosquito bites at once, the lovers shrieked and leapt to their feet, setting up their little pup tent in record time. Every night thereafter, their lovemaking took place in the romantic confines of their cozy, insect-free tent.

Walter and Bernice always had a satisfying sex life, but they were forever after most passionate in the boundary waters. As they prepared for their annual trip, they looked forward to the peace of the wilderness, the beauty of the surrounding, and the excitement of their lovemaking. As their children were born, the trips became family vacations, but always Walter and Berniece put their own pup tent a little further away from camp than necessary.

Their kids learned to canoe from the duffer's position in the middle of the canoe and were carrying canoes over their heads before their ages reached the double digits. The boundary waters trips were real family vacations as all of the pets came along, too. Walter was dreaming about the year they had their basset hound along as well as two little blue budgie birds. The budgies' names were Atlantic and Pacific, and in Walter's dream, he was telling a scary story around the campfire, the one about the hook dangling from the passenger's door handle. None of the kids were listening to him because they were laughing at Atlantic biting on Bernice's glasses. Every time she would try to reprimand the bird, he would tweet at her so convincingly that you would swear there were words somewhere in the musical tweets, and the kids laughed harder and harder.

The tweeting grew more and more expressive and off in the distance another bird tweeted back in response. In his dreamy state, Walter thought at first it was Pacific tweeting back to Atlantic, but gradually the dampness causing Walter's bones to ache brought him slowly to his senses. The dream faded and Walter opened his eyes to see the bright red cardinal in the branches above him leaning forward and back using his tail to keep his balance as the breeze blew through the sky. The birds' conversation was so expressive. One ended the phrase lifted at the end as though asking a question, the other responded as though asking a question back. Then the bird overhead repeated the phrase but this time going down at the end as if answering the question and his conversant did the same. All around there were different squawks, screeches, tweets, and twills. The mournful cooing of the aptly-named mourning dove, whoo-who-who-who, caused Walter's heart to actually ache with the significance of what he was feeling.

He lay there high up in the oak tree feeling one with nature all around him and he felt unafraid. He thought about what a good life he had lived, how lucky he had been in love and in life. He wasn't famous or particularly important to anyone anymore, he hadn't won the Nobel prize nor had a vaccination named after him. But he had been a decent person who appreciated his life and enjoyed it practically every step of the way. He'd had a terrific childhood, fortunate in its simplicity as most childhood memories seemed to be. He had respected his parents and helped care for them in their later years. He had loved his wife as best he knew how and had been a good provider for his family. He enjoyed his job and told his kids to try to find something they liked to do just as much so they, like him, would never have to 'work' a day in their lives. A nuthatch, unaware of Walter's presence, shuttled down the trunk of the tree inches from where Walter lay, and he admired its fine markings as it chirped rhythmically in conjunction with its movements. Walter smiled in his contentedness and thought to himself, I have lived a good life. A woman's voice shouting from far below snapped him out of his reverie.

"Yoo-hoo, Walter, wake up dear, and send down your little basket so I can put a nice, hot breakfast in it for you," Marge Peterson yelled. "I brought the Opossum Falls Digest, too."

"I wasn't asleep," he hollered guiltily, "and what the heck are you doing up so early?" Walter felt his phone vibrating in his pocket. Struggling to sit up, he reached for his glasses and put them on so he could answer the phone. He smiled when he saw it was Marge calling. "Good, now we don't have to shout at one another."

The old neighbors chatted pleasantly over their cell phones throughout breakfast, Walter sitting high up in the oak tree wolfing down the delicious waffles with homemade maple syrup, bacon, sausage, and scrambled eggs with onion and tomatoes in it; Marge sitting below him in a lawn chair she'd brought along sipping on coffee from her thermos. She told him how he had been all over the evening news the previous night and they talked about his long term plans. She scolded him for launching such a foolish protest with winter right around the corner. Her thermostat had dipped down below forty degrees earlier that morning. When she asked if there was anything she could do for him at home, or anything in particular she could bring him, he thanked her and said that what she had done for him that morning was just about the most wonderful, neighborly thing possible.

"I've sure enjoyed being your neighbor all these years, Marge, yours and Charles'."

"Funny how we never knew that they would go first leaving the two of us to figure out how to carry on on our own." Marge felt close to tears. It felt very intimate speaking to Walter over the phone but being able to look at him from a distance, too. "Berniece would get a kick out of what you're doing, Walter; she'd be real proud of you, too."

"Thanks, Marge."

Chapter 19

It was late morning by the time Emma Grabow finished all of her errands in town, so she ended up driving a few miles over the speed limit to get home, something she very rarely did. Glancing in the rearview mirror, there wasn't a single vehicle around as far as her eye could see so she felt quite safe in her little indiscretion. She was feeling frustrated after her latest run-in with Walter and anxious to get home to fix lunch before Pete arrived.

As she carried the groceries into the house, she felt satisfied with how things had gone at Pick and Pay. Naturally, Emma had heard the rumors about the Fischer girl being pregnant. She braced herself for all of the holier-than-thou comments that were sure to follow, the slandering of the girl's reputation, the speculation as to the paternity, the advice on what should be done after the birth. Over the years, the inevitable unplanned pregnancies occurred in Opossum Falls. Making babies was a perfectly natural human activity, after all. Emma was forced to listen in silence. Her own teenage pregnancy was still a secret from her community as well as a source of pain to Emma even after all these years. Seeing Shannon's little belly growing every time she visited the grocery store, observing the quiet dignity the young woman showed in her expectant state, studying the reactions of her fellow townsmen to the fact that this girl was not about to cower in shame over the result of her actions, Emma felt relief. More than relief, Emma realized that she felt glad.

Emma put the hot water on to boil while she laid the table for lunch. She thought about how the naysayers so often spoke louder than the optimists. The notion that history would go on repeating itself ad nauseam was beaten into our heads so much that we came to believe it almost wasn't worth the effort trying to change for good. We were doomed to suffer the same fate as each and every civilization before ours that had ever tried to spread its wings had suffered. Emma poured the boiling water over the tomatoes to scald them, peeled them, and put them in the blender while she thought about how much things had changed. She reflected on how ashamed she had been made to feel by becoming pregnant while not yet married. They had made her feel that her pregnancy was such a dirty secret that she had to be hidden from society. Worst of all, she had not been allowed any say about her baby's life. Tears sprang to Emma's eyes, and she patted them with the dishtowel as she marveled at how much her heart ached over the injustice of it all and how angry it still made her feel. Taking a deep breath, she reminded herself that at least young, pregnant girls like Shannon Fischer would never be subjected to the humiliation and pain at having no part in the decision of her child's life.

Emma had waited in Shannon's line at the grocery store even though the woman ahead of her had a cart over laden with groceries, much of it fruits and vegetables that had to be weighed and keyed in individually by Shannon. When that pleasant woman named Laney had called over the aisle that her checkout lane was free, Emma had declined and said she would wait right where she was, thank you. After Shannon had greeted her and begun to scan her groceries, Emma asked her what school activities she would be involved in now that the volleyball season was over, not mentioning, of course, that Shannon's pregnancy made any physical activity finished for her regardless what season it was. Shannon said that she was editor of the year book and that they were hoping to be able to afford extra pages in the yearbook which would be full of highlights of the news from around the world, the country, and, Shannon had gushed, she would even like to include pages from the Opossum Falls' Digest.

Pleased with Shannon's answer, Emma had paid for her groceries, and then she had handed over a check to Shannon and said, "Please accept this contribution for your yearbook."

Shannon had automatically reached out to take the check, but when she saw all of the zeros on it, her mouth had dropped open as she looked up at Emma and said, "Holy Shit!" before she slapped her hand over her mouth.

Emma had actually laughed telling her not to worry, she hoped the yearbook would turn out exactly as Shannon hoped it would. Then she had handed her another, considerably smaller but still significant check and said, lowering her voice, "And this, my dear, is only for you. It doesn't need to go any further than just the two of us. I want you to use it in any way at all to make your pregnancy easier for you. Buy maternity clothes, vitamin e oil to help prevent stretch marks, books on what to expect when you're expecting. Do you know what you intend to do with the baby?"

"I, no, I'm not completely sure what I've decided yet, Mrs. Grabow," Shannon was too stunned over the two checks she held in her hand to consider how rude Emma's question was.

Relieved to hear Shannon refer to the decision as her own, Emma said simply, "That's alright, I'm sure you'll make the right decision. You are the only one who can. You're the mother. Good luck, my dear." Emma felt as if a weight had been removed from her chest as she walked out of the grocery store, her chin held high.

Driving to the property she was planning to sell to Wal-Mart to see what all of the hoopla over Walter Fassbinder was, she felt another weight descending upon her chest again. There were cars lined up all along the highway. Emma slowed down but kept going until she reached the giant oak tree which was where the people were gathered. "Good god, it's like a circus!" she murmured under her breath. And indeed, a couple of tents had been erected, vans sporting logos from various television stations parked beneath them. There were a few mini-campers selling pronto pups, tacos in a bag, and mini donuts. Emma had to keep driving as there was no place to pull off the highway, but when she got to the last parked car, she pulled in front of it and parked, then walked back to the tree.

WCCO had aired their coverage on Walter last night, and today being a Saturday, everybody and their grandma had come out to see the excitement, many from as far away as the cities. There were also a couple more television stations and some radio stations, too, all trying to interview Walter. Protestors from other causes had gathered, too, to share some of the limelight that Walter was creating. A group carrying PETA signs, People for the Ethical Treatment of Animals, were milling near the base of the tree. Emma looked up and saw Walter calmly sitting in his lawn chair flipping through a newspaper. "Lower your basket, Walter, I've brought you lunch," Emma hollered up at him. "I stopped at the deli in Pick and Pay and brought you MEAT sandwiches and whatnot."

"She's not with PETA," one of the protesters explained to a reporter.

"I sure as hell am," Emma retorted as she put the lunch sack in the basket Walter had lowered, giving it a tug so he knew he could crank it back up. "In fact, I am PITA! That's Pain In The Ass, people." Some locals milling nearby knew Emma, of course, and soon the reporters knew who she was, too. Soon, there were microphones being shoved into her face and Emma was bombarded with questions. One young, red-headed reporter in the back of the crowd shouted, "Are you going to force Mr. Fassbinder out of the tree, m'am, so Wal-Mart can start building?"

"My property has not yet been sold to Wal-Mart. Walter is my fellow-townsman and we've known each other practically all of our lives. If he wants to camp out in my oak tree, that's fine with me," Emma turned around to leave.

"Thanks for lunch, Emma!" Walter shouted from high up in his perch. Emma waved her arm high in acknowledgement without turning around and marched back to her car looking neither left nor right.

Glancing out her kitchen window, Emma saw Pete's truck coming down her driveway, so she put the cheese sandwiches in the frying pan to begin grilling them. The tomato basil soup with fresh herbs from her garden was simmering on the stove. She could hear Pete chatting with the Gonzalez boys before he came to the door. They were laughing about Jingle Bells and all of his clones again. Surprisingly, they had found homes for all but one of the lookalikes. Emma had a mind to take it down to the PETA folks milling around Walter and let them take care of the stray, give them a chance to practice what they preached.

"Knock-knock," Pete said as he pushed open the back door. Emma liked it that he no longer felt he had to ring the bell and stand there waiting for her to come and let him in. Over lunch Pete told her that, indeed, the results from the lab proved that there had been herbicide drift onto her vineyard and that the culprit was Roundup, just as they had suspected. Pete's job now was to go around and interview the owners of the surrounding farms and look at their history of applying herbicides to their fields, what they had sprayed and when, to try to determine who the guilty party was. This would take some time, Pete warned her, so she was not to expect results any time soon. Pete, of course, was drawing this entire process out as much as he could to give himself more time to spend with Laney. He explained that he was heading to Bloomington for the week-end to visit his folks but that he would be back on Monday to begin the interviews. As he was speaking, Pete reached into his pocket and pulled out his cell phone, apologizing as he explained that it had been vibrating all during lunch so he figured he'd better take a look.

"Speak of the devil," he said, "It's my dad calling now." Pete's face paled as he listened to the voice on the other end. After repeated exclamations, ending with, "I'm on my way," he turned to Emma and said in a voice filled with emotion, "My mom….she, she just died."

Emma gave Pete a hug but said nothing. There were no words when one received news like this, so why bother. Death was the shadow we all lived under every single day of our lives though we so seldom talked about it. When the flame of life was extinguished it put each one of us one step closer to losing our own. We might spend a little more time watching sunrises and sunsets, and take a bit more care being kind to one another, but before we knew it we were back to normal frowning into the mirror over the wretchedness of having gained another pound or two. Turning quickly so Pete could wipe his tears unnoticed, Emma went to the counter and said, "Give me a minute to put the soup in a container for you to take with you along with the apple pie I was planning to serve for dessert. Dealing with death is a very social experience, and you'll have visitors to feed."

Pete had already put Emma's cooler full of food in the back of his truck when he walked back down the sidewalk and told Emma he was going to bring the last of the lookalike cats to his dad. When Emma asked if he was sure this was the right time to deal with a new pet, Pete explained why he thought it was exactly the right time. His dad had been taking care of his mom with her Alzheimer's for so long that he would surely feel absolutely lost without someone to take care of. He wasn't equating a cat to his mom, of course, but his dad had grown up on a farm with lots of animals around so taking care of one would be second nature to him. More importantly, it would be good for him and it would mean he wasn't completely alone. Isn't that what every one of us was trying to avoid? After telling Pete to take the cat food and kitty litter, too, so his dad wouldn't have to worry about that, Emma sat with Jingle Bells on her lap, appreciating his companionship and knowing that what Pete had said was absolutely right.

Laney squealed as Michael smiled at his big sister and she ran to grab the camera. "Gabby, do it again!" She commanded. The moment was lost, however, and no matter how many times Gabby jumped up and said "Boo!" her infant brother wasn't about to smile again. "That's okay honey; I don't need a picture of it to remember that was Michael's first smile! You were the one to first get your baby brother to smile! I'm gonna write that in his baby book even!"

Gabby saw Michael's eyes begin to droop and she yelled, "Boo!" once again, startling him so that he began to cry. "Okay, that was good, honey, but you can stop now. No more scaring Michael, okay?" and she reached to take her son out of the electric swing. Her son. Laney marveled at the fact that she now had a son and that she had actually thought she wouldn't be able to love this baby as much as she loved Gabby. Looking over at Gabby now as she held her doll imitating everything Laney did with Michael, she couldn't get over how grown up she suddenly seemed. The day before Michael was born, Laney had thought of Gabby as just a baby. The second Michael Joseph was born, such an easy, by the book delivery that Scott was even the one who got to cut the umbilical cord, Gabby seemed huge. How quickly they'd forgotten what it was like to have an infant around! From the moment her midwife laid Michael on her chest and she'd asked Scott, "What is it?" and he'd mumbled, completely caught up in the miracle of the moment, "I don't know," and they had lifted him up to see that it was the boy Laney had known all along he was, she was head over heels in love with him.

How lucky they were to have their precious baby boy! Now their little family felt truly complete. Michael Joseph was the complete opposite baby to Gabby. Very hesitant around strangers, he seldom interacted with anyone except his own family. Happy to let his big sister garner all of the attention, he loved watching her antics and his eyes followed her everywhere. They dubbed him, 'the silent observer' because that was how he spent his days, studying his big sister's actions.

Lately, he seemed to have gotten his days and nights mixed up. Taking her midwife's advice, Laney was doing everything she could to keep Michael awake during the day so that he might sleep better at night. Rather than putting him down for a nap, they tried to keep him awake for as long as possible. Gabby had been more than happy to help with her 'Operation: Keep Michael Awake during the day so he'll sleep at night', assignment.

Propping Michael next to his sister on the couch, Laney held the camera and filmed the two of them as Gabby pretended to read from the Where's Spot *book.*

She knew the book by heart, so she read each page while lifting up the paper to look for the missing dog. Michael's serious brown eyes studied every page, too. On the final page when Spot is at last found, Gabby squealed with delight so loudly that it made Michael smile again, and this time Laney did catch it on the camera.

Gabby was so thrilled with her accomplishment that she patted Michael on the head in her enthusiasm but whacked the poor little guy a bit too vigorously. Michael's smile immediately crumpled into tears, and soon his wails of hurt were inconsolable. The depth of his grief as he looked at Gabby while he cried caused Laney to put the camera down to pick him up to console him. Rocking Michael in her arms, Laney felt the weight of her baby on her chest as she slowly awoke from her dream. The pressure was so great, she was afraid that her heart would break in two. Holding nothing in her arms but her pillow, she lay in bed and looked up at the ceiling, wondering how she would find the strength to get out of bed.

Chapter 20

Brandon Hopkins was obsessed. The more he replayed his raid at Minnesota's Sugar Beet Cooperative back in his mind, the more he was absolutely certain that there were some undocumented workers who had gotten away during the singing of that patriotic song. He pounded his steering wheel in frustration as he drove down the street. His supervisor had obviously been disappointed in him when he'd reported that all of the paperwork had been in order and that every single employee at the factory had papers that were legitimate. But when he tried to tell his boss that he was sure some of them had snuck out the backdoor because, he emphasized this with feeling, Brandon had been completely alone with no back up, his boss had told him to stop beating a dead horse and to resign himself to the fact that he, Brandon, had been wrong about the factory and that everyone there was on the up and up. Brandon grit his teeth in anger and pulled up to the Chit Chat for some lunch.

It was a quiet, middle of the week, day. Brandon sat at the counter and ordered a patty melt with extra fries. Marty Bleak was just paying his bill, so when he noticed Brandon's uniform, he sat next to him and said, "One of my best friends is a cop. He told me about this couple that he pulled over one day, for speeding.

Walking up to the driver's window, the officer said, "You were going at least 75 in a 55 mile an hour zone."

The Man says: "No sir, I was going 60."

His wife leans over so the officer can see her and butts in: "Oh, Chester. You were going 80."

Officer: "I'm also going to give you a ticket for your broken tail light."

Man: "Broken tail light? I didn't know I had a broken tail light!"

Wife: "Oh, Chester. You've known about that tail light for weeks."

Officer: "I'm also going to give you a citation for not wearing your seat belt."

Man: "But I just took it off when you were walking up to the car."

Wife: "Oh, Chester. You never wear your seat belt."

The man turns to his wife and yells: "Shut your damn mouth!"

The officer turns to the woman and asks, "M'am, does your husband talk to you this way all the time?"

Wife: "No, officer, only when he's drunk."

Getting barely a grunt out of Agent Hopkins in reply, Marty raised his eyebrows at Bianca in mock consternation and he headed out the door.

When Bianca set the patty melt with extra fries in front of Brandon, he suddenly grabbed her wrist between his thumb and forefinger, "Do you have papers?"

"What?" she asked completely startled and she tried to pull her arm away, but Brandon pinched even harder.

At the end of the counter in his usual seat, Dick McGhee looked up from reading the paper to watch.

"I'm asking for your papers. Let me see them, NOW!" Brandon released her wrist with a flourish.

"I am a citizen of the United States, if that's what you're asking. But don't you have to have some sort of probable cause to start demanding to see someone's proof of citizenship or have our individual rights totally disappeared since 9/11?"

"Citizen of the U.S.A, I'll just bet you are!"

Dick had ambled over to stand behind Brandon and asked, "Is there some kind of problem here? Bianca? Everything alright?"

Brandon answered, "I'm asking to see this Mexican's papers to see if it's legal for her to be working here or not. Not that it's any of your business."

"Actually, it is my business. Ms. Gonzalez is my client." Dick pulled a business card out of the front pocket of his shirt and laid it on the counter next to Brandon's plate. Brandon picked up the patty melt and took a huge bite. Some of the burger's juice slid down his chin and dripped onto the card while he leaned over to read it.

"Mr. McGhee." He pushed the contents of the patty melt over into one cheek and continued talking while he chewed, "Is your client illegal or isn't she?"

"First of all, you are aware that 'illegal' is a uselessly vague term in this situation. The 11th amendment affirms that neither the federal government nor state governments may deny to any person within its jurisdiction the equal protection of the laws. So, an undocumented immigrant may have violated immigration requirements but is still a legal person under the law. It would be better if you used the correct label of 'undocumented immigrant' which clearly states the offense as someone residing in the U.S. without proper documentation rather than the unclear and even misleading term 'illegal.'"

Dick hoisted up his pants while he carried on. "With regards to my client, Bianca, she was born in Texas and has lived in this country her entire life, paying taxes just like the rest of us," He spoke respectfully despite what he thought about the agent. He had tipped his head to Bianca signaling to her that she should carry on with her work. Brandon opened his mouth wide and took another enormous bite out of his sandwich while Dick stood and waited for him to finish chewing.

"You sure about that, Mr." he peered down at the business card, "McGhee?" Brandon picked up his pop and took a long sip out of the straw all the while noisily chewing up the burger in this mouth.

"Yes, sir, same as her husband, her children, and the nephews staying with her, too." Dick realized he was probably sharing more information than was necessary, but he wanted this ICE agent to have as much evidence as possible so he could walk away from the Gonzalez family, and hopefully the whole town, without causing any more trouble.

Smearing four fries at once around the catsup on his plate, Brandon shoved them into his mouth and nodded at Dick. He appreciated the lawyer treating him deferentially. "Alright then," he spoke with his maw full of food again. Dick walked back over to his spot at the other end of the counter and continued reading the paper. When Brandon finished his lunch, he paid his bill and left. Bianca walked over to Dick to thank him for intervening. She placed a large slice of lemon meringue pie in front of him and told him it was on the house and that if she ever did need a lawyer, he would definitely be the one she would go to.

"Right, like when you need me to oversee the papers of the Chit Chat when you buy it from Tom and Betty."

"Oh Dick, I'd have to win the lottery, first. But wouldn't that be just the ticket?" Bianca sighed as she washed down the counter, thinking of the changes she would make inside the Chit Chat if it really was hers.

Brandon stood in front of the Chit Chat and popped a couple Tums into his mouth, burping as he did so. He was going to pay for those fries and patty melt later, he just knew it; he was prone to heartburn but he just couldn't resist anything deep fried. He looked up and down the sidewalk still feeling like he was on the warpath. He was sick of being jerked around when he knew this town was seething with aliens. He heard the friendly toot of a car horn and looked down to see a woman with a stroller crossing the street. Obviously the driver of the car had hooted to let her know it was okay for her to cross, that he would wait. Brandon squinted his eyes as he realized she was crossing in the middle of the street, and that she looked Mexican. He climbed back into his car, put his flashing lights on, and drove down the street to pull up next to the woman. The panic in her eyes when she turned her head and realized that he was stopping for her told Brandon he'd gotten himself a winner at last.

Laney was walking home from work when she saw the commotion on the street and heard the wailing of the frantic woman. Instantly, her own panic started enveloping her as she felt herself immediately sucked back into The Event, and she began trembling all over. The woman's cries grew louder and more desperate however, forcing Laney back into the present. Anxious to be of assistance to help avert anything like the trouble she herself had experienced, Laney made herself walk up to the official-looking car. The woman had been rattling away in Spanish but when she saw Laney, she reached for her with both hands and said, in English, "Please, to call Juan Carlos Ramirez, is his granddaughter." The woman used her chin to point down at Isabella Rose.

Laney looked down to see the little girl perched forward in the stroller because the back was full of groceries. She had just waited on them at Pick and Pay and she'd given the little girl a sucker for being so good. She was still sucking on the candy, but whereas before her eyes had been sparkling with childhood innocence, now they were luminous with fear as she didn't understand what was going on around her. When her caretaker pleaded with the officer to at least let her say good-bye and he'd told her to hurry up then, she had taken out the sucker and asked, "Tia Juanita, what is it?" and she'd begun to cry.

Tia Juanita had crouched down so she was eye level with her. Tears were streaming down her cheeks, but she spoke in a strong, clear voice now. "You be a good girl now, my Isabella, my angelita," she said pronouncing 'you' like 'Jew', "I have to go away for awhile, but I know you'll keep being my preciosa, my good little girl, alright? When you say your prayers before bed, look out at the beautiful, night sky and find the biggest, brightest star and that will be me, Tia Juanita, shining down on you and sending you my love. Good-bye, little Izzy, adios!" She showered the little girl with kisses as she continued to cry.

"No, Tia Juanita, no, no!" The little girl was screaming now and struggling to get out of the stroller.

Brandon was forcing Tia Juanita into the back of the car while she was still yelling to Isabella Rose, "You go with the nice lady, and she'll take care of you now." Isabella Rose was fighting Laney hard now trying to get to the car, wanting to chase after it as it pulled away. Laney lifted the little girl, who was bigger than she'd originally thought, into her arms and held onto her tightly while she screamed and struggled to get out of Laney's embrace. Laney, terrified both for the girl and for herself, comforted the girl with sweet whispers in her ear while she patted her back, then started the familiar 'mother's sway' back and forth, back and forth, to calm their beating hearts.

Soon the news spread quickly around town that the detestable ICE agent had found someone to put into detention. Tia Juanita had no legal status and, after a long battle with the immigration court, would be sent back across the border. Laney had held Isabella Rose in her arms until her sobs turned to whimpers and then she'd managed to distract her by bribing her with a butterscotch sundae from the Chit Chat. Bianca called Juan Carlos and told him the news. They sat in the booth by the window with their sundaes, Laney with her butterscotch, Isabella Rose asking for chocolate instead. While Laney was still trembling from witnessing such a traumatic scene, she marveled at the ability of the young to suffer a traumatic event and apparently move on. The little five-year-old girl had looked at her with such trust in her big, brown eyes. Now she was chatting away telling her all about her abuelito, where they lived, and the names and colors of the houses of everyone who lived on their street. She had just made Laney laugh by starting to list all of the animals in the neighborhood. She said that one of the neighbors had a dog named Justin, after Justin Bieber of course, because he had such cute, shaggy hair. When Laney had asked what kind of dog it was, she thought she'd said a poodle.

"No," Izzy shook her head slowly back and forth, "a 'poo' dog. Abuelito won't let me say the real name." When Laney promised she wouldn't tell, Izzy had leaned forward and whispered, "A shit zoo." Laney had laughed out loud at a Shih Tzu named after the Bieb. The girl started giggling, too, covering her mouth with both of her chubby, little hands. Her little fingernails had been painted a hot pink color and Laney realized with a stab in the chest that it had most likely been the deported nanny who had done the polishing.

Juan Carlos jingled the bell over the Chit Chat door as he walked in, and he quickly spotted his granddaughter. He walked over and slid into the booth next to her. As if he had turned on a faucet, tears began to stream out of Isabella Rose's eyes and she wrapped her arms around Juan Carlo's neck saying, "He took Tia! The mean man took Tia Juanita! Please make him bring her back, Abuelito, please, please, please." Juan Carlos mouthed the words, "Thank you," at Laney as he gently carried his granddaughter out of the restaurant and home, where he would try to explain immigration rules to a five year old. He didn't know how to make it right that the only mother figure she had ever known had been forcibly dragged away from her like a criminal when all she had done was fulfill a need in their makeshift family's home.

Therese Dotray-Tulloch

Chapter 21

Walter blew on his fingers as he tried to warm them. Damn, it was cold up in the tree. Still not even November yet, but at night the temperature dropped into the twenties. He'd have to ask Marty to get him some more hand warmers from Just Screw It tomorrow. He was sitting up in his lawn chair reading *Giants of the Earth* with the help of an itty-bitty night light attached to the book. He was covered from head to toe in layers trying to keep warm except for one of his hands which he needed free to be able to turn the pages. He'd just realized the practicality of those gloves that had the removable finger tips. He'd have to see if he could order some for the shop just in time for the winter.

He was really enjoying his book. What a terrific storyteller Ole Rolvaag was. Walter congratulated himself on choosing such a classic book to read while he sat up in protest in his oak tree. If he was starting to feel sorry for himself in his remoteness and the cold, just reading the painful story of Per Hansa and his miserable wife Beret made him aware of how fortunate he was to be living more than a hundred years after the Norwegian and German settlers to their area. Now that was isolation! Not to mention the locusts. Walter had just read about the immigrant children of that generation and how they quickly became estranged from the old ways of the country they had left behind. He thought of the Hispanic teenagers in Opossum Falls and how history does repeat itself.

He had heard about Juan Carlos' live-in help being deported and how hard it was on Juan Carlos' little granddaughter, Isabella Rose. For god's sake, this country was made up of immigrants. How could those living just decades after the fact have forgotten all of that so determinedly and somehow come to feel that they had the right to live in this land but no one else did? How did they think they came across these privileges except for the fact that their ancestors were brave enough to have left their lands to become immigrants themselves?

Walter yawned and decided to call it a night. He went and stood in the corner and peed into the large plastic pop bottle he used just for this purpose. He had a separate bucket system he used for his more serious bathroom duty now as everyone was making such a stink about it, no pun intended. Marty had complained loudly and frequently about emptying Walter's waste, but with his irrepressible humor, he'd forbidden Walter to use the empty apple juice bottle to pee in just in case Marty got them mixed up!

Walter put his gloves back on and shuffled over to his mattress to climb carefully into his down sleeping bag. He grunted out loud when he bent down all the while he struggled to get into the sleeping bag. He'd learned that it was better to wiggle his way into the bag with the zipper already up than to climb in first and then try to zip up the bag. His fingers were so stiff with arthritis these days that securing the zipper between his crooked fingers while he was already in the bag had proved to be nearly impossible.

He was feeling awfully stiff. The blowup mattress wasn't proving to be quite as comfortable as Walter had hoped it would be, and the cool nights were beginning to take their toll. Walter had been living up in the tree for over two weeks. The Opossum Falls Digest had just done another interview on him and they'd asked him how long he intended to stay up in there. He had boasted that he would stay up there as long as it took. He was not going to let Wal-Mart chop down this tree and if it took Walter living up in the tree for the rest of his life, then so be it.

The tree removal company had spent the first couple of days on site with Walter sitting up in the tree. They had all of their equipment with them ready to complete the arduous task of limb by limb, amputating the oak tree and finally cutting down its trunk flush to the ground so no sign of its existence would be left behind at all. The lumberjacks had sat around laughing and playing cards waiting for word on what they should do. Walter had to admit that he was very relieved the loggers weren't willing to endanger his life by cutting down the tree with him in it. The police also, drove by from time to time to check on Walter and to make sure the chopping down of the tree did not start with Walter up in it. After three days of the lumberjacks purportedly getting paid for sitting on their bums playing poker, they must have gotten word to go away and not to come back until called. Score one for Walter.

The majority of the people in Opossum Falls seemed to be on Walter's side, and they treated his experience of living up in the oak tree as a sort of celebration. The big events in town were the Fourth of July, the county fair, and the holiday parade in early December to kick off the holiday shopping season. Walter had chosen to spend time up in the tree during a void season, as it were, so the community appreciated having an event to celebrate, and they wholeheartedly embraced the opportunity Walter presented to them.

The teachers at school began to assign projects having to do with famous tree protestors, called 'tree sitters'. The students would come to Walter for current quotes to add to the authenticity of their reports. One student wrote a paper about the very first tree sitter ever recorded which happened back in 1978 in New Zealand. Another wrote about the first American tree sitter, Mikal Jakubal, who sat in a Douglas fir tree in 1985. Another wrote about the tree-sitters' camp in Berkeley, California because it was the longest tree-sit in history. The protestors sat, presumably taking turns, for three years in the oak trees on the Pacific coast from 2006 to 2009. Walter learned from another student about the highest tree sit so far which took place in Tasmania,

Australia. The sitter spent fifty-one days two hundred thirteen feet high in a giant Eucalyptus tree nicknamed Gandalf's Staff. Shannon Fischer came and read her entire paper out loud to Walter about Julia Butterfly Hill who sat in the six hundred-year-old giant redwood tree she had named Luna for seven hundred thirty-eight days. Both Julia and Luna survived. Walter loved hearing these stories with happy endings.

The reports written about activists who had died during their tree sits were not so interesting to Walter. He concentrated instead on the idea of naming the oak tree. The eucalyptus tree in Tasmania was obviously named after Gandalf from the *Lord of the Rings* which was being filmed nearby at the time. Walter couldn't think of a recent movie made in Minnesota but Judy Garland had been born in Minnesota so he could call the tree Dorothy. He had always really enjoyed the Little House on the Prairie television series (he had to admit he'd never read the books; he preferred the Hardy Boys) so he thought he could name the tree Charles Ingalls or better yet, Michael Landon, the good-looking actor who'd played the part.

A couple of the elementary school teachers sent home permission slips the parents signed which allowed the children to come on a field trip to visit Walter sitting in his tree. The students brought bag lunches and sat around under the tree, thrilled to be out of the classroom on such a beautiful, fall day. They went home and told their parents how fine-looking the tree was that Walter was sitting in and how they didn't think it should be cut down, either.

The high school science teacher got permission to hold class one day under Walter's oak tree. While it wasn't the time of year that he normally worked on Field Biology, he shifted things around a bit in his curriculum so he could take the opportunity to teach the kids something about trees. The history teacher gave his kids the assignment to write about Walter's oak tree beginning with when it first began to grow and to describe Opossum Falls and its inhabitants at that time.

The grown-ups in town were taking ownership of Walter's situation, too. Ladies at the churches in town got together to work out a meal schedule for Walter. The Methodists took breakfast, the Catholics lunch, and the Lutherans dinner. Sometimes Walter had barely finished visiting with the Methodist bearing egg bake for breakfast, when the Catholic bringing a pork sandwich with sauerkraut and dumplings for lunch arrived. Walter would not want Berniece to be able to read his mind on this, but he could say without a doubt that he had never eaten so well in his life before. Three hot meals a day, each one a labor of love designed to impress not only Walter but each other as well because they had to know, after all, who had recently brought Walter what. They couldn't have him eating liver and onions two days in a row now, could they?

Owning a hardware-store business in a small town meant that Walter knew practically everybody in town. It would be different if he owned the butcher shop, for example; then he might not know the vegetarians or vegans in town, not that there were very many of those. But who doesn't at some point or other find the need to visit the hardware store? People who frequent a hardware store aren't usually in the mood to browse either. It's not like the dress shop where you need to walk around and take a look at all of the dresses on the racks before choosing some to try on. The hardware store patron is usually smack dab in the middle of a project: painting a room, unclogging the drain, building a bookshelf, changing a light bulb. He or she is not interested in browsing the aisle to find the right screw size. They preferred to walk straight through the door and ask Walter for assistance.

Walter had been helping people at Just Screw It for so long that practically the whole town was on a first name basis with him. When word got round that he was up in the oak tree protesting its removal and Wal-Mart's building on the spot, they all wanted to do something to help him. Walter had visitors all day long. Henry Johnson brought the chess board every afternoon and set it up so Walter could look right down on it from his lawn chair up in the tree and tell Henry what piece to move where. Dick McGhee had offered to represent Walter and had sorted out any trespassing issues with Emma already. He checked in on Walter daily, too. Someone had brought a patio table with chairs so whoever was bringing a meal could stay and visit.

Of course, not all of his visitors were positive experiences. Jeanine Westerly had stormed over the first day shouting what in the hell did he think he was doing? Had he turned *Amish?* He was using a cell phone, wasn't he, which showed he was for progress of a fashion, so why the hell was he trying to prevent the inevitable development of Wal-Mart moving into town? Had he gone native? (Walter had no idea what she'd meant by that. He'd looked down and noticed he'd left his fly open but he was pretty sure Jeanine couldn't see that from where she was standing, but he'd zipped up nonetheless.) There were a couple other people from town who heckled him a bit. Old man Glickson shouted at him for a while before his daughter came and dragged him away. He owned the building company that was bidding for the Wal-Mart project. Sister Beatrice of the Bleeding Heart shouted the rosary for a few hours nonstop one morning, but she was suffering from dementia so he didn't mind about that. A few teenage boys threw eggs at Walter one night, but he called Dusty who drove the boys over to Walter's house the next day and made them rake his entire lawn for free. The boys had been back to visit Walter a few times; no hard feelings there, either.

Once darkness descended, Walter was pretty much on his own. The evenings were getting cooler now and it wasn't much fun for anyone to sit outside in the dark talking to Walter up in the tree where they couldn't even see him. The trouble was, it was getting dark earlier and earlier now, too. By six o'clock, Walter had to put on his reading light if he wanted to read. He didn't even want to think about Day Light Savings time which occurred at the end of the month.

Walter listened to the news on the radio. He'd gotten a kick out of it when he'd heard about himself for the first time over the radio. Besides the Opossum Falls Digest, however, Walter wasn't news anymore beyond his own town. None of the news stations had gotten a response from Wal-Mart at all, either. Walter wondered what their strategy was going to be. The day that Emma had visited Walter, she had been in the news, too, as the owner of the land the tree was on that Wal-Mart was allegedly in the midst of purchasing. Because they couldn't get her to say anything negative about Walter, they had stopped trying to interview her. It wasn't news when Emma kept saying Walter could sit up in her tree for as long as he wanted to.

The friends of the library had a group of volunteers who delivered books to the homebound so Walter's name was added to the list and he had a steady stream of books coming and going. He read at night till his eyes got too droopy and he read first thing in the morning just as soon as he woke up.

Truth be told, Walter sure did wish that his tree sitting had taken place in the spring rather than in the fall. Winter was fast approaching and Walter was not looking forward to being up there during the thirty below temperatures and even less to the blizzard conditions. He listened to the sounds of the crickets rubbing their legs together creating the comforting, nostalgic sound which always meant fall to him. It also meant death to so many living things when the cold of winter set in. Soon, it would be too cold for the crickets, too.

Walter lay in his sleeping bag hoping that tonight his sleep would be without adventure. Since Berniece died, Walter had begun to suffer from an ailment he had not experienced since he was a little boy. He had begun to walk in his sleep. He had grown up with his mother telling funny stories about Walter walking about in the middle of the night, able to carry on intelligible conversations and looking to all the world as if he were wide awake. He never remembered a thing about it the following day. They had to lock the doors because he tried to wander. Hearing the front door shut in the middle of one such night, Walter's Dad had hurried out to find Walter walking straight into the cornfield where he could have been lost for days. Another night, the chickens were squawking loudly because Walter was busy disturbing them to look in their roosts for eggs.

After marrying Berniece, Walter's night wanderings had stopped. She had been an anchor to him in so many positive ways. A month or so after her death, Walter found some leftovers from the fridge left out when he was sure he'd put them away. Then he woke to find a load of laundry separated with the darks neatly placed inside the oven. Walter started barricading his bedroom door and he was fine. He had hoped that the difficulty of getting in and out of the sleeping bag would hinder any attempt to get up while he was tree sitting in the oak tree, and so far that had proven to be the case. He had woken up one night with his sleeping bag more twisted than usual and on the floor right next to his air mattress so he wondered if perhaps his ol' unconscious had tried to take him for a walk that night but had been thwarted by the tricky sleeping apparatus. He was grateful for that.

The first tweets of the earliest of the morning birds tweaked the edges of Walter's sleeping conscience. He carried on in the blissful slumber that was so necessary to humans that when deprived of it, people became totally deranged and were as psychotic as if they were on hallucinogenic drugs. The long whistle of another bird stirred him momentarily into consciousness but soon he was breathing heavily again still sound asleep. As more birds awakened, their calls became more numerous and they reached his ears from near and far, now across the field, now right above his own head. The variety of the calls was intoxicating to Walter even though it was nearly the end of the season and most of the songbirds had already left and gone south. He knew that the sparrows, bluebirds, and robins would soon be seeking warming climates. The cedar waxwings, chickadees, cardinals, nuthatches, and blue jays would keep Walter company all throughout the winter, but hopefully he would not be up in the tree that long.

The robin tweeted a couple of crystal clear notes in a melodious sequence; far off the phrase was repeated. Back and forth the musical phrase was tossed, each vocalization pulling Walter nearer and nearer to consciousness. He had been in the middle of a rather bizarre dream. Berniece was in it with him and they were apparently on some sort of dog-sledding expedition. Berniece had been laughing joyfully and shouting to the six or eight huskies prancing friskily and easily pulling her on her skis. She was skillfully guiding them, leaning this way and that on her skis as they made their way through the enchanting pine trees wearing layers of sparkling snow. In the dream, Walter was falling farther and farther behind. His hands were freezing and he kept shouting at his dogs to mush, mush, but the dogs pulling Walter's sleigh were basset hounds and they couldn't keep up with the Alaskan huskies at all.

Pulled fully out of his dream now, Walter felt that twinge of sadness when he realized it was a dream and that Berniece, of course, was no longer there. Then he chuckled at the incongruity of his dream and wondered what Freud would have had to tell him about it. He wriggled his fingers a bit to get the circulation back in them. They were frozen stiff and Walter knew it was no wonder he was dreaming about being cold. His cantankerous old bladder which called attention to itself more and more frequently with each passing year was making itself painful again so Walter knew he would have to get up and empty it. The brilliant red cardinal which initially had been so shy of him now sat and sang on the branch right above him. Walter spoke to the bird, "Well, I'm still here. Another day above ground is already a good day, right, Red?" and he painstakingly pushed himself up off the mattress.

Feeling the ache in his swollen joints as he forced them to move, Walter thought to himself that death, at his age, was not a bad thing to contemplate either. He had enjoyed his life, for the most part. He had known love, his life had had meaning, and he was proud of his children and the children they were now raising. If his family remembered him with love, fond memories, and a sense of pride in his life, that was as fine a legacy as he could ever want. Groaning loudly with pleasure as he began to pee and feeling relief in his over-extended bladder, Walter wondered what the Methodists would be bringing for breakfast.

Therese Dotray-Tulloch

Chapter 22

Displeased with the big chunks of corn flakes that still remained in the large, zip-lock bag, Emma rolled the rolling pin back and forth over the bag until all of the flakes were thoroughly crushed. She dumped the contents over the tuna hot dish, took the small saucepan of melted butter off the stove, drizzled it over the crushed flakes, then put the casserole in the oven and set the timer. As she took out the ingredients for a salad to accompany the hot dish, her mind wandered over her plan of attack. Slicing the tomatoes and cucumbers, she thought about how the process of creating a meal had always been such a comfort to her. She had loved cooking for Otto throughout their marriage. He may not have been the most complimentary of men, but he ate whatever she put in front of him and had often asked for seconds. What better compliment could there be than that?

She had missed cooking for someone else. After Otto's death, she must have gotten a little depressed, although she never would have admitted that at the time. She started eating tins of soup for lunch and Lean Cuisines for dinner. One night, she was having a portion of

Chicken Alfredo with a side of the soggiest broccoli she had ever tasted. The meal was so bland she felt like it was hardly worth the effort to lift the fork to put the tasteless gruel in her mouth. She had suddenly stood up with some of her old spirit reclaimed, dumped the packaged food into the garbage, and strode out to the chicken coop to gather some fresh eggs. She had found some bacon in the freezer and had cooked bacon and eggs for supper. She couldn't believe how delicious it was. The next day, she had slaughtered her fattest chicken and slow-roasted it with rosemary and butter. She had eaten what she could and divided the rest into freezable containers. That had been the start of her return to good cooking. She enjoyed the therapeutic results that creating delicious meals brought to her as well as the culinary delights she stocked her freezer with.

Having Pete Oetzmann around so much had given her an even more renewed sense of the joy of cooking. Like Otto, he was a good eater who always cleaned his plate, but, unlike Otto, may he rest in peace, he was extremely generous with his compliments. Pete had been eating with her all week while he went around interviewing the neighbors to try to get to the bottom of the Roundup drift. She wasn't sure why he was bothering when Emma felt sure it was Eric Hanson. She practically remembered the windy day it had happened, too. But she approved of Pete's thoroughness, and she appreciated his company. Besides, ever since his mom's death and the subsequent discovery of his adoption, Emma had been flummoxed, to put it mildly, and the more time she spent with Pete the better it was for her.

Pete was not interviewing around the neighborhood today, however. He and Laney Anderson were actually out working in the vineyard. Emma peered out the window but the grapevines were too high for her to see the two of them out there working. Never mind, they had agreed to come in to lunch at noon. She was surprised and pleased when Pete had asked if it would be alright for him and Laney to come and remove the grapes damaged by the herbicide drift. Emma had planned to just leave them rotting on the vines as they would have come off with the early spring pruning. At that time, all but the two hardiest buds on each vine were left to be trained along the trellises to hopefully produce a prolific amount of grapes. Pete felt differently, however. Taking his job with the Department of Agriculture seriously, Pete had admitted to Emma that he'd never worked with a vineyard owner before. He had been spending his evenings, well, when he wasn't able to be with Laney, researching cold climate grapes.

During his investigation, he'd discovered that it could be potentially harmful to the future of the vineyard to leave rotting grapes to winter on the vines. If the winter turned out to be mild, the grapes could become harbingers of disease. The best way to prevent that from happening would be to remove the damaged grapes. Pete had told Laney that he was proposing to spend the day in the vineyard and she had asked if she could help, too. She didn't tell Pete it was because she missed having a big garden to care for like she used to have and how living in an apartment made that impossible. Pete had been so delighted at the prospect of spending the day with Laney working side by side in the vineyard that he never even questioned why. He was over the moon because she wanted to spend time with him.

Emma removed a couple of the chilled hard-boiled eggs from the fridge, gave one a big crack on the counter, easily slipped it out of its shell and began slicing it, replaying in her mind the conversation with Pete that had led to her clandestine plans. Pete had stayed in Bloomington with his dad throughout the funeral. Apparently, the service for Pete's mom had been a real celebration of her life. When someone had Alzheimer's, it seemed to be easier for families to accept their loved one's death. They had actually already mourned the death of the person they loved; the stranger inhabiting their loved one's body was simply a cruel, painful reminder of the fact that the one they knew was no longer there. Such was the case with Pete's mom. All of her friends and extended family had gathered to share memories and stories of her life.

It was while having a conversation with his mom's ancient Aunt Mildred that Pete first heard of the stunning revelation. Aunt Mildred was just over a hundred years old; Pete had driven home back in June for her one hundredth birthday celebration. She was a feisty old bird who still had all of her faculties about her, or so Pete had thought. At the luncheon following the funeral, Pete had brought Aunt Mildred a small sampling of some of the many bars and cakes people had generously brought. Putting the entire square of lemon poppy seed cake in her mouth, Aunt Mildred's lips were smacking as she told Pete she would never forget how happy his mom was on the day they had delivered him to her. Pete handed her a napkin as he corrected her, "You mean, when my mom delivered *me*."

"No, Peter," Aunt Mildred continued, a poppy seed stuck right between her two front teeth, "when *they* delivered you to your *mom*. The Lutheran Home Society, or some such group, I can't remember exactly which one it was. Your dear mother had been trying for a baby for so long! Her childbearing years were actually over by then when suddenly this beautiful, blond baby boy arrived! You were much blonder then, Peter. I remember it as if it were yesterday, your mom holding you as if you were the most fragile creature on earth. You weren't, of course. You were a strapping little fella, strong as an ox. She fell in love with you the moment she laid eyes on you." Pete had been called away then to say good-bye to some departing guests just as Aunt Mildred was pushing every layer of the entire seven-layer bar into her mouth, unknowingly scraping a chocolate chip off onto her top lip.

Pete had been tempted to confront his Dad about it before he'd left him the day after the funeral but he couldn't bear to add any more grief to his Dad's plate at that time. Besides, it couldn't be true, could it? Aunt Mildred apparently was not quite as cognizant as they thought she was, that was all. Why would Pete's parents have lied to him all these years? Pete found himself looking hard at his father as he was saying good-bye, trying desperately to see some physical similarity between the two of them to put his recent misgivings to rest. His father's short stature and his broad, flat face certainly didn't reassure tall, fine-featured Pete that his suspicions were misdirected at all.

Pete had shared the story with Emma over coffee one morning before he'd headed out to interview more neighbors. For a grown man, Pete had looked awfully boyish and vulnerable as he'd told Emma how confused it made him feel. Right on the heels of losing his mom, to learn the peculiar news that she may not have been his birth mother at all? Emma had offered words of understanding and sympathy at the same time as offering him more coffee. As he'd held out his cup for Emma to fill, the reel of life froze in mid-frame as Emma's hand clutching the coffee pot and Pete's holding his cup were stilled side by side. Emma's heart leapt up to her throat as she saw the masculine version of her own hand attached to Pete's wrist: thin fingers with the large, bulbous knuckles beneath smallish, flat nails. When Emma had subsequently overfilled the cup, Pete had jumped up as hot coffee scalded his hand and Emma had a chance to compose herself as she rushed to get a wet cloth.

It came to her then, who it was that Pete had reminded her of all this time; he was the younger version of her own father. The way he cocked his head when he was listening to you to really take into consideration what you were saying, the fine line between his eyebrows, even the lanky walk was just like her father's had been as if his limbs were too long to control properly. Emma somehow managed to hold it together until Pete had finally been on his way. She'd shut the door behind him and collapsed into the nearest chair, her heart beating wildly as she'd asked herself, "Could it really be true? Could Pete Oetzmann be the little blond boy she'd given birth to thirty-seven years ago?"

Fluctuating between being one hundred percent convinced that it was true to thinking she needed to have her head examined because the odds of her own son casually walking back into her life were so absurdly unlikely, Emma finally could stand it no more. She'd decided she had to know or she would drive herself crazy with speculation. After researching online exactly what she needed to do, she'd driven to Snyder's in Olivia and purchased an Identigene Kit. All she needed to do was to collect a couple of samples to test Pete's DNA. She would mail Pete's samples as well as two of her own back to the company. Within two days she would be able to see the results online.

Emma had managed to confiscate a piece of gum Pete had been chewing which he took out before eating. Today she intended to extricate a piece of hair. She had scraped the inside of her cheek and put her samples in the envelopes already. After she got a piece of Pete's hair, she would mail in the evidence and wait with bated breath to find out if Pete Oetzmann was who she already knew him to be, her own son.

When Laney and Pete came in for lunch, Emma's opportunity presented itself immediately. Laney had gone to use the powder room. Pete had pulled off his hat and his hair stood up on end. Emma had laughed and handed him a comb saying in a lowered voice, "If you're trying to make any headway in your relationship with Laney, I suggest you tidy yourself up a bit." He gratefully took the comb she handed to him and voila, she had her specimen trapped ingenuously between the teeth of her comb.

Therese Dotray-Tulloch

Her dreams instantly found her back outside, but instead of in a vineyard, she was in a vegetable garden harvesting bountiful yields. Laney was kneeling on the rectangle of inch-thick foam with wavy edges digging up the last of the carrots. Michael was still napping so Laney had the Fisher-Price monitor in her sweatshirt pocket so she would be able to hear him once he woke up. Gabby had woken up from her nap already and was in the garden with Laney. She had brought a couple of Barbie dolls out to the garden with her and Laney could hear her sweet little voice as she played. Gabby ran to the deck to get the shoebox she used for the Barbie's bed. She ran back to the garden to put them in it. Sitting back on her heels, Laney watched her and thought how funny it was that Gabby so seldom walked but was always running instead as if there was too much living to be done to waste any of it by moving slowly.

Gabby was tucking the Barbie dolls in for a nap now and covering them with a Kleenex for a blanket. She was singing Edelweiss to them. Scott always sang that to Gabby when he was tucking her in. It was charming to hear Gabby singing it, making up the words as she went along. Now Gabby came over to help her mom. Laney asked her to pick the cherry tomatoes and she handed her the basket to put them in. Back and forth they chatted as they worked in the warm September sun. They had had a little cocker spaniel that had recently been hit by a car and killed. This had been tragic for the family and they had all cried at Buster's passing. When Gabby had carried on, crying excessively, Laney had said to her after a while, "That's enough now, Gabby. Don't think about Buster anymore."

Gabby had responded, "But I have to think about Buster, Mommy. Otherwise, how will he know how much I loved him?"

They were talking about Buster now. They had listed all of their favorite things about him and now they were talking about their least favorite things about the shaggy little puppy. Suddenly, Gabby screamed and started wailing, calling for Laney's help. Laney jumped up to find Gabby in the cucumber patch. She had gotten pricked by one of the thorny bits on the cucumber skin. Laney told her to hold still so she could remove the sliver. Gabby was afraid to let Laney near her hand in fear she would make it hurt even more.

"Trust me, Gabby," Laney had said, "Turn your head the other way so you don't have to look. There! Look! It's out already!" Laney had started tickling Gabby and soon she was howling with laughter and begging Laney to stop. They collapsed on their backs in the shade of the tomato plants. Gabby was running her thumb

over the spot where Laney had removed the thorn. "Mommy, I don't want you to die like Buster." When Laney had assured her that she wasn't going to die, Gabby had persisted. "But how do you know?"

Laney gazed up at the brilliant blue sky with majestic clouds looking to be permanently fixed in it and wondered how to reassure her little girl without lying. Unable to come up with a way, she used the universal reason parents had used for centuries all over the world and said simply, "Because I just know. So you don't have to worry about that, alright? Now," she pointed to one of the clouds, "I think that cloud looks just like an elephant. See how that part could be the trunk?"

They had lain there pointing out objects in the sky until Laney heard something over the monitor. At the same time, Gabby had jumped up and said, "Oh, listen, Mommy," She had cocked her head so enchantingly with her eyebrows raised expectantly; "Can't you hear them? My Barbie's are just waking up, too!"

Laney gathered up the vegetables while Gabby retrieved her shoebox. "Hold on a second, Gabby," Laney had said and she'd run into the house to retrieve her camera. "Be right there, Michael," Laney had shouted toward Michael's bedroom door which, of course, only made him cry even harder in frustration. She raced back outside and posed Gabby in front of her voluminous cosmos flowers in all different shades of pink and purple. The sun was shining so beautifully, it lit up the flowers and Gabby's smiling face ethereally.

"Come on, Mommy, you get in the picture, too," Gabby had said, and Laney had laughed at how savvy kids were these days about cameras. Laney sat on the ground with Gabby on her lap as she held out the camera and snapped their picture. Gabby immediately took the camera to see how the photo had turned out. Her little eyebrows furrowed in concentration. The photo obviously met with her approval as she said, "Look, Mommy! We're both smiling!"

"That's because we're so happy!" Laney had said as she hugged her. Laney felt the weight of Gabby on her chest as she slowly awoke from her dream. The pressure was so great, she was afraid that her heart wouldn't be able to take it. Holding nothing in her arms but her pillow, she lay in bed and looked up at the ceiling, not knowing how she would find the strength to get out of bed and face another day.

Chapter 23

Hitting the snooze button for the third time, Marge turned onto her side and promised herself that she would get up in five more minutes. She had stayed up half the night reading again so she wasn't surprised at all that she was having such a hard time waking up this morning. She was reading *Cutting for Stone* by Abraham Verghese and, despite its heavily detailed medical leanings, she couldn't put it down. She could practically hear the soft Indian accent of Marion, the half-British, half-Indian doctor raised in Ethiopia, the narrator. The way the story pulled her right in, and oh, the tragedy of poor Thomas Stone's life; it was truly heart-wrenching. It was fantastic that books could enrich one's life so much. Without leaving her bedroom, Marge truly felt as though she had just been on a journey half way around the world to Africa and that she now knew more about performing surgery and practicing hospitals than she ever thought she would. As she did whenever she encountered a book that made her life more enhanced and interesting, Marge vowed that she would write to the author to let him know it. 'You made me cry', she always wanted to tell them, 'you created emotions inside of me so powerful that they could no longer be contained and they seeped out of my eyes as sensational droplets of feeling'. She had wept somewhere around three a.m. when Ghosh died. Her eyes filled with tears even now as she remembered again the cancer that claimed his life. Then she thought about Charles' death by cancer, too. The sun was just beginning to highlight the deep crimson and burnt orange of the tree outside her window as Marge recognized the therapeutic value of reading. It gave her a chance to cry over the death of a character and throw in some tears from her own loss, too.

Her alarm buzzed again, five minutes having passed, and this time Marge sat up and reached over to shut it off for good. She felt a little guilty as she set her simple, less than ten dollar alarm clock that she'd bought from Just Screw It down in front of the complicated, probably more than one hundred dollar iPod speaker system her son Zach had given her for Christmas. He had even thoughtfully loaded the iPod with some of her favorite music, telling her that she could wake up to Vivaldi's Spring Movement every morning if she wanted to. Too convoluted, she thought as she swung her legs over the side of the mattress; perhaps if it just had some buttons she could push she wouldn't be so hesitant about it. She found something unsettling about these modern gadgets that just went dark and put themselves to sleep when not being used. She wanted to be able to turn things on or off at will.

Marge was about to step into the shower when she remembered that she had no water. She had developed a leak somewhere between her kitchen sink and the dishwasher on the other end of the counter so she had shut off the water. Her maple floor was already beginning to buckle a little over where the water was pooling. She got dressed in a soft grey cashmere sweater over a dark grey skirt and back-combed her hair a little to freshen it up, as she was unable to shower. Today was testing for hearing day at school and Marge volunteered every year to help out at the elementary school. She was just about to pour her coffee when there was a soft tapping sound at the back door.

Juan Carlos held up a small white bag, "I'll trade you a donut from Donna's for a cup of coffee from Marge's. I stopped at Just Screw It and picked up the part you need for the leak under your sink. I thought I'd get here early enough to fix it before you had to leave." Marge smiled when she saw her favorite donut, a cake donut with maple frosting, touched that Juan Carlos remembered that from the last time they had had donuts together. Such a simple matter, perhaps, but more flattering to Marge than if he had brought her a ten thousand dollar diamond ring. Knowing someone's favorite donut, or ice cream, or musician said, 'you're important to me. I remember what you say'.

It was a tight fit wedging himself underneath the kitchen sink to get at the leaking pipe. Juan Carlos stood up again to remove his tool belt as well as his bulging wallet, then he shimmied back underneath the cupboard again. Marge poured a second cup of coffee and chatted with Juan Carlos while he worked, keeping an eye on the clock so she wouldn't be late for the hearing tests. She asked about his granddaughter and how she was coping without her caregiver, Tia Juanita. Izzy missed her a lot and apparently was not happy at all to be going to the neighbors for daycare until Juan Carlos could work out something better. The neighbor had three little ones of her own to care for and seemed to take care of a couple of other babies as well. The normally cheerful Isabella now cried every morning when he dropped her off there. Marge clucked in sympathy as she spoke about the resilience of children when the phone rang. Marge answered and spoke briefly before hanging up. For the second time that morning, her eyes filled with tears.

"Oh god, Juan Carlos, we have to go quickly." Her voice sounded so anguished that Juan Carlos sat up without thinking and banged his head on the s-shaped pipe. He rubbed his head while he asked what was wrong.

"It's Walter. It seems he's fallen out of the tree," she said hollowly.

Stunned, they decided they had to go to the site to see if there was anything they could do to help. Juan Carlos had left his truck parked out by the curb. He was thinking about the state of the interior of his vehicle and whether or not it was as cluttered as usual, or if he had recently made a half-hearted sweep to empty it of pop cans, fast-food bags and what have you, when Marge said, "Let's take my car. You drive."

It was such a simple statement. But it was to have such far-reaching consequences.

Juan Carlos backed the Toyota out of the garage and drove to the proposed Wal-Mart site. Marge's heart was racing as she thought with horror about the implications of Walter falling out of the tree. She couldn't even imagine it. Her stomach felt sick as she glanced over at Juan Carlos. She appreciated his silence; there was certainly nothing to say, at this point, and she was grateful for the respectful quiet. Juan Carlos put on his blinker and turned left onto the highway. Immediately, he noticed a flashing red light in his rearview mirror. He eased his foot off of the gas and began to pull over onto the shoulder. Marge started to ask what he was doing when she noticed the reflection of the red lights in her own side mirror. "Well, you certainly weren't speeding, so we don't have to worry about that," she said to calm him.

"Driver's license and proof of insurance, please."

Marge's hands were shaking as she reached into the glove compartment to find the car's insurance papers. She leaned across Juan Carlos to hand the officer her papers, saying, "Officer, we've heard about an accident our friend was in. Can we please just be on our way?"

Brandon Hopkins hackles went up right away. What was with this town, anyway? He didn't get any respect no matter which way he turned. He was still feeling so pissed off at his failure at the sugar beet factory and was vigilantly stalking the third of the population in town that were of Hispanic origin. Seeing Juan Carlos driving such a nice car had definitely caught his eye. He leaned down to see Marge in the passenger seat.

"Not so fast. You're missing a tail light," He scrutinized the insurance papers then repeated to Juan Carlos, "Driver's license."

Juan Carlos had checked his back pockets twice trying to stay calm as he tried to figure out why his wallet wasn't there. After Brandon repeated his request, Juan Carlos suddenly remembered that he'd removed his wallet to climb under the kitchen sink at Marge's. He was saying, "Officer, I can explain…."

Brandon's eyes gleamed with pleasure as he gruffly commanded Juan Carlos to step out of the car.

"This is an emergency," Juan Carlos explained, as he stepped out of the car, "In my hurry, I left my wallet on the kitchen counter. I know right where it is. We can go immediately to get it."

"Hands on the car, now!" Brandon yelled as he turned Juan Carlos around and began frisking him unnecessarily roughly. Then he barked at Marge to get back in the car when she tried to get out to explain the situation. When Brandon ignored her, she started to threaten him.

"You have no right!" Marge was yelling through the window as Brandon began handcuffing Juan Carlos.

"No, *he* has no rights," Brandon said, "As an illegal alien he has no rights in this country and will soon be on his way back over the border. Say 'bye-bye' now," Brandon said rudely as he walked Juan Carlos over to the back of his car.

Marge could hear Juan Carlos saying in a remarkably calm and reasonable voice, "I am an American citizen. I have a driver's license, a social security number. You have no right to arrest me."

"Well, muchacho, you don't have any papers on you so I'm afraid you don't have any rights as far as I'm concerned. It's illegal to drive without your driver's license with you in this country; did you know that, smart guy?" Brandon shoved him into the back seat. Marge watched in shock as the car did a U-turn on the highway and drove away.

She sat there for a moment in disbelief. What had just happened? It was all her fault. She knew as soon as she presented Juan Carlos' billfold with his driver's license down at the station, he'd be released. She could picture it in her kitchen sitting right on the countertop next to his tool belt. But, what about Walter? She just had to go see if he was alright. Hoping that Juan Carlos would understand and would know that she would be on her way just after checking on Walter, she stepped out of the car to walk around to the driver's side.

Marge drove cautiously the rest of the way, remembering belatedly that she was supposed to be at the school right now testing the children's hearing. Picturing that scene in her mind felt so inviting and secure. She would be sitting in the library helping the students place the headphones on their heads which they would be laughing at; they were used to their little ear buds these days. She would instruct them to raise their left hand every time they heard a beep. They would be so sweet and trusting, most of them. Even the ones who she could tell raised their hands whether or not they heard, mostly because their timing was off, still melted her heart as they tried to avoid the stigma of being different, of having a weakness. She wished she were there right now instead of here, she thought to herself as pulled up next to Marty Bleak's hearse.

Marty was about to pull away but when he saw Marge, he got out and gave her a big hug in sympathy, saying, "The Methodists found him when they turned up with his breakfast pizza. I don't think he missed much today as far as breakfast goes but don't repeat that."

"Is Walter gone?" Marge covered her cheeks with her hands like a child surprised. She should have known he wouldn't be able to survive a fall from that height but she had not thought of Walter possibly being gone. She couldn't bring herself to say 'dead'. She gestured to the hearse. "Is he in there?"

"I'm afraid so. The ambulance got here the same time as I did, but he'd been dead for a couple of hours already so there didn't seem to be any point in their taking him, did there? The police and firemen were here, too. They scoped out the area and even used their ladder to climb up to the tree house, but there's no sign of foul play at all. It looks pretty straight forward; seems he just fell out of the tree."

"Poor Walter, I can hardly believe it."

"He died immediately from the impact, you know. There was just the tiniest dribble of blood under his mouth so we know his heart stopped beating instantly after his neck broke when he landed. There's consolation in that, knowing Walter didn't suffer," Marty's voice choked up on the last words and Marge saw that, for all of his familiarity with death, he was greatly moved by his friend's tragic ending. She hugged him again as they both wept quietly. There were no words necessary as the initial recognition of grief settled upon them. Walter's life was now complete. The final mystery of how his life would end, when and where he would die was no longer unknown. Memories of Walter would now be forever linked with the fact that he died an unusual death. Falling out of a tree while protesting against Wal-Mart's opening in Opossum Falls was part of Walter's legacy now. In such a way, he would always be remembered.

Marge thought about his now parentless children. She felt badly for them knowing that the normalcy of this day was about to change for them. Were they experiencing any sense of unease, she wondered. If they were in tune with life on any other level, did they feel Walter's spirit leaving this world? Perhaps the shudder of recognition passed through them but they pushed it aside to concentrate instead on merging with the traffic or making sure the kids remembered their lunches. Later, when they learned of their father's passing, would they think, 'I knew. I felt him pass through me as he left this world.' Now, final last words between them would be remembered, their last Christmas, his ultimate birthday.

Marge thought of the last breakfast she had shared here with Walter chatting over cell phones while she sat beneath him under the tree. She was glad she had that last experience with Walter, just two friends enjoying the start of a new day together. It would turn out to be one of Walter's last, but she was glad she didn't know that then.

Marty sighed heavily and said, "Well, I guess I'll give Walter one last ride through town on my way home. He wants to be cremated, you know, so I'll drive past his house now, the hardware store, the Chit Chat, and the rest of his old haunts before putting him on ice till his kids get here and have the chance to say good-bye."

"You're a good friend, Marty. We're lucky to have such a good soul taking care of our physical remains once our spirits have left our bodies behind. Thank you."

When Marty's hearse pulled away, Marge was tempted to walk over to the group of neighbors and friends milling around talking softly amongst themselves. She would have liked to have heard what they knew and to talk about the funeral luncheon. She was worried about Juan Carlos however, so she gave a little wave while shaking her head sadly, and she got back in her car to drive straight to the police station.

Dusty was glad to see her. He told her they were just about to call Walter's family and wondered if she thought it would be easier if the news came from her. Marge felt her stomach drop and she would have loved to have said no, that the police could call the family themselves. Then she thought of her own children and if the situation were reversed. Of course Walter's children would rather hear the news from her, their neighbor whom they'd grown up with, a friend to the family. She sat down at the desk and agreed to call them. But first, could she explain about Juan Carlos?

"Who's Juan Carlos?" Dusty asked.

Marge's heart skipped a beat as she explained the situation but Dusty just shook his head and said that no one had brought a Hispanic in to the station, legal or not. Dusty speculated that it wasn't a cop who had pulled them over but rather an ICE agent, most likely the infamous Brandon Hopkins. "If that's the case, Mrs. Peterson, then I'm afraid I have some more bad news. If Hopkins didn't bring your friend here, then that means he took him straight to ICE headquarters in Willmar. ICE operates under a different set of rules you know. Since 9/11, they can hold folks for up to five days without arresting them. Or ship them back to their country of origin if they're not citizens. But all of that is outside of our jurisdiction and I'm afraid I can't help you."

Marge felt her stomach clench again. Oh dear, Juan Carlos, she thought miserably, what have I gotten you into?

Taking a deep breath, she picked up the phone to call Walter's children.

The phone started ringing but Laney had no intention of getting up to answer it. She was sitting in the rocking chair in Michael's room, a feverish baby in her arms who had finally fallen asleep out of sheer exhaustion. She was not about to risk waking him again to answer the phone. She knew it was probably Scott calling from Las Vegas where he was attending a bachelor party with one of their college friends. He was being sweet to check in. She'd call him back once she laid Michael down in his crib, if she ever got the chance.

Michael had displayed none of his usual contented nature all day. He had woken up with his nose all stuffed up and had seemed crabby about it all day. Not even Gabby could get him to laugh even though she tried all of her usual tricks. She got the littlest hint of a smile out of him when she got out Mr. Potato Head and stuck the ear where the nose should be, the mouth where the eye should be, and the eyes where the ears should be. Other than that, he was grouchy all day. It wasn't until evening, however, that he started coughing and Laney noticed he'd developed a temperature. Why did it always seem to be over the week-end or during the evening when the kids got sick? She debated taking him to the emergency room but she knew what that was like at Fairview. She was afraid she would expose the kids to much worse by being there, so instead she gave Michael some liquid Tylenol for infants and hoped that would help him sleep through the night. She had put him down twice already, but his stuffed nose and dry coughing had woken him up shortly afterward. She had rubbed Vicks on his chest and cranked up the humidifier in his room. Now she was rocking him again and felt relieved when he'd drifted off to an uneasy sleep.

Gabby was sound asleep in her own room, her doll Anna nestled in her arms. With Scott out of town, she'd promised Gabby a girls' night in; well, with Michael too, of course. They'd had pizza and popcorn in front of the TV watching the Little Mermaid. Afterward, Gabby had asked if they could watch a Gabby movie. She loved watching home videos of herself growing up. They put on the one of Gabby's second birthday when she'd gotten Buster as a birthday present. In the video, Gabby was in bed when they brought her the traditional birthday breakfast in bed accompanied by a big box wrapped in brightly colored wrapping paper with a huge powder-blue bow on top. Scott was carrying the box carefully as he set it down in front of Gabby on the bed. Lifting off the lid of the box, Gabby laughed delightedly when the little six-week old cocker spaniel poked his head eagerly out of the box he had just been put in moments before out in the hallway outside of Gabby's bedroom.

"Mommy, can I get another puppy? I don't think Buster would mind. I think he wants me to get a puppy, don't you Mommy?"

Gabby had been sitting next to Laney who was holding Michael and she looked up at her with her big blue eyes with long blond lashes framing them. Her soft, blond curls lay this way and that on her head, and her long, flannel nightgown with big, soft pink flowers splashed across it made her look adorable. Laney put her arm around her and kissed the top of her head. "I think we should get another puppy, too. We'll talk to Daddy about it when he gets home, alright? Now, go choose a book so I can read to you before it gets too late."

Gabby sat on the floor in front of her bookshelf and ran through every single book on her shelf, saying, 'nope' to every book she passed. Finally, she brought two of them over and said that Michael had to choose. Michael was sound asleep at this point, but Gabby still held the books in front of him pretending that he was involved in the decision. She set down Are You My Mommy? *and held up* I Wish I Were a Butterfly, *saying, "Michael chose this one!"*

"Michael is so lucky to have you for his big sister!" Laney said, smiling at how sweetly Gabby included Michael in everything they did. She knew it wouldn't last forever and someday the siblings probably wouldn't believe the stories when Laney told them how well they had gotten along as children, but for now, she enjoyed every loving moment. After reading the sweet story, she turned to the last page and Gabby recited the last line by heart, which is a picture of a cricket playing beautiful violin music, "I wish I were a cricket! Mommy, can I play the violin soon?"

Gabby had just started taking violin lessons, but so far she was only allowed to practice on a box with a wooden stick for a bow. Laney reminded her that her teacher, Jacqueline, said she had to get perfect position with the box first and then she could use her violin. It was called a 1/16th size violin and was the cutest little instrument Laney had ever seen. She put Michael down at last and tucked Gabby in, too. "Sweet dreams, sweetheart. I love you!"

"I love you more!" They repeated this phrase as they did every night until Laney walked out the door.

Laney pressed speed dial number two to call Scott. His voice sounded slightly slurred; she could tell he'd been drinking. It was a bachelor party after all, so she wasn't the least surprised by this. She told him about her day and he did the same. She said she was probably in for a long night as Michael was all stuffed up. He sounded genuinely sad for her and said he wished he were home so he could help take care of Michael, too. Laney knew that he meant it. Scott was a great dad;

he loved being a parent just as much as Laney did. She got off the phone by telling him not to worry and that he should enjoy himself while he was there, in moderation, of course. She was looking forward to having him home tomorrow. She was planning to spend the evening in the bathtub surrounded by bubbles, sipping red wine and reading a good book while Scott was on parenting duty alone.

She sat for a moment with her phone in her hand after hearing her husband tell her that he loved her. Laney's heart felt so full at that moment. She was living a dream. She had a beautiful home, two perfect children, and a wonderful man to share her life with. Laney felt a shadow of fear skitter across her chest and she thought for a moment that she was about to jinx it. Everything was so perfect, but how could it possibly last?

Just then, she heard Michael crying from his bedroom again. Okay, she said to herself as she pushed herself up to see to her baby, maybe perfect isn't the right word. But I would say that I'm living life to the fullest. She lifted Michael out of his crib and sat with him in the rocking chair humming soothingly to him. She felt the weight of her baby on her chest as she slowly awoke from her dream. The pressure was so great; she thought her heart would break in two. Holding nothing in her arms but her pillow, she lay in bed and looked up at the ceiling, not knowing how she would find the strength to get out of bed and face another day.

Therese Dotray-Tulloch

Chapter 24

Cath and Laney just looked at each other without saying a word for a good, long minute after the door clicked closed. Their eyebrows were raised in wonderment until finally Cath slapped a hand over her mouth and whispered, "Oh my god, what just happened here?" She jumped from her chair, knocking it over behind her and she ran to the other side of the table and grabbed Laney's hands, pulling her out of her chair to dance with her around the tiny kitchen.

"Shhhhh, you'll wake the neighbors!"

"Laney, it's after nine in the morning. If the old biddies are still asleep, then we're doing them a favor. They need to wake up!" Cath twirled Laney around a couple more times laughing as she did so. They collapsed back into their chairs, Cath asking, "What just happened here? Laney, please, tell me I'm not misunderstanding this."

Laney and Cath were planning on going to Walter's funeral together. Cath was picking Laney up so she wouldn't have to carry the pan of bars she'd made for the funeral luncheon on the walk to the church. Cath had said she would come early to have coffee with Laney first.

When Laney heard the soft tapping on her door, she assumed it was Cath and had hollered from her bathroom to come on in, the door was open. She'd been surprised to see Shannon Fischer standing hesitantly inside of the door when she walked out. She obviously had something on her mind.

Shannon was playing hooky from school that morning. She was only missing two classes, because after that everyone was excused to attend Walter Fassbinder's funeral. This was an unusual decision for the school, but the administration felt it would seem unfair to deny the students the chance to attend Walter's funeral. Most of them had spent time with him while he was up in the tree with one class or another, and of course, he was known from the hardware store, too. Immediately after the funeral, the students were expected back in school or detention would be given.

Shannon told Laney she had just been accepted to Gustavus College in St. Peter. She was thrilled to have received a scholarship, too. Laney smiled at her enthusiasm and remembered her own excitement when she had gotten her Gustie acceptance letter. Just then, Laney's door flew open and Cath was saying "I couldn't resist. I picked up a couple of cappuccinos from the Last Chapter, not that your coffee isn't good, Laney, it's just that I can never resist a cappuccino. Oh, hello," she said when she noticed that Laney wasn't alone.

Laney introduced Cath to Shannon. As with most people who live in a small town, the two had obviously seen each other around. Shannon had most likely checked out Cath's items before at the grocery store, but still, it was polite to be sure they knew each other's names. Shannon looked apologetic and was about to leave when Laney asked her to stay, saying she had had enough caffeine that morning already and that Shannon should have her cappuccino so it wouldn't go to waste. When they sat in the kitchen around Laney's small table, they chatted about Walter and how much the town was going to miss him. He was such a character.

"But you know, underneath that salty persona, he really had a heart of gold," Cath said, chin in her hand, "When I was in Just Screw It once, just after one of my miscarriages, a woman checking out in front of me had a little baby with her who wouldn't stop crying. She'd rolled her eyes at me and said in a whiny voice, 'I should sit in front of the high school with him; that would scare the kids into using birth control.' When she left, Walter had said something like, 'Some people don't deserve to have kids.' and I burst into tears. He was so kind to me. He turned the Open sign above the door around to Closed, sat me down in the back room, and, after hearing my sad tale, poured us each a shot of some awful-tasting blackberry brandy that he kept behind the counter for just such occasions." There was an awkward silence for a moment.

Shannon suddenly burst out, "I'm pregnant, you know."

Whether Cath had known or not, she didn't let on. She most likely had as there was a lot of time to chat when she was highlighting someone's hair, and Cath knew most of the gossip in town. She just nodded her head and asked Shannon how she was feeling. Shannon said much better now that the first trimester was over. She asked Cath then whether she'd ever been pregnant, after the miscarriages, she clarified. When Cath told her about her stillborn child, they all three bowed their heads and a silence prevailed for a while. Cath thought about the horror of that day, Laney about the day she had given birth to Gabby, and Shannon said a prayer that her baby wouldn't be stillborn. She placed her hand over her stomach. Watching Shannon's protective movement, Cath smiled wistfully, "I had a lot of miscarriages after that. I don't seem to be able to carry children of my own." She brightened then and said, "But that's okay, because now we're looking to adopt. There is a baby out there with our name on it, we just have to find him….or her."

The tiny kitchen was suspended in time for a moment and it felt as though there was no air in the room at all. A hush filled the room. Laney felt tingles as she saw Shannon and Cath looking at one another as the significance of their situations and their meeting at this time dawned on them both. No one spoke. Shannon slowly removed her hand from her stomach and reached over to take Cath's hand. She drew it carefully to her and placed it on her stomach. Cath's eyes filled with tears, and as if she'd been holding her breath, she gasped then and pulled her hand away from Shannon's baby as if she'd been scalded. "Shannon, don't do this to me. You have no idea."

Seeming far older than her years, Shannon had nodded and told Cath that she knew exactly what she was doing. She explained to Cath that she had been so torn between giving her baby up for adoption and keeping it. She had just decided that morning that she was going to go to Gustavus Adolphus College and to do that she needed to give her baby up for adoption. She had wanted to talk to Laney about it first because Laney had been such a good friend to her throughout her pregnancy. "And, here we are," she concluded.

"Shannon, do you believe in destiny?" Cath asked, finally. When she'd nodded solemnly, Cath had reached back over and placed her hand gently on Shannon's swollen belly, her eyes filling with tears. After a while, Shannon had said that she wanted to tell her parents about it first and that she would be in touch. She had left Laney and Cath to hop around like a couple of two year olds crying very grown up tears of joy.

~~~~~~~~~~~~~~~~~~~~~~~~~~~~~~~~~

Checking to be sure *Grabow* was clearly marked on both the pan and the lid, Emma used the hot pad holders and was about to carry her chicken a la king out to the car. The hot dish was heavy in her arms and she felt an ache in her lower back. She was not looking forward to this. She would much rather sit at home with another cup of coffee and go online to check on the results of her Identigene test. Today was the first day the results would be available to her. Her stomach twisted in knots as she thought about it. Soon, she would know if Pete Oetzmann's DNA matched her own.

At a time like this, it would have been nice to have a son to take her to Walter's funeral. She just knew she was going to be treated like the town pariah. She had been sorely tempted to sit the funeral out and pay her respects to Walter privately. But Emma Grabow had never been one to shy away from adversity. She just wished she didn't have to go to the funeral alone.

The truth of the matter was that Walter had already succeeded. The day Emma had stopped to talk to Walter, up in that lovely, old oak tree, Emma had had a change of heart. That old fool had gotten her to thinking and she had decided he was right. Emma had been losing interest in sealing the deal with Wal-Mart, anyway. She hadn't liked the way they were handling the negotiations. It always had to be their way or the highway. The way that the town had come together to protest the retail giant, all those little David's against Goliath had tickled Emma pink. Emma sympathized with the little guy much more than with the big one. She had been trying to find a way to bow out of the deal gracefully without losing face. Seeing Walter up in the tree had given her just the excuse she needed. She loved the idea of saving the life of the majestic old oak tree. Emma placed her thumb and finger over her eyelids and pressed down as if to stop them from shedding the tears she had felt building up. It was all her fault that Walter was dead. Her excuse was that she had been distracted with the idea of her son coming back into her life, but truth be told, there was no excuse. She had procrastinated too long in making the announcement that the Wal-Mart deal was off and that Walter's tree was safe. Now Walter was gone because of it. Emma wondered exactly how she was going to sit through the funeral alone, much less attend the luncheon, all the while feeling the daggers of everyone's eyes upon her; her, the cause of Walter's death. She said a silent prayer for strength. Emma wasn't particularly religious. She probably most closely emulated the Japanese religion in that she spoke most of her prayers to Otto, like now, asking Otto to keep her strong through the difficult day ahead of her.

There was rapid-fire knocking on her door interrupting Emma's musing, and she hastened to answer, setting her hot dish down. Manuel stood next to Alonso holding a cat. Emma frowned at the cat scrutinizing it carefully before saying, "Come on in, Jingle Bells." Noticing how nicely dressed the boys were and realizing that it was a school day, she asked, "What are you two doing out of school?"

"Tia Bianca said we could skip school to go to the funeral with you today. She said if you wanted us to, that is."

Manuel spoke from behind his older brother, "And she said we'd be in the casa de los perros if we say even one word during the funeral, right 'Lonso?"

Emma felt tears behind her eyelids again but this time, she let them fall. They were tears of gratitude; somehow, those tears felt good dampening her cheeks. She told the boys to put their bikes round the back before getting into the car and she picked up her hot dish again.

Everything felt much lighter to Emma now.

~~~~~~~~~~~~~~~~~~~~~~~~~~~~~~~

If a stranger had driven through town on the day of Walter's funeral, he would have thought Opossum Falls a dismal place indeed, and might have felt bereft for the death of small town America. Every shop was closed that morning, including the Chamber of Commerce, the bakery, the café, and the bookstore. If an accountant were needed, none would be found, nor a lawyer, optometrist, dentist, or plumber. Even the school appeared to be empty with no children playing on the playground.

Rather than bemoaning the death of this small town, however, the stranger should have been saluting it for remaining stalwart in these changing times when we are often viewed as a nation that doesn't even know its own neighbors. They were all neighbors in Opossum Falls, and they were all gathered together to honor one of their own.

The German Lutheran church was packed for Walter's funeral. Pastor Fischer had told the altar boys to bring up all of the folding chairs from the basement and these were lined up in the side aisles. The balcony had quickly filled up, too, with the choir rather reluctantly, and with great sighs, moving their music stands over to one side of the choir loft so the congregation had enough seats. Little white cloths were draped over the first three pews on both sides of the aisles to reserve them for Walter's family on one side and the Honor Guard on the other. The smell of coffee brewing in the giant urns in the kitchen wafted up through the air ducts reminding everyone of the luncheon to follow; a few of those attending found their minds wandering to the wonderful variety of hot dishes soon to be chosen from. There were swallows heard around the church as mouths unintentionally began to water.

The Honor Guard, in all their feathered finery, walked solemnly down the center aisle and stood at attention. Soon, soft sniffles could be heard as Walter's children, bearing the urn containing Walter's remains, began their slow, somber walk between the Honor Guard to the front of the church. The grandchildren following were not able to hold back their tears and one little granddaughter, struggling mightily to hold in her sobs, cried plaintively the entire way down the aisle. This unleashed a torrent of tears throughout the church, and rustling sounds were heard as women dug in the purses for their tiny packages of tissue, kindly sharing them with any woman within arm's reach. It was a relief when Pastor Fisher finally walked down the aisle and the choir started to sing 'God, Our Help in Ages Past'. Most of the congregation was too choked up to join in, so the choir was on its own.

Pastor Fischer looked out on the crowded church as the Honor Guard filed into their seats. He saw his daughter Shannon sitting with the other seniors in her class, and she smiled sadly up at him. His voice was rich and deep as he recited Psalm 23, "Even though I walk through the valley of the shadow of death, I will fear no evil, for you are with me; your rod and your staff, they comfort me. Surely goodness and love will follow me all the days of my life, and I will dwell in the house of the Lord forever."

As funeral services go, Walter's was a good send off, for sure. A couple of his grandchildren had just finished playing a beautiful Amazing Grace duet on their violins. Once again, the tissues were in demand. One of Walter's daughters stood at the lectern and gave a touching eulogy that included a brief outline of his life, sharing a few sweet stories of living with Walter as Dad, commenting on the abiding love her parents shared all throughout their marriage, and even mentioning the Blackberry Brandy he always kept on hand for special occasions causing Cath to nudge Laney with her elbow. She ended by repeating Walter's oft-quoted phrase that he might not have been a rich man monetarily, but he surely was a rich man in all of the ways that counted.

After she took her seat, many were surprised when Marty Bleak took her place. "I'm Marty Bleak, and I'm honored to be here today as funeral director and, more importantly, Walter Fassbinder's friend. When he and Berniece were making their funeral arrangements a few years back, he made me promise to share this story with you today.

One day, I got a call at the funeral home from a gentleman who told me his wife had died and could I come collect the body. I assured him I could and asked for his address. He told me Eucalyptus Street and when I asked him to spell it, he paused for a moment and then said gruffly, 'Oh hell, I'll drag her over to Elm, and

There was a silence throughout the congregation that Pastor Fischer found he was a little envious of; he could never get the church this quiet. The high school kids looked at one another with mouths agape, the honor guard, who had sat through more than their share of eulogies that, truth be told, had all begun to sound exactly alike, struggled to control their facial expressions, and one of the altar boys clapped his hand over his mouth to hide his grin. Suddenly, one of Walter's daughters guffawed loudly. A moment later, the rest of the church joined in, and soon the tissues were used to wipe away the tears of laughter. Marty walked down from the altar, tipped an imaginary hat to the large brass urn containing Walter's remains, and went back to his usual funeral director's position in the back of the church. The organist started the familiar chords to 'How Great Thou Art', and the entire congregation joined in, singing wholeheartedly, as Walter's family escorted him from the church.

Marty had one more surprise up his sleeve, but this one he came up with on his own. Had Walter known the oak tree was where his life would end, Marty felt sure he would have suggested this addendum to his funeral, too. The funeral procession left the church, headlights blazing. It was a chilly, overcast day, so the headlights shone out like beacons on an otherwise dull day. On the way to Oak Ridge Cemetery west of town, Marty drove the hearse with dozens of cars following past the site of Walter's death. The deep crimson leaves on the magnificent old oak tree lit up as though on fire as the headlights shone upon them. Emma, driving in the procession with Alonso and Manuel, was so glad she had made them remove the 'for sale' sign as well as the 'future site of Wal-Mart' sign. Perhaps his family would take comfort in that and see that Walter hadn't died in vain.

At Oak Ridge Cemetery, taps was played by one of the high school girls, and the rifle party consisting of five Honor Guard paid tribute to Walter with a three volley salute during which the grandkids covered their ears. Pastor Fischer said a few final words as the urn was lowered into the ground, ending with how fitting it was that Walter's remains were to be kept at Oak Ridge as fighting for the life of an oak tree was how he had died.

Back in the church basement, a handful of Lutheran ladies had stayed behind to prepare for the luncheon. They worked with the precision of a well-tuned assembly line as they put together the smorgasbord of donated dishes. Plates, silverware, and napkins were at the start of the banquet table immediately inside the door closest to the stairway from the parking lot. Cold dishes came first: lettuce and seven-layered salads, coleslaw, cold cuts, raw veggies, and a colorful selection of jell-o salads from lime green to cherry red and all colors of the rainbow in between. Next came the casserole dishes of tuna and hamburger hot dish, chicken a la king, lasagna, cheesy potatoes and the crock pots filled with meatballs, chicken wings, mini wieners and shrimp wrapped in bacon. They cut up the pans and pans of desserts and put together massive trays of a variety of brownies, seven-layer, rice crispy, mint, peanut, and special k bars as well as yellow cakes with chocolate frosting and German-chocolate cakes with coconut frosting, all cut into one-inch pieces so no one felt guilty about sampling as many as three or four. The platters were distributed one to a table throughout the church basement. Thermoses of coffee were filled from the urns and these, too, were dispersed on the tables. The cups were left on a table of their own at the end of the buffet line so those wanting coffee could pick one up and dangle it from their pinky while they balanced their over laden plate full of food between two hands. Tepid water was available in small pitchers next to the coffee cup for the children.

The mourners arrived and quickly formed two lines, one on either side of the buffet table so that in no time at all it seemed everyone had their plate. The church basement ladies removed empty serving dishes and put out new ones as the lines went through, excusing themselves to slide in and out of the mourners at the table some of whom, it couldn't be denied, behaved like pigs at a trough. The women recognized each other's serving dishes and sometimes, as in Claudia Mueller's case because she always brought the same thing to every funeral, deviled eggs, the contents as well. They took pride when their dish was emptied faster than others on the table and they chose carefully whose to sample so they could tell one another later how delicious their dish had been. Pastor Fischer had slipped in through the side door and was allowed to butt in line so he could offer up a prayer of thanks to God. He had his prayer memorized now to avoid the debacle of the Zimmermann funeral when he had thanked Wolfgang for his death so they could all enjoy such a delicious banquet.

Marge stood at the sink washing the Pyrex dishes and crock pots that were already empty. They would be placed on a table by the exit so the women could just pick them up on their way out. Laney came and stood by her, telling Marge that her shift was up and she should get in line and join the other ladies to eat. Cath had suggested to Laney that it was time for the younger generation of women to step up and start helping out, too. Laney had agreed and stayed to help in the kitchen.

"I'd rather just keep busy, Laney. If I stop working, I'll start thinking about how sad and worried I am. Here," Marge handed her a dish towel, "you dry the dishes and carry them out to the dining room and save me the trip. We can visit while we work."

Laney got busy drying the dishes. "I still can't believe Walter's gone. You've known him for such a long time; I can only imagine how sad you are. But what are you worried about? Unless it's none of my business…"

"No, it's alright. I'm worried about a friend of mine. The strangest thing happened. Actually, you know who it is, Laney. Remember Juan Carlos?"

"Of course, he's the grandpa to that sweet little girl whose nanny got arrested."

"Arrested and sent back to Mexico. She wasn't a citizen here. Well, it seems as if the same thing has happened to Juan Carlos." Marge explained what had happened on the morning of Walter's death, how Juan Carlos was stopped without his billfold, and how he had since fallen off the face of the earth as far as Marge was concerned. She was sick with worry because she knew he would never abandon his granddaughter willingly. She had contacted ICE and every law enforcement agency she could think of but she had hit a brick wall. Juan Carlos had disappeared.

Laney carefully dried the porcelain dish with the hand-painted rooster on the bottom. "Do you still have his billfold? Maybe there would be some sort of a clue in there."

"I didn't even think of that," Marge dried off her hands on her apron. "Let's take a look. I have it right here in my purse." They went over to the shelf where all of the women in the kitchen stuffed their purses.

Marge extricated her deep purple leather handbag from the pile and pulled out Juan Carlos' wallet. "I feel guilty looking through it like this," Marge was saying when her cell phone vibrated in her purse. She handed Laney the wallet and dug out her phone. "Oh dear, seven missed calls. I forgot I had turned it down during church." She took the call and grabbed on to Laney's arm as she repeated, "Oh dear, oh no. I'll be right over."

"What is it?"

"That was the daycare lady who was taking care of Isabella Rose. What an unpleasant woman, let me tell you. I already told her that I would pay her for all of this overtime until Juan Carlos turns up. I even offered to take the little girl myself as soon as the funeral was over. She keeps threatening to turn Izzy over to child services. Now she said she can't find her. Juan Carlos had told me how unhappy Izzy was there, so I'm hoping she may just be hiding or something, I don't know. I'm going over there to see."

Just then, Laney noticed a tall, young man with laugh lines on either side of kind-looking eyes come into the kitchen. Walter's son came up to Marge and said, "There you are, Mrs. Peterson. My sisters and I were hoping you'd come sit with us for a while before some of them have to head back to the cities. We won't be doing anything about the house right away, and we don't want to impose on you, but we're hoping you could keep an eye on things for us till we figure out what we're going to do with it. Do you have a minute?"

Marge hesitated for a moment till Laney put a hand on her arm. "Give me the daycare address and I'll go check. I mean, if it's walking distance. You stay and talk to Walter's family." She smiled over at him.

Marge knew Laney didn't have a car. "Do you drive?" When Laney nodded her head, Marge fished her keys out of her purse, gave her the daycare address and told her where she'd parked her Toyota. It wasn't until she was opening the car door that Laney realized that she still had Juan Carlos' wallet in her hand. She shoved it into her coat pocket and drove over to Hickory Street where the daycare lady lived.

There was a sleek, black vehicle parked in front of the extremely rundown, one and a half-storey house. It was in the oldest section of town and had been there when there had simply been a dirt track in front of it rather than the paved street. It had been white, but most of the paint had faded away to nothing so it now looked almost abandoned. Two of the green shutters were missing on one window which gave the appearance of the house winking. All of the shades were drawn and the cement on the bottom step was crumbling. Laney could hear the TV blaring as she walked up the sidewalk. A smell of rotting garbage got stronger as she got closer to the house, and she saw the likely culprits were a couple of black garbage bags leaning against the side of the house.

She was raising her hand to knock when the screen door swung open and a woman wearing a grey suit, listless brown hair falling to her shoulders, greeted her, "Mrs. Peterson, I'm Violet Knox with Child Protection Services. I'm here to remove," she glanced down at the paper she was holding, "Isabella Rose Ramirez into our protective custody. If you have any idea of her whereabouts, you must tell us immediately or risk being charged with withholding information."

Laney stepped up to the top step and entered the porch. She didn't like the advantage the portly woman had enjoyed looking down upon her. "I'm not Marge Peterson, I'm afraid. She couldn't come. I have no idea where the little girl is. I'm here as a friend of the family to see if there is anything I can do to help." She couldn't hide the annoyance from her voice but she didn't really care.

The woman looked Laney up and down and without apologizing, continued, "We understand that the girl's parents are dead and her grandfather is being held in jail. Daycare is not responsible for her well-being at this point, so we're stepping in. I'm here to take her to a foster family. If I can find her, that is."

The sound of a door slamming followed by shouts issued from inside the house, "Just wait until I find you. You're gonna regret this."

"Yeah, miserable Isabel," a squeaky boy's voice hollered just before the volume on the TV was turned up even louder.

"Thank you anyway," the government agent said, handing Laney her card. "If you do hear anything, please give me a call immediately." She went back inside the shoddy home.

Laney got back into Marge's car and sat with her hands on the steering wheel. No wonder the poor little girl was missing. She remembered how sweetly the woman called Tia Juanita had treated the little girl when they were in the grocery store and when she had had to say good-bye to her. What a nightmare to go from such a loving caregiver to this hellhole. As she slowly pulled away from the curb, she saw the Child Protection agent walk down the sidewalk and get into her car. Laney turned the opposite way from the highway driving slowly until she saw the black car turn toward the main road. Then Laney drove around the block and slowly drove through the alley behind the daycare house. She parked on the sidewalk and walked down the alley.

She could still hear the TV blaring and she hoped her suspicions were right. This daycare woman wasn't looking too hard for Isabella Rose; she was probably glad not to have to worry about her anymore. Laney approached the garbage bags. She was right. She did see a small tennis shoe protruding between the garbage bag and the house. She spoke quietly, telling a white lie in the hopes that the little girl would come with her. "Isabella Rose, it's me, Laney. Remember, we had a sundae together at the Chit Chat? I'm here to take you to Tia Juanita. She misses you so much. But shhh, you must be quiet, okay?"

Laney listened to the sounds of the TV inside of the house and waited. She looked around, feeling conspicuous talking to a bag of garbage and hoped none of the neighbors were looking out of their windows. She could only imagine how scared Isabella Rose was, however, so she waited. The smell seeping out of the garbage was awful; she didn't know how the girl could stand it. Finally, her foot moved a little, the garbage bag rustled and tipped over, and the dirty, tear-stained face of Isabella Rose peered up at her. She looked so miserable and slovenly, Laney could hardly believe she was the same little girl she had seen looking neat as a pin with her thick, wavy, black hair pulled into ponytails when she had been with Tia Juanita. Isabella Rose's tears rolled down her cheeks as she whispered, "Will you really take me to Tia Juanita?" and when Laney nodded her head, the little girl's face crumpled. Sensing the dam was about to break and Isabella Rose would soon be wailing, Laney whispered, "Come on." She grabbed the little girl's hand and they walked quickly and quietly back to the alley.

"Hey, it's Izzy! Ma, I found her! The little brat is out here," the boy's squeaky voice called from the back porch. Before Laney could even think about it, she scooped up the little girl and ran with her back to Marge's car, the boy's voice shouting from behind them as she hastily drove off.

Chapter 25

Laney kept right on driving past Marge Peterson's house when she saw the same sleek, black car that the Child Protection Service agent was driving now parked in Marge's driveway. She glanced back at Isabella Rose strapped into the back seat but knew that her head was too low for her to have been seen even if the woman had been looking out for them. She drove to her apartment, her mind racing as she tried to decide what to do. She parked the car in the parking lot alongside her apartment building and shut off the motor.

"Is this where Tia Juanita is?" The voice was so tiny, full of fear and doubt that Laney had to wonder what had happened to the poor little thing since she'd seen her last.

"No, this is where I live."

"But you said you'd take me to Tia Juanita. You pr-promised!" Isabella Rose's face scrunched up again as tears leaked out of her eyes.

"I know I did, honey, I just have to think a minute. I have to find out exactly how to get to Tia Juanita's, okay?"

"Where's abuelito? I want my grandpa!" She began to cry even harder.

The mention of Juan Carlos reminded Laney that she held his wallet in her pocket. Murmuring soothing words to Isabella Rose, she pulled out the wallet and opened it, apologizing in advance for invading his privacy but knowing Juan Carlos would want her to do whatever it took to keep his granddaughter safe. She rifled through it seeing his driver's license, a couple of credit cards, and a picture of Isabella Rose that was a couple of years old. She opened up the money section and saw a couple of twenties, some ones, and what looked like a deposit slip. Opening it, she saw it was a money order. Juan Carlos had wired money just a couple of days ago to a Juanita Monzalez in Piedras Negras, Mexico.

The sound of a car door slamming caused Laney to look up. Violet Knox was walking briskly up the sidewalk to Laney's apartment building. Laney froze with fear, willing the woman to keep moving and not to turn her head to look toward the parking lot. Just then, a squad car pulled up right behind the sleek, black car. Violet turned at the sound of the engine and waited on the sidewalk for the police officer to join her. Together they walked up to Laney's apartment building and went inside.

Isabella Rose was crying softly now, saying "I want Tia, I want abuelito," in a childish, singsong mantra. Laney knew they had come to take the little girl. She thought of all that Izzy had already been through and of what lay ahead for her. She would be put into the hands of strangers again. She could get lost in the foster care nightmare. ICE was known to hold people in custody for weeks without anyone ever knowing where they were. What if Juan Carlos had been deported and Isabella Rose remained separated from her family forever? She thought about her own little girl's tragedy which she could do nothing about, The Event that was never far from Laney's mind. Here was a little girl she could help. She turned the key in the ignition and put the car into gear.

Isabella Rose looked over at her, "Are we going to Tia Juanita now?"

"Yes, Izzy, that's exactly where we're going."

Isabella Rose wasn't an orphan and didn't deserve to be separated from the woman who had basically been like a mother to her these past four years. With Juan Carlos temporarily out of the picture, Laney saw no other recourse than to reunite Izzy with Tia Juanita, no matter what it took.

She plugged Piedras Negras into the GPS on her cell phone as she drove south on the highway and saw that it was just under fourteen hundred miles away. She took a deep breath and sighed, realizing for the first time that she was actually driving! She hadn't been able to drive since The Event. Every time she even thought about glancing into the rear view mirror, she felt sick to her stomach. Now she had been driving for a good half hour already and had checked out the rear view mirror numerous times thinking nothing of it. It must be true then, what they say about the passage of time. She blinked back tears as it occurred to her that she was beginning to move on. Why did she feel guilty about that?

Laney glanced over at Isabella Rose curled up into a little ball sound asleep in the back seat. She would drive as far as she could before stopping to fill up with gas and purchasing something to eat plus plenty of energy drinks to keep her going. She'd try to get through Kansas before stopping in Oklahoma at a roadside rest to snatch a few hours of sleep. Would the police be looking for her? She considered calling Marge to explain the situation to her, but she didn't want to put her into jeopardy by being affiliated with Laney's crazy scheme. She knew Marge well enough to know that she wouldn't worry about Laney having her car.

It was late afternoon the following day when Laney was making her way through Eagle Pass, Texas toward the International Bridge over the Rio Grande which would take her into Piedras Negras, Mexico. Her plan was to find the Western Union office where Juan Carlos had wired the money and hopefully be able to trace Tia Juanita down that way. She looked back at Isabella Rose and smiled at the way her little tongue poked out of the corner of her mouth as she concentrated on her coloring. It was purple from eating fruit roll-ups. They had bought snacks, crayons and coloring books at one of the stops along the way. The little girl was a good traveler and the trip had turned into an enjoyable adventure for both of them. The flash of red caught

Laney's eye in her rear view mirror and she swore under her breath. "Laney!" Isabella Rose exclaimed, "That's a bad word!"

"I know, honey, don't repeat it." She put her blinker on and slowly pulled over to the side of road, her heart racing. "Listen, we're being pulled over by the police. Izzy, don't say anything about where we're going, okay? We don't want him to stop us from getting to Tia Juanita's, okay? Just smile at the nice officer if he talks to you." Laney took a deep breath and tried to calm herself as she waited for the police officer to get out of his car.

After asking for her driver's license and insurance, the officer strolled back to the squad car to plug the information into his computer. The next thing Laney knew, she grabbed Izzy and ran. She supposed she should take some small amount of satisfaction from knowing that when the time came, she didn't hesitate. She bent down, looked straight into the chocolate-brown orbs that gazed back at her so trustingly, and hissed, "Let's go!"

Holding on tightly to the chubby little hand still sticky from unraveling fruit roll-ups, she grabbed her purse and ran straight into the marketplace. She couldn't do anything to cover her noticeably blond curls, but the little girl's shiny black hair fit right in with the hordes of humanity conducting business in the typically-busy outdoor market. By the time the police officer looked up from entering her driver's license information into his computer, she was long gone.

As the officer rushed into the crowd, glancing left and right while standing on tiptoe to see farther into the impenetrable crowd, he chided himself for allowing her pretty face to cause him to let down his guard. The shoppers closed in around him. Glancing down at the little, plastic driver's license he still held in his hand, he memorized her name. "Alright, Helena Elizabeth Anderson, let's see what you've got going on to cause you to run from an officer of the law like this," he said.

~~~~~~~~~~~~~~~~~~~~~~~~~~~~~~~~~~~~~

Marge frowned as she hung up the phone, saying to herself, "Oh dear, Laney, what have I gotten you into?" Marge felt as though every friend she had was somehow involved in trouble as soon as they came into contact with her; first Juan Carlos and now Laney.

The police officer on the other end of the line had called from Texas, the town of Eagle something. He said he had pulled the driver of her Toyota over because there was a taillight out, but when he'd asked for her driver's license, the woman had fled on foot taking her little girl with her. Discovering that the car was registered in Marge's name, he was calling to ask if her car had been stolen or if she could explain why the driver had fled. Marge imagined Laney had fled the officer to avoid being arrested for kidnapping a child. But what in the world was she doing in Texas?

Therese Dotray-Tulloch

Chapter 26

Her computer had just come to life when she heard the familiar knock on her back door which could only mean that it was the Gonzalez brothers. Emma was actually delighted to be delayed. This was the day she was finally going online to check on Pete's DNA. While she had initially been so eager for the results, now that the time had come, she didn't mind a bit putting them off a while longer. "I've been meaning to ask you," she said to the boys when she pulled open the door, "are you tapping 'La Cucaracha' when you knock on my door?"

"What?!" they answered in unison. Alonso carried on, "No, that's Miley! You know, Miley Cyrus, used to be Hannah Montana? It's her sexy song, 'Can't Be Tamed'," and the boys started dancing around, acting it out for her. When they finished, they apologized for being late for work but said they'd had to stop to watch the excitement on Main Street before biking out of town. When Emma asked what excitement, they told her the extraordinary news that Jeanine Westerly had been arrested. Emma scolded them and said that it was not right to tell lies, surely they were exaggerating. They assured her that, no, it wasn't an exaggeration if they saw Dusty walk out of the Chamber of Commerce with Jeanine Westerly beside him with her hands held behind her in handcuffs. The reporter from the Opossum Falls Digest was taking a picture so that was the proof that they weren't lying. It would even be in the newspaper! Emma turned on the local radio station and sure enough, the top news story was of Jeanine's arrest.

Jeanine had turned up at the hospital in Olivia the previous night with burns on both of her hands. Her explanation had been that she'd been lighting the grill on her deck and accidently squirted charcoal fluid all over her hands. When she went to light the grill, her hands had caught on fire, too. The next morning, Karen had called Dusty and asked him to come down to Just Screw It. Something strange had happened. Karen had walked into work and found the back window broken. Inside the hardware store, she'd found an empty wine bottle that had obviously been thrown through the window. It had a partially burned washcloth inside.

Dusty had arrived at the hardware store and picked up the bottle. "A gas bomb," he'd said, holding the crude, ineffectual weapon in his hand. Earlier that morning, while Dusty had been enjoying a donut at Donna's, Jeanine had stopped by for her morning donut and coffee. Her bandaged hands had caused quite a stir and she'd tried to slough it off as though it had been nothing. Later, holding the wine bottle in his hand, he'd surmised what had happened. Jeanine had lit the rag inside the wine bottle, but as she'd thrown it through the window, the gas had spilled onto her hands, burning them. Luckily, without enough gas, the flame had burnt itself out on the floor of the hardware store with no harm done other than the broken window.

Dusty had left Karen and walked straight to the Chamber of Commerce. He told Jeanine that she might as well confess as the whole thing had been captured on the video camera Walter had installed after his front window had been broken.

"What? I had no idea Walter had put in a video camera!"

"So, are you admitting to the crime then, Jeanine? This one and all of the other attacks on the local businesses in town? Why, Jeanine? What was it all for? Why create hardship for the businesses that, let's face it, pay your salary. Furthermore, why persecute Walter when he's already dead?"

Jeanine squinted her eyes and looked as though she was attempting an Elvis impersonation as she curled back her lip. "These businesses that pay my salary, as you so snidely point out, are also holding me back from gaining the biggest coup of my career by signing Wal-Mart up to enhance the dismal retail options we have in this pathetic excuse for a town. And Walter! Saint Walter to all of you. His death was the nail in the coffin for any hopes I still had for getting Wal-Mart here. Grabow withdrew the property, hadn't you heard? There's no place for Wal-Mart to build now even if they wanted to come here. All of my dreams just went down in flames so I wanted Walter's dream to go down in flames, too. And I'd do it again, too, don't think that I wouldn't."

Dusty put the handcuffs on and escorted Jeanine out the door. Karen had been busy calling the newspaper to be sure they caught a picture of Jeanine in handcuffs. "By the way," Dusty said as he led Jeanine away, "Walter did talk about installing a video camera but he never did get around to it. It was probably a good decision, too, don't you know."

Emma could put it off no longer. She brewed herself one last cup of coffee. She had the individual pod machine now so every cup was fresh. She selected Velvet Hammer, a delicious dark roast. Then she sat down in her office just off of the kitchen, hit the button on her computer, and waited for it to come to life again. She went immediately to the website before she could distract herself by checking her email. With trembling fingers, she punched in her user name and password. Before she even had time to take a sip of coffee, the test results popped onto her screen and Emma had her answer.

Therese Dotray-Tulloch

Chapter 27

Laney and Isabella Rose found their way onto the Port of Entry Bridge One after passing through the flea market in Eagle Pass. The fourteen foot high metal fence passing through downtown for over a mile was a real eyesore and spoke loudly of the determination to keep the two countries separate. Walking through a parking lot at the entrance to the bridge, Laney joined a group of Americans exiting a bus. Holding on to Izzy's hand, she made conversation with some of them and discovered they were snowbirds from Minnesota living in a trailer park in Texas for the winter months. They were heading into Piedras Negras to enjoy margaritas at happy hour as well as some nachos. They informed Laney that Piedras Negras was the only place on earth where she could get the original nacho.

Laney paid the fifty cents it cost for her and Izzy to walk across the bridge under the sign Bienvenidos a Piedras Negras, Coahuila; Mexico. All the while, Laney laughed and conversed with her new friends so that when the Mexican customs official on the bridge, who knew this group well, waved them through with a friendly wave, Laney entered

Mexico, too. Promising she would try to join them at Jalisco's later, she climbed into a taxi so she and Izzy could make their way to the Western Union.

Tracking down Tia Juanita was even easier than Laney had hoped. The serious young man working behind the iron barred counter initially said that he couldn't help her. When she explained that Isabella Rose was the little girl that Tia Juanita had been caring for and living with for the past four years, his grave visage transformed into a smiling, beaming face. Introducing himself as Arturo, he said that not only did he know Tia Juanita, but she was his wife's cousin's mother-in-law and he would take Laney to her just as soon as he finished work in about forty-five minutes. He suggested they walk over to Our Lady of Guadalupe and then to the Plaza de los Heroes. He would join them at the statue of Christopher Columbus.

It felt good to be out of the car walking around the old Mexican town. Piedras Negras looked just like Laney thought a Mexican town should look. They bought some pozole and tostada, and Izzy got a real kick out of feeding the leftovers to the pigeons. Soon Arturo met them and escorted them down narrow side streets through a labyrinth of winding roads with whitewashed houses and colorful doors lining both sides of the street. He explained that he was taking them to his wife's cousins house because Tia Juanita was staying with them, temporarily, it seemed, because she was planning to return to the states soon. Laney hoped this meant that Tia Juanita would soon be in possession of legal status and not that she was planning to sneak across the border. That could be so dangerous and often even deadly.

They stopped in front of a house with a shiny red door. Arturo lifted the heavy knocker in the middle of the door and rapped twice. Laney could hear footsteps echoing down the corridor before the door swung open and Arturo began speaking in rapid Spanish. She could only make out a word or two but caught the names Tia Juanita, Isabella Rose, and Minnesota. The woman invited them in. The corridor was at least twenty degrees cooler than outside. It was dark inside with no lights on, but after they had walked through the corridor, they came out on an enchanting courtyard filled with flowers and a meandering brick path complete with a charming little fountain where the soothing sounds of trickling water dribbled out of the mouth of the stone fish in the middle of the fountain. Tia Juanita was working in the kitchen, Arturo explained unnecessarily to Laney. She was insisting on earning her room and board.

Tia Juanita walked into the courtyard drying her hands on the white dish towel tied around her waist. When she saw Isabella Rose, she screamed 'Dios Mio' throwing her arms up into the air and running to her, crying, hollering, and laughing all at once as she rocked the little girl back and forth in a massive hug. "Why are you crying, Tia?" Izzy asked, "Aren't you happy I'm here?" She patted Tia Juanita's cheeks with both of her hands. Seeing them reunited, Laney felt her heart swelling with happiness and pride. She was so proud of herself for getting Izzy back to Tia Juanita.

Laney insisted that she couldn't stay. She left phone numbers and all relevant information with them and promised Tia Juanita that she would keep her posted as to Juan Carlos' situation. Tia Juanita had started crying all over again when she heard that her employer was lost in the bowels of ICE's clutches. Hadn't he just wired her money until she was able to figure out a way to get back to Minnesota?

They had to fetch Isabella Rose so Laney could say good-bye to her. There were other children living in the house and Izzy had already run off with them to play. Laney could tell that she was going to be so much better off here than she likely would have been back in Minnesota. At any rate, Laney had to convince herself of that to make the difficulties ahead of her worthwhile. Arturo walked her back to the main street where she could easily catch a taxi back to the border. They shook hands firmly as they said good-bye

The Quality Inn of Piedras Negras was the closest hotel to the International Bridge. Laney bought a colorful Mexican dress at one of the kiosks outside and a few toiletries from the shop inside of the hotel. The sky was just beginning to turn a brilliant pink off to the west. The sun had already set and darkness was descending. Laney was so tired, she thought perhaps tonight she would sleep so soundly that she wouldn't be awakened by her dreams. She couldn't seem to be able to turn down the air conditioning, so it was freezing in her room, but before she could crawl under the covers, she knew she had to make the phone call.

Wishing she had a happy-hour margarita, she sat on the edge of the bed and felt practically paralyzed. It was as if her mind was separate from her body and she couldn't coordinate the two of them together. But there was no putting it off any longer. She held her cell phone in her hand and pushed speed dial number two. The wonder in his voice as he answered her call with, "My god, Laney, is it really you?" made her answer stick in her throat. She knew the rich timbre of his voice so well. It brought back every emotion under the sun: happiness, love, pleasure, excitement, wonder, and, ultimately, pain, sorrow, horror. She felt herself beginning to spiral backward to the frozen state she had only recently pulled herself out of. She dug her fingernails into the palms of her hands to keep herself in the present and sat up on the edge of the bed. "It's me, Scott. I need your help."

Chapter 28

The ball sank through the net without touching the rim at all giving the Awesome Opossums three more points on the board. The fans leapt to their feet as one while thunderous applause erupted. The cheerleaders stood high on their tip toes throwing their arms around while clutching the black and red pompoms. Jesus Maria hadn't even stood still to see his shot go in. He'd turned around to head back to the other end of the gym. He always knew when his shots were going in; they felt just right. That was one of those shots. If he could stop just at the right three-point line spot and count on his teammates to hold back his opponents, he knew he just needed a fraction of a second to put the ball in. He was quickly finding out that he could depend on his teammates. He looked at Coach Martin as he ran by, to receive any instructions he may have had for him. Coach had just nodded his approval and shouted at Jesus Maria's teammates to hustle down the court.

Shannon Fischer stood underneath the Awesome Opossums' basket and hit the button to review the previous picture on the camera. Yes, she'd gotten it. She had trained the camera on the exact spot she knew Jesus Maria liked to shoot from and waited. Just as she'd anticipated, he appeared in the viewfinder and she'd snapped the perfect shot. Jesus Maria's feet were a foot off the ground and the ball had just left his fingertips but was still visible in the frame. Although Shannon was there as a yearbook representative, she would be offering this picture to the Opossum Falls Digest. The whistle blew as a timeout was called and Shannon snapped a few pictures of the band as they fired up and played a rousing song throughout the timeout. When the game resumed, she took some more pictures, snapping some of the cheerleaders, too, even though she thought they were not only silly but annoying, too.

The first home game of the basketball season was always well attended, but tonight the gym was filled to capacity. Opossum Falls was playing their arch rival and next door neighbor, the Bold Warriors. Bold was the acronym for the nearby towns of Bird Island, Olivia, and Lake Lillian school district, so fans of both teams filled up the gym. The Awesome Opossums' school colors were red with black while Bold's colors were black with red. There wasn't a fan in the crowd who wasn't decked out in black and red. The Bold mascot, a fierce-looking warrior, made the Awesome Opossum's mascot look rather pathetic, especially because he played the part the way he'd been trained to, freezing every so often as an opossum would before scurrying off to the sidelines.

Anita sat on the bottom bleacher with the rest of the high school kids on the Awesome Opossum side of the gym feeling torn between being fiercely proud of her brother Jesus Maria and sadly disappointed for her boyfriend, Matthew Stevenson, sitting next to her on the bottom bleacher, crutches on the floor beneath them. Jesus Maria had stepped up to fill Matthew's position as the guard bringing the ball down the court. His stardom was the direct result of Matthew's misfortune at the sugar beet piling station. Anita felt her loyalties divided in two. After yet another perfectly swished three pointer, some of the freshman held up signs with his name spelled out like this, "Hey, Zeus, hey Zeus!" The crowd leapt to their feet again shouting, pronouncing his name just like that, "Jesus, Jesus!" Matthew put his arm around Anita and pulled her close to him so he could whisper in her ear above the roar of the crowd. "It's okay, Anita. You can be happy for your brother, you know. I am. Truly!"

Anita looked at Matthew and felt love welling up inside of her. Although the crowd hollered all around them, she felt as though the two of them were enclosed in their own private enclave. His generosity and understanding touched her deeply. She kissed his cheek before jumping up with the rest of the crowd, proudly shouting her big brother's name.

~~~~~~~~~~~~~~~~~~~~~~~~~~~~~~~~

Emma finished the last sip of her coffee still staring at the results on the computer screen. It didn't seem possible that after all of these years, something as simple as a strand of hair or a bit of saliva could prove that she was someone's mother, that she was, in fact, Pete's mother. The moment was too big for her to take in all at once. She felt as though even the slightest movement might spoil it for her, make the positive results on the screen disappear. Emma felt a waterfall of emotions gushing down upon her. Most powerful of all was a profound sense of relief. She realized that for the past thirty-seven years she had been worrying about her son. Her fear was that he hadn't actually lived, that he had died and his death had been hidden from her. Her nightmare was that he had fallen into a bad family, a home lacking in love. Knowing now that Pete had been raised by devoted parents who had given him a truly wonderful life, that he had grown into a responsible, productive adult, made Emma happy beyond words. Her sense of relief inflated her so much that she couldn't move. Emma began to wonder how different her life would have been had she not spent it worrying, even on a subconscious level, and mourning the loss of her son. Perhaps she would have been a completely different person, a nicer one, even.

Now that he had been found, she had no idea what she was going to do about it. Emma wished that Pete hadn't just lost his mother, although, had it not been for comments made by an aged aunt at his mom's funeral, perhaps Emma would never have known the truth about their relationship. She tried to think back on the moment she'd first met Pete. Shouldn't her heart have spoken the truth to her during that fateful meeting? Shouldn't she have recognized the man to be the boy she had given birth to decades earlier; shouldn't she have known on some unspoken level that Pete was her son? Her son. Emma felt her smile muscles tire and realized that she had been smiling ever since she first read the Identigene results on her computer.

She saved the page on her computer where the blessed results were listed. Typing away at her keyboard, she soon found the phone number she was looking for. She picked up her phone to call the one man who knew Pete well enough to be able to advise her on what she should do next.

~~~~~~~~~~~~~~~~~~~~~~~~~~~~~~~

Stepping out of the shower of her tiny bathroom at the Quality Inn, Laney wished for the umpteenth time that there was some way to turn down the air conditioning. She had slept soundly after having snatched only a few hours of sleep on the drive down to Mexico, but when she'd woken up from her dream, the tip of her nose had been frozen even though her head was completely buried underneath the scratchy wool blanket. Laney hated having to use blankets in hotel rooms. Sheets, she knew, were, as a rule, washed, but blankets were used over and again and without being cleaned. Laney had the regrettable habit of picturing the least attractive person she saw in the hotel lobby as the last person to have slept in her bed. If she traveled more, she would be one of those people who carried around their own bed linens just to be comfortable.

She combed her fingers through her hair, knowing that once she stepped out of this freezing cold hotel room, it would dry quickly. She examined her face in the mirror as she brushed her teeth imagining the first moments of her and Scott seeing one another for the first time in over two years. She had aged, she was sure of that as she noted the way her eyelids were looser now and there were the beginning shadows of wrinkles about to make an entrance onto her face. But she hadn't fallen completely apart, she knew Scott would be happy to see that. She tied the sash around the waist of the peasant dress with the intricate crocheted hem and neckline feeling a little foolish now for her impromptu purchase last night but knowing she couldn't bear to spend another day in the outfit she'd put on for Walter's funeral. Had that really been just a couple of days ago? It felt like weeks.

Laney ordered a café con leche at the coffee shop next to the Quality Inn. She sat at an outside table while she waited for Scott. She couldn't believe he would be able to get here so quickly. Right after their phone call last night, he'd hopped into his car and driven directly to Opossum Falls, to Parkview Estates, where she'd already alerted her apartment manager to let him into her apartment. He procured her passport and caught an early morning flight on United Airlines to Del Rio International Airport via Dallas. Her problem of how to get back into the United States should be solved, but she wondered if she would be arrested immediately upon arrival for, what would the charge be, resisting arrest? She still had no idea why the police officer had been pulling her over yesterday in Eagle Pass, but she just knew that she had had to get away with Isabella Rose. She hoped she wouldn't be charged with kidnapping, that would be a serious federal offense, but, if Laney were honest with herself, she actually had to admit that it felt good to be worried about something. It made her feel as though she were actually still alive.

Laney felt the bittersweet conflict of emotions as she recognized that the pain of The Event was subsiding. For the first time, Laney became aware that she was alive and she wasn't saddened by the realization. Feeling eyes upon her, she glanced up at the tall, handsome man who was looking at her, concern written all over his craggy face. He was wearing a well-cut navy blue suit, a yellow and gray striped tie, and carrying a leather satchel. He tipped his head slightly to the side as he looked down on her, a wistful little smile pulling at the corner of his mouth. The powerful current of the tragedy they shared had prevented them from getting close to one another after The Event, as if they were each a magnet and no matter how hard they tried, they were prevented from being together; the force was too strong. "Laney," Scott said softly, and she stood up to give her ex-husband a hug.

They walked across Eagle Pass Bridge One and easily re-entered the United States. The bridge was not nearly as crowded as Laney had observed it being all morning when it had been full of Mexican students walking to their schools in Texas, shoppers eager to fill their shopping bags with items they couldn't find across the border, day-trippers visiting family. Now the customs agents had time to chitchat.

The bald man with rich, chocolate skin asked Laney and Scott if they'd had a nice time in Mexico, flipped through their passports, then said warmly, "Welcome home, Mr. and Mrs. Anderson." They walked to Scott's rental car in the adjacent parking lot.

After picking up the keys from the police station in Eagle Pass, Scott drove Laney to the impound lot to pick up Marge Peterson's car. The police officer, who had stopped Laney because the car had a tail light missing, met them there. Scott introduced himself as Laney's lawyer. The officer was very disappointed in her, he'd scolded. Running away from an officer of the law was a serious crime. She could have been shot. She could be sent to jail. The officer was looking at Laney with kindness and pity and she knew then that he had seen her record, he had read about the crime she had been tried for. When he had found out from Marge that her car hadn't been stolen, he'd given her a ticket for parking in a no parking zone and impounded the car, but that was all.

"You have a tail light that needs replacing. Be sure to fix it before you drive back to Minnesota." They had paid Laney's fine, thanked the officer profusely, and left.

Laney was relieved that there wasn't a warrant out for her arrest for kidnapping, either. She called Marge and told her to let Child Protection know that Isabella Rose was in Mexico staying with 'relatives' until things were sorted out with Juan Carlos. Marge assured Laney she could keep her car as long as she liked but that she needed Juan Carlos' billfold back as soon as possible. She needed his driver's license to establish his identification and therefore to help prove his citizenship. Laney asked Scott to send the billfold to Marge as soon as he got back to Minnesota that afternoon.

Laney assured Scott that she would be just fine driving back to Minnesota on her own, that it would be nice not being in a hurry this time, that she planned to stop in Oklahoma City to spend the night and even take time to visit the site of the Federal Building bombing and view the memorial set up there. She'd always wanted to see that. Scott made her promise to stop at a garage to get the tail light fixed.

Facing each other in the front seat of the rental car, their eyes spoke the volumes they would never be able to say out loud. Laney finally asked, "How's Melinda?"

"She's well. She sends greetings. Tyler is starting to crawl, so she's busy chasing after him.

"Crawling already? Wow!" There were so many questions Laney was desperate to ask, but she had no idea how to begin.

Scott pulled out his phone and hit a few buttons until a picture appeared on the screen. He handed the phone over for Laney to see. It was a beautiful family picture of Scott, his second wife, Melinda, and two boys. Laney bit her lips, struggling grievously to hold in her sob. Her eyes flooded with tears as she nodded her head when Scott spoke.

"That's Michael holding Tyler. Michael. Your son. Our son, Laney. He asks after you, you know, because we keep your picture right beside his bed. He'd like to see you. Don't you think it's time?"

Therese Dotray-Tulloch

The hard mattress on the bed at Oklahoma City's Sheraton Hotel caused Laney to toss and turn. She dreamed she was holding Michael in her arms. His fever had risen dramatically and he had spent the night coughing and crying. Laney had held him in the rocking chair most of the night, drifting off to sleep for snatches of minutes at a time. She'd called the clinic first thing in the morning and made an appointment.

Gabby had come running into the kitchen as soon as she'd woken up, bursting with her usual enthusiasm for life. She dragged her doll Anna behind her and sat her in the chair at the little, blue, kid-sized table. She tied a bib around her neck and asked her doll, "What kind of cereal do you want today?" Laney put cereal bowls out and told Gabby to eat quickly and get dressed; they had to take Michael to see the doctor.

It was cool enough out to warrant jackets. Laney bundled up Michael first while he cried miserably. She stood there holding Gabby's jacket, telling her to hurry up. Gabby finally came running out of her room with Anna all wrapped up in a blanket explaining that she had a fever, too, and needed to see the doctor. Laney had a terrific headache and wondered if she was coming down with the same flu that Michael had. She paused for a moment thinking, if it is flu, maybe I shouldn't even take him to the doctor? Sometimes the responsibilities of motherhood were so overwhelming. Laney couldn't stop thinking about the story of the child who had recently died of meningitis, the implication in the newspaper article being that if the mother had taken him to the doctor sooner, perhaps death could have been avoided. She picked up Michael and held the door open for Gabby as they walked through the garage to the van. After putting both of the kids into their car seats in the second seat, Laney folded the stroller and lifted it into the back of the van.

Their doctor was on the third floor. Laney used her Greco stroller they'd gotten when Gabby was born. It was only a single, but when the seat was put down, Laney had Gabby sit in the back with Michael lying down in front of her and it worked perfectly for the two of them. It was a little more crowded with three as Gabby insisted Anna had to squeeze in, too, for her doctor appointment. The waiting room was crowded. Gabby quickly made friends with another little boy about her age while they played together pushing beads around a complicated wire contraption on the kids' table. Laney smiled as she overheard Gabby telling him they were going to get a dog. When they were called into the examining room, Gabby asked if she could keep playing out in the waiting room, but Laney insisted she come with them. She didn't want to be worrying about her and she never knew how long she'd have to wait before the doctor came into the room.

Before long, the doctor examined Michael, took a swab from his throat to check for strep, and prescribed an antibiotic. Michael screamed the entire ride down in the elevator. The elderly couple riding down with them were not amused when Gabby managed to punch the second floor button before Laney could stop her, so they stood there as the doors slowly opened on the empty second floor, waited for what seemed like an eternity, then finally ever so slowly closed again. "He's got some lungs on him," the man said, gesturing with his head towards Michael while the woman stared straight ahead, her lips pursed so tightly Laney imagined the fine wrinkles surrounding her mouth were permanent.

"We're getting a dog!" Gabby said, smiling happily up at the couple.

"You'll really have your hands full then," the man said grumpily as they hurried out of the elevator. Laney couldn't resist immaturely rolling her eyes as she maneuvered the stroller backwards out of the elevator while appreciating now the slow-moving doors. In the lobby, she struggled to put Michael's jacket back on as his cries grew louder and more frustrated.

"It's okay, honey, come on, Michael, we'll get your medicine and you'll feel better real soon." Laney turned to see Gabby just about to hit the elevator button again.

"Gabby, get over here NOW and let me put your coat on." She was rougher than usual as she hastily pulled on Gabby's jacket, zipped it up, and lifted her into the back of the stroller.

Laney was halfway through the first door when Gabby yelled, "Mommy! Don't forget Anna!" Laney left the stroller where it was and ran to pick up the doll reclining against the garbage bin next to the elevator doors. She tossed her into the stroller. Soon Gabby was mimicking, "Shhhhh, don't cry Anna. We'll get your medicine and you'll feel better real soon."

The wind had picked up and the icy chill was a glimpsing reminder of the winter season fast approaching. Laney stopped at the back of the mini-van. She lifted Michael up reminding Gabby to scoot forward so the stroller wouldn't tip backward. Michael's cries grew louder as he fought Laney while she strapped him into the car seat. She was trying to decide which pharmacy to go to, Walgreen's was closer but CVS had the drive-thru so she wouldn't have to struggle with the stroller again when she put the van in reverse and started backing up. There was a slight resistance so Laney pushed down more firmly on the gas pedal. There was a rocking motion as one of the back tires on the van laboriously drove over something. Laney creased her forehead in thought as she tried to remember if there was a cement parking barrier behind her. She heard a horn honking then, one long blast as someone laid on the horn. There was a woman screaming and running towards Laney from the other end of the parking lot. 'My god, is she being attacked?' thought Laney as she pushed the gear shift into park and started opening her door.

"The stroller," the woman was running with both arms over her head reminding Laney for some odd reason of the disjointed movements on the dance floor during the playing of YMCA. "You ran over the stroller." Her shrieking voice was hysterical.

In the same way that movies become annoying when the slow motion speed is implemented during crucial stages to be sure to catch the viewers' attention, Laney felt a switch was pulled and every frame of the story of her life in this scene started playing in sluggish measure. Laney's first unhurried thought was that this woman had stupidly left her stroller all the way over on this side of the parking lot behind Laney's van. Then she glanced in the backseat and thought, quite unsuspectingly, 'where's Gabby?' Stepping down from the van, her foot landed on top of the small wheel from the front of the stroller which was twirling about, separated from the rest of the carriage. Even when Laney saw the doll, Anna, splayed out face forward in a rather unnatural pose, she managed to hold the gates of panic closed. Her mind did not want to accept what it was seeing. To believe what her eyes beheld was an awfulness too much for any human being to acknowledge, so therefore her conscious state remained calm and tried to come up with other, more reasonable explanations for the horrific sight at the back of her van. The stroller demolished, so much blood, Gabby.

Sitting on the tarmac, cradling the limp form of her little girl, Gabby's partially crushed skull resting in her lap, Laney heard the incessant screams with irritation before she realized the pain-filled sobs were coming out of her. Medical staff from the clinic were pressing white towels down on Gabby's head to try to stem the flow of blood staining Laney's jeans before the ambulance arrived. The color of the blood was so red, redder than Laney would have thought it would be.

Laney had already clambered into the back of the ambulance, as wild as a mother bear about to be separated from its cub, when the YMCA dancer shouted that she would follow them to the hospital with Laney's other child, the baby bellowing from the back seat of the van. In that moment, Laney thought of Michael the way she would not be able to stop herself from thinking about him again, as the child she didn't run over, the lucky one she'd taken out of the stroller first. God help her, there were times when she wished it weren't so.

She rocked back and forth in the back of the ambulance while they did everything they could to stop Gabby's life from flowing out of her sweet little body. From years born of habit, Laney felt herself swaying and patting the back of the baby she held not even aware that it was only Anna, Gabby's much loved doll, the only baby Gabby would ever get to love and care for. Laney felt the weight of her baby on her chest as she slowly awoke from her dream. Her pillow was wet with tears. Laney pushed herself up out of bed. It was time.

Chapter 29

Laney walked from the Sheraton towards the softly glowing lights of the Outdoor Symbolic Memorial on the grounds where the Alfred P. Murrah Federal Building had once stood in Oklahoma City. The sign said, *"We come here to remember those who were killed, those who survived and those changed forever...May this memorial offer comfort, strength, peace, hope, and serenity."* The peaceful quietude beckoned to Laney. She sat on the cement tier alongside of the tranquil Reflecting Pool standing where Fifth Street had once stood. Laney looked across its sparkling water to the Field of Empty Chairs. Each elegant, hauntingly lighted up chair represented one of the one hundred sixty-eight lives lost during the senseless bombing on April 19, 1995. Visiting the museum the previous day, Laney had learned that nineteen of those who'd lost their lives were children under the age of six, just like her own little Gabby. She sat across from the nineteen smaller chairs which each bore the name of one of the children who had died there. She thought this would be a good place to try to come to terms with her own loss in the company of so many other tragic victims.

Laney drew in a shaky breath as she allowed herself to think about Gabby. Thinking about her had caused so much pain that Laney had taught herself the only way to survive was to banish all thoughts of Gabby from her mind. The problem with that was that Laney found herself guilty of killing Gabby not only at the time of the accident but also on the day she was born. Gabby's short, precious little life deserved to be honored, and Laney could only do that by remembering it first. She would never, ever be able to forgive herself, but, Laney thought hopefully, if she could at last stop blaming herself, then maybe she could allow herself to recognize the child she still had, her son, Michael. Scott had told her she had punished herself long enough. Both of her children did not have to be lost to her. It was time to be a mother again.

Gabby's heart had managed to keep beating for two more days after the accident. She had had such genuine zest for life, no wonder her heart refused to give up. A few hours after the accident, the doctor had told Laney that Gabby was brain dead. He had seemed like such a kind man, his thinning, white hair looking tussled as he ran his hand over it, using the time to find a way to put into words the ghastly truth that, because of a mother's negligence, because she was so arrogant as to take the lives of her children for granted, because she forgot to think about her daughter, she abandoned that child behind her vehicle to be run over, crushed by a massive, black, rubber tire rising up and over her, because of a mother's carelessness, her daughter's brain was dead.

Laney remembered how her own brain had rejected the term, how she had stared into the kindly doctor's eyes hoping she had misunderstood, looking for some sign of hope, seeing only profound sadness. She thought of Gabby's enduring optimism, her insatiable curiosity, her innate flirtatiousness, her unconditional love. How does her brain being dead fit into all she already knew about her daughter?

The hospital was full of friends and family. Scott flew back from Vegas by late afternoon. When he arrived and appeared at the end of the hospital corridor, everyone else faded away and disappeared until it was just the two of them. As Scott walked towards her, she saw the muscle in his jaw twitching as he worked hard to control his emotions. She was crying, "Oh, god, Scott, I'm so sorry," while he was saying, "Stop it, Laney, you don't have to apologize. How is she? Is Gabby alright?" He could not control what was behind his eyes, however, and it was there that Laney saw the awful truth. Their marriage could not survive. How would Scott ever be able to forgive her for killing their child?

It wasn't until weeks after the funeral that Laney realized the prescription for antibiotics for Michael's fever was never filled. The whole point of their being out that day in the first place, and Michael's fever and its medication was simply forgotten. If only she had stayed home that day. Michael would have gotten over his fever. Gabby would still be alive. If only.....

Gazing out at the Reflecting Pool, Laney told herself that she had to stop that now. She had to accept what had happened. She forced herself to continue remembering The Event.

Gabby's body was a goldmine of healthy body parts. She and Scott tearfully agreed that bits and pieces of Gabby could be used to keep others alive, to enhance their lives, to give sight. They kept her alive while teams of physicians stepped in to harvest what Gabby's little body yielded. While standing near the fire exit, Laney desperately wanting a cigarette, even though it had been years since she'd smoked, and even though she'd only been a casual smoker, she overheard some nurses who must have been involved in the organ removal say, "Her kidneys looked awesome! They're both on their way to new homes already." Laney had stared through the cloudy glass door and felt as if she were dreaming.

The kindhearted doctor laid his hand on Laney's and said that it was time to say their good-byes. All she could think of was that the skin on his hand seemed to have way more age spots than she would have thought by looking at his face. She was baffled by her mind's betrayal, by its insistence on ignoring her emotional state by continuing to function as her mind always had; it was inquisitive, thoughtful, a little quirky. And yet, her mind had failed her during the critical moment when it should have reminded her that she wasn't finished, she'd left unfinished business there in the back of her van, she still had to take her daughter out of the stroller and tuck her safely into her car seat, out of the dangers inherent in a parking lot. Instead, her wits had failed her and now Gabby was brain dead.

It used to be that the beating heart set the standard for what constituted life. A beating heart meant you were alive. At some point, we decided that, wait a minute, the heart is important and all, keeping the blood circulating around the body, but it was actually our brains that made us who we were. If our brain died, we might as well be dead, too. There was no such thing as heart dead or liver dead or kidney dead. Everyone knew, however, that brain dead meant sayonara. Gabby's brain was dead because Laney ran over it. And now it was time for Scott and Laney to tell her good-bye.

The last organ to go was Gabby's heart. The compassionate woman in charge of the organ donations had asked Laney and Scott if they were interested in a list of the recipients of Gabby's life-saving organs. Laney had cringed in horror at the thought. In a heartbeat, if Laney could have, she would have ripped out every one of the recipients' own heart, liver, kidneys and eyeballs if it meant she could bring her own daughter back to life. To possess their addresses had the potential to turn her into a stalker, hunting down what was left of her daughter. She could not handle that information; she did not want to know.

The surgeons had arrived to remove Gabby's heart. Scott had said, "Come on Laney, they've come to take Gabby's heart. Time to say good-bye," and she had thought that was one sentence she would never, ever have to hear in her lifetime. The medical assistants wouldn't meet their eyes as they walked past. Laney and Scott sat on either side of Gabby's bed, each holding one of her precious little hands in their own. Laney looked down on the polish that was just barely visible on her tiny fingernails. Gabby had chosen it for its name as much as the color: Cha Ch'ing Cherry. "How do we do this?" Laney had thought. She kept wishing she could wake up from the nightmare her life had become.

Finally, they had had to drag Laney away. She couldn't bear to let go of Gabby's still warm little hand. Sitting at the site of the Oklahoma City bombing, tears running freely down her cheeks, Laney couldn't help but think that it was her own guilt over the accident that had made it so hard for her to let go of Gabby. She, Laney, had killed her own daughter, the most precious thing in the world to her. She was still trying to figure out how to go on from there.

She took a deep breath as she looked at the Gates of Time at the Oklahoma Federal Building Memorial. The glowing lights shone brightly through the early dawn hours. The majestic arches framed the moment of destruction at the site when the bomb had gone off in 1995. The East Gate has the numbers 9:01 and the innocence of the city before the attack. The 9:03 on the West Gate signifies the hope that came after. The concept of time for Laney had become something to simply get through since Gabby's death. She felt a stirring within herself and knew that was beginning to change. She was coming back to life. She wanted to acknowledge her own gates of time, the memorial etched into her heart marking the date of Gabby's death. Life would always be measured before The Event and after. But at last Laney was able to actually call it what it was: a horrible, tragic accident, a death, the loss of her child's life. She needed to walk through the gates of time and move on now.

There was an elm tree on the Memorial sight called The Survivor Tree. It had born witness to the violence and withstood the full force of the bombing. It stood there majestically as the sun began its slow ascent in the east symbolizing resilience. Laney walked over to the tree, placed her palm against its ridged bark and tried to garner some of the energy it carried within its sturdy trunk. She, too, was a survivor. She had learned how to endure; now it was time to learn how to live again. Laney walked around the orchard surrounding the Survivor Tree to the children's area. After the blast, children from around the world had sent cards of sympathy and love. The wall of tiles painted by children was a testimony to the healing process which was possible even after such tragedy.

Finally, Laney walked over to the fence which had initially been installed to protect the site of the Murrah Building. Immediately after the bombing, people began to leave articles there in sympathy, tokens of love and of hope. Everything from flags, flowers, wreaths, tee shirts, pictures, and poems were placed on the fence. There were over sixty thousand items which had been left there which were kept in the archives. There was still more than two hundred feet of the original fence standing for people like Laney who needed the opportunity to leave a token of remembrance and hope.

Laney opened her billfold and carefully removed the swatch of scarlet material with tiny purple and yellow buds adorned with little green leaves on it. She held it to her nose and breathed deeply though any lingering scent of Gabby had long since diminished. This had been the shirt Gabby had put on to wear on the morning of her death. It had matching black stretch pants to go with it sporting the same tiny rosebuds on it. Laney had carried this scrap with her to remind herself not to forget her daughter's death so that if she started to have a good time or feel happiness, the swatch was to remind her that Gabby was dead and that she was in mourning. Laney knew she didn't need the reminder anymore. And to honor her daughter's death, she needed to live again.

Laney also pulled out a picture of Gabby she had in her billfold. It was the one she had taken in the garden in front of the colorful cosmos right before Gabby had insisted that Laney get into the picture, too. The beauty of the flowers couldn't even begin to compare to Gabby's radiance. Laney used her finger to trace Gabby's gold-strewn curls, her sparkling blue eyes, graceful upturned nose and laughing mouth. She drew the photo closer and kissed it gently. Laney felt her heart bursting with gratitude for the years she had had with such an angel of light, love and happiness. She took out a pen and wrote on the back of the picture, *Gabrielle Rose Anderson, she will always be loved, and she will never be forgotten.* She attached the picture and the swatch of material onto the fence. She wept for a moment as she said good-bye to Gabby one more time, then she turned, straightened her shoulders, and walked away. This would not be the last time that Laney shed tears for Gabby, but at last she felt she was able to say good-bye. She drove back to Minnesota with plans to begin to live again.

Chapter 30

Pete struggled to extricate all of the mail from the tiny little box allocated to him by the apartment complex. He threw it into his backpack without taking time to read it. He saw that he had what looked to be a card from Emma Grabow, and he smiled to himself thinking it was most likely a thank you card. Everything had turned out well for Emma and her vineyard and Pete was inexplicably jubilant about it. The culprit who had inadvertently sprayed Roundup on Emma's grapes, killing the fruit before it had had time to grow, turned out not to be her neighbor Eric Hanson after all. There were co-op farming fields well west of Emma Grabow's vineyard. They had hired a helicopter service to spray their fields at the crucial time to avoid 'root madness,' an aptly named disease which turned the bulbous tap root into many small roots making the crop economically unprocessable. There had been very little wind that day which was probably why they had chosen it as the day to spray. Right at the end of the job, however, as the helicopter was making its final pass through the last segment of the field, a gusty wind had appeared from the west blowing a blast of deadly herbicide onto Emma's Frontenac Gris.

Pete and his crew had been able to narrow down the window of damage done to the grapes to have occurred right when the co-op was spraying. After presenting the documentation to the co-op, it had basically admitted guilt and said it would definitely prefer to pay a settlement to Emma than end up in court. At their next meeting, they planned to come to an agreement and would likely be ready to settle. All Emma had to do was to assess the monetary loss of her crop that year and to submit the amount prior to their meeting so they could come to a decision for how much to write the check. Pete was happy for Emma. They were planning to go out to celebrate once the check actually came in, Emma's treat.

Pete left Fargo on Interstate 94 heading east toward the Twin Cities. It would take him about four hours to get to his dad's place in Bloomington. He would have been tempted to swing by Opossum Falls on the way had Laney been there, but he'd heard she was still driving back from her spontaneous trip to Mexico. Pete hoped he'd be able to drive through to see her on the way back to Fargo. He was ready to ask her if she was interested in going forward with their relationship. He knew that they were friends, but Pete wanted more than that. He had never felt this way about a woman before. He thought that Laney felt something for him, too, but whatever the big secret was that she didn't want him to know about was definitely holding her back. Pete speculated on what it might be.

Something had happened to Laney which must have put her in the media spotlight. There was something about it which had put her in trouble with the law. Pete wondered why he didn't just Google Laney's name and find out the truth. If he were honest with himself, he would admit that a part of him was afraid to find out. What if she was a serial killer? He scoffed, knowing that the Laney he knew had one of the tenderest hearts he'd ever encountered. He knew she wasn't a killer. He also knew that the reason he didn't research her past on the internet was because he wanted her to tell him herself. She would do that because she trusted him; Pete wanted to be sure that he was worthy of that trust.

The miles flew by as he raced along the freeway. Soon he would be at his dad's. He wondered what it was his dad wanted to discuss with him. He'd said that it was something he wanted to talk about in person. He speculated that perhaps it had something to do with what Aunt Mildred had said about his being adopted. It would be good to get it out in the open. Pete was glad that the element of surprise was already over so that if his dad did break the news to him, he wouldn't be too surprised. In fact, he'd already had time to plan his response and he knew just what he wanted to say.

Pete had the good fortune to have had one the happiest childhoods of anyone he knew. He always felt like he had the best parents in the whole world. Sure, his parents had seemed a bit old compared to the younger moms and dads his friends had, and when he was young, he'd often wished that he had a brother or a sister. But other than that, he had always known he was the luckiest kid around. He still felt that way. His parents were the best. If Pete had been adopted, well, so what? That didn't change anything one bit. He loved his mom and dad just as much or even more than he always had, knowing how hard they'd worked to get him. And he couldn't wait to tell that to his dad.

~~~~~~~~~~~~~~~~~~~~~~~~~~~~~~~~~

Marge hung up the phone and absentmindedly scratched the top of Pumpkin's head. He had leaped onto her lap the second she sat down. She had been so relieved to hear from Laney that all was fine and that Isabella Rose was safely reunited with Tia Juanita. She hadn't realized that Laney had the courage to act so spontaneously for the sake of a child. When Marge realized that Laney could have been caught and charged with kidnapping, she had been worried sick. She was therefore extremely relieved to learn that all was well. Laney had left Oklahoma City that morning but was driving to Minneapolis before returning with Marge's car to Opossum Falls. She felt terrible about inconveniencing Marge by leaving her without a car, but Marge assured her that it was no problem.

Marge thought about the missing taillight and all of the grief it had caused. She thought of Charles and how she had taken for granted all of the things he had always done for her without her appreciating it. Well, she had definitely learned her lesson and never again would she let a detail like a missing taillight go.

Now, if only she would hear something from Juan Carlos. It had been
five days since Walter had died and they had been on their way to see
him when Juan Carlos had disappeared. Marge had searched high and
low for Juan Carlos but, for all intents and purposes, he had fallen off
the face of the earth. Marge was horrified that something like this
could happen to an American citizen in the United States. She was
consumed with guilt that it had been completely her fault Juan Carlos
found himself in this predicament. What had happened to an
individual's rights? She had been aware things had changed since
9/11, but she had had no idea how much.

After countless hours on the phone calling county jails and detention
centers throughout Minnesota to try to locate Juan Carlos'
whereabouts, Marge had finally found an attorney who specialized in
immigration law. Actually, she found a whole family of them. The
Vaquero Law Office consisted of Mom and Pop and their two
extremely handsome sons. Born of a Colombian father and an
American mother, they combined the best of both nationalities, were
bilingual, and together with their parents had quite a reputation for
serving the needs of the multitude of migrants in the Twin Cities and
surrounding area. Vaquero had told Marge the bad news first. Until
Juan Carlos was processed, ICE would not be obligated to give out his
location nor even have to allow him to make a phone call. Obviously,
the fact that Juan Carlos had no driver's license on him made the ICE
agent believe that he was an undocumented immigrant. Having no
driver's license was one of the easiest ways to identify illegals. Juan
Carlos could be sitting in a county jail; the first thirty-six hours would
have been under a probable cause hold. After that, ICE most likely
placed an ICE hold on him whereby he would be forced to sit
indefinitely still without the possibility of contacting family, his lawyer,
or anyone. After several days had passed, however, he had to be
processed into the system. After processing, Juan Carlos would at last
be able to make a phone call. The Vaqueros were putting the word
out that they were representing Juan Carlos. Once ICE became aware
of that, they would allow the Vaqueros to get information and find out
which county jail was holding their client.

Marge had received Juan Carlos' billfold from Scott via Federal
Express so now she had his driver's license. As soon as she got the
call either from Juan Carlos or the Vaqueros, she would be on the

road with it, ready to prove Juan Carlos' legal status.

~~~~~~~~~~~~~~~~~~~~~~~~~~~~~~~

'Don't look now, but the wicked 'you-know-who' from the west is marching without her broomstick right this way," Henry Johnson said as he sat at the Chit Chat counter. He pulled the newest edition of the Opossum Falls' Digest up to his face and peered around it. Dick McGhee glanced at his watch and issued an expletive, hastily rising and buttoning his suit jacket. The button pulled tightly, the threads through the buttonhole straining mightily to hold the button in place. All of those hair-thin strands of thread miraculously doing the job were an excellent example of strength in numbers.

"Do you want me to distract the old biddy while you sneak out the back door?" Marty Bleak asked, glancing up from his beef commercial. "I have a new Ole and Lena joke about golf clubs and being left-handed, oh, and death, of course." Dick chuckled and said that wouldn't be necessary when the little bell tinkled above the door and Emma Grabow strode in.

"Dick, I've been standing outside of your office door for three and a half minutes already. I expect to dock that from your exorbitant fee," Emma's eyes were drawn to Dick's stomach and the tension caused as he buttoned his suit jacket.

"Beg your pardon, Mrs. Grabow. I just had some business here to finish up with Marty. Let's head back to my office now, shall we?"

"Right," she said skeptically. Seeing Bianca balancing three plates as she came from the kitchen, Emma greeted her warmly, "Thank you for the Tostada soup you sent with your nephews. It felt divine on my sore throat. Those boys are such good workers, Bianca. You should be proud of them. They're emptying out the old storage shed for me now and making such progress!"

"You're welcome, Mrs. Grabow. Thank you for employing them. Working for you has really helped keep them out of trouble. And they love all of the animals and the extra money they get selling the eggs. They're saving up for an X-Box, if you can believe it."

"Oh, they won't have any time for that. The Helping Hands 4-H Club meets next week and I've already signed them up. They're spending so much time on the farm, they might as well have the fun of competing at the fair. You can never start too early working on 4H projects."

Bianca laughed approvingly and said good-bye as Dick and Emma walked across the street to his office.

Emma had a lot to discuss with Dick. Now that she had an heir, she changed her will so that Pete would ultimately inherit the farm. She also wanted to discuss the windfall she would soon be receiving from the Co-op to compensate for her lost grape harvest. She had decided exactly how she wanted to spend it. Dick was handling the purchase for her and she wanted to get the wheels in motion. Lastly, Emma decided that it was time someone spoke out and told Dick that the jokes he always told at the Sugar Beet Pageant needed to be okayed by people who perhaps had, how could she say it, better 'taste' than he did. She had made up a list of names of people who she thought would be willing to serve on the committee. Furthermore, she had brought a half dozen Bell Jars labeled Dick's Joke Jar which she thought should be distributed at high-traffic areas around town so people could actually submit jokes they thought would be appropriate.

Dick advised Emma regarding her will and the purchase she wanted to make on Main Street, and he accepted her suggestion about the joke jar. Emma shook his hand firmly as she stood up to leave. Striding towards the door, she turned so abruptly, Dick had to quickly wipe the grin off of his face that he had been hiding throughout the entire meeting. "One last thing," Emma said, "I suggest you either lay off of dessert from the Chit Chat from now on, or go ahead and buy the bigger size the next time you're shopping for a suit at the Men's Warehouse. Good day."

Dick waited until he saw Emma walk to her car and drive away down Main Street before he let himself bellow with laughter. He felt so good after his meeting with Emma that he decided to walk across the street again and treat himself to a piece of pumpkin pie, leaving his suit jacket unbuttoned this time.

Chapter 31

Pete said good-night to his dad and decided to put on his jacket and walk around the neighborhood to think about what they had discussed. There was a real chill in the air and the clouds were thick and gray, hanging so low in the sky they looked like they could be touched by just reaching up on tip toe. They looked voluminous and threatening. In fact, the weathermen were predicting the first snowfall of the season to be a heavy one. Pete felt a cacophony of memories from his childhood circle around him as he walked the memory-filled streets of his youth. He could practically hear the voices of his friends as they raced their bikes up and down the street, listen to the shouts after the school bus had dropped them off and they all scattered to their own homes, feel the pleasant thump of the baseball landing in the mitt as he and his dad played catch for hours on the front lawn.

They had had their best talks when throwing the baseball back and forth. There was something about the effort of throwing and catching the ball well that lent itself to words and meanings, too. The connection they felt with one another standing out on the lawn went far beyond the mutual pleasure they gained from playing baseball. It seemed so much easier for women who loved to talk and share their feelings and hug one another. It was harder for men, the idea of sharing thoughts. Much easier to be doing something, like concentrating on throwing the ball well and holding your mitt in the right spot to catch it, while important things were discussed. Over the years, Pete and his dad had come to understand that when one of them said, "Play some catch?" it could well mean they had something on their mind.

It had been too cold to play catch this evening, so Pete and his dad had used the novel responsibility of cleaning up the kitchen to make the difficult task of talking about Pete's adoption easier. Pete's dad had taken out one of the last of the hot dishes for supper that had been brought over when his mom had died. They had checked the name taped to the bottom of the casserole dish with masking tape so they knew it had come from one of their neighbors. That hadn't made it any more palatable, however, and Pete had had a hard time of it; the French-cut style green beans with hamburger and tinned mushrooms all held together with a thick white sauce, none of which had much flavor, made Pete struggle with the pretense of eating any of it. He worried about his dad who, as far as he knew, had never spent any time in the kitchen at all while Pete's mom was alive. It seemed he'd been living off the food they'd filled the freezer with from the funeral. He sure did wolf down the disgusting hot dish at dinner. Pete wasn't sure what his dad would do when the neighbors' handouts ran out.

Helping his dad clean up in the kitchen had confirmed his suspicions that his parent's marriage was of the old school where the kitchen belonged to the wife. "Where do you think we should put this?" was a phrase Pete's dad must have asked a dozen times while the two of them tried to organize the kitchen; obviously, this was the first time it had been attempted since the funeral. In between sorting out the serving spoons from the knives and forks and the hot pad holders from the dishcloths, Pete's dad talked about the happiest day of their lives: the day they'd adopted Pete. He explained how they'd always meant to tell him but the right time never seemed to present itself. Pete was surprised when his dad admitted that he still probably wouldn't be talking to Pete about it if his birth mother hadn't called.

"What? What birth mother?" He supposed it sounded silly, but Pete truly hadn't given any thought to the notion that he had a 'birth' mother. There was the moment of birth and there was the rest of his life. His thoughts, from as far back as he could remember, dwelt on his 'life' mother then. Even now, his initial reaction was to avoid the concept of a birth mother altogether. He did not want to be disloyal in any fashion to the woman who had been his mother in every possible sense of the word except for the one physical act of giving birth. As if reading his thoughts while awkwardly wiping off the kitchen table, spreading bread crumbs onto the floor while doing so, Pete's dad continued.

"I think mom would be happy your birth mom is coming into your life now. Especially, you know, now that she's no longer here. I mean, no mother wants to leave her child parentless, no matter what age they are. So, I think she'd be glad you still had a mom, if you know what I mean. Anyhow, this woman called me up out of the blue, said she gave birth to you thirty-some years ago, thanked me for being your dad, and asked what did I think about her telling you who she was. She was asking my permission, far as I could make out.

I thought it might be kind of awkward for you especially as how we'd never even talked to you about being adopted and all. I told her to write you a letter. I put down the phone and picked it up again to call you, knowing the time had come to tell you the truth." His dad was practically wearing a spot out into the table top where he kept wiping it down with the dishrag. His fist clenched and unclenched and Pete wished they were tossing the baseball around.

He paused in sweeping the kitchen floor and leaned the broom against the counter. In a gesture he was much more comfortable doing with his mom than with his dad, he put his hands on his dad's shoulders and said, "You know what the truth is, dad? You and mom have been the best parents ever. Knowing that I was adopted doesn't change a thing about that. I am so glad you and mom were my folks." As the two men hugged awkwardly for a moment, Pete said, "I love you, dad," which his dad repeated gruffly and then excused himself to watch the ten o'clock news.

Reflecting on the evening as Pete walked around the neighborhood, he quickly rounded the corner back toward his parents' home. The air was starting to hurt a little when he breathed it deeply into his lungs. He knew that, in spring, this same temperature would feel balmy to him and he would likely have his jacket off already. His blood had thinned over the summer and the twenty-five degree temperature felt cold to him.

Pete was also walking quickly because he realized that he wanted to check the mail at his dad's house; he smiled a little sadly at how quickly he had changed from calling it his *parents'* house to now calling it his *dad's*. Maybe the letter had already arrived for him from the woman who'd called 'out of the blue.' Letting himself in the front door, Pete flipped through the stack of mail his father had left on the long, narrow table in the foyer. Nothing for Pete. As he flipped through the mail, Pete remembered his own mail that he'd grabbed just as he'd left Fargo. It must have fallen to the floor on the passenger side of the front seat. Pete walked back out to his car and carried the mail inside. Once again, he flipped through the mail and found nothing out of the ordinary. His heart had begun to beat faster in anticipation and he couldn't help but feel a little disappointed. He set aside his bills, junk mail, and the card from Emma for later.

The news was over on the television and Pete's dad had fallen asleep in front of it. Pete's mom had always told his dad that it was a good thing when he could fall asleep during the news; it meant there wasn't anything too horrendous going on which would keep them awake like watching those Twin Towers fall over and over again. Pete sat and listened to Jay Leno's monologue before waking his dad so that the two of them could put out the lights, head up to their respective rooms and get some sleep.

Pete had planned to spend the morning helping his dad pack up his mom's things from the bedroom, but his dad kept putting him off. After trying to get started several times, he finally asked again, but his dad adamantly refused his help. Pete hadn't intended to overstep his bounds, but apparently he had because it was one of the few times that he could ever remember his dad actually showing anger.

"Dad, just let me help you empty her clothes, and shoes, and stuff from the closet. It can't be good for you to keep seeing all of that every time you go in there." The slam of knuckles on the kitchen table made Pete jump.

"You can't presume to know what's good for me or not. Until you've lived with the same woman for almost fifty goddamn years, slept with her every night, shared a closet with her, then you can't assume to tell me when it's a good time to remove what's left of her from my bedroom. Until then, stay the hell out of my closet."

Pete had apologized and after a few awkward moments, they had settled down to sending out thank you cards to everyone who had sent cards, food, and attended the funeral. Pete had never seen his dad address an envelope by hand before. All of the birthday cards he'd received over the years had come from his mom. It was a cheerless task, but they worked through the morning until it was done.

When his dad went to a Lion's Club meeting, Pete got out his laptop to work on some of his own business. He opened his mail, and was stunned to find the letter from Emma was not a thank you card at all.

There was another envelope inside of the first one on which Emma had written, *Please don't open until after you've spoken to your dad.* Pete sat at the kitchen table with his long legs splayed out in front of him, holding the envelope in his hand. The cup of coffee he poured got cold as he opened the envelope and read what Emma had written.

Dear Pete,

I have dreamed of this moment my whole life. I have always wondered how you were, imagined each stage of your life as you went through it, imagined where you were, if you were well. It makes me almost unbearably glad to finally know you, to see how happy you've been. It is a miracle I had long given up on, the opportunity to know my son. Forgive me; I'm getting ahead of myself. I need to start at the beginning. But I'm not going to tear up this sheet and throw it away like I've already done to the countless other copies of this letter I have begun. So here goes.

Pete, I am your mother, the woman who gave birth to you 37 years ago. I was only 18 years old at the time, and in those days, in a small town, it was not acceptable to deliver a baby out of wedlock and raise it as your own. Your father was a nice boy also only 18. He never knew he was a father. I have lost touch with him after all these many years but I will be happy to give you his name if you would like to look him up.

Therese Dotray-Tulloch

My parents forced me to go to Minneapolis to give you up for adoption. I was too young to fight them. I never forgave them, however, and I tried to track you down but was unsuccessful.

I've never been much of one to believe in miracles, but the way you came back into my life can be described as no less than miraculous. The first day that I met you when you stood on my lawn talking about herbicide drift, I felt a familiarity which I couldn't put my finger on. When you came home from the funeral with the story of your aunt spilling the beans about your adoption, it hit me like a brick that you could be my son. I'm a little embarrassed to admit that I had your DNA tested without you knowing it. I would do it again in a heartbeat. The results are sure, we're a match.

I expect you are feeling overwhelmed by this information. Please don't feel that any action is required on your part. While I feel infinitely comforted by the fact that we already were friends even before I found out that you were my son, I understand that you may not share the same interest that I do in forming a relationship. I am already sleeping so much better at night knowing that my son is alright.

Your dad and I have talked and he is the one who encouraged me to write this letter. I would like to extend an open invitation to the two of you for dinner here at the farm whenever you think you are ready. The ball is in your court.

Emma Grabow

Pete didn't move for a while after reading the astonishing letter. Then he picked it up and read it over a couple more times. Emma Grabow, his birth mother? He suddenly had a million questions, but he knew he had plenty of time to ask them. He needed to absorb the unexpected news and he knew he wasn't up to talking to Emma yet. He did pick up his phone, however, and ordered a delivery of flowers to Emma Grabow in Opossum Falls. When the florist asked if he would like to include a message, he paused for a moment before responding, "Sure. Just say, with love from your son."

Hanging up, he saw that he had a text message. He grinned broadly when he saw that it was from Laney.

Chapter 32

The drive back to Minnesota was a therapeutic one for Laney. She kept the radio off and took advantage of the long ribbon of interstate to evaluate and organize her life. Her emotional good-bye to the spirit of her daughter, Gabby, freed her in ways she never would have imagined. As if a heavy, morbid weight were lifted off her chest and grey gloom pinched from her future, she felt as though she could breathe easier now. Gabby. She drew in a quick, startled breath as she realized she could think about her without her eyes immediately filling with tears. "I'll never forget you, Gabby," she said out loud in the silence of Marge's car. She smiled at how good it felt, how right, for her to talk to her daughter. She inhaled deeply and felt, for the first time since that awful morning of The Event, that she had the strength to survive. And now she wanted to see her son.

Halfway through the state of Kansas, a light dusting of snow covered the countryside which gradually became inches as she drove through Iowa into Minnesota. The sun sat low in the sky casting long, reaching shadows of the leafless trees she passed along the highway.

There was such an aching beauty to the intricate designs of the bare branches stretching up to the brilliant blue sky. The trees appeared dead in their absence of foliage but, of course, they were simply dormant. In a few months, the advent of spring would sprout buds upon the brittle branches holding the promise of the blossoming of life. Deep inside, Laney felt the stirrings of her own rebirth beginning to bud. As the sun slipped below the horizon, the Western sky began to blush, first a soft, delicate rosy color soon turning to shocking, dazzling pink. The winter season awarded those who suffered through it with the most spectacular sunsets of the year, stunning in their brilliance and generous in their duration. Long after the sun had set and the sky was nearly dark, a gorgeous rosy hue shone up directly above where the sun had gone down shining as brightly as though a spotlight were glowing from below that speck on the horizon. The beauty from her left window illuminated Laney's trip the rest of the way home.

Laney spent a few long-overdue days with her parents. She had spoken with them weekly since Gabby's death, but the conversations never went beyond simply reassuring one another that they were alright. Her parents wanted desperately to relieve their daughter's pain, but that simply wasn't possible. Being together had become too hurtful on both sides, so Laney had simply stayed away. The look of relief on her mother's face at the door caused Laney to feel a rush of guilt at the never-ending pain she had caused to those she loved. The two women sobbed as they embraced and likely would have carried on for hours had her father not stood in the hallway clearing his throat saying, "Good to have you home, Laney," as he gave her a warm, long hug. Being with them gave her the strength she needed to continue on her path to wellness.

She had called Mr. Schluter at Pick and Pay after she'd left town with Izzy and asked if she could have some time off. While not happy about it, he had nonetheless told her she would have her job waiting for her when she got back as he'd appreciated her loyalty up till then. She'd asked Marge if she could keep her car for just a few days longer. With still no word from Juan Carlos, Marge was worried sick but said she was fine without her car for the time being. She'd called Cath and told her how much she was looking forward to another night of bottomless glasses of wine and soul sharing. Not feeling confident enough to call, she sent Pete a text telling him that she was alright and asking how he was doing. She'd barely pressed the send button when her phone played "You've got a friend in me," the song Pete had programmed into her phone to ring when it was his phone calling. She was smiling as she answered. Surprised to learn he was also in the Twin Cities, she agreed to meet him for dinner near Calhoun Square.

The Uptown area was crowded as usual, so Laney ended up practically parking at Lake Calhoun before she found a spot. She was late as she hurried down Thirty-First Street to reach the tiny neighborhood restaurant. Pete was standing outside waiting for her; the initial touch of their lips was icy cold from the chilly night air. Clinging hungrily to each other, their mouths quickly heated up as they pressed firmly against each another. Laney placed her hand on Pete's chest and gently pushed him back.

"Holy mackerel! I missed you, too, Laney."

Laney smiled and leaned in to softly touch her lips to Pete's once more. "We have a lot of catching up to do."

"Actually, I'm beginning to see the benefits of short separations from time to time." While Pete leaned in for another kiss, Laney pushed him away and said she was freezing and starving, so they headed into Lucia's.

Pete dug right into his hanger steak with mashed potatoes and asparagus while Laney lingered over her beautifully-presented dinner. She was savoring the seared arctic char, leek pancakes and roasted peppers with zucchini in a delicately herbed yogurt sauce. Pete had hung on every word as Laney had told him about Juan Carlos' arrest, Isabella Rose's misery, their impromptu trip to Mexico, and finally about finding Tia Juanita. After the waitress had served their artisan cheese plate with grape juice drizzled over it, Laney sat back in her chair struggling to find a way to share the secrets of her past with the man she had a feeling was going to be an important part of her future. At a loss for words, she finally sighed and said simply, "There are some things that you have a right to know about me, Pete." After a long pause, she went on, "First of all, I have a son."

Pete gazed into those pain-filled blue eyes, grateful to be hearing her story at last and said, "Well, I *am* a son. I mean, of course I am, but I just found out that I am the son of someone we both know." Laney's eyebrows arched in surprise. "But, you first, Laney. I've been waiting a long time to hear your story." He reached across the table and held her hand while she told him the story of Gabby's life from the moment she gave birth to her to the tragic split second she unwittingly took her life away again. She shed a few tears in the telling, of course, and Pete, too, felt his eyes fill as he struggled to keep the horror from his face. No wonder Laney walked around with a heart broken in grief. They sat in silence after Laney described the hospital room where she had to be dragged away from Gabby so the organ harvest could begin. Pete couldn't be silent, however, when Laney described how the police had come then to arrest her for Criminal Vehicular Homicide in the death of her daughter.

"Those sons of bitches, my god! Couldn't they see you were suffering enough as it was?"

"No. I mean, of course it was unbearable at the time. I wanted to be the one who had died. And then I was glad that they had arrested me. I felt that I deserved that, too. Now I just see that they were doing their job. Gabby deserved that. They stayed the sentence eventually, and I was put on probation, but that's finished now, too.

That's why I freaked out over the reporters looking for the scoop on Walter when he first went up the oak tree. I had been hounded for so long after Gabby's death. Even after I was released from the hospital, they were there shoving their microphones into my face, snapping pictures. I went to Opossum Falls for a lot of reasons, but one of them was to hide. After a while, I began to let my guard down and I practically felt safe. The day the reporters showed up scared me out of my wits."

Finally, Laney told Pete about the breakdown of her marriage to Scott not long after the loss of their child. She didn't blame Scott at all; in fact, she still felt very close to him. She simply had been unable to forgive herself for causing Gabby's death and she couldn't bear to see the loss in Scott's eyes for the rest of her life. Furthermore, she felt incapable of being a mother to their little boy. Since then, Scott had married a wonderful woman named Melinda who up until now had been raising Michael as her own son; they also had another boy of their own. For the first time since The Event, however, Laney felt able to be a part of her son's life again.

Pete offered to be with Laney the following day when she went to see
Michael. She said she appreciated the offer and that she would
consider it, but somehow she felt as though she should be alone when
she reunited with her son at last.

Over cappuccinos and Lucia's legendary chocolate chip cookies, Laney
insisted that Pete explain his news about 'being someone's son'. He
didn't want to change the subject but she begged him to, saying that
she was tired of talking about herself. She was shocked to learn that
Emma Grabow had given birth to Pete. There was a distinct flutter in
her stomach when Pete smiled wryly and said, "I guess I'll have to
spend lots and lots of time in Opossum Falls now, you know, getting
to know her better and all."

He reached across the table and slowly slipped his fingers through
Laney's until they were tightly entwined while they looked deeply into
each other's eyes. Her voice was soft as she murmured with a smile,
"So, now, you're 'For Opossum Falls,' too, hmmm? Walter would be
glad to know it."

~~~~~~~~~~~~~~~~~~~~~~~~~~~~~~~~~

Marge grunted as she threw her weight behind the stick shift to get it
into gear. Hell's bells, she thought, if the situation weren't so serious,
the fact that she was trying to drive a stick shift again after a hiatus of
some fifty years might be funny. The truck jerked a couple of times
while she tried to ease her left foot off of the clutch. Rubbing the
back of her neck to soothe her nearly whiplashed muscles, she
reminded herself to be grateful that Minnesota was mostly flat as a
pancake, and then quickly put her hand back on the shift to move into
a higher gear. Honestly, she'd forgotten how much you had to
concentrate when driving a stick, constantly listening for the whine of
the engine as it cried its need to move up a gear. Her left foot and
right arm were already exhausted from the unusual exercise and she
was barely five miles out of Opossum Falls. She glanced over at the
passenger seat to be sure she had not forgotten Juan Carlos' billfold
which had been returned to her by Federal Express, thanks to Scott

Anderson. All of the jerking around caused by her unfamiliarity driving with the clutch had lodged the wallet in the seat fold, but Marge felt reassured to see it there.

She had gotten the call at last from Myrna Vaquero telling her that ICE had informed them of Juan Carlos' whereabouts. They were planning to process him that morning, so Marge was hightailing it over there to prove his identity and let them know he was a U.S. citizen by showing them his driver's license and social security card. It was a crime that this could have been done five days ago if anyone had simply cared enough to listen to Juan Carlos. Marge gripped the wheel in anger as she thought how all of this should have been avoided. Of course, she was feeling guilty, too, that it was all her fault. If only she hadn't asked Juan Carlos to drive her car in the panic of the moment when she'd learned about Walter's fall. She sighed thinking about all of the 'if only's' throughout one's lifetime; surely, they would fill the pages of an entire book.

Marge drove straight South on highway six. She stayed in the middle of the road as much as she could as the edges of the road shone with an icy veneer. When she saw another car approaching, she slowed down and carefully stayed in her lane. Soon she was snaking down to the Minnesota River. The river was gradually freezing from the outer banks inward so the movement of water was reduced to a thin stream in the middle of the tributary. The bare branches of the trees near the river bottom sparkled with the early morning hoar frost, white ice crystals that had formed after the cold clear night when heat loss to the open sky caused the branches to become colder than the surrounding air. The glittering phenomenon occurred only a few times per winter and was so dazzling that normally Marge would have pulled over to marvel at the magical formations, snapping pictures to document winter in all its glory. Now, however, she concentrated on downshifting as she descended to the bottom to ford the river then struggled to shift smoothly as she ascended up the other side. For a moment, she wanted to kill Laney for still being in possession of her car. Driving Juan Carlos' truck was not what she had in mind when she imagined herself arriving swiftly to his rescue when he was finally found.

Marge crossed the line into Redwood County. It was only about twenty-five miles from Opossum Falls to Redwood Falls, so soon Marge was approaching the picturesque little town and searching for

Third Street. The historic town of just over five thousand was situated on the original site of the Dakota Indian Reservation where the early settlers had tried to corral the natives. Present-day Christmas decorations glittered from the lamp posts creating a charming, Thomas Kincaid-like ambiance throughout the homey little village.

Marge wondered if Juan Carlos had been here in Redwood Falls for all this time. She had called around to all of the county jails in the first days of Juan Carlos' wrongful detainment. She wracked her brain trying to remember is she'd talked to the sheriff of Redwood County or not. She scolded herself for not physically driving around the entire state of Minnesota searching out every jail cell, but then the truck jerked violently again as she slowed down without shifting and she knew she would soon end up in the hospital with recurrent whiplash if she had to drive for much longer. She promised herself to appreciate the magnificent invention of automatic gears the next time she ventured out in her own car again. She drove past the brick Redwood County Courthouse and wondered what the strange-looking emblem on the top of the building was; it looked rather like a sheep's horn. She circled around the Courthouse Square until she arrived at the Sheriff's office which housed the county jail.

There was a parking space directly in front, but it would require her to parallel park. Marge hesitated for a millisecond, just long enough for the truck to begin to shudder, so she put her foot on the gas to drive to a more easily accessible parking space. It was completely on the other side of the square, but at least all she had to do was pull forward into the spot. She thrust her feet down onto the clutch and brake and hastily turned the keys to the off position to yank them out of the ignition. She was so relieved not to be driving anymore but was too nervous about the condition in which she might find Juan Carlos to revel very much in her arrival.

Marge grabbed her purse and Juan Carlos' billfold and began walking across the square. The trees were strung with Christmas lights creating a cheery scene. Marge tried to calm herself by appreciating the pretty square as she walked across it, glad she had worn comfortable, warm boots as she stepped over the small pile of snow left behind by the snowplow. She walked briskly across the street. As

Therese Dotray-Tulloch

she pushed open the door to the sheriff's office, she stomped her feet on the brown service mat to shake off any slush before she walked in any farther.

Chapter 33

Waking up to the unfamiliar but wonderful feeling of a warm, breathing human chest for a pillow, Marge lay still and reveled in the comforting serenity. She admired the look of her pale hand against Juan Carlos bronze-colored stomach and she bit her lips at the stirring deep within her which the sensuous sight evoked. Marge smiled to herself as she thought about Charles, her husband of so many years and her previous love-making partner. What would Charles think if he were alive and able to give his opinion? Of course, if he were alive, then Marge wouldn't be here in the arms of her lover; she would be home in her familiar bed with dear Charles snoring beside her. She sensed a profound awareness settle over her as she felt tremendously alive. She stretched out her fingers and felt herself tingling all over as though every hair on her entire body was standing on end. Her senses were fully alert and she felt her heart beating steadily within her. She recognized what she was feeling: she was happy. How lovely to recognize within herself the elusive but all-powerful sensation of happiness.

Late last night after Juan Carlos had carefully removed all of her clothes and had slowly made love to her in the soft light of the street lamp shining into the hotel room, Marge had called him her Latin Lover, and he had chuckled, a low rumble emitting from his chest. He'd accused her of using him to fulfill a fantasy as she had told him all about her lifelong crush on Antonio Banderas.

Through the stillness of the early morning, Marge listened to the sound of a car crunching over the snow on Bridge Street in front of the Redwood Valley Lodge thinking how she couldn't have planned a more perfect reunion with Juan Carlos if she'd tried. But, of course, she hadn't planned this; when she had parked in Redwood Falls, she'd merely left the lights on in his truck causing the battery to go dead. For so long she had driven cars which automatically turned the headlights on and off that she had totally forgotten to shut them off on the truck after she'd turned them on as she'd driven through the dark river bottom. Ignoring completely the Triple A card slipped dependably in the wallet inside of her purse, Marge had agreed with Juan Carlos that it was best to walk over to the Redwood Valley Lodge and deal with finding a jump for the truck in the morning. The desire she read in his eyes was matched only by her own. The anticipation of their first time making love taking place in a hotel room heightened the appeal; being in a place free of memories was also beneficial. They had walked to Chumly's first. Lingering over the hamburgers and root beer the restaurant was famous for, Juan Carlos had told Marge all about his five days in the Redwood County Jail.

On that fateful morning, Brandon had driven Juan Carlos straight to Redwood Falls and dumped him on the rookie Deputy Sheriff on duty without explanation. Within the shady ICE handbook's vague mention of holding a suspect for up to five days without charging them, Brandon took refuge and abandoned Juan Carlos until the fifth day. Much as Juan Carlos had tried to explain to the Redwood County officials that he was an American Citizen and could easily prove it, they claimed that because the ICE agent declared he had been driving without a license and was officially in ICE jurisdiction, there was nothing they could do about it.

If he hadn't been worried about Isabella Rose, it wouldn't have been half bad residing in the Redwood County Jail. There was a reasonable sized T.V., three meals a day, and access to pencil, paper, and reading materials. As it was, Juan Carlos was worried sick about Izzy. She must have been so frightened by his absence; she had already lost too many people she loved. He was frustrated beyond measure to not be allowed to call his granddaughter's caretaker to explain his circumstances. And what was his situation? He was an American citizen of Hispanic origin who, in helping out a friend, had left his driver's license behind. Five days in jail for the negligent act of driving without his driver's license in his possession. What had this country come to?

It had taken every measure of Juan Carlos' willpower to remain civil to ICE Agent Hopkins when he finally darkened the doorway of Juan Carlos' cell. Arrogantly informing Juan Carlos that he had already called his immigration lawyer, Juan Carlos stated through gritted teeth that he had no need of an immigration lawyer as he was not an immigrant. He used his one allotted phone call to Isabella Rose's daycare where he was given the devastating news that his granddaughter had run away but that they'd heard she was safe in Mexico. He suffered another agonizing hour until, to his astonishment, Marge appeared, thanks to the Vaqueros' informing her of Juan Carlos' whereabouts, waving his driver's license and social security card at the Deputy Sheriff and gaining Juan Carlos' immediate release. She had quickly assured him that Isabella Rose was safely and happily residing temporarily with her beloved Tia Juanita, thanks to Laney's quick thinking and long driving. Juan Carlos had so many questions, Marge was still answering them as they walked to Chumly's and all throughout dinner. When Marge's cell phone had rung and she saw that it was the Vaquero Law Office, she handed the phone to Juan Carlos telling him that he needed to talk to them. ICE Agent Hopkins was out of control and his treatment of Juan Carlos needed to be publicized.

Juan Carlos groaned and tightened his arms around Marge. "Am I dreaming?" he murmured as he buried his face in her hair. "I was afraid of who they might arrest and put in jail with me, but perhaps I was foolish to have dreaded it." Marge laughed as she snuggled more deeply into Juan Carlos' embrace, deciding not to mention that there was a distinct possibility his truck may have been towed due to the snow removal trucks she heard rumbling through the town. Oh well, they would surely have jumper cables at the tow lot. Until then, Marge planned to take full advantage of one of the hidden secrets a winter storm presented unbeknownst to those residing in warmer climes: the opportunity to feel no guilt whatsoever for snuggling warmly indoors while the blustery weather whirled away on the other side of the wall.

Epilogue

ICE Agent Brandon Hopkins felt his heart rate increase as he approached Opossum Falls. He turned onto Main Street and drove slowly while he looked left and right searching for anyone he knew. The street was crowded with pedestrians made up of a familiar small town mix of old farmer's in bib overalls, stylish young moms in platform sandals pushing strollers with Gap-clothed toddlers, and middle-aged Hispanics dressed to the nines in vibrant colors of shiny fabrics in tight skirts which flattered their full figures. The atmosphere was festive as the annual pageant was soon to begin. The screech from his passenger caused Brandon to jump, but he did as he was told and eased into the next available parking spot.

"Oh, my gosh, there it is, just like my cousin said," Liliana Gonzalez squealed, clapping her hands together with glee. "Look, look at the sign, doesn't that look nice?"

Brandon turned off the ignition and lowered his head to look past Liliana through her window, reading the sign out loud, "Yup, there it is alright: Gonzalez's Chit Chat Restaurant. Wait, what? Does that say 'Chit-Chat-Charla'?"

Liliana laughed as she pulled down the visor and looked in the mirror to reapply more glossy lipstick of the aptly-named color *Siren*. She carefully bit her lips together and moved them around a little, then blotted them on a Kleenex and pouted into the mirror once more to be sure the application was complete. "Oh, that's so cute! 'Charla' means 'chat' in Spanish, see? Chit-Chat-Charla, the best Mexican restaurant in Renville County," Liliana read from the bottom of the sign. She wiped a trace of lipstick off her front tooth while a little frown line appeared between her delicate eyebrows plucked so drastically they were scarcely more than two thin lines perched high above her rich brown eyes causing her to look permanently surprised. "My cousins could have reached a little further than just Renville County, don't you think, mi amor? Perhaps, the 'best Mexican Restaurant in Southern Minnesota,' no?"

"I say, let's go find out. We have just enough time for a grande burrito before the pageant begins," Brandon said as he quickly stepped out of the car to hurry around to the passenger side to open the door for Liliana. He admired her shapely calf above her sexy red shoes with the precariously high heels as he reached for her hand to help her out of the car. He couldn't resist a quick peck as he drew her near him, then he quickly straightened and gallantly stuck out his elbow so Liliana could hold on to him as they walked into the Chit-Chat-Charla.

Bianca and Liliana both shrieked in unison as they ran toward each other and air kissed a few times. Ever since Emma Grabow had purchased the Chit Chat from Tom and Betty Larson and given it to the Gonzalez's, Bianca had been beaming. Emma had said that keeping Bianca and her wonderful cooking in town was her gift to Opossum Falls.

After hugs and exclamations of delight, Bianca finally turned to Brandon, her eyes sparkling with good humor as she shook the hand of her husband's cousin's fiancé, the infamous ICE agent turned Hispanic advocate, if the rumors were to be believed. Even so, she took a perverse amount of pleasure in noting the hot pink lipstick staining his upper lip, which she was sure no one in all of Opossum

Falls would be considerate enough to tell Agent Hopkins about, to save him from the embarrassment he would suffer when he finally looked in a mirror and saw how ridiculous he appeared. He may be a kinder, gentler ICE agent now, but still.

Last fall, when Brandon's Immigration and Customs Enforcement supervisors heard of his unlawful detainment of Juan Carlos, a legal United States' citizen, they felt pressured to enforce some form of disciplinary action upon him. The reputation of ICE had recently suffered from shocking revelations from the Michigan office, and the public was already rightfully displeased with the Agency. The Assistant Director of the Detroit ICE office had just been sentenced to thirty-seven months in prison for receiving bribes and defrauding the United States. Roy Bailey had confessed to accepting cash and other valuable items including, in one instance, landscaping work to be done at his house, in return for benefits to illegal immigrants to which they were not entitled. Furthermore, one of Bailey's employees, ICE Detention Officer Patrick Wynne, was allowed to systematically steal hundreds of thousands of dollars in cash from nearly five hundred immigration detainees over the course of four years, for which he was sentenced to serve almost five years in prison following an embezzlement plea.

This desire to demonstrate that Agent Hopkins was not getting away with his wrongful vigilante behavior was heightened due to the unseemly amount of publicity Juan Carlos' case received. The publicity started with the Opossum Falls Digest, the Minneapolis Tribune, and then, once Izzy's Youtube video of her singing "A Year Without Rain" went viral, even to the New York Times. The much maligned government agency had to be quick to show the world that discipline of ICE agents acting out of line was swift and appropriate.

Brandon was initially assigned to participate in the 'Sentence to Serve' program, picking up trash, and painting over the remarkably beautiful graffiti found throughout the inner city of St. Paul. While he was furious, at first, over the humiliation he was forced to endure performing manual labor which he felt was far beneath his dignity, after a few weeks, Brandon was surprised to find he was experiencing enormous job satisfaction. Taking garbage bags full of trash he had collected along the banks of the Mississippi River to the dump made him feel prouder of himself than months of illegal alien chasing had ever done. It was during the Cinco de Mayo Fiesta week-end, however, that his life had changed forever.

He was stationed at Our Lady of Guadalupe Catholic Church in St. Paul to assist in the extensive West Side preparations and to be on hand during the parade to prevent the toddler turnout from being trampled. He first noticed Liliana Gonzalez when she was in front of the church stringing up the colorful, massive flowers made of tissue paper. Her thick, shiny black hair shone in the sunlight over her soft emerald green, tightly-fitted suit. She was wearing sturdy, black high-heeled shoes while climbing up a step ladder to attach the bright yellow blossoms to the wall, rattling away in vivacious Spanish to the two teenage boys assisting her. The boys were bent over the cardboard box filled with flowers and didn't notice the ladder slowly tilting over to one side. Liliana screamed and was just about to topple to the ground when, suddenly, Brandon was swooping her into his arms holding on to her closely while the ladder clattered harmlessly onto its side.

"Ay, dios mio," Liliana exclaimed breathlessly, gazing with delight into Brandon's startled eyes before throwing her head back to laugh heartily, exposing her silkily smooth caramel colored neck, "You look more frightened than I feel, mister…."

Enjoying the feel of her round, firm womanly bottom in his arms, Brandon was rendered speechless and stood there looking helplessly into Liliana's eyes until he was embarrassed to feel a tightness in his jeans resulting from the pleasure he was getting from holding her in his arms. "Er, Hopkins….it's Hopkins. But, please, call me Brandon," he said haltingly as he hastily dropped her legs so she was standing on her feet. She still had her arms circled around his neck so she fell into him when she landed on her feet and the two boys whistled and clapped, congratulating Brandon on his chivalry. Hurriedly stepping away from her, Brandon bent over pretending to search in the box full of paper flowers to try to hide his erection. He mumbled something about being at her service to help with decorations and anything else she needed from him over the course of the Cinco de Mayo celebrations while Liliana smiled in response.

Easily surpassing the service hours expected from him, Brandon stayed by Liliana's side throughout the entire preparation for and celebration of the Cinco de Mayo festivities that long, lovely week-end in St. Paul. Insisting that Brandon taste his first churro, Liliana placed it between his teeth as she stood on tiptoe to watch and see what he thought of the warm, sugary, slightly crunchy pastry. When he reciprocated and fed her a churro in return, he thought he would die with desire; she made the act of biting and chewing the donut look so sensuous. Breathless, right then and there he asked her to marry him underneath the garish string of lights with the sounds of the Mariachi band's guitarron strumming in the background. Liliana laughed and didn't take him seriously, at first, but the following week-end when Brandon took her to Boca Chica Restaurante and got down on one knee, cupping a tiny silk box up to her which contained a sweetly delicate engagement ring, she realized with delight that he was sincere. While the violinist in the restaurant's Mariachi band played Guantanamera, the only Spanish song Brandon knew to request, Liliana responded affirmatively to his proposal, her eyes shining with tears of happiness.

No one was more surprised by Brandon's complete reversal in behavior and performance than the Vaqueros. Brandon had turned up with a bottle of Aguardiente at Vaquero Law Office late one afternoon to apologize to them personally for his treatment of their client, Juan Carlos. With the spicy, licorice liquor relaxing their tongues, they ended up visiting long into the evening and discovering some mutual passions. The Vaquero males learned that Brandon not only shared their love for soccer but in particular that he, too, was a huge Ricardo Izecson fan, feeling sure that the Brazilian known as 'Kaka' would go on to become the best soccer player in the world.

When Myrna Vaquero grew bored with talk of the footballers, she pulled out her current knitting project and began clicking away on her needles. Brandon came over to compliment her even stitches and expressed his appreciation for her garter and stockinette stitch cable pattern. Myrna was astonished that the hardened ICE agent was also an ardent knitter for which he gave all of the credit to his paternal grandmother. She had spent many hours taking care of Brandon when he was a delinquent teenager, and they had discovered knitting was something they enjoyed doing together while watching reruns of *The*

Simpsons on her small twenty-six inch screen TV.

From that day, Brandon's relationship with the Vaqueros grew to be a mutually beneficial one and he became the ICE agent they turned to more and more for help with their immigration cases. Getting to know Liliana, her extended family and friends and understanding firsthand the problems facing them, Agent Hopkins, in turn, used the Vaqueros in his surprisingly increasing role as advocate for the Hispanic population.

It was weeks later when they realized that Liliana was Anthony Gonzalez' cousin and that coincidentally, Brandon had dined often in the restaurant which Bianca and Anthony now owned in Opossum Falls. Reluctantly confessing to Liliana his appalling behavior in Opossum Falls the previous year, Brandon set off on a path to make up for the mistakes of his past.

~~~~~~~~~~~~~~~~~~~~~~~~~~~~~~~~~

The 78th Sugar Beet Days Festival began on a gorgeous fall day following nearly a week of rain, but no one had complained about the rain because the farmers knew the soil needed it after the particularly dry summer. The sugar beet harvest would be a muddy one, however, and the chains were taken out of storage and kept handy for when the tractors and loading trucks got stuck in the muck. The first day of the festival, the sun was out but already sitting lower in the sky in the northern hemisphere as the shorter days of winter loomed on the horizon. Laney was glad she had bought the little red sweatshirt for Michael to wear to his first Sugar Beet Days Festival.

This year's festival logo was obviously inspired by Michael Jackson, and the volunteers were all wearing dark red tee shirts with a strikingly-white glove holding a tulip-shaped sugar beet with bold letters underneath the glove spelling out "Beet It". The Sugar Beet Days buttons, the wearing of which was required to attend any of the week-end's festivities, sported the same logo. There had been some interesting runners up in the logo selection process which made the decision a difficult one for the Festival board. Someone had submitted a beautiful drawing of the oak tree Walter had protested and ultimately died in, with sugar beets dangling from the ends of the bare branches like ornaments on a Christmas tree. Someone else had proposed a take-off of the town's new "For Opossum Falls" motto and written 'For Opossum Falls Sugar Beets' inside of a red circle. Mayor Jens Jenson's secret favorite was the large mouth with rather bad teeth, a wisecrack about the negative effects of sugar, and the sugar beet poised in front of it as if the mouth were about to bite into it like an apple. Publicly, he admonished the contestant who entered such a logo for its harmful publicity to the sugar beet industry.

Laney and Pete walked on either side of Michael with his little arms stretched high as he held on to each of their hands. Every fourth step, Michael would clasp more tightly and lift up his feet squealing, "Wheeeee!" while they swung him forward and his feet landed with a plop onto the sidewalk. Thanks to the wonderful innocence of children, Michael had warmly welcomed Laney into his life, and Pete as well, with nothing but delight to have two more people showering him with love and attention. Scott and Melinda retained permanent custody, but Michael loved his monthly visits to Opossum Falls.

Years from now, when Michael turned thirteen and was at the humiliating stage all boys must go through on the road to manhood, when voices vacillate between deep rumbles and sudden screeches, splotchy, oozing pimples drip from shiny faces, and female classmates turn into goddesses while they remain remarkably small and delicate, Laney would tell him the awful role she had played in his big sister's death. Michael had always been told that he had an older sister who had died suddenly at the clinic when Michael was just a baby. One day, Laney would explain what had really happened.

Michael saw the beet red cotton candy booth and began begging for a stick. While Laney took him to stand in line, Pete stopped to chat with Juan Carlos in front of Just Screw It. After Walter's death, his family was feeling heartbroken at having to close the hardware store their father had built into such a strong representation of small town survival. With the building and inventory paid for, they really had no desire nor need to sell it, but none of them were interested or able to return to Opossum Falls to run the business. Marge took advantage of her position of influence within the Fassbinder family as close neighbor and confident to suggest that they sell the business to Juan Carlos for a mere pittance. He was delighted to take over the business and was still able to do landscaping work on the side as Karen claimed she came with the building and stayed on working behind the counter at the hardware store.

The dairy booth was set up on Main Street selling popular sugar beet milkshakes. The sign above the stand read, 'Got Beet?' The Beet Run, the annual 5k run and the Tour de Beet, the 15, 30, and 60 mile bike rides which would take place over the week end had booths open for registration. There was also a place to sign up for the highly competitive Beet Eating contest, as well as a huge tent set up to accept the variety of dishes entered in the Beet Tasting contest ranging from Buttered Beets and Pickled Beets to Bacon-wrapped Beets and Beet Mousse.

Emma Grabow stood behind a table where she was accepting entries of homemade bottles of wine for the first ever wine tasting competition in Opossum Falls. While some of the wines were, indeed, made from sugar beets, they didn't have to be, and the variety of fruit used to make the wines ranged from rhubarb to gooseberry with some grape varietals thrown in, too. Pete's Dad was helping Emma out in the booth as he'd driven up to experience his first ever Sugar Beet Days' Festival. Pete wasn't quite sure what to make of the amount of time Emma and his Dad spent together, but they sure seemed to enjoy one another's company. Pete had a feeling that Opossum Falls might become his Dad's home one day, too.

 When Laney, Pete, and Michael walked past, Pete reminded Emma that first thing Monday morning he was coming with the crew to take down the netting that had been protecting Emma's grapes from the gratuitous feasting by every bird in Renville County. As soon as the netting was taken down, the grape harvest would begin. Pete was using this year's vacation from work to harvest Emma's grapes. He had wanted to use them to go on a honeymoon with Laney, but she'd said she would rather use the money to make some improvements on the new home they had recently purchased and to save the honeymoon for another year. They had bought Walter's old home and were now happy to be next door neighbors of Marge and Juan Carlos. Truthfully, Pete had already decided that he was ready to resign from his position with the Department of Agriculture to become a fulltime viticulturist. He wanted to be sure this year's harvest was as fruitful as he anticipated it would be before he turned in his resignation. He was excited to add some new varietals of grapes to Emma's vineyard the following spring, and she was thrilled to be able to work side by side with her son. Pete was very fond of Emma as had been long before he learned that she had given birth to him. They were both enjoying one another's presence in each other's lives and, Pete had to admit, the vineyard added a lot to the already sweet relationship.

Living next to Marge and Juan Carlos was beneficial when they had Michael visiting because he and Isabella Rose loved to play together. In fact, even when Michael wasn't there, Izzy was a regular visitor at their house due to the close bonds Laney and Izzy had formed on their adventure to Mexico. Juan Carlos had been so glad to be reunited with his granddaughter again. Izzy had loved being in Mexico with Tia Juanita although she had naturally missed her grandfather a lot.

One of Tia Juanita's nephews had videotaped Izzy singing a beautiful rendition of Selena Gomez' 'Year Without Rain' in both English and Spanish just as Selena is able to do. She dedicated the song to her 'Grandpa in jail in Minnesota' and looked dolefully into the camera as she held her arms out wide singing, "A day without you, is like a day without rain," and she would wiggle her fingers downwards like raindrops falling. When it kept getting hits on Youtube, it quickly went viral, and the negative fallout from all of the online comments blaming the government for wrongfully separating a little girl from her care-giving grandpa was huge. The government paid Juan Carlos an undisclosed sum in reparation for his five days in jail as a result of the publicity from the video, and he and Marge drove down to Mexico to bring Izzy back home with them.

At the festival, Michael was just about finished with his cotton candy when they rounded the corner to see the long line to get into the pageant snaking down the street. Laney knew Cath would be saving a spot in line, so they carried on walking, greeting many they knew who were waiting in line in the festive atmosphere. At last they spotted Cath and Eric pushing a stroller with only a dozen people ahead of them in line waiting at the door. They greeted one another with hugs and kisses as Cath complimented Laney on her sassy skirt with her stylish boots and Laney exclaimed over the baby. Michael immediately started playing peek-a-boo with Ida while she squealed with delight.

Shannon Fischer had not only agreed to let the Hanson's adopt her baby, she had also asked Cath to be with her at the hospital when she gave birth. For Cath, who had participated in far too many pregnancies with heartbreaking endings, this was more than she could have ever dreamed of. Cath began taking Shannon to her doctor appointments; the first time she saw the baby on the ultrasound monitor, she cried so hard her mascara and eyeliner formed into an eerily melting mask; the fact that Cath didn't care about her appearance at all but merely raved on and on about the magic of seeing the healthy fetus convinced Shannon she was making the right decision for her baby.

The night that Cath got the call that Shannon was ready to head to the hospital had followed an unseasonably warm day in the middle of March, so the fog blanketing the road only enhanced the surrealness of the night. Cath was the perfect coach for Shannon all through the long labor, holding her hand, bringing her ice chips, walking her up and down the corridor between contractions, distracting her with music and stories. When at last the baby's head crowned, Shannon drew Cath's hand down between her legs so she could touch her daughter while she was still in the passage of the womb, being in contact with her from the earliest moment possible.

Dick McGee came soon after the baby was born, and the adoption papers were signed. Shannon had been adamant in her instructions to Cath that after she left the hospital, she wanted no more contact with the baby. She felt it would be far too painful, and besides, she didn't want Cath to feel she was peering over her shoulder and judging her parenting skills. Not only would she be leaving Opossum Falls as soon as she graduated to head to St. Peter, but her parents were leaving town, too, as her father had been assigned to serve in a parish way up north in Embarrass, Minnesota. Shannon knew she was making the right decision; Cath and Eric would be wonderful parents and her little girl would grow up in a home where she was truly wanted.

On a whim, Cath named the baby Ida as her birth date was on the ides of March. The two women were dreading the final moment when Shannon would put her baby forever and always into Cath's arms when inexplicably, Dick McGee began to speak:

"There was a woman who arrived at the doctor's office with a baby. She was taken into the examining room to wait for the doctor. After the doctor examined the baby he said that he thought the baby was too skinny. "Is he breastfed or on the bottle?" Doc asked.

"Oh, he's breastfed," the woman replied.

"Please strip down to your waist," the doctor said.

She took off her blouse and her bra and sat on the examining table while the doctor started pressing, kneading, and pinching both breasts for several, long minutes giving her a very detailed, thorough examination. Afterwards, he told her to get dressed and he said, "No wonder this baby is so thin. You don't have any milk."

The woman smiled contentedly and said, "Of course I don't, I'm his aunt.....but I'm sure glad I brought him in!"

There was a long moment of quiet while Dick gathered up his briefcase and quietly let himself out of the room. Shannon and Cath looked at each other in astonishment before Shannon said, "Oh my god," and her shoulders started to shake as she began to giggle. Cath joined her, laughing so hard she collapsed onto Shannon's bed. Only when Shannon started to moan that laughing hurt her bottom did the two try to pull themselves together. They looked in each other's eyes. There was nothing to say then, the moment was too big to be expressed in words. Bravely, neither of them cried as Shannon stretched out her arms with baby Ida nestled in her pastel blanket for Cath to reach out to take her, and she walked out of the room.

~~~~~~~~~~~~~~~~~~~~~~~~~~~~~~~~

The pageant doors opened at last and the crowd filed excitedly in as they rushed to find seats. Leaving the stroller at the back of the auditorium, they slid into a row with enough seats for all of them. Up ahead, they saw Bianca surrounded by lots of relatives, all there to cheer on Anita Beatrice. It didn't take long for everyone to get seated and soon the lights were dimming and the pageant was about to begin. There was a lot of excited murmuring throughout the auditorium, much of it dedicated to speculation as to whose joke Dick McGee had chosen to tell while the judges' votes were being tallied at the end of the pageant. Laney smiled warmly at Cath knowing how excited she was to be acknowledged as 'former sugar beet' royalty this year. She planned to stand up proudly with baby Ida in her arms.

The first contestant set the bar high with a beautiful medley from the *Phantom of the Opera* which she performed by alternately singing the haunting melody or drawing it out on her violin. From there, the pageant moved swiftly along with the remaining contestants showing off a variety of talents including tap dancing, singing, poetry reading, oboe playing, and, a first for the Sugar Beet Pageant, dart throwing. The contestant was pretty good, too, landing three bull's-eyes in a row. She should have stopped while she was ahead, however, because the next throw after that popped a balloon onstage which startled Sister Beatrice of the Bleeding Heart so much it gave her the hiccups. The rest of the pageant sounded like it was being performed to a metronome as Sister hiccupped along.

Bianca's daughter, Anita Beatrice, performed a dramatic flamenco dance in honor of her great grandmother's heritage. In a gorgeous black and red costume with an intricately designed, full skirt which flowed out and dazzled the audience, Anita twirled and clapped her castanets. She danced through the sequences of the traditional flamenco dance, enthusing the audience so much that they joined in and clapped along, something the judges always reacted very positively to, resulting in extra points for the contestant.

After each contestant answered a question, introduced her parents, and walked in figure eights around the stage, the judges cast their final votes. While they were being tallied, Dick McGee walked on stage. After thanking everyone for all of their hard work, announcing the highlights of the events happening during the Sugar Beet Days' Festival, and generally schmoozing with the audience, Dick at last began telling the long anticipated joke:

"Two guys were hanging out on a hot September afternoon with their dogs. After a while, one of them wiped his sweaty brow and said, "Let's go over to that bar and get something to drink."

His friend said, "We can't. We've got our dogs with us."

"Watch this," his pal said, as he began to put on sunglasses. He walked into the bar while his friend peered through the window in the door carefully observing the

unfolding situation.

The bartender looked up and said, "Sorry, man, no pets allowed."

"But this is my seeing-eye dog." The bartender proceeded to serve the man a drink.

His buddy licked his dry lips and thought, what the heck; he'd give it a try. He put on a pair of sunglasses and walked into the bar. Once again, the bartender looked up and said, "Sorry pal, no pets allowed."

"But this is my seeing-eye dog," he replied.

The bartender said, "A Chihuahua is a seeing-eye dog?"

The man replied indignantly, "They gave me a Chihuahua!?!"

When the laughter died down, the contestants filed back onto the stage. Holding hands, they waited anxiously while last year's royalty made their farewell speeches and showed a video of the highlights of the preceding year. At last, they announced the winners of this year's Sugar Beet Pageant. After the first and second princesses were crowned as well as Miss Congeniality, the remaining contestants held hands once more as the drum roll played. When Anita Beatrice was crowned Sugar Beet Queen, there was enthusiastic applause from the entire audience. Not only was she a very well-liked young woman around town, her talent had been excellent, she was beautiful, she would be an excellent ambassador for Opossum Falls, and, she was the first Hispanic ever to wear the Sugar Beet crown. The Gonzalez family, including ICE Agent Hopkins, rushed the stage to congratulate Anita Beatrice.

~~~~~~~~~~~~~~~~~~~~~~~~~~~~~~~~~~

After the pageant, everyone headed to the park to celebrate and enjoy the rest of the first evening of the festival. Laney, Pete, and Michael had tacos-in-a-bag for dinner. They let Michael go on a few kiddies' rides and ended the night with the three of them riding the Ferris wheel. It was a beautiful, star-filled night. Laney remembered the Ferris wheel ride she'd taken with Gabby, and her heart ached for an instant. She knew these moments of sadness when remembering

Gabby would be with her for the rest of her life. As they waited at the top of the wheel for the riders below to get off, Laney placed her forefinger over her lips to let Pete know that Michael had fallen asleep after all the excitement of the evening. Pete reached across the sleeping boy and held Laney's hand. She looked over at the man she loved and would soon marry and mouthed the words, "I love you." As the Ferris wheel began to move again and Laney's stomach lurched with the excitement of the movement, she knew she was being given a second chance to be alive again, as a woman, a mom, and a wife. Pete squeezed her fingers in rapid succession and pointed to the north. There, shuddering magically, were the pulsating northern lights in all of their brilliantly-colored glory. Laney gripped Pete's hand in return as her eyes filled with tears and her heart trembled with joy.

For Opossum Falls

Therese Dotray-Tulloch

Acknowledgements

I am so fortunate to have such supportive family and friends encouraging and helping me in my writing endeavors. Thank you to Mary and Lisardo Baquero for sharing their knowledge and experience concerning immigration. Thank you to my awesome readers: Lucinda Tulloch, Travis Rose, Kareena Tulloch, Cindy Curtis, Jacqueline Tulloch, Mary Brahs, Jon Megahan, Bette Traxler, Jessie Bappe, Kathy Mesenbourg, John Dotray, and Alastair Tulloch.

As always, a very special thanks to Timothy, without whom none of this would be possible.

Therese Dotray-Tulloch

This book is a work of fiction. Names, characters, places, and incidents either are products of the author's imagination or are used fictitiously. Any resemblance to actual events or locales or persons, living or dead, is entirely coincidental.

14166129R00184

Made in the USA
Charleston, SC
24 August 2012